blessed monsters

ALSO BY

EMILY A. DUNCAN

WICKED SAINTS
(SOMETHING DARK AND HOLY: BOOK 1)

RUTHLESS GODS
(SOMETHING DARK AND HOLY: BOOK 2)

blessed monsters

SOMETHING DARK AND HOLY: BOOK 3

EMILY A. DUNCAN

WEDNESDAY BOOKS
NEW YORK

This is a work of fiction. All of the characters, organizations, and events portrayed in this novel are either products of the author's imagination or are used fictitiously.

First published in the United States by Wednesday Books, an imprint of St. Martin's Publishing Group

BLESSED MONSTERS. Copyright © 2021 by Emily A. Duncan. All rights reserved. Printed in the United States of America. For information, address St. Martin's Publishing Group, 120 Broadway, New York, NY 10271.

www.wednesdaybooks.com

Book design by Anna Gorovoy
Map illustration by Rhys Davies
Endpaper art © Shutterstock.com

Library of Congress Cataloging-in-Publication Data

Names: Duncan, Emily A., author.
Title: Blessed monsters / Emily A. Duncan.
Description: First edition. | New York : Wednesday Books, 2021. | Series:
    Something dark and holy ; book 3 | Audience: Ages 13–18.
Identifiers: LCCN 2020048571 | ISBN 9781250195722 (hardcover) |
    ISBN 9781250195746 (ebook) | ISBN 978-1-250-81967-3 (international edition,
    sold outside the U.S., subject to rights availability)
Subjects: CYAC: Fairy tales. | Magic—Fiction. | Monsters—Fiction. |
    Princes—Fiction. | Kings, queens, rulers, etc.—Fiction.
Classification: LCC PZ8.D917 Ble 2021 | DDC [Fic]—dc23
LC record available at https://lccn.loc.gov/2020048571

Our books may be purchased in bulk for promotional, educational, or business use. Please contact your local bookseller or the Macmillan Corporate and Premium Sales Department at 1-800-221-7945, extension 5442, or by email at MacmillanSpecialMarkets@macmillan.com.

First U.S. Edition: 2021
First International Edition: 2021

10 9 8 7 6 5 4 3 2 1

For Thao, who said,
"I think Malachiasz should get a book."

Disputed
Borderland

Lakelands

Kazatov

Cathedral

Palace

⊕ Grazyk

Tvir

TRANAVIA

Rosni-
Ovorisk

Tanów

Kyętri

Salt Mines

Łaszczów

Haa'ti

LIDNADO

Narjeen

Rhys Davies

blessed monsters

prologue

THE BOY EATEN
BY THE WOOD

This was a mistake.

Rashid was alone, in a dark forest that pried and pulled and tried its very best to rip him to pieces, and all he could think was, *This was a mistake.*

Don't worry, it only wants those of us with magic, Nadya had told him, in a tone he did not want to contemplate, her gaze pinned on Malachiasz.

This was a mistake.

He had buried it deep—long abandoned, but never forgotten—that was a mistake, too. It was too late for regret. Too late to wish that he had taken a different path. When Parijahan had shaken him awake to run, he should have said no. If only he had remained ignorant to politics and its intricacies, remained what he was supposed to be: a guard and a captive, nothing more. The if onlys spread out like a spiderweb, a hundred thousand different avenues where he could have chosen differently, and he wouldn't be

here. He wouldn't be remembering what he had forced into darkness, waking it from its slumber.

He kept moving, boots crunching through underbrush, wishing he had a torch or a fancy blood mage spell to spin light into the air. He paused and grazed upon that sleeping power but pulled away.

No magic. And of no consequence. A guard and a captive and a boy from the desert who was in over his head.

If he stopped, the vines would curl around his ankles, tightening, whispering that it was better to stay. Wouldn't he like to learn, finally, what it was that settled beneath his skin, waiting to break forth?

He slashed at a vine and kept moving. No and no and no. The trees—broad and vast as the eighteen pillars in the temple where he had been hidden away as a child—were slowly closing in. The spaces between them becoming so narrow that soon he would be trapped. Dying here would be his fate.

Rashid had wanted to die under the sun.

He flinched at a shivering underneath his skin, slithering within his forearm. He swallowed back bile as something broke forth. Green and wormlike and splitting across his arm. He blinked. A stem. Flowers burst forth, crimson and burgundy and pale violet and *dripping with blood.*

Rashid refused to let the whimper that had settled in his chest escape.

Crack. He whirled, coming face-to-face with a creature that he could not immediately put a name to. He didn't know the monsters that lurked in Kalyazin's corners, but this one was familiar. Hunched over, just shy of walking upright. Long claws tipped humanlike hands, and it walked on deerlike hooves. The head was that of a deer skull if deer had that many . . . teeth. Flowers, acrid and rotting and roiling with maggots, dripped from its antlers.

Oh. The word came to him.

Leshy. A forest guardian. One of Nadya's preferred threats—to leave them all to the *leshy* that she claimed one of her gods commanded.

Rashid couldn't fathom any god commanding this being. He couldn't fathom this not being a god itself. But he had a very wobbly understanding of what the Kalyazi considered gods.

He took a step back, knocking into a tree. The openings had closed. Nowhere to run. He pressed flush against the trunk.

Words came crawling and scratching out of a throat dormant for centuries. They were strange and uncomfortable and unfathomable to him, yet they pierced deep into his core.

Escape was no longer possible.

His fate was sealed.

The forest only feeds on those with magic.

The forest would eat every single one of their doomed group before it turned on the rest of the world. Because they had set it free from its prison and it had been waiting a very long time to feed.

1

MALACHIASZ CZECHOWICZ

There is music at the end of the universe. Chyrnog's songs that push like roiling worms into the brain and slowly take apart the mind. A weakening before consumption.

—The Volokhtaznikon

Malachiasz Czechowicz woke up in bloodstained snow. The cold of death was a needle that dug deep into bone, and he remained still, eyes closed, ice soaking into the last tatters of his clothes, until his skin warmed.

He shivered only once, as the cold from the snow became more present than that of the grave, doing his best to shove past his disorientation. Had he—?

Yes.

He had died. The last thing he had seen was Nadya, streaked with blood and tears, churning with spent power and clutching him. Then darkness, but not quiet. No peace.

He was afraid to move, afraid to disturb whatever tenuous

silence had wrenched him away from the ledge. He shouldn't be breathing.

His fingertips were blackened with what he hoped was magic and not frostbite. He let his iron claws slide back into his nail beds and nearly cried with relief that he *could*. He didn't feel like himself, but he hadn't felt like himself in a long time.

He was going to die here.

He blinked. Considered how he already had. He touched the wound at his chest. It wasn't bleeding, but it was certainly a gaping hole that led straight to his heart.

He shouldn't be alive.

At his edges were echoes of transcendence, and he wasn't prepared to return to that state. Becoming a god was a bit of a lottery, he had found, and chaos was a not entirely pleasant lottery to win. As sweet as the thrill of power might have been, the pain of his bones shattering only to reform only to break free of his skin was a little too near for his taste. If he pressed out—just a bit—he could feel where he became something more. It was a series of steps before the fall, and the illusion that he was consciously in control of it was one he would like to maintain for as long as he could.

He had only killed one god.

There were many more to go.

"Well, boy." A horrible voice slithered through the back of Malachiasz's skull. His vision blanked out. No bleak mountainside of white and white and white. No more anything. Only darkness.

Malachiasz had known horrors. He knew the sounds of nightmares and chaos. The feeling of burning coals raked over skin, of knives under fingernails, of living shadows taking him apart and putting him back together in the wrong order. He knew pain. He knew chaos. He *was* chaos.

But chaos—chaos was small and rational at the foot of this.

This was all those terrors combined and wrapped into something much worse. Two words, small, insignificant, yet with them came an invisible shackle binding his wrists, a collar around his throat. A promise.

Well, Malachiasz replied, trying to be the Black Vulture and not the terrified boy. *This won't do at all.*

It was the wrong move, and the voice gave a scraping laugh. A starburst of pain rattled across Malachiasz's vision, sparking the darkness with bursts of light. He was so young before whatever had taken him.

"*I am tired of mortals who think they can fight me,*" the voice said. "*I have been waiting a long time for you. But there will be time for that, time for everything, time for exactly what I wish. This is our introduction, you see.*"

Malachiasz's heart was pounding so hard he thought it might give up in his chest, and at least that would stop the horror.

Hard to have an introduction when I don't know your name.

"*Earn it.*"

Malachiasz didn't know how he had made it off the mountain. He was outside the strange church, every part of him aching, the forest creeping, taking, rotting within him.

He had grown used to his vision splitting every time a cluster of eyes opened on his body. He was used to his shifting chaos. But this pain was darker, and there was nothing for him to do but grit his teeth and press through it.

The church was made of wood—had it been stone before? He needed a place to get out of the cold, to feel *something.* The door opened easily at his touch. He closed it behind him, relishing the silence.

Moss crept along the floor and up the walls over the old icons. He could feel the forest pulling at his fraying edges, trying its very best to unravel him, as it ate and ate. It had nearly succeeded once. He stepped across the hallway and closed the door to the stairway leading to the well. He didn't want to think about what Nadya had done.

The crunch of bones underneath his boots was loud as he followed a hall to the sanctuary. He bypassed it, hoping to find a smaller room to hole up in until he felt warm.

Maybe he would never feel warm again.

It took time, stepping through rotting plants and brittle bones, to find the room that would have housed the caretaker of the church. There was an oven in the corner. Malachiasz filled it with shattered bits of furniture and reached for his spell book. It wasn't at his hip. Neither was the dagger he'd carried for years. Frustration and anxiety and blistering fear overcame him all at once and he thudded heavily to the ground, squeezing his eyes shut. He let out a long, shuddering breath.

He buried his face in his hands and tried not to bring back the voice. He suspected the being was always there, watching. Waiting to overwhelm him further. Forcing his eyes closed did little, a cluster of them opening on his hand and disorienting him.

When he had snapped past the mortal bonds tying him to this realm of reality, a lot had been made clear that had been taken by the Vultures. Things he had lost. Was any of it real?

He remembered the boy with the scar on his eye. And dragging books into the boy's room after a failed assassination attempt. Spending his days wandering the palace until the boy pulled him back to lessons.

His *brother.*

Serefin. His murderer.

Family was something Malachiasz had yearned for but now wished to forget. Better to have the false family he had built for himself to replace the one wrenched away. Reconciling this was too difficult.

His time in the forest was hazy. It had clawed at him long before they'd reached Tzanelivki. The moment they left the monastery and moved into Dozvlatovya, it began its assault, wanting to devour him. Serefin had been distant as they traveled through the forest, constantly taken by fits, his eyes bleeding. And if he—*or Nadya*—had shown signs of malicious intent, Malachiasz was too distracted to notice.

Yet he didn't understand. Why had Nadya saved him when confronted by her goddess? Why let him taste the terrifying expanse of her magic?

Malachiasz had the power of a god but it was nothing, inconsequential, to what the Kalyazi girl with hair like snow could have if she knew how to wield it. The thought was as thrilling as it was terrifying. It would have been better had she not betrayed him. But he had betrayed her, too. They had spent the past year willfully kicking each other at any glimmer of weakness. She was the enemy, perhaps it had been foolish to think she would ever be anything else.

He tugged on a bone knotted in his hair. He still had a few relics, their power thrumming under his fingertips, and he could break them. Push past his consciousness, his mortal body. *Transcend.* But that was, quite possibly, the last thing he wanted to do.

He stared blankly at the cold oven, realizing he was useless without his spell book. But even if he had it, would it work? What had Nadya done?

Frustrated, he slashed the back of his hand with an iron claw, hoping he was wrong and that she hadn't destroyed everything— hadn't betrayed him so fully.

But there was no magic in his spilt blood. There was nothing.

He swallowed hard, staring at the blood dripping down his hand and fighting tears. What good was he without his magic? What was the point of him? He was nothing but a monster. He still had *some* magic, something far past blood magic, and he could feel it if he pressed. But using it was tapping into chaos and he wasn't sure he had the control for it.

Malachiasz shivered. He was freezing and it was growing harder to ignore the ripples of pain each time his body shifted. At least it had quieted back down to what he was used to, eyes and mouths and twitching. No extraneous limbs or spines in the wrong places.

All his life he'd had a goal, for things to not be so bad, and he could always see that light at the end of the darkness, even as it grew farther away with each step he took.

Now it had gone out and he wasn't sure what he was fighting for—if there was anything *to* fight for.

Taszni nem Malachiasz Czechowicz.

He couldn't let himself fall—he didn't know if he could return from that place of chaos—but his edges were fraying, the presence sliding forward with a scrape. And there was no stopping it.

The dark was far past that of the Salt Mines—that place where no light touched. This was destruction. This was entropy.

Awareness was a transient concept. Unimportant. Insignificant. The god had pulled him here. Call it what it was, he supposed. His ideals might have to be compromised. But he knew with perfect clarity that this was not one of the gods he had declared war against.

"No."

Then what?

"Older, greater, far more powerful."

His bones cracked as he was forced into chaos. Breaking only to be reforged. Steel puncturing through his skin. Teeth slicing through him. Eyes blinking open and fractured vision and how far could it go? How much more could he withstand? How much could he be altered until nothing left of him was human?

"Fighting is hardly in your best interest. We will work so well together, you and I."

Malachiasz didn't know how to respond—he had no mouth to speak in that moment. He only had panic and fear and clarity—perfect clarity.

Let this play out. Let him hear what this god had to say.

"Ah, surrender—I knew you were clever. I knew if only you listened, you would see."

It wasn't surrender; it was biding time. Malachiasz knew what to do with those who thought themselves capable of manipulating him. He'd known how to handle Izak, and he could handle this.

Except . . . he had not known how to handle Nadya. An error of a heart he did not know he still possessed. No more mistakes with that—not with her.

But he could make this look like a surrendering of will. He could play this game.

He also had no way to argue. Chaos was an entrapment, it forced him into its will and he was powerless before it. He had known what transcendence could do to him. He had studied enough to know it would either kill him or turn him into something so much greater, but there was no way to predict the result. And the chaos, it was fitting, but it was a punishment, a prison.

Malachiasz did not allow himself the luxury of regret, and, forced back into divinity, his body breaking under the weight and power of this being, this god, he let himself taste it. He had made so many mistakes, told so many lies, and here he was at the end of the universe—a god in power. A boy, broken. So damn tired.

"I know what you want. Listen. It would be less painful for you to not force my hand."

What did Malachiasz want? Once, it had been clear, but then his path had crashed into a girl from Kalyazin who was clever and vicious and nothing like he'd thought those backward people were, a girl so wrapped around the finger of a goddess who only meant to use her, and Malachiasz's grand ambitions had altered. He hadn't killed Marzenya because he'd wanted to topple Kalyazin's divine empire, he had done it because she'd forced Nadya to watch him break into pieces. Because she had led Nadya to her own destruction—merely her tool to wipe the magic from Tranavia. Because he couldn't stand to watch as the goddess snuffed out Nadya's vibrant spark because she had dared turn it in a new direction.

Nadya would never forgive him, but he didn't know if he could forgive her, either.

Maybe this was all that was left. He had killed one god and he would kill more.

And so, he listened.

"Very good." The god's voice was marked with approval. *"Together, we will plunge this world into darkness in order to bring the light."*

What is it you want from me?

"You have power—divine and mortal—and I need it to remake this world anew before I scatter your bones on the edges of my domain."

Oh good . . . I have only ever wanted to bring peace to my country.

"Is that all you wish?"

So much had changed, so much of *him* had changed. What had always seemed clear was murky. But, in the end, yes. He yearned for the same thing, no matter its shape. He wanted peace. He wanted no one else to suffer in the acutely specific ways he had. Not with the Vultures—they weren't going anywhere—but because of this war, this unending madness.

There was more he wanted, quiet things he couldn't admit, because to admit them would be to tempt fate against them. Except there was nothing left for him with Nadya. He needed to close off the shattered pieces of his blackened heart. If he didn't, he would find his way to her again. If she had been willing to take everything away from him, and he had been willing to take everything from her, what was left?

I only want peace, he finally repeated.

"A noble goal. Lofty. What a hero." The voice was snide.

I know what I am, Malachiasz snapped. He didn't need to be reminded of what he had done.

"You don't, not really. But we will go on that journey, you and I, and I will break you if I must."

Malachiasz scowled. *I ask again, what is it you want?*

"Your being exists in ideal circumstances. And I have already given you the tools you will need to put the first steps into motion."

He frowned, uncertain where this would lead. *The first steps . . . killing another god?*

"I knew there was a reason I chose you." The voice was smug as it let Malachiasz go.

2

NADEZHDA

LAPTEVA

Out of Svoyatovi Yeremey Meledin's mouth came
twelve hundred snakes. When the last snake fell, the
last word spoken, he died.

— Vasiliev's Book of Saints

Light filtered in through the dirty farmhouse windows, illuminating the dust motes that hung in the air. Nadya picked at the bandages wrapping her hands, the temptation to pull them off strong.

It had been fourteen days since she had fallen off the side of a mountain and lost everything. Only a fortnight. To say she had spent every moment of it wallowing would be too gentle.

She pulled at the fraying cuff of her dress to avoid tearing at her bandages.

Rashid sat down next to her at the small table, cradling two cups of tea in his hand. Nadya took them, waiting for him to settle. He gave her a grateful smile, tucking a lock

of long black hair behind his ear. His wrist was carefully splinted. Cuts were scattered across his hands and face, and a handful of ugly gashes along his forearms that Nadya didn't want to consider. She hadn't asked what had happened to him in the forest; he hadn't offered to tell.

None of them would talk. The horrors were too fresh, and Nadya couldn't fool herself into thinking that what the others had gone through hadn't been as terrible as her experience. They may have gotten out alive—well, most of them—but they had all lost something. The forest ate and ate and ate.

Nadya had nothing left.

The door opened with a crash and Nadya's tea jostled as someone kicked the back of her chair.

"All right, *kovoishka,* time's up." Yekaterina Vodyanova threw herself down in the chair across the table. She eyed the teacups before standing and abruptly leaving the room.

Nadya frowned, puzzled, before the *tsarevna* returned with a wine bottle—gods only knew where she had found it—that she casually placed on the table before dropping into her chair, kicking it back, and putting her feet up on the seat beside her.

Katya's black hair curled, tangled, around her shoulders. A long cut was healing on her cheek, promising a scar. She was in a soldier's uniform sans jacket, her black boots and cream blouse uncomfortably clean. Pristine and untouched.

"I've given you time. I'm done being patient," Katya continued. Her gaze flicked to Rashid. "If you would also like to share, I'm all ears."

"Considering our friend who was all eyes, thank you for that truly terrible image," Rashid replied.

Nadya couldn't decide whether she wanted to laugh or sob. The only thing she knew for sure was, she didn't want to talk.

Her god was dead.

Malachiasz had killed Marzenya, and she had given him the means. How would the others retaliate for that transgression?

Since then, they had been ignoring her completely. It was a

different emptiness than before. She had touched each kind of abandonment, categorized them all. This was new, more painful than when she couldn't feel them at all. Or was it easier? She didn't know. The very fabric of the world had altered, the universe tilted sharply on its axis. And it was her fault. She had broken everything.

"Don't make me order you, *kovoishka*." Katya took a long drink from the wine bottle and regarded Nadya with careful scrutiny, taking in the fading bruises from Marzenya's touch that stained her skin.

Even now Nadya could feel her skin splitting open underneath her goddess's fingertips. The warmth of Malachiasz's blood on her hands.

"It wouldn't make a difference," she said, skimming her fingertip around the rim of her cup.

Katya's eyes narrowed. They had been waiting for soldiers from the nearest garrison for weeks without sign of them. Nadya guessed they were still too close to the forest to be found, but Katya didn't seem ready to give up. Regardless, what could Katya do to her?

Many things, but not here, not now. Not when all she had was the power of her name and some weak magic she barely knew how to use. But if Katya thought it would be useful to know the horrors that haunted her, who was Nadya to stop her?

"A god is dead," Nadya said quietly. "And many of the fallen gods have risen. The rest have decided we're not worth the trouble."

"That's impossible."

"You will find a great number of impossibilities have become possible." Nadya flexed her corrupted hand.

Katya didn't appear appeased. "I don't have time for your theological riddles."

"I'm not giving you any. Marzenya died. Velyos and the others—" she waved a hand "—were set free. I have no answers because no one ever bothered to tell me any of this existed in the first place."

"So, you went and crashed through every wall placed before you and toppled what little stability we had," Katya said derisively.

I was a complacent little soldier, she thought. *Fighting a people who were naught but monsters. Ask no questions, act on the faith that everything you have been told is absolute truth. Until you realize it was all lies. What did they expect I would do if I found out? Continue on as I had, I suppose.*

"You should put a glove over that." Katya frowned in disgust, her eyes on Nadya's hand.

Nadya made a thoughtful noise. It horrified her once, this blackened claw, when the corruption had begun, but now, horror wasn't the word for it.

"How does one kill a god?" Katya murmured.

"Become one," Nadya replied, her voice hollow. It haunted her. A god of chaos was a fitting shape for a boy like Malachiasz, but it was a terrible, monstrous, ever shifting, ever churning horror. The madness they had been thrust into since that night in the cathedral, forever ago, made all the more sense. Chaos had gripped the world the night a god of chaos had been born. It was inevitable. All that had happened with her heart, broken and bloodied and pulled to him, was inevitable, too. His gentle hands and careful smiles had not been enough to mask his true horror.

"But that would mean . . ."

"I don't know," Nadya whispered. "He's dead, too."

Katya did a bad job of masking her delight. Nadya felt like she'd been punched in the chest.

"I didn't think the drunkard could do it."

Rashid tensed, and Nadya nearly reached out to hold him back but remained still. Anything the *tsarevna* received for her callousness she deserved. But was it even that? Why shouldn't she celebrate the death of Kalyazin's deadliest enemy?

Instead, Nadya tucked away the implication that Katya and Serefin had been planning something together. No wonder Katya had been there. A princess masquerading as a Vulture hunter, and what a prize Malachiasz made.

Except Nadya had carried the blade that murdered him. Had Pelageya known who it would be used on when she gave it to her?

She had been warned the mountains would destroy him, but she hadn't realized, not truly, how final the destruction would be.

"Did you not notice that he hasn't been around?" Rashid asked incredulously.

Katya rolled her eyes. "That wouldn't mean anything, and you know it. We don't know where the forest spat out Serefin and Kacper—"

"*If* the forest spat out Serefin and Kacper," Nadya muttered.

"—and I wasn't about to indulge my hope," Katya continued, ignoring her. "I can't say I'm particularly sorry. Though, I was promised his teeth and he did have nice teeth."

"Shut up."

An eyebrow quirked. "It's a very bad look, mourning the Black Vulture."

"I don't care."

"You don't, but you should. I won't be able to protect you from those who will blame you for what's happened."

"Which part? His death, or Marzenya's, or maybe stripping the blood magic from Tranavia?"

Katya paled. She lowered her feet off the table, a little less cavalier.

"What do you want from me?" Nadya asked.

"That should be obvious. If—if that boy, gods, both those boys, did what you say, you're the only one who can do *anything*."

"I just fell off a mountain after watching the boy I love kill my goddess and then be murdered. Katya, I don't want to help anyone do anything."

Katya winced.

"Don't you dare say anything about Malachiasz's teeth."

"I wasn't going to." Katya sighed heavily. "I won't lie to you and say I'm sorry he's dead. But you're grieving and I'm sorry for that."

"Gods, you're terrible at this."

Katya shrugged. "He's killed thousands of Kalyazi on his own, not including what his cult has done in his name."

"Stop talking about him."

Katya ran both hands through her hair, standing. She started pacing.

"What do you mean you stripped blood magic from Tranavia?"

Nadya wasn't sure. Marzenya had implied that they simply would not remember how to cast magic anymore. She didn't know if that meant they could relearn it, or if it was gone entirely. Malachiasz's panic implied the latter.

"I don't know."

Katya's gaze went to the window. "We have to leave," she said, in a whisper so low Nadya almost missed it.

She exchanged a glance with Rashid. Katya didn't say anything more, grabbing the wine bottle and dashing out the door.

"That was useless," Nadya said, sipping her tea. "How does the world turn when the gods decide it's no longer worth their attention?" She frowned. "How do we reconcile the gaze of gods who have gone mad in the dark?"

"I did not sign up for these kinds of conversations," Rashid replied cheerfully.

She shot him a wan smile. The door to the other room opened. Arms wrapped around her neck, someone resting their chin in her hair from behind. She knew it was Parijahan, but the glimpse of black hair made her heart jolt.

Nadya didn't know how to survive constantly having the people she loved returned to her, only to lose them again. First Kostya, then Malachiasz. Who else would be ripped away?

"You should both leave," she said, tilting her head against Parijahan's arm, twining her fingers between the other girl's. "Go back to Akola before this gets worse."

The look on Rashid's face as he glanced up at Parijahan—hope and a plaintive entreaty—was not lost on Nadya. This wasn't their fight, their gods. They could walk away unscathed. Nadya desperately wanted them to so she wouldn't face losing them as well.

Parijahan sighed.

"They want you home," Rashid said, his voice soft.

A lot made sense in those words. Why Parijahan had been upset on the journey through Kalyazin. But it didn't explain the private conversations with Malachiasz, their frustration with each other. Parijahan was running from something in Akola, Nadya assumed whatever it was couldn't *possibly* be as bad as facing this oncoming storm.

"No, they don't," she replied. "Flowery messages singing forgiveness are only ever lies."

"Your cousins wouldn't—"

"Rashid, don't be foolish."

Nadya frowned.

"It's die here or die there."

"You should consider it," Nadya said softly.

Parijahan's arms tightened around her. "I'm not leaving you, Nadya. Not after that. Not after losing him."

"He was already lost," Nadya murmured. "I knew the forest would kill him, I just didn't know it would happen like that."

Parijahan went very still. Rashid eyed her strangely. Why shouldn't she take the blame? She had known from the beginning that he wouldn't return from the Tachilvnik Wood. No, she hadn't expected him to die by Serefin's hand, but it was the inevitable coming to pass. She had played his game against him and he had lost.

And she ended up all the more broken.

"Even if you intended . . ." Parijahan trailed off.

"I intended it," Nadya said. "And I regret it. But there's no changing it."

The door flew open. Katya, and one flustered blood mage being dragged by the wrist.

"Sit," Katya said.

Ostyia glared, not sitting until the *tsarevna* did. Her black hair, already jagged and uneven at her chin and forehead, looked disastrous, and she hadn't bothered with an eye patch, leaving the scarred void of her eye socket visible.

She muttered a curse under her breath in Tranavian, pulled her spell book from her hip and dropped it onto the table. Tense silence stretched throughout the room.

Fresh cuts were scattered across Ostyia's forearms, haphazard and messy, sluggishly bleeding in a way she had chosen to ignore.

"It's not working," she hissed.

"Try," Katya urged.

"Wait," Nadya said, but she was silenced by a glare from Katya. She sat back in her chair.

Ostyia shook her head. She flipped her spell book open, frowning deeply. "I can't even *read it*." Her voice cracked.

"May I?" Nadya asked, reaching tentatively for the spell book.

Ostyia nodded. Nadya flipped it around and found pages upon pages of text she could read—it was definitely in Tranavian—but the words didn't totally make sense, like some element was missing.

"It looks like nonsense to me," Ostyia said.

"We're leaving," Katya announced. "You've all wallowed long enough. We're going to Komyazalov. I need to speak with my father."

Nadya swallowed hard, meeting Ostyia's gaze from across the table. The Tranavian girl was clearly thinking the same thing: she did not want to meet the *tsar*.

SEREFIN
MELESKI

*There are no lies and no truths to Velyos. It's all one
and the same. Words are words are words, and words
are meaningless.*

—The Letters of Włodzimierz

Serefin Meleski should have succumbed to his wounds. As a
fever burned through him, he contemplated more than once
how nice it would be to simply give up.

He didn't know where he was when he finally came out
of it. He woke to darkness and cold. Someone was curled
up next to him—which wasn't like him *at all*—and his shattered world started to piece together when he realized it was
Kacper. He touched the bandages over his left eye—or, eye
socket, rather. It hurt, an ache like a thousand headaches at
once, but he no longer felt like he was being stabbed in the
brain.

He could still feel his brother's blood on his hands, the
god's will smothering his own and shoving him down to use

his body for its own ends. He hadn't lost control since. And it had only taken tearing out his own eye.

A paltry trade, all things considered.

He nestled down and pressed his forehead against the back of Kacper's neck, hoping to finish out the night with no more nightmares.

But he was back at the front and it was so *loud*. Screams and crying and so much blood. An arrow zipped past his face, grazing his cheek, and there was blood on his face. His friend Hanna was being cut into pieces by Kalyazi blades, moving too fast to be real.

Serefin shot awake as a blade was aimed for him. He shivered, raking a hand through his hair, trying to remind himself that he wasn't at the front, and hadn't been in some time. He was soaked with sweat. His gasps for air gave way to tremors and he buried his head against his knees and tried his hardest not to break.

"Oh, good morning," Kacper mumbled, his voice scratchy with sleep in a way that sent a different kind of warmth rushing through Serefin, no less feverish. And, "It was only a bad dream."

"That doesn't really help when it actually happened," Serefin muttered, before lifting his head.

Kacper squinted at the light filtering in through the hastily tied tent. "Ah, we overslept." His brown skin was warm, his edges rumpled and soft, and his black curls were messy. "You look like you're feeling better," Kacper said, a hopeful note in his voice.

Not only had they overslept, they shouldn't have *both* slept through the night without someone keeping watch—but it was growing harder and harder to care.

Serefin nodded, fingers fluttering near his bandage. "The fever broke. Maybe this thing won't kill me."

"Or lack thereof, of a thing," Kacper said.

"Get out of my bed."

Kacper laughed softly. He sat up and clambered over Serefin to dig through his pack. "Not a bed. Take that off," he said.

Serefin hated this part, but he dutifully untied the cloth and carefully unwound it from his head, freeing the rest of the bandages covering the remnants of his left eye. Kacper returned with fresh bandages. He paused, taking Serefin's face between his hands.

"How bad is it, really?" Serefin asked. He had been avoiding anything even remotely reflective.

"Charmingly rakish," Kacper replied a little too easily.

Serefin lifted an eyebrow.

Kacper's fingers traced the cuts on Serefin's face where his fingernails had dug and dug. His touch was featherlight, and it was all Serefin could do not to pull him back down onto the bedrolls.

"They'll scar," Kacper murmured. He touched a cut that ended at the corner of Serefin's mouth. It pulled at his lips as it healed. "This is going to be all some people see."

Serefin closed his eye.

"Not me, though," Kacper continued, his voice very low.

He gently pulled the last bandage away. He was quiet for a beat too long. Serefin opened his eye—the old healer had sewn his other eyelid shut until the socket healed.

"Kacper?"

Kacper blinked. He lowered his hands. "Sorry," he said. "The swelling has gone down. Does it hurt?"

"Blood and bone, yes." Constantly. A ceaseless headache that varied in levels of intensity.

Kacper hesitated before gingerly cupping Serefin's cheek. "You made it out, that's what matters."

"Oh, so it's *very bad*."

Kacper's continued silence was not reassuring.

"*Kacper.*"

"Your eye never went back to normal," he finally said. "I guess I keep thinking it will."

Serefin wasn't so optimistic. Moths still clouded around him. Something was *off*. Like he had been taken apart and put back together in the wrong order. Being snapped across the continent by the whim of a god had not been kind to him.

Kacper cleaned the socket carefully before bandaging Serefin up. He kissed his forehead.

They had left the tiny Kalyazi village weeks ago, even though Serefin had been in no state to travel. The last thing he wanted was to be trapped in Kalyazin with no way home, but that appeared to be his terrifying new reality. He had no idea what was happening at the front or at court.

Kacper sat back on his heels and shoved extra bandages back into his pack. He tied his tunic and picked up his military jacket, frowning at it quizzically.

"Don't wear it," Serefin said. He gathered his tangled hair in his hands—when had it gotten so long?—and tied it back.

Kacper sat down next to him, pulling his boots on. Serefin pressed his face against Kacper's shoulder. Kacper tensed for a heartbeat before he rested his head against Serefin's. That was how it always was, a beat of hesitation where uncertainty flickered in Kacper. Serefin had grown deft at catching it.

He'd known Kacper for three years, but it was three years of chaos. The things a person learned about another during long days on a battlefield and long nights of excruciating routine watches were deeply specific. He knew Kacper had grown up in Zowecz, one of the southern Tranavian provinces. He was one of the youngest of five and nearly all his siblings had done time at the front before returning home to the farm. But Kacper hated getting dirty and didn't really think farm work would suit him. He loved plants, but not the growing—rather, the effect they could have on a person. Poisons, specifically. The broad strokes of a person's life were easy to paint in the quiet moments between brushes with death out at the front.

Kacper busied himself lacing his boots and Serefin lifted his head to study the side of his face, wondering about the little things he didn't know. He was very good at getting to know every soldier under his command's broad strokes, but the little things? Those were hard for him.

Serefin didn't have friends. He didn't really know how. Ostyia was all he had because they'd been attached at the hip as children and mutually decided that was how it should be always. She'd gone to war because he was being sent.

And with Kacper . . . sure, if he thought about it, he could remember when he'd promoted Kacper and pulled him into his inner circle. He remembered when the formality finally broke between them. It had been a slow build. Kacper warming up to telling jokes at Serefin's expense, cracking him across the face during a training drill and laughing instead of immediately apologizing, treating him like a *person* and not the *prince.* It had been gradual, this thing between them, whatever it was that burned through him when Kacper smiled. He hadn't realized how much he trusted Kacper until the chaos in Grazyk when he repeatedly turned to Kacper to keep him grounded.

So, what was the hesitation?

He reached up, brushing his fingers against Kacper's jaw, rough with a few days of stubble.

"Ser—?"

Serefin caught the end of his name with his lips. Kacper made a low plaintive sound, one hand lifting to curl against Serefin's neck, thumb brushing up his throat.

He wanted to *know* Kacper in a way that he was too aware he simply didn't yet. And he wished they weren't in a situation so deeply antithetical to making that happen.

"What was that for?" Kacper asked breathlessly when he broke away.

"Why do you always tense when I touch you?"

Kacper blinked, visibly startled. "What?"

Serefin backtracked, looking away. This was going to start something. "N-no, I—never mind—"

"Serefin, wait," Kacper said, turning Serefin's face back toward his. "I didn't realize I did."

"Oh."

"It's because you're the *king.*"

It was not the answer Serefin wanted to hear. "I'm just Serefin," he said, a little desperately.

"I know. You are. But you're also not."

Serefin pursed his lips, tugging away. They needed to get moving. Kacper scowled.

"No, you're shutting down on me, don't do that," Kacper said, sounding frustrated. "Can we talk about this?"

"What's there to talk about?"

"A lot, actually."

"It's too much trouble."

"It is. But it shouldn't be. I don't *care* about that." Kacper took Serefin's hand, stroking the inside of his palm with his fingertips, before releasing it. "I'm sorry. I'll be more aware of how I respond. And it would be nice if you remember that I'm breaking a thousand different rules with this and it might take a little getting used to."

"What rules?"

"Don't act dense, Serefin. You need an heir. Your court hated my proximity to you enough as it was."

Serefin sighed. He had spent so long thinking the crown would never pass to him that the things he *should* keep in mind never occurred to him. Not that he cared much about the heir problem. Not that he cared about the opinions of his court, either, but Kacper cared because Kacper had to. Serefin wondered, not for the first time, if he had done more harm than good dragging Kacper into this life. "There may be no Tranavia to return to, so."

"Deflecting by way of catastrophizing is a great strategy," Kacper replied dryly.

Serefin shot him a look. He closed his eye, knuckling the bridge of his nose. "I'm sorry," he whispered. He buried his face in his hands, immediately drawing back at the shooting pain. "Ow."

"You just came out of a fortnight-long fever, so I can't really be *too* upset with you." Kacper kissed his cheek. "We both need to get better at talking, I think."

"Gross."

"I'm going to leave you here. I'm walking back to Tranavia without you. I'll be the king."

Serefin grinned. "That's *treasonous*."

"I guess I commit treason now."

But the jokes made Serefin relax, which was what Kacper always managed to do. He squeezed Serefin's hand.

"What are you actually worried about?" Kacper asked, his voice low and gentle, and it felt like an unfair question. Serefin was worried about *everything*.

He was worried that if—*if if if*—they made it back, this would be over for all the reasons Kacper was worried about. He was worried that Ostyia wasn't with them and he didn't know if she was alive. He was worried that every single thing they'd done had been in vain.

He was worried they were going to die, and he would never know all the things about Kacper that he didn't know yet.

"Do you think the priestess was telling the truth about Tranavia?" he asked. It was a horrifying thought that blood magic was gone as if it had never been in the first place.

Kacper's eyes narrowed. "I don't know," he said after a long pause. He picked up his spell book and his brow creased. He held it out to Serefin.

Serefin swallowed hard. "That's yours."

"I . . ." Kacper trailed off. "That feels right, but—" he shook his head "—it's also wrong? I don't know what to do with it."

"Kacper, you've known how to use magic your whole life."

Another reason Serefin was terrified of returning to Tranavia. What had happened to make Kacper forget such an intrinsic part of himself? Why could Serefin remember? Why had he been spared?

"I can tell something is missing." He tilted his head. "But I don't know what it is."

Tranavia was built on blood magic. The country would crumble without the small spells everyone used without thinking. Serefin couldn't confront how he might not have a country to go home to. Kalyazin could very well already be moving in to raze it to the earth.

But shouldn't he try to save it? After everything? He'd likely lost the throne to Ruminski, but he could take that back. The noble was no more than a nuisance, those who followed him would eventually have their self-interests turn them back to Serefin. Court politics were the least of Serefin's concerns. If he went back to Grazyk, he worried he would be letting something even worse fester.

Kalyazin wasn't his problem. Their capricious gods were not his problem.

But . . .

What had he set free? What had he done? He wasn't so naive as to think that the consequences of his actions would stay in Kalyazin, that he could go home and forget about it while this nightmarish kingdom burned. Katya had warned them that no one would be safe if one of the elder gods returned and Serefin had a bad feeling he knew what the second god he had been dealing with truly was. He had cast that voice out, but that didn't mean it was contained, or powerless.

"I don't know what to do," he said.

"I can't say I do, either," Kacper agreed.

"But you're my voice of reason!"

"I'm not feeling particularly reasonable right now."

"I don't think we can go back to Tranavia yet," Serefin said, wanting to drop his head into his hands.

"We don't even know who survived, and if they did, where they are. And what are our options? Nadya, who knows you killed Malachiasz and will definitely murder you for it—"

"She won't."

"Stunningly optimistic of you when she was in love with him. That leaves the *tsarevna*."

Serefin liked Katya, which was alarming but perhaps spoke to his weariness. He had spent the past three years killing Kalyazi for a cause he thought was perfectly justified. He wouldn't take back everything he had done in the name of the war effort, but he was ready for it to end. He didn't really think he could fight with the same conviction, and maybe that was thanks to one dry Kalyazi cleric and one snotty *tsarevna*. He was fine with that.

But Tranavia had been rendered completely powerless. And that did not sit well. He wanted a truce, not to surrender. He had his pride.

"We don't know if Ostyia survived," Serefin said quietly.

Kacper closed his eyes, something in him clearly giving up.

"I can't leave her here, Kacper."

"No, you can't," he agreed. "She'll take out your other eye if you do. But if she didn't . . ."

"Stop."

"You have to face reality."

"No. *No*. You—" He poked his finger against Kacper's chest. "—and Ostyia and I have been through hellfire and back and we have survived too much to be defeated by that damned forest and those miserable gods."

Kacper lifted his hand, threading his fingers through Serefin's, whose heart kicked traitorously in response.

"We're going to find her. Then we're going home." Serefin had been so delirious for weeks and now everything was so *clear*.

"How are you going to find her, Ser?"

"Magic."

Kacper was quiet. Serefin hated the look in his dark eyes; it was far too close to pity. He took his spell book and flipped it open. His heart immediately dropped.

It was indecipherable.

Suddenly he was too hot and too cold all at once, like his fever had returned in full force. He let out a shaky breath. Kacper put a steadying hand on his arm.

He knew these spells, had worked with an apprentice book binder to put them together; the girl had spent the whole time looking like she was going to faint at the prospect of writing the king's spells for him. And he couldn't read any of them.

This can't be happening.

"Well. This is strange," he said, voice strangled. "How can I remember how it works and you can't?" He pulled his *szitelka* out of its sheath and cut a careful line down his forearm.

"Careful," Kacper murmured.

"Probably not the wisest move to bleed on a random spell." Serefin contemplated. He glanced at Kacper, a calming exchange, and shrugged. He tilted his forearm and let blood drip onto the pages. The seconds stretched to minutes.

Serefin had not been spared, after all.

4

MALACHIASZ
CZECHOWICZ

*It's blood boiling underneath skin. Teeth tearing flesh.
It doesn't end. It never ends. We made a mistake. We
made a mistake. We made a mistake.*
—Fragment of a journal entry
by Svoyatova Orya Gorelova

Malachiasz woke to darkness. His first instinct was to panic because not again *not again*. But the air didn't taste like copper and terror. He wasn't in the dank depths of the Salt Mines. But he also wasn't in the church room.

And he wasn't alone.

A door creaked open, and a knife of light landed on him. The smell of burning flesh filled his nostrils, and too late he realized it was his. He scrambled back, knocking into boxes and something that rattled. His body gave out on him and he ended up crumpled on the ground, too weak to run or strike, when a hooded figure entered. Face in shadow, they crouched in front of Malachiasz, a hand breaking free from

the folds of their robe to tilt his chin up. He was being scrutinized and he hated it. He hated feeling weak; hated being this vulnerable.

The figure muttered something in Kalyazi that Malachiasz couldn't parse and he blinked, puzzled. He was fluent in the language, especially after Nadya's refusal to speak in Tranavian if she didn't absolutely have to.

"Where am I?" he asked, stupidly, in Tranavian, his voice hoarse. A misstep.

The figure grabbed him by the throat. Malachiasz shut down, instinct finally winning out. Teeth sharpening in his mouth, the world closing in as his focus narrowed. A spike of iron split from his wrist and he lashed out at the figure, who caught the spike on the palm of their hand, and silently, slowly pushed down until it broke to the other side. The hand on his throat tightened its grip and he was pulled abruptly into the light.

It *burned*.

Malachiasz coughed, spitting up blood as he tried desperately to move back into the darkness and the figure held him down. His skin was bare, the shirt he'd been wearing long since rendered into tatters by his shifting body, and his flesh was sizzling like hot oil. Eventually he was let go and kicked back into the shadows. He slunk away like the wounded animal he was.

When he next woke, it was in the tiny room in the church, the oven still cold and dormant in the corner. He retched, spitting out a mouthful of bile.

Scorched flesh ran up his arm, bubbling into blisters. He gritted his teeth, hissing against the pain. Light flickered in through the shattered window and he carefully moved out of its way. After some consideration, he tentatively stretched his fingers out underneath the beams.

He jerked his hand back, squeezing his eyes shut against the white heat—the terror of what this meant. Against the ripple of chaos shuddering through him as his control slipped.

Taszni nem Malachiasz Czechowicz.

Taszni nem Malachiasz Czechowicz.

Taszni nem Malachiasz Czechowicz.

He needed to get out of here. Figure out this new . . . development. Had that dream been *real*? Was he not alone? Blood and bone, he hoped he was alone.

"Never truly alone."

Malachiasz buried his head in his hands, his breath coming in pained, shuddery gasps. He was going to die here if he remained, or worse.

He wasn't used to not knowing what to do. There had always been a next step, more to reach for, something else to gain when everything came crashing down. The ashes could always be swept aside to reveal a greater path.

Now, when he pushed the ashes away all he found was darkness.

He didn't want to live in the darkness. As close as he may be with it, he didn't like the dark. He scrambled to his feet, deciding to find someplace less likely to burn him. He'd wait out the rest of the day before he made his escape. To where, he could figure out later.

And if the voice in his head wanted him to kill another god, he could see that into being. But what was he dealing with? What kind of god would taint themselves with a heretic like him?

"It's your heresy that makes you so compelling," the voice said.

Malachiasz winced. None of his thoughts were safe, then. That was . . . less than ideal.

"Heresy is too simple a term. It is your denial of reality that makes you so interesting. Your power, your cleverness, your ruthlessness, all things I can use."

Malachiasz would have to be willing. He knew that much. Nadya's gods couldn't force her hand, not truly, they could only suggest and grant power.

"Oh, that is precious," the voice said, sounding like a sigh and a groan and death and death and death.

Malachiasz stumbled as pain lanced through his head at the base of his skull. He put a hand on the wall to steady himself.

Suddenly he was sitting down, a hairsbreadth away from the

light, a needling feeling to edge closer, to let it bathe his face, and *burn.*

"I can make you do whatever I wish. You have no choice but to comply. I am not like the pretenders. I am more, I am greater."

Malachiasz swallowed hard. His body sagged as he was released. He shoved away from the light.

Serefin had been dealing with a Kalyazi god in his head—had he managed to break that off? Was he even alive? Malachiasz couldn't decide whether he hoped the boy, the king, *his brother* was dead, or if he hoped he'd done what he set out to do and had torn himself away from malevolent powers too great to fathom.

No, not that. Not unfathomable. Malachiasz was near that state, too, wasn't he? A sidestep into the void, and he could touch the chaos he had power over. Nothing could truly control chaos, though, it did as it willed. Malachiasz was a channel and a vessel but he could harness it, at least; he could point it in the right direction.

He had what he wanted but nothing was *right.* There had to be another step forward. Surely all the pieces could not have fallen so fast.

The Vultures. He needed to get back to the Vultures. He needed to go home.

To do what? To what end? He didn't even know if he could get out of this forest. It was idly chewing at the back of his mind. And he let it, if it wanted his madness, it could have it.

He blinked, confused. He wasn't in the church anymore. Like he had been taken apart, scattered, and reformed somewhere . . . else.

The clearing.

He swore softly, spinning in a slow arc to take in his surroundings. It did not look as it had when he had been here with Nadya. There had been forty statues in a ring, each more grotesque and bewildering than the last.

There hadn't been an altar in the center. Or bones scattered around the clearing, shattered skulls and broken ribs. No fresh blood scrawled in a pattern along the stones.

A black decay had begun creeping up the base of the statues. One was completely consumed. The figure had captivated Nadya when she was here. Marzenya, then. Mold dripped out the many eyes and sharp mouths of the statues.

I wish this didn't terrify the shit out of me, Malachiasz thought idly. It would be fascinating if he didn't feel like he was going to tremble himself into an early grave. Although he *had* already died, he supposed.

"Many have died, many will die, many are dying as we speak. You are not nearly as special as you think."

Special enough that you're here, Malachiasz shot back petulantly. He moved toward the altar, though he sensed that wasn't the wisest decision. *You clearly need me.*

He picked up a cracked skull, mostly in one piece. The person it belonged to must have died from a pronounced blow to the head.

Why me? Aside from my cleverness. I'm hardly going to make this easy for you.

"When the lives of paltry mortals are spread out before me, why would I not choose the one who has consistently altered the course of the world with little regard to life?"

Malachiasz winced. That was true enough.

"The one who tells himself that it's all for a greater cause but relishes fear and chaos and blood."

He absently rubbed his thumb over the skull. It *was* for a greater cause. What would have changed had he not taken the Vultures? Or if he had not . . . lied to Nadya again?

Except she had been lying right back.

Why had he thought coming to this place had only been about her magic? Because if he had been in her situation it would have been the singular force driving him?

Instead she had wrenched away the only thing that had ever truly mattered to him. All to pull him down and salt the earth behind her. It was fair, ruthless even, and he'd be impressed if he wasn't so furious.

"Do you hate her for it?"

The question caught Malachiasz off guard. Did he?

Yes. A little, a lot. Too much, not enough. He hated that it had surprised him. He hated that it *hurt*, that he had allowed himself to be vulnerable to that kind of pain. That he had let himself love her. It was supposed to be a game, an act, a layering of truths over lies so she trusted him enough to do as he wanted, but somewhere it got muddled and he forgot he was pretending.

He wished for indifference. Hatred burned too hot, too close, and it would be better to forget the Kalyazi girl who had broken so much. Indifference would mean a concrete answer to what he might do if he ever saw her again.

At the moment, he didn't know whether it would be better to run her through or . . .

He didn't know what the other option was. Let her kill him? She would try after what he had done. A betrayal for a betrayal. It was fair, rational. This cycle of theirs would burn forever. This was why a war between their peoples had churned for so long; there was nothing else, and there never would be.

The change he had been fighting for would never happen. His was a doomed quest, hopeless.

"Yes," the voice confirmed, gleeful.

Malachiasz almost rolled his eyes. He set the skull down on the altar, careful, though he wasn't sure why. *Do you think reminding me what I already know will make me turn to a being I have spent my whole life fighting against? You're supposed to be a god—be better than this.* Appealing to his emotions wouldn't work. He knew when he was being toyed with.

A tremor before the shift; he closed his eyes so when others opened, it wasn't as jarring. There was no way to get used to this and still retain some measure of humanity, and it was the latter he'd been so willing to lose, only to discover that it wasn't the case at all once he'd lost it entirely.

As much as he might hate her—or hate that he didn't—what Nadya had done for him was something he would never be able to repay her for. Because he *had* miscalculated the spell—it *had* driven him farther than he expected, and if she hadn't gone into the Salt Mines to throttle him back into a bare semblance of human, he would still be down there. He would be gone.

He remembered what he had done in that state. Leaving the mines for the battlefield, rending apart his enemies, cementing his place in Kalyazi stories of what monsters Tranavians truly were. There was no regret there. One vibrant Kalyazi girl didn't make up for the rest.

"Is that what you want? Better? Fine. This game can be played until you realize that fighting what I wish is futile. If you must be broken, I will break you."

Malachiasz didn't have a chance to point out that he was already broken before he shattered.

It was cold and dark, and he knew this cold, this darkness. He had been here before, a different time, under different circumstances. But he had forgotten this part, forgotten everything, because that was the way the Vultures wanted it. They wanted children to be blank slates, nothing but vessels for the magic that would be embedded in their skin. It was a closely held secret, how Vultures were made, but there were no secrets kept from the Black Vulture. He knew struggling was useless.

Agony, a searing heat that flashed to cold and back, too fast, too much, a boiling, a flash burn, a block of ice pressed down, down, down against skin. Repeated, unending, until a snapping point. There was always a snapping point. Everyone broke in the end.

Bones fractured, shattered, melded back together to be stronger than iron, harder than steel, and sharpened, so sharp. One wrong move will part flesh until they adapt, until they learn to control what they have become.

A baptism of dark magic and cold iron and blood.

But he wasn't in that place anymore; he was more, he was greater.

No, he wasn't. Not really. He was still that boy, confused and afraid and uncertain. Now he had all this power that could be twisted and formed and turned against him.

His spine fissured. The weight of heavy wings dragged at his shoulders and he tried to stop the changes—once upon a time he had control over them. Once, he could bend them to his will. When had that changed? His *feet* shifted and iron punched through his skin as he drew further and further down. Less human, less human, *less*.

5

SEREFIN

MELESKI

Siblings abandoned at a monastery deep in the forests, Svoyatovi Kliment and Svoyatova Frosya Ylechukov grew up to infiltrate the Tranavian ranks where they were eventually martyred by the heretics.
—Vasiliev's Book of Saints

Serefin couldn't remember traveling this far south. He re-membered everything from after the forest—well, mostly, a few days were blurred by his fever—and they couldn't have walked as far south as they were.

"The forest spat us out close to its border," Kacper ex-plained with a shrug that said he wasn't going to interrogate the weirdness, only be grateful the forest had let them out at all.

But Serefin *wanted* to interrogate the weirdness. Because everything and nothing had changed. He felt like he was biding time. If he had shattered anything by tearing out his

eye, it had been the connection to the nameless voice, but then, what about Velyos?

"It's true. I've been quite put out by it."

Serefin was careful not to react to the return of the reedy voice he loathed so much. A shudder ran through him all the same.

Is there no way to be rid of you? He had done everything, and it wasn't enough. Still haunted by some know-it-all Kalyazi deity.

"Oh, no, you succeeded. Claim broken, bonds snapped, all that and more. You're free, little Tranavian! But once you hear the voices of my kind, well, that *doesn't stop."*

Serefin took the slightest comfort that the situation could be much worse. Still, less than ideal. *No more visions?*

"No more visions. Did you not like them? I thought they were such fun. It had been so long since I was able to play. I'm disappointed that you didn't enjoy our time together. But the maiming really wasn't necessary in our situation."

Serefin disagreed. He refused to live under the will of a god who could physically control him like Chyrnog or twist his mind and yank him across the continent like Velyos. He refused to live by the whim of *any* gods. *It was worth it.*

"Yes, well, Chyrnog is . . . like that."

Serefin shivered at the name. He didn't want to remember that feeling of his control being wrenched away.

But you can't do what he did?

"Oh, no, not anymore. Don't even want to! Isn't that nice of me?"

He made me kill my brother.

"You were planning on doing that," Velyos noted.

Serefin struggled not to flinch. That wasn't the *point*. Yes, Serefin *had* been planning it. Malachiasz was volatile, a wild card who couldn't be trusted and needed to be dealt with. When it came down to it, though, Serefin hadn't actually wanted to deal with him *like that*. He had lost so much already. It wasn't enough that the blood of his father was on his hands, now he was stained with his brother's blood, too.

How was he supposed to live with himself?

How was he going to face his mother—if he ever made it home?

He didn't know how he was supposed to go to her and admit that the son she had lost to the Vultures could have returned—Malachiasz had stood before Serefin on that mountain top, terrified and in tears and ready to go *home*—and Serefin had killed him.

He couldn't face her. He could barely face himself. Knowing that some kind of order had been returned to the world with Malachiasz's death wasn't enough to assuage the guilt. That Malachiasz had literally been the cause of Serefin's murder wasn't enough either, somehow.

"Serefin?"

He jolted at Kacper's voice. "What?"

Kacper was eyeing him, clearly trying to appear nonchalant and failing utterly. He was worried. He shook his head slightly. "I don't like when you go quiet," he said.

Serefin glanced around, realizing how silent everything was. The roads were empty. They were exposed and had no magic to defend themselves. The alternative, though, was the forest that hemmed in the road on either side, and Serefin was done traveling through forests for the next ten years at least.

"Sorry," Serefin said, shooting Kacper a wry smile. "I will endeavor to maintain a constant stream of chatter from here on out."

"Wait, no—"

"I can start, well, on any topic. I was always told I had an alarming wit at court."

"I don't think they meant that as a compliment—"

"I also have an *incredible* collection of lurid ditties rattling in my brain."

"Please, never say the words *lurid ditties* in front of me ever—"

"I can also start in on my unfathomable collection of jokes, with a warning that I picked most of them up from Lieutenant Winarski when I was a very impressionable sixteen years old."

Kacper paused. "Wasn't he—?"

"Of a deeply questionable emotional and mental state, yes. They are not good jokes."

Kacper's face broke into a weary grin. Serefin was not going to ruin the moment by telling Kacper that he could still hear Velyos. It truly was incredibly unseemly for a Tranavian king to be talking to a Kalyazi god—

"Not a god."

Oh, shut up.

Serefin would have to figure out how to close himself off so Velyos didn't chime in on every errant thought. At least he had broken off the greater bond. It was a relief to know his maiming had meant something. That was nice.

"I was thinking," Serefin said softly. "We need to figure out how to get back to the capital and into Grazyk without Ruminski finding out." He felt bad lying to Kacper, but, well, he *could have* been thinking about that, right?

"I wish we had been able to free Żaneta," Kacper mused.

So did Serefin, but that wasn't in the cards. He wondered if it even would have fixed anything, if Malachiasz had been telling the truth that she needed time to adapt. He didn't know how the Vultures were made, but Malachiasz had seemed earnest about that, at least.

Suddenly Serefin tripped on a hole he'd thought was several steps away, Kacper barely catching his arm and keeping him on his feet. His depth perception was shot, and while he would eventually adjust, he couldn't help feeling useless.

"Careful," Kacper murmured, but didn't pull away.

Serefin kept waiting for it, surprised when he slid his hand down Serefin's arm, twining their fingers together. It was almost as if things were normal—or at least not quite so broken as they truly were.

A snap sounded within the forest, too loud to be an animal. Serefin cursed softly, dropping Kacper's hand and reaching futilely for his spell book.

They exchanged a glance.

They had gone from two of the deadliest blood mages in

Tranavia to two boys trapped in an enemy kingdom. A king and his lieutenant. Easy prey.

And what manner of creatures had awoken in Kalyazin? Malachiasz had torn down the wall separating that damned forest from the hellish place hiding within it. What had escaped? What had they done on that mountain?

He wanted to place the blame on Nadya and Malachiasz but so much of it was his own damn fault.

"You were only doing as I asked," Velyos said, sounding petulant.

Serefin didn't deign to respond. He had done what he had been forced to, and he rather thought that was different.

Another snap within the trees. Someone was moving through the underbrush toward the road.

Serefin's hand fell away from his spell book. He gestured for Kacper to relax. Perhaps they were dealing with mortal foes.

Can't you, I don't know, help?

"No—no, you had your chance with me, and you made your stance perfectly clear. I can do nothing and that's your own fault."

Serefin sighed. He had worked so hard to get rid of the god's influence, he supposed he couldn't very well complain about the god mostly leaving him alone.

Still . . . it would be nice to know what they were dealing with.

"Drop any weapons you have," a young voice called from within the trees. Serefin frowned, glancing at Kacper.

Kacper shrugged but relaxed slightly.

Serefin tossed his *szitelka* into the dirt, gesturing for Kacper to do the same. He did, scowling.

"That can't possibly be it."

"I assure you, dear," Serefin said, not bothering to mask the Tranavian accent from his Kalyazi. "That's it."

A girl—Serefin's age—with pale skin and blond hair cropped close to her scalp slipped out of the forest. Her bow was drawn halfway, arrow pointed at Serefin's throat. "Coins. Into the dirt with the blade."

"You're about to be disappointed," Kacper muttered, tossing his light purse dramatically beside Serefin's *szitelka*.

Nothing more than highway robbers. Losing their coin and blades was less than ideal, but survivable. Those were trivialities.

She nudged the bow at Serefin, and he shrugged.

"I've got nothing. Are you alone?"

One eyebrow lifted. She wore a tunic in a neutral gray, the edges frayed, a tear in the neckline. There were holes in her coat and her leggings, and the soles of her boots looked like they were barely hanging on.

"We have nothing else to—"

"Your ring." She gestured with her bow to Serefin's little finger.

Kacper tensed. Serefin's hand curled into a fist. The signet ring was one of the only things he had left—it was all he had of his authority; the hammered iron crown had been lost in the forest. The girl had no idea what she was asking, but thanks to Serefin's response, she knew it was *wanted*.

She smiled. "Drop it."

"I'm afraid we need to reach a different agreement," Serefin said.

Her arm pulled back, the bow taut. Her aim needn't even be good for the arrow to punch through Serefin's throat, and dying by choking on his own blood wasn't particularly how he wanted to die.

But this was only one girl. Serefin could take her. The moths around Serefin had been idle, unnoticeable, but when his alarm spiked, so did they, bursting up in a cloud.

The girl jumped back. And more than a dozen arrows visibly trained on Serefin and Kacper as the girl's companions finally made themselves known. Serefin sighed, lifting his hands.

"I won't ask again," she said.

"But I certainly will refuse again!" Serefin said cheerfully, a bead of sweat dripping down his back. He didn't *quite* know how to talk his way out of this one. Before the forest—before Kalyazin—he would have been able to. He could've charmed the bow out of this girl's hands and walked away with her coin, but he didn't know what he could possibly say to make it worth lowering her bow. She had likely spent the better part of the long winter starving.

"Take the coin, take the blades," he said, more seriously. "Leave the ring, it's nothing more than iron."

Her gaze flicked to his hand, unconvinced, but she smiled.

"Take them," she said. "There's use for them yet."

"Wait, no, I don't—" But before Serefin could finish, something sharp pricked his neck.

He dropped to the ground, unconscious.

Serefin woke to the taste of blood in his mouth and a pounding headache. He was soaked to his skin and *freezing*. His disorientation lasted only long enough for him to open his eye. He immediately closed it, pretending to be asleep.

All this time in Kalyazin and *now* they had been captured by highway thieves? It would be funny if it weren't so damn sad.

The cords that bound his ankles and wrists were too tight and his extremities felt fuzzy from the lack of circulation. Uncomfortable, but not the end of the world. The weight of his signet ring remained on his little finger, a massive relief. Why hadn't the girl taken it, if she was that desperate?

Of course, if she *was* that desperate, he would be dead on the road, not tied up and left out in the wet snow to gather water in his ears.

He almost tried to sit up, better to get this over with, but he heard the low murmur of voices and decided to wait this one out.

As he listened, he became increasingly disappointed. The chatter was utterly useless. One of the girls was lamenting about a girl she'd left behind in her village and she was being thoroughly teased for it. Serefin sighed internally. So much for these being Kalyazi agents of war. He had been certain everything they'd been avoiding since the mountain was catching up with them, but maybe not. These were just tired Kalyazi thieves who wanted to make a few quick coins off some boys on the road.

Though that didn't explain why they had been taken alive.

He opened his eye a slit. It wasn't yet dark.

"It was all well and good to spend your nights gossiping like *babas* when we were in Dovribinski," the girl who'd threatened him said, "but if you keep this up, you're going to bring the whole wood down on our heads and we're in *kashyvhes* country."

"*Kashyvhes* country," one of the men said derisively. "You and your children's stories, Olya."

"I won't pray around your tent tonight, then," Olya said blandly. "You can go without any blessings. I'm not sure they would hold anyway—blessings aren't like flies, you know, they don't stick to shit."

The whole group erupted into jeers, and Serefin couldn't help but feel nervous. He knew how dangerous these woods could be, and he didn't particularly want to be visited by a *striczki* while he was hog-tied on the damn ground.

"I thought I told Tsezar to put the Tranavians in a tent," Olya said, sounding tired, annoyed, and disgusted all at once, which Serefin thought was rather impressive.

"Why should they get a dry canvas over their heads?" a woman's voice asked.

"Because I don't want them dead," Olya replied wearily. "And the pale one looks like he's ready to drop at any second. Put them both in the tent. *Baba* Zhikovnya can decide if they're worth anything."

There was the sound of someone spitting. Then the hard smack of flesh as, presumably, Olya smacked the spitter.

"I didn't come here to deal in your witch flesh trade," a man said.

"Go back to your starving village then, Stepan, and see if I care," Olya snapped. "Get them inside."

Serefin chewed on the inside of his lip, thinking. He could draw enough blood and—

He sighed. He was thinking like a blood mage and that wouldn't do him any good. He still had *something*, could feel some power under his skin, but maybe that was Velyos' work. He didn't want to rely on Velyos for anything.

"You may have to," Velyos said pointedly.

Why couldn't the god have gone away when he'd torn out his eye?

"Because that was you breaking the connection with Chyrnog, mostly. And with me, but I had you in a different way than he did. It's fine, I'm not offended. I got what I wanted."

And what did you want? Serefin's curiosity won out.

Velyos had wanted to wake other fallen gods who had been banished like him, for vengeance, but what did that mean?

Was the death of that goddess part of your plan?

"I am not saddened to see her go. I expected to take a more direct route for her death, I was not expecting the Vulture to do it for me."

You feel sadness?

"No."

Serefin shifted his shoulders, attempting to relieve some of the tension in them.

"What I want is simple, and you have essentially given it to me. Me and my ilk were banished, and I wanted that undone. I wanted my revenge on Marzenya for the banishment, and she is dead."

What about Chyrnog?

"Well, I can't say that his goals and mine align."

Serefin felt a chill. *What does he want?*

"The death of the sun, of the world, renewal."

Serefin pressed his head down into the dirt a little more. What had he done?

But . . . couldn't the gods not work without mortal intervention? Maybe all was not lost. Maybe the god hadn't found a human to claim. Serefin would have to hold to that.

He wanted to go home but running was useless. Everything would catch up to him. These problems wouldn't stay localized in Kalyazin, and it would fall on Tranavia all the faster because his was the country of heretics.

"I'm so proud. You're finally catching on!"

This is all your fault, Serefin thought morosely.

"I wanted freedom and Marzenya to pay. I have those things and I am now content to watch."

Serefin frowned. *But what about the vision? What about the ash and blood and . . . and . . .*

"The burning?"

It seemed then like you were giving me a warning.

"A warning of the inevitable, perhaps."

Serefin withdrew, building a wall between himself and the god. Velyos wanted this chaos, and there was no trusting this god to point him in a direction that wouldn't be catastrophic. Surely something could be done, but Serefin wasn't going to figure out what from a god.

He didn't know the havoc the fallen gods were wreaking, but it couldn't be good, and he would hear about it soon enough.

If he survived this, of course.

But if gods could be set free, that meant they could be bound. What if they could be bound again? The Kalyazi would have thoughts about that, but their precious gods would turn on them soon, and they'd see it was the only way.

Though he supposed he shouldn't expect them all to be as rational as Nadya.

Olya finally wandered over, loosening the ropes on Serefin's wrists.

"You're already out an eye," she said. "You don't need to be out both your hands as well."

"Oh, all the better for me to hold the hilt of the blade you'll kill me with?" Serefin replied cheerfully.

"If I wanted you dead, you'd be dead," she said dryly as she moved back to the others.

But he was able to work his way into a sitting position and inch over to Kacper, who eyed him with some bemusement.

"You have a type," Kacper noted.

"I'm not going to like where this is going, am I?"

"Your type is girls who could very easily kill you and definitely want to."

"And pretty boys who are nice to me," Serefin finished for him. "And would also like to kill me."

Kacper made a thoughtful, vaguely disbelieving sound, but grinned. "My life *would* be much easier with you dead."

"Are you allowed to say that about your ki—?"

Kacper elbowed him hard. He wheezed.

"Are you allowed to do *that*?"

"I better be," Kacper muttered. A flicker of worry crossed his face. "Am I?"

"Obviously." He slumped against Kacper's shoulder, tilting his head to kiss his neck. "You can do whatever you want. Within reason."

"*Oh.*"

"No coups, please."

"I'll try to restrain myself, but no promises."

Serefin laughed softly.

"You'll be a good king," Kacper said softly, so softly Serefin wasn't sure he was supposed to hear it.

Serefin's face heated. He didn't know if Kacper was right. It was something Serefin had never thought he was allowed to want, never mind that he was the prince. He was supposed to die on a battlefield in Kalyazin.

"I hope so," Serefin whispered, because that was all he had. A fragile thread of hope that he wouldn't die in the kingdom of his enemies and could pull his country out of the mess they had found themselves in—so much of it his fault.

The evening twilight cast the wood in a strange, dim light, and Serefin had a terrible feeling they were being dragged into the forest they had already escaped. He could feel it gnawing at his edges, the awareness of a greater force that wanted to take him apart again.

"Olya, look at this," one of the thieves called across the camp. She was inspecting a tree, holding a torch close to the bark, a frown on her face.

Olya got up with exaggerated exasperation, but her expression changed as she inspected the tree.

"Keep away from it," she warned. "I don't like it."

"What is it?" the girl asked.

Olya shook her head.

"If you dragged us all the way out here to be eaten by witch magic . . ." One of the other thieves grumbled.

"Shut *up*, Stepan," Olya snapped, but she sounded rattled.

Serefin and Kacper exchanged a glance.

Olya turned, her gaze lighting on the two Tranavian boys. Her eyes narrowed. She gestured to a nearby Kalyazi, who hauled Serefin to his feet and shoved him in the direction of the tree.

"You don't have to be so handsy," Serefin protested. "Buy me a drink first." But his heart fell when he saw what they'd discovered in the eerie dim.

Something was eating the trees alive. Like mold, a black infection creeping along the bark and worming its way deeper. After peering too long, Serefin was overwhelmed with the sudden desire to plunge his hand in. He was oddly grateful his wrists were tied.

"Were any of the trees we passed on the way like this?" Olya asked the girl.

She shook her head, eyeing Serefin.

"I'm not sure why you've brought me over," he said serenely.

"You're a blood mage with a godstouched eye," Olya replied, her voice flat.

Serefin froze, stomach clenching. His fingers twitched uselessly, wanting to cover his eye.

"Untie my hands," he said.

"You think me a fool?" Olya replied evenly.

He didn't. In fact, he was beginning to think she was much more than a simple thief. Serefin was infinitely tired of bossy, magic-touched Kalyazi girls.

"How do you expect me to—" He was interrupted when a choir of screams rang through the trees. A cacophonous echo, surrounding them. A thousand terrified screeches.

A bird, large and black, thudded to the ground at their feet, a scream tearing through it before it cut off, silenced and dead.

Serefin swallowed hard, dread coiling through him as he lifted his gaze to where hundreds of birds perched in the tree branches.

All of them screaming.

The group lost three quarters of their members that night. They argued for hours about acrid mold and screaming, dying birds. Olya wearily attempted to explain that they were nowhere near Tachilvnik; the horrors of the deep wood could not travel this far.

Serefin kept the truth to himself. The rush of old power, dark magic, ravenous and mad, sweeping past them. Clawing and biting and so very, very hungry.

Instead, he leaned against Kacper, resting his head on his shoulder, and listened to them argue. Most left, complaining of cursed magic and muttering how nothing good could ever come from treating with Tranavian demons, even if they were tied up. Only the girl, an old man, and a boy about Serefin's age—twitchy in a shadowy way that reminded Serefin of Malachiasz—stayed.

The boy was excited about the horror, in an unsettling, morbid way. Olya took his enthusiasm with weary patience, as if used to it.

"The witches will have an explanation," was all she said.

"It's not witch magic," the boy insisted. He had the look of the people from the very north of Kalyazin. Straight black hair tied back but still managing to hang in his face, and narrow dark eyes.

Serefin tilted his head slightly to glance up at Kacper, who was frowning.

Olya crouched down, poking a dead bird with a stick.

"It's not blood magic either," she replied, casting a look at Serefin and Kacper.

Serefin shrugged. He was trying his best not to think about the screams still ringing in his head.

Chyrnog was gone. Serefin wanted to be relieved, but he didn't know where he had ended up, and so long as his dreams were

tainted by a massive doorway and arms and hands, grasping, clawing at him, he would worry.

"The witches will know," Olya said. "The witches have to know."

"When did it become witches, plural?" Kacper asked, voice soft.

Serefin shook his head. "This might not be the worst situation
for us to be in."

He could *feel* Kacper's incredulity and he didn't particularly
want to explain with the Kalyazi in earshot. He sighed.

"Magic," he whispered.

Kacper rolled his eyes. "Magic is what got us into this mess."

"And magic will get us out."

6

NADEZHDA

LAPTEVA

Marzenya has gone silent. I cut my palms, I bleed over
her altars, I weep. There is nothing. She does not care.
She will let this world burn.

—Passage from the personal journals
of Sofka Greshneva

Nadya was startled by how cold it was when she left the farmhouse. But of course it was cold. Nothing had changed.

What happened when a god died—was murdered? Would Marzenya's domains—magic and winter and death—change anywhere else, or only Kalyazin? How much power did the gods have over the world, truly?

Nadya had no answers, and she was beginning to wonder if she should stop looking for them. That was what had gotten her in this mess to begin with. If she had gone with Anna to Komyazalov instead of Grazyk, how much would be different? She wouldn't be dreading the capital; she knew that much. She wouldn't feel the icy chill of fear grasping

at her spine at the mere thought of the seat of the church and the Matriarch.

She had never met the Matriarch. Magdalena Fedoseyeva, the head of the Church, the mouthpiece through which the gods touched the world now that the world had no clerics. Or maybe she had—she had been to Komyazalov once, when she was so young she could barely remember it. She didn't think that really counted. But the Church was hiding things from her. They were afraid of her. It wasn't a difficult leap to realize all signs pointed to the Matriarch.

Would she know what Nadya had done? That Marzenya was dead? That Nadya had failed so utterly as Kalyazin's cleric?

She didn't want to find out.

Nadya wasn't running away—though she did consider it—when she wandered out of the small village and into the woods. A part of her never wanted to step into thickly wooded terrain again, but she wanted someplace where peace was a guarantee. Where no one would stare at her hand and ask questions. She wanted . . . to test a theory.

She didn't know for certain how many fallen gods were free. Katya—while knowledgeable—gave vague responses when asked, making it clear she didn't know, either. Fine with Nadya. The *tsarevna* already had too much power over her and she didn't want to give her anything *more* that could be used against her. She knew the mistakes she had made; she knew her list of crimes had grown since fleeing the monastery.

She didn't trust Katya. Maybe it was uncharitable, but the *tsarevna* had spent her life hunting Vultures and studying the occult only to meet Nadya—a girl, who was supposed to be divine, dabbling in darkness and leading the worst of the Vultures, the boy she loved, to the seat of the gods. Nadya's intentions didn't matter, to Katya it was her fault Marzenya was dead, because Nadya had given Malachiasz the chance to strike.

But not going to Katya meant Nadya had no idea how many

gods existed outside the twenty she had devoted her life to. It was an uncomfortable thought. A frozen bite of wind raced around her, spinning dead leaves through the air, as she ran her hand down her prayer beads. Useless. Nothing but a wooden necklace with sentimental value. Her grief slammed into her, and she considered not going back.

What if she kept walking? Past Komyazalov, past the far western border, to Česke Zin or Rumenovać. Somewhere no one would know her name or her story. Somewhere her gods had different faces and names and it wouldn't matter, so much, that she had once been able to talk to them and still failed.

"Ah, there you are."

She jumped at the nearby voice. Perched on a rotten tree stump was a figure cloaked in black, with hair like the depths of an acrid swamp. Their skin was sallow, lips thin, eyes large and dark and impossibly sad.

"Ljubica," Nadya said.

"Hello, little cleric." The fallen god grinned, revealing sharp teeth—like those of a poisonous fish.

"Not a cleric."

"Not a cleric, not a witch, not divine, not mortal." Ljubica rolled their eyes. "What are you?"

"Not interested in playing these games."

"Not fun!"

Nadya pressed her lips together. She had come here to try to commune with one of the fallen gods, but she was realizing this was another impulsive mistake to add to her tidy collection. This would only pull her further into this nightmare. All she wanted was to escape. To wake up.

She wanted Malachiasz and Marzenya to not be dead.

What she wanted did not matter.

She moved past Ljubica's tree stump. After a beat, Ljubica let out an irritated huff and their footsteps crunched through the leaves after her.

Heavy footfalls for a god, Nadya thought absently. She had no idea what Ljubica was the god of. She also didn't understand why she could *see* them. That's not how this worked.

"You have a mortal form," Nadya observed.

"It's nice, isn't it? I'm quite fond of it. It could be different. What will get you to truly talk to me, I wonder?" The figure in Nadya's peripheral vision changed. Blond and freckled with full, red lips. "No?" Ljubica spun in front of Nadya, forcing her to stop.

Nadya gasped, her heart in her throat, because the figure was taller, lithe and pale, with a pile of long black hair and knife sharp features.

"Don't you dare," she whispered.

"He bled all over that divine mountain. We all know what he was."

Heat prickled Nadya's eyes. She wasn't going to cry. Not here. Not ever again. Certainly not for him.

Ljubica grinned but they were wearing his face and a sob broke from deep in Nadya's chest. She shoved past Ljubica.

"Your tears are exactly what I want," Ljubica said with a blissful sigh. "Let's make a deal, you and I, for you have so many tears to give and I have been thirsty for so very long."

No more deals. No more listening to gods who only wanted Nadya for their petty games. No more trusting pretty Tranavian boys with sly smiles.

"No."

"You can't do this on your own," Ljubica said.

Nadya risked turning back. The god didn't look like him any-more. They were back to their normal form. She didn't like the way her heart wrenched at the loss because she had wanted to see him one more time.

"No. I'm done being manipulated. You can all find some other mortal to torture."

Silence fell on the wood. Not a complete silence—the birds were too loud in the treetops. Something rustled nearby and Na-dya couldn't help but think about the rumors of dragons Katya kept bringing to dinner. It would be quite a fate for her, to survive so much only to be killed in the woods by a mythical creature. Fitting, really.

"You are not wholly mortal, though. Isn't that right?"

Nadya closed her eyes. Stars and oblivion and an ocean of dark water. "I don't want answers." She had thought that was all she wanted—to know what she was, why she was different, why it was so necessary for those she trusted to lie to her for eighteen years.

"I don't think that's true, either."

And maybe it wasn't. But answers might break her and she had so little strength left.

"I don't want to be anything else," Nadya said softly.

Ljubica nodded. "That Tranavian king set us free. You set us free. Velyos set us free."

"How many of you?"

"Five of us retained our minds after being locked away."

The implications of their words chilled Nadya. That meant there were others that did not.

"Who are they?"

"Myself, Cvjetko, Zlatana, Zvezdan, and Velyos, of course."

"Of course," Nadya murmured. "What happens now?" she asked pathetically.

Ljubica smiled serenely. "Chaos."

Nadya was left standing alone in a clearing, her corrupted hand clutched to her chest. She closed her eyes. It was so *quiet*. She had grown mostly used to the quiet since that night in the cathedral in Grazyk, but there had been potential, then, for the quiet to cease. No more.

She could sense the *wrong* in the earth beneath her feet. The loosening of the ties that bound the world into its careful order. The witch had told her that the gods' retributions on the mortal world were made in small movements. They needed people to push along their plans, and people could only do so much.

But Ljubica's tangible presence meant these five weren't so bound. And the others might not stay so bound.

So, Nadya's theory, whatever it was worth, was accurate, though she wasn't quite sure what to do with that information. She almost wanted to talk to Velyos. He had started this whole mess. Except she didn't know how to reach these five like she had reached her gods. She didn't have symbols to ascribe to them; she didn't have a tether that she could grasp.

A tree branch snapped. Nadya whirled, reaching for—

What? What did she have? Her fingers closed over the hilt of one of her *voryens*, an almost blinding pain in her hollowed palm followed.

She was relieved it *wasn't* a dragon that stepped out through the brush. Her relief was short lived as a starved wolf watched her with gold, hungry eyes.

It was huge. Nadya had seen plenty of wolves near the monastery while growing up, but none of them had been *this* big. It was unnatural. What primordial monstrosities walked the earth because of their recklessness?

Her recklessness.

She shifted her *voryen* in her grip, wincing as warm liquid slid down her palm. Malachiasz's claws had punched clean through her hands and the wounds were slow to heal. She held out a hand, remembering how the *rusalki* had responded to her, the way her blood had hummed when they had fought the *Lichni'voda*. Could that work here, too?

A growl rippled through the clearing. The wolf's fur was matted with dirt and dark with dried blood. Her fingers stretched toward it. The growl grew to a snarl. Nadya drew her hand back, fear icing her veins. One didn't run from wolves; they were too fast. The trees surrounding her were impossible to climb—their branches too far out of reach. She had to fight.

All she had was one *voryen*, that was it.

That's not remotely true. The voice was hers, yet not, and it jarred Nadya enough to focus, to dart away when the wolf lunged, jaws snapping a hair away from her arm. But she didn't want to reach for the dark water. To use that power was to admit that even if she had been a cleric once, it was not all she was.

The palm of her corrupted hand, wounded and aching, grew warm as the wolf circled her, salivating at the anticipation of a meal. She sensed the coil in its muscles, the rippling of its fur before it struck again.

Nadya knelt at the edge of a churning ocean. Desperate, she plunged her hand under the icy water.

A wall of power, shimmering in the light, slammed up before her. The wolf crashed into it and yelped, rearing back. A wealth of pure magic, a drowning. The taste of iron and ashes. Time slowed around her, and she clenched a fist. The wolf let out another distressed yelp as its body went rigid.

It would be so easy to kill the beast. The thought was dispassionate. Nadya felt like she was watching herself from afar. Another inch of tension, tightening her fist a little more, and she could crush the beast's bones as easily as if they were twigs. White flames licked up her corrupted hand, catching on her sleeve.

Her vision shifted and she could see far more than she should. The beast—not a beast, only a wolf, an ancient creature that had prowled the forests for hundreds of years—and its ravaging hunger covered up an old nobility. Nadya could not find the cruelty within herself to snuff it out. She dropped the magic with a gasp, considered further, and slammed a heavy blow of power down on the wolf to knock it unconscious.

Then she fled.

She patted out the flames on her sleeve, breathing hard. It was foolish to leave the wolf alive. Stupid. It was too close to the village. But old things had woken, were set free, and she didn't know if the right move was eradicating them. And if it was, she was afraid of how using that power made her feel. Like she was someone else, something else, and cruelty was nothing but a pleasantry for her. She had done enough cruel things that maybe it was. The echoes of Malachiasz's voice telling her how well she wore cruelty were too near. She didn't want to force herself further down that path than she had already gone.

She winced at the raw, seeping wound on her right palm.

Using her magic had obliterated the bandages on her hands. With a start she realized the left had healed, spiral scar punctuated by the place where Malachiasz had pierced her.

A sense of *wrong* came over her. Warily, she moved toward a copse of trees that seemed darker than the rest. Like shadows were eating at their bases and slowly chewing their way up.

She brushed a hand against one. The bark fell away, crumbling at her touch and revealing pale white underneath. Sap the color of dark blood oozed down the tree.

Oh, this is bad. Her first instinct was to clutch at her necklace. Vaclav would know what was going on. With a sinking feeling it hit her fully that she had no one. She was completely alone.

No gods, no goddess, no obnoxious, anxious Tranavian boy with too many answers.

Just Nadya.

Just a girl and the eldritch well of magic that had made its home inside her at the end of the world.

interlude i

PARIJAHAN

SIROOSI

Parijahan could not think of a single time when Rashid had been as upset with her as he was now.

"It's not that you told Malachiasz," he said, rigid with anger. "I understand that. It's that you didn't tell *me*."

She had withheld everything from him. The missives, the letters, the reports that kept finding their way to her. All begging for her return. All whispering that her particular transgression would be forgiven, her status secure, and everything would go back to the way it was before she had run.

Nadya had left the house without a word, unreadable. Ostyia left not long after, Katya following. Parijahan sat down across from Rashid. She had been avoiding him—avoiding this—since the forest.

The notes from her Travash were spread out on the table before him, and she couldn't stop watching the way he was rubbing at his forearms, at the strange markings and terrible

gashes scattered across his brown skin that didn't seem to be healing.

"Did you tell him everything?" Rashid asked.

Parijahan shook her head. "He would have made it obvious if I had."

He tilted his head in agreement. Cold fury was pouring off him in waves. She refused to let him see how rattled she was by his response. She deserved it, but they would get nowhere if they sat here and fought.

"What were you planning with him?" Rashid asked. "Don't tell me it was nothing."

She eyed him warily. He looked exhausted. His black hair, kept long, was tied back, which only made the shadows under his dark eyes more pronounced. She had known Rashid most of her life. He'd been by her side the entire time. She hadn't intended to keep him in the dark.

"Do you remember your home before you came to Paalmidesh?" she asked.

He frowned at her for turning a question back on him. He gave a hesitant nod. It was not the answer she wanted, but she waited, watching as he decided whether to speak. He had told her what little he could recall of his family, but she wanted something deeper. When the tension in Akola finally came to a head, she needed to know: Would he be with her, or would he be with Yanzin Zadar?

"It's only pieces. There's little to remember," he replied. "Why didn't you trust me, Parj? What did I do?"

It had nothing to do with him. If anything, it had everything to do with what *she* and *her* country had done.

His rich, warm eyes were wounded as they searched her face. "Oh," he said, some measure of disgust in his voice.

"Malachiasz was a neutral party," she said softly. "I never want to put you in a position where you have to make that kind of choice."

"I was never *given* that choice," he pointed out.

She winced.

"Now I make that choice every day. I stay here, with you, instead of going home. Could I even do that? You're the *prasīt*, I suppose you could have me hunted down for running."

"Rashid."

"You chose not to trust me," he snapped. "What were you planning?"

"A way to save Akola from the civil war that is on the horizon," she said, lifting her chin, daring him to tell her what she wanted was wrong.

There was a gulf between them, and it was made from the fractures threatening to shatter Akola back into the five countries that had formed it. A faulty bridge—made from the backs of the people of Yanzin Zadar, broken under the weight of Paalmideshi rule—between them.

He blinked at her, faltering slightly.

"Yes, the unification is failing, and my father is dying," she murmured, aware it had never really been successful. "I thought there would be a way to save it. That maybe Malachiasz could help. And, yes, I was worried that if given the choice to go home to your people, you would take it, and I couldn't bear to lose you. It was selfish."

Rashid rubbed his hands over his face and was silent. Parijahan looked away, gaze darting around the farmhouse, the soft golden light of the setting sun casting it in unearthly shadows. She looked anywhere but at him.

"Parj . . . I don't think there's a way *to* save it."

"That is exactly what Malachiasz said. But that means a civil war."

"A civil war that you could stop if you returned home?"

That was . . . also what Malachiasz had suggested. She shook her head. They were past the point of no return. Paalmidesh had been sucking the other countries dry and her Travash was at fault. If she went home, she would be assassinated long before she could fix her family's mistakes.

"Malachiasz had a lot of convoluted suggestions that required poisoning choice nobility at very specific times to create a rather impressive domino effect that would eventually leave the Siroosi Travash standing."

Rashid snorted.

"And I would lead the Travash," she said, her voice growing quiet. "And I don't want that."

"What about—"

The door opened, and he broke off. Parijahan looked up, hoping for Nadya, but found the *tsarevna* instead. She moved to hastily gather the papers on the table, but Katya had already seen them. The *tsarevna* sat down with them, eyeing the ephemera before leaning back.

"You're a long way from home," she observed. "And you're not who you say you are."

"I'm exactly who I say I am," Parijahan replied.

"An Akolan *prasīt* in a known kingdom of chaos and you can talk to the cleric when no one else can."

"Nadya needs time," Parijahan said. "Give it to her." Parijahan had lost one of her closest friends on that mountain, but Nadya had lost much more. It would be a long time before she came back from that, if she ever did.

"We don't have time." Katya sighed, tying her dark curls back. "I need to know why you're here so when we reach the Silver Court I can explain to my father why I've dragged a *prasīt* into the heart of our country. I would like to keep your Travash from claiming I've kidnapped you and declaring war."

"They wouldn't declare war," Parijahan said. "Not over me."

"I would not be so certain."

"They wouldn't declare war over me because it would mean moving resources that are necessary in case of an internal conflict," Parijahan explained.

Katya's eyebrows rose. Parijahan had never lied about why she was in Kalyazin, but she had also never told the entire truth. It was easy to talk of vengeance. It made sense to those like Malachiasz, or

Nadya, whose worlds were born of violence. It was a perfectly reasonable explanation why an Akolan would willingly be in such unforgiving countries as theirs. But there was so much Parijahan was running from, and she wasn't ready to stop running. Her grandmother was the real ruler of Akola, not her father, and Zohreh would do anything to keep that stranglehold on her family, on the country.

Parijahan had grown up thinking she was safe from her grandmother's machinations. She'd never been expected to take over the Travash. She'd had her sister, Taraneh, and Arman, her older brother. But then Taraneh had been married to a Tranavian, effectively removing her from the line to rule, and Arman had gone to the desert mages and never returned. Parijahan was not so optimistic as to think he was still alive.

That left Parijahan with the weight of a fractured country on her shoulders. A weight she did not want. A weight no one wanted her to have, either.

She thought she'd been *fixing* things when she left. No one wanted her on the throne. Her grandmother had dismissed her as too headstrong to be of any use long ago. What had changed?

Rashid lifted his eyebrows at her after a pointed look at the *tsarevna*. She had never seen him so dimmed, his cheerfulness tempered in a way that was painful. She didn't know what he had gone through in the forest—she was too scared to ask. That was the first time she had been separated from him in years, and it was a divide they couldn't quite cross. But then, she had already planted the seeds of their rift by not telling him that her father was dying and what it meant for Akola.

He wanted to go home, and she couldn't follow him. If he left her now it would break her heart, but she wouldn't stop him.

"Give me something, *anything*," Katya said. "I'm not the enemy. I'd simply like to avoid an international incident."

"Akola knows what I've done and why I left. What they don't know is why I chose to remain here. Akola isn't going to turn on

Kalyazin or Tranavia, trust me. We have our own issues. But if you want to give your court an excuse, tell them a portion of the truth. I'm here to help you fix your disastrous kingdoms."

"But that's only a portion?"

Parijahan could feel Rashid's dark eyes focus on her face.

"It's enough."

Parijahan's time in that damn forest had been strange and uncomfortable, and now she was marked like her friends and it wouldn't be easy to escape. She knew what she had seen, what was required of her, though she wasn't sure how anything would be possible without . . . she swallowed thickly. No matter.

7

MALACHIASZ CZECHOWICZ

A churning, unending horror, pulling back in on himself as he feeds on whatever he can find, even his own body.

—The Volokhtaznikon

He couldn't stop *shaking*. Try as he might, he couldn't get warm, couldn't stop the anxious tremors that had molded alongside a shivering hard enough to rattle his bones.

Taszni nem Malachiasz Czechowicz. Not again. Please, no more. He would do what he had to—anything.

He couldn't escape the fact that he wanted to *live* and to hold onto a scrap of himself as he did. It didn't need to be much—only a piece—and that god had threatened to rip everything away, more than he ever thought he had to lose. Strip away all that was *Malachiasz* until he was nothing but a soulless vessel.

It wouldn't do. Malachiasz was a god in his own right,

and he wouldn't be controlled like this. If it took cooperation, so be it. He would suffer; he would survive. If he was alive, he could change things.

Of course, that had been his driving philosophy for ages, and nothing had changed. Tranavia and Kalyazin would be locked in this war forever, because that was what they knew. It was comfortable, even. Both sides would make demands the other would be unwilling to concede. He didn't see a way forward.

Maybe once he would have considered Nadya a possibility. Someone who wanted to find a compromise. They believed in different things, but he was drawn to her, and she to him. Her company was a comfort he'd never had before. He *liked* being around her, liked arguing about theology and what that meant for the world. She made him consider things he never had, and as much as he might fight against that, he found it fascinating, he found *her* fascinating.

And it had been sufficiently demolished. She would only make things worse, not better, not as she was—who she was.

"Are you so confident in your knowledge of what that girl is?" the voice asked, sounding curious.

Malachiasz winced, but ultimately ignored him. Him? Was that right? Was that even possible? Was it so easy and simple to ascribe human traits to this being?

"No," the voice said, amused. *"But it doesn't particularly matter either way to me."*

He had woken up in a sanctuary at the church, one claimed by the forest. Thick, poisonous-looking grasses grew up and around the remains of benches. Bones rested amidst the growth, maggots crawling in the underbrush, as if dead things, too, were scattered in this place. Malachiasz got to his feet, shuddering and flicking maggots off his skin.

He tugged a hand through his hair, fingers catching on beads and relics knotted in the strands, and he considered ripping the bones out—so much disaster from such small things—but he might have use of them yet, and it had cost him so much to get them.

His chest tightened and he coughed, the pain in his lungs—in a dark part of him—heightening for a heartbeat until it eased. He spat out a mouthful of blood. There was a shiver of eyes and teeth and bone, and then everything settled. Temporary peace.

All he wanted was to sleep and let the worms and maggots take him because that would be better than what he had left.

He supposed getting out of the forest was the first step; figuring out how to take down the rest of the pantheon without destroying himself could wait until he was free of this wood that kept trying to pry him open.

The last time he'd eaten or even had water was before he'd woken up on the mountain. He was constantly dizzy, light-headed. There wasn't much he could do other than hope he came across a stream—when the sun went down and he was finally able to leave this damned place—that wasn't poisoned and hope for the best. He wasn't about to eat anything here. Everything was *festering*.

He tried not to panic at the thought of not feeling sunlight ever again.

Unsure what possessed him, he ventured down to the strange well in the basement. The pale flowers had wilted to withered grotesque husks. He found his jacket balled up in the corner and picked it up with a sigh, tugging it on. He didn't want to think about when he'd first grabbed it in a panic the night he'd fled Tranavia.

Malachiasz hadn't been particularly well liked among the Vultures. They underestimated him, assumed because he was anxious that he was useless—but eventually he'd earned their respect. That was what truly mattered in the cult. Rozá had tried to undermine him at every step, like he'd undermined Łucja until the day he had challenged and killed her. Except Rozá never would have openly challenged him. She wasn't like him. The moment he'd taken Łucja's head from her shoulders had been so very sweet.

Łucja, the last Black Vulture, had held the cult in her grip for a very long time, systematically destroying any Vulture who dared oppose her. She had been calculating and ruthless, but she had no *ambition*.

Tranavia had come to know Malachiasz as the most ruthless

and calculating Black Vulture the cult had ever known. They would remember him; they would never remember her.

Hadn't that been his goal? All those nights when he had planned, when he had stumbled in front of her, over and over, convincing her that he was weak and useless and only good for a punching bag. The more she saw him as a pathetic failure of a boy, barely a Vulture, the easier it would be to take her down. And he'd been correct.

He hadn't done it for notoriety—though that was nice. He had done it because he wanted to change things. Because he was frustrated with his order's passivity, with Tranavia's—with the *world's*—and could not abide Łucja's inaction any longer.

He was surprised by his sudden yearning to be back on that damn throne and dealing with petty court matters. He hadn't asked to become the monster that he was and for so long he had hated it. His fingers brushed the scars that lined his forearms. He didn't know when his feelings had changed; when he'd embraced what he was.

He found himself at the edge of the pool of blood, eyeing the uncomfortably still surface. Had Nadya known what would happen when she stepped into the well? He held his hand out over the surface, not daring to touch it. Could he reverse what she had done?

It had to have been here. There were gaps. He didn't know what had happened to her between the wall falling and arriving at the temple, but this was where something had been wrenched away.

He reached for his spell book. A beat of panic, constricting his chest, tugging at his lungs so hard he started coughing when his fingers found nothing. There was no way to get used to it. That spell book was his entire life and it was gone. A chronicle of every spell he had written, every sketch he had drawn of Nadya and his friends, everything. If he had it, there was a chance he could reverse what Nadya had done, or at least have a starting point to understanding. All he needed was something to start with. Anything broken could be fixed, he had to believe that.

If only for his own sake.

NADEZHDA LAPTEVA

Lev returned last night. From Tachilvnik, supposedly.
I don't know. He won't speak. Can't. No one there but
the gods, he scrawled it on a piece of paper, but then he
showed me . . . They'd cut out his tongue.
— Passage from the personal journals
of Sofka Greshneva

Nadya didn't enjoy riding. She *especially* didn't enjoy riding through forest roads with nothing to do but feel the shifting of the world around her. She tried blocking it out, but the trees looked different, in a way that she couldn't put words to, and the air tasted strange. Everything was broken, wrong. She kept waiting for, what, the end of the world?

"When we get to Komyazalov, we can regroup," Katya said confidently, when Nadya inquired what she was planning, and it didn't sound like false confidence this time.

Nadya was quiet in response, gazing up at the trees. The

last time she checked, they were doing their best to scrape free from the long harsh winter, a dull green that wanted so desperately to be brighter. Now they were blackened and dead and spiderwebs hung from them, with ribbons of shredded flesh caught in their branches.

She squeezed her eyes shut, pressing her fists against them. She breathed out slowly, waiting for a voice that wasn't hers, for anything. But there was only deafening silence.

When she opened her eyes, the trees were green once more, but she knew that wasn't true. This was only the beginning. That strange mold on the trees wasn't an illusion, the spiderwebs weren't illusions. She was seeing some other realm that existed woven into the edges of hers. And those edges had frayed.

She didn't want to wait until Komyazalov for answers. She didn't think she would *get* answers in Komyazalov, where the Matriarch resided. The woman who'd almost certainly had a hand in keeping Nadya in the dark her whole life wouldn't help her. Nor would she be safe in a place where what she was could condemn her to death.

But maybe they would be right to sentence her thus. With each passing hour, she could feel herself edging closer to that dark water. Using it in the forest, on that wolf, was unlike anything she had ever known. *Good,* even. As terrifying as that was, it was inevitable. She was always going to end up here; this was always going to happen.

Maybe that was why the Church had lied to her. Why they had tried so hard to keep her in the dark. They suspected what she was. Something darker than a cleric, worse than a mage. Something *else*.

The magic from that well of dark water felt, if not the same as the feeling she had around Ljubica, then worse. If that was even possible.

There had been whispers of things worse than the fallen gods. Older beings. The clearing and the statues around it—*that* was how using this power made her feel. The same dread horror; the same terrible inevitability. She knew, now, who five of those other statues had been, but that left *fifteen*. Fifteen beings unaccounted for and unknown, and that didn't sit well with her. Were they dead? Or were they biding their time?

Would the fallen gods unleash something even older and darker?

Was that what she was?

The thought was too much, too far. But she couldn't deny being connected to that clearing, not anymore.

After a long day of travel, they set up camp for the evening, and Nadya wandered away, watching as the forest shifted around her vision. Growing darker, the normal sounds of the wood turning to screams. She shivered, glancing back at the others, but they didn't notice. Except Rashid. He flinched every time *something* in the woods screamed. He caught her gaze and she tilted her head. He got up and followed her into the woods.

"You can sense it, can't you?" she asked.

Rashid gazed up at the trees in silence before he spoke, the timbre of his voice rough. "It might be time to tell you the truth."

Her heart dropped. Not him, he couldn't be lying to her, *too.* She couldn't take another betrayal.

Rashid caught the look on her face, something flickering over his that she couldn't parse. It quickly morphed to careful reassurance. "No, no, don't worry, those were the wrong words to use. I . . ." He trailed off, considering his hands, flexing his fingers. "I was taken into the Siroosi Travash when I showed signs of power. It runs in my family, magic, but we tend to ignore it because it's always been easily ignored."

"What kind of magic?"

"Well, that's the thing, isn't it? You Northerners have it all laid out so carefully. Magic from the gods or magic from blood and while that's *mostly* true—even the mages in Akola draw blood for their power, but you Kalyazi never realized because they don't venture out from the deep deserts—it doesn't work the way the north has decided. We knew to keep quiet when Kalyazin turned on Tranavia because any divergence in how our power worked would put a target on us as well."

Nadya winced.

"But it's easy to ignore the spark of power, let it grow dormant and disappear, and that's what my family did. Because my grandfather made a mistake that would cost him my uncle and ultimately, me. And it meant we ended up in a Travash that has poisoned the country for years. Because that Travash wanted mages, as many as possible, before they were taken into the deserts and hidden away as is tradition."

"But magic is changing," Nadya whispered, realizing what he was telling her.

He nodded. "The roads have been broken. Katya has magic that doesn't fit. *You* have magic that doesn't fit. So much that has happened just . . ."

"Doesn't fit," she said softly. It was something she was struggling to reconcile. If her entire world had been based on lies, how did magic—something that was supposed to be based in immutable truths that did not change—end up so different and wild and unpredictable? "Do you think it's because those gods were set free?"

Rashid shrugged. "I couldn't feel it until now. My power had gone dormant because I forced it to, and that forest . . ." He shivered. "I was barely trained, and I don't really know what would happen were I to use my magic. Parijahan knew—she's always known—but when I was taken into her Travash, she convinced her grandmother that she needed a guard and who better than the fresh mage from Yanzin Zadar? I didn't want to use my power—didn't want it trained—and so I didn't, and it wasn't, and I think I have made a terrible mistake."

Nadya thought of the way Parijahan had been for the past year. Closed and anxious, constantly tugging Malachiasz away from the group like she was planning something.

"They wanted mages but were fine with not training you?"

"It's not about the magic," Rashid replied. "It's about being able to claim to the other Travasha that they had an army of mages in their employ. If asked for proof there were enough that could do something flashy and be convincing, they never needed me."

"I never should have asked any of you to come with me into that forest," Nadya murmured.

"Probably not," Rashid agreed. "Malachiasz would've followed you anyway."

"Not if I had told him the truth."

Rashid cast her a long look. "Even then."

"Don't. Don't try to make out like there was something between us more than constant betrayal now that he's gone. This isn't about him anymore. What's going on with Parijahan?"

Rashid sighed, and in it was far more than he was willing to say. "Her family is after her."

"I gathered that."

"I don't know how much longer she can keep running without her family sparking something drastic."

"Right."

"The least of your concerns," Rashid said wryly.

"No, it's not that, it's just . . . another problem I don't know how to solve."

"Nadya, have you ever considered that maybe you don't have to fix the world all by yourself?"

She groaned.

"You're, what, eighteen? Why should you be responsible for the entire world?"

"Because I'm the one who broke it."

"No, you weren't. It's been broken and it will continue to be broken because people are broken, mad creatures who will always do terrible things."

"It's not that simple."

"It's not, you're right, because people are infuriatingly complicated and capable of doing wonderful things all the same."

Tears flooded her eyes. "I don't know what else I'm supposed to do," she whispered. "I lost my goddess and I lost Malachiasz and I think the thing worse than being pulled in two different directions is having both suddenly vanish. There's nothing left." She rubbed furiously at her eyes. She wasn't going to *cry*.

Rashid's hands circled her wrists. "You're allowed to grieve," he said. "I am."

"He doesn't deserve it." Marzenya didn't, either, but that wasn't really a conversation to be had with Rashid.

"Maybe not. But I loved that boy so damn much and he didn't deserve that, either. It's not really about that, I don't think. You can't ever deserve love."

"Stop trying to make things better. Nothing is ever going to get better."

"That's not true, Nadya."

She shot him a dry look, but she appreciated his relentless optimism here at the end of everything.

Another scream tore through the forest and Rashid flinched, shuddering hard.

"You get used to it," Nadya said.

"I'm not sure I want to."

"Did Malachiasz know?"

He frowned, anger flickering over his features. "Parijahan says she never told him, but I think she was lying." Rashid paused, smiling sadly. "I still don't know a damned thing about what I can do and there's not really anyone who can help me."

"What about Ostyia?"

"Would she want to?"

Nadya considered this. Ostyia had never been particularly hostile to her—or Parijahan from what she could recall—and she didn't seem to mind Rashid's company.

"Hard to say, but I think so. It would mean Katya would find out, though."

"How did *that* happen?"

"I don't think anything has happened yet, but if you're making bets on it with Parj, my money says Katya would love nothing more than a scandal from involving herself with a Tranavian general."

"Listen—"

"I will never let you live those bets down." A thoughtful pause passed between them. "I'll help if I can, but I doubt your magic works anything like mine."

"The girl I met on the mountains would have killed me for daring to have power different from hers."

"The girl on the mountains got everything wrong," Nadya replied, trying to keep the acute melancholy out of her voice and failing. "And she died a long time ago."

Nadya couldn't sleep. She let one watch run into the next, not bothering to wake anyone. The forest was mostly calm except for the screams—but nothing seemed to be coming of those.

Suddenly the taste of magic grew thick in the air, and she was slammed into the ground before she could get to her feet.

There you are. Iron claws clamped around her neck, a heavy weight against her chest, and a voice hissed, chaotic and wrong, in her ear. "What have you *done,* little cleric?"

A fall of black hair against pale skin and Nadya's heart lurched even though she knew it was not him.

"Żywia."

"Where is he?" Żywia perched on Nadya's chest, her eyes pitch black, her teeth iron needles in her mouth.

Nadya wheezed. "Get off me," she whispered fiercely. "And shut up before you wake everyone." Katya would kill her on sight.

Żywia stilled, eyes returning to Nadya's face. She tried not to think about how the Vulture looked like she could be Malachiasz's sibling. Though that honor was, apparently, Serefin's.

And Nadya had said nothing. She had put the pieces together long before the forest picked Malachiasz apart. She could have told him; she *should* have told him. She knew it ate at him, not knowing who his family was. But he didn't like Serefin and wouldn't have reacted well to her suspicions. So, she kept it to herself until it became far too late.

Fear shot through Żywia's expression. "Where is he?" she asked. Her confidence had drained away, and she sounded lost and scared.

Nadya let her head fall back against the ground. Żywia scrambled off and she sat up.

"Not here," Nadya said, standing.

The Vulture eyed her warily as she held out her hand. Nadya didn't know what she was doing anymore, but she had done enough to Tranavia, anything more was baseless cruelty. Malachiasz was Żywia's friend and she had to tell her that he was gone. Just punishment.

The Vulture took her hand, iron claws slowly receding. Nadya hauled her to her feet and turned her in the direction of the forest. "Go," she whispered. "I'll meet you shortly." After she disappeared into the trees, Nadya woke Rashid to take watch and slipped away when he wasn't looking. She didn't doubt that he was aware of her leaving.

The forest around her was a terrifying, suffocating darkness that pressed down at her chest. She wasn't entirely sure how far Żywia had gone until something rustled in branches above her.

"Taking high ground really isn't necessary," Nadya said. "I'm not going to harm you."

Żywia slid on the branch she was perched on until she was hanging upside down in front of Nadya. "I don't trust you."

"You shouldn't."

A trickle of blood dripped down the Vulture's face, starting from the corner of her mouth. Could she use magic still? What did wrenching blood magic away from Tranavia mean for the Vultures, who were *made* of magic?

"Something broke in the air," Żywia said, her voice holding the chaotic note of *wrongness* that came whenever the Vultures were closer to monster than person. "Something broke and our Black Vulture is gone. You'd better talk fast, little cleric, because I'm not feeling particularly kind and I would very much like to kill you."

Nadya lifted her chin. She couldn't crumble at every mention of him. "Your Tranavian king killed his brother," she said.

Żywia frowned, head tilting, before understanding sparked in her eyes. She closed them for a heartbeat. "Of course they are."

"They had the same eyes," Nadya mused, unable to hide the tremor of fear in her voice as she waited for the Vulture to react fully.

Żywia pressed her hands to her temples, still hanging. "How did it happen?"

"He was stabbed in the heart with a relic."

The Vulture frowned. Her eyes opened and she stared at Nadya for a long time. She carefully cut a line down the back of her hand with an iron claw. Nadya tried not to wince.

"That is impossible," Żywia said.

I wish. But did she? There had been no other way for this to end. No matter how strongly her heart was pulled to him; he had been everything she was born to destroy, and so she had.

"I know you Vultures are functionally immortal—"

Żywia scoffed. Nadya ignored her.

She could still feel the warmth of his bloody fingers against her lips. "He's dead, Żywia." Her voice cracked. The Vulture's eyes flew open at the sound.

Nadya only had seconds to react as the Vulture struck. She moved fast, shooting to her feet and away right as the Vulture snapped. Żywia whirled, crouched, baring her rows and rows of iron teeth. Nadya swallowed hard. She wasn't so lucky a second time, Żywia slamming into her and throwing her to the ground.

She raked her corrupted hand against Żywia, and the Vulture hissed, immediately scrambling back, a pained whimper escaping her. Nadya watched in horror as her torn flesh rippled. Eyes flickered open and closed along her arm. She slammed a hand over the cuts, staring at Nadya wide-eyed.

"What *are you*?"

Nadya shook her head slowly. She clenched her hand into a fist, her claws digging into her palm, blood trickling between her fingers.

A series of sluggishly bleeding cuts raked down Żywia's arm from her shoulder, but no more eyes. What had that been?

"It doesn't make sense," she murmured. "That's not how we die."

Nadya didn't know how to kill a Vulture, but dying from a relic wound made sense to her. "What's happening with the Vultures?"

Żywia glared, a shiver of anxiety cracking through her. For all the Vultures had been twisted into monsters they were still painfully human. Żywia shook her head. "Why should I tell you?"

"Because we're past this war deciding our fates," Nadya replied, wishing she could say she had tried to save Malachiasz. Wishing she had.

Żywia lifted her chin and Nadya recognized something in her expression that cut down to her bones. A girl, grieving. What had he done to trap so many under his spell that their lives were so altered by his death? It seemed wrong, that so terrible a boy could leave behind so much hurt.

"Another turning of the war is on the horizon," Żywia finally said. "I won't be able to stop it. I don't know if I want to. The Vultures have always rested tenuously at the edge of chaos and now—"

There was noise from the direction of the camp. Nadya stood.

"Get out of here. There's *Voldah Gorovni* in our group."

Żywia gave her a dirty look. "Of course there are."

Nadya sighed. It was useless explaining that she had nothing to do with Katya's presence. None of it mattered.

Żywia eyed the cuts on her arm dubiously. Then she glanced from Nadya to her corrupted hand before disappearing into the darkness.

Nadya tugged at the end of her braid, chewing on her lower lip. Divinity twisted mortal flesh—but Vultures weren't entirely mortal, so what was that?

She was no better than the Vultures she had spent her life thinking were abominations.

Katya stepped through the trees, her hand on the hilt of her sword. "You shouldn't be out here," she said.

"I can handle whatever these woods spit out," Nadya replied wearily.

"Even so," Katya said softly. She was looking at Nadya's hand with narrowed eyes.

Maybe Malachiasz was right and her hand was a product of corrupted divinity, an allowance of a taste when she had freed Velyos. That night she had set free a part of herself she never would have known had she not bled for power and treated in heresy. She'd found the dark water in a place where she never should have trespassed. When she considered all the pieces of herself that were different, wrong, they all came from pushing back at the structures of her life that had been presented as immutable truth.

If only she knew what to do with those revelations.

"If I go to Komyazalov, can you guarantee me your protection?" Nadya asked. She was too cautious to think she would have another Brother Ivan in her future. The Matriarch and the capital city would not be so kind toward her transgressions.

"Why would you need that?" Katya asked.

Nadya shot her a dry look. "Don't pretend. I'm not the cleric that was promised to Kalyazin. I'm not the one to stop this chaos."

If anything, I've made it so much worse.

Katya scoffed. "You've stripped heretic magic from the world—"

"And caused the death of a god."

"—and the death of the worst Black Vulture we've ever known." Nadya flinched.

Katya was oblivious. "The Vulture killed Marzenya and he's dead."

But he killed her with my help. She was sick of being lied to, controlled. She'd wanted out from underneath Marzenya's thumb.

Thunder rippled through the sky. Katya lifted her head. "Can you still feel them?"

"The gods?"

Katya nodded.

"Yes and no. They've turned away. They won't talk to me. I think they're . . . preparing for something. It's not like when my access to them was blocked off, this is willful. Are the fallen gods truly that deadly?"

"I wish I knew," Katya said. "I wish we had more than some apocryphal texts that are vague at best and meaningless at worst. I don't know, Nadya. I don't know what's to come." A strange expression flickered over her face. "Were you talking to someone out here?"

"No."

It was clear Katya didn't believe her.

"What is the Matriarch like?" she asked.

Katya lifted an eyebrow. She eyed Nadya in silence, deciding whether she wanted to discuss this with her. Whether Nadya was worthy. It stung to know the *tsarevna* didn't trust her, but she hadn't exactly earned it.

"Is she why you're asking for protection?" Katya finally asked.

Nadya hesitated, then gave a small nod.

"I see." The *tsarevna* leaned back against the same tree Żywia had been hanging from. "She and I do not get along."

A knot formed in the pit of Nadya's stomach. This was not what she wanted to hear.

"She can be . . . draconic. She's the high mouthpiece of the gods, her words are law within the Church." Katya's eyes studied Nadya's face. "She has been quite gleeful in eradicating all magic not divinely appointed from Kalyazin."

And *there* it was. The confirmation Nadya needed. Katya's gaze strayed to Nadya's hand.

"You think she'll go after you," she said.

"Katya . . . I don't . . ." Nadya sighed. "Yes. I do."

Katya took that with a carefully neutral expression. Nadya had no idea where she stood with her.

"Is it because of the Black Vulture?" she asked. "Is he why you've strayed so far that you think the Matriarch would hang you?"

"I think I'd be put on a pyre, actually," Nadya said. "No. He helped. I'll grant him that. He asked some very pointed questions that I had no answers for, but . . . I would have ended up here without him."

Nadya had no idea if that was true but had to believe it. Otherwise it gave far too much power to a boy who had too much to begin with. But she would have posed those same questions for herself eventually. She was too damn curious, and it was her down-fall.

"I'll do my best, Nadya," Katya said, after a long pause between them stretched out into the cold air.

Katya turned back toward camp as glimmers of dawn began to break through the trees, and Nadya touched the ink-stained skin of her left hand, fearing what was to come.

9

MALACHIASZ CZECHOWICZ

*His fingers clawing, grasping, scraping at anything he
can rake into his maw to sate his unending hunger.*
—The Volokhtaznikon

Malachiasz wasn't used to being alone. Even in the Salt Mines
there were other Vultures—aside from the isolation of the
mines themselves. Any other time he surrounded himself with
people. It never eased the loneliness fully, but it was tempered:
Vultures, Rashid and Parijahan and an odd group of Kalyazi
renegades, Nadya . . .

He closed his eyes and abruptly collapsed amidst the acrid, rotting flowers, his knees going liquid. He didn't dare
prod at the magic that bound them, but he doubted his
death had broken it. There was too much. Too much magic
that was not his and not under his control. The thread of
Nadya's weird, dark power. Chyrnog's touch heavy upon
him. All of it the same and he didn't understand why.

He raked his hands through his hair. He should be dead.

He *died*. A part of him was still on that mountain and he wouldn't ever get it back. And what was the cost of his return?

How old was the god that had Malachiasz? What had it seen? Done?

What had it consumed?

The thought struck him like a thunderclap. *Consume.* He thought of his hunger. Constant, gnawing, eternal. He thought of the darkness, absolute and complete.

Malachiasz considered what he had become.

Judging by the silence, the god wasn't *always* paying attention. It wasn't always listening. That was important. So what if he couldn't fight it? It didn't have him completely. He wondered if it had slept for so long it was left weak. Weak, maybe weak wasn't the word, but it hadn't yet obliterated Malachiasz.

He needed answers. He needed to—

"Start by getting out of here," he asserted, standing.

Ignoring the shifting of his body, he made his way up the stairs. It was dark outside, blessedly so, and though he didn't want to leave the church—he was safe here, protected from the forest—he knew he must.

How did I even get here? he thought. Dragged into divine nonsense. He should have stayed in Grazyk. He shouldn't have left the mines. He shouldn't have listened to Nadya.

He shouldn't have loved her.

Well, that's over.

He needed to stop thinking about her, the last thing he wanted was her knowing he was alive. Better she think him dead. Better she live with her righteous—so she thought—fury. He was so tired. Still so much farther to go.

Still so much farther to fall.

The gnawing hunger chewing at the core of him was *more*, somehow, than simply not having had food in a while. It was ancient and old and altogether too familiar. He had to ignore it or else it would drive him mad.

The forest didn't bother him when he finally left the sanctuary of the church. It was too dark, the trees oppressive and too close together, the cold wind cutting straight through his jacket and down into his bones.

When he stumbled into a clearing with a squat hut in the center, he gave a heavy sigh of recognition. He considered turning right back around and going deeper into the forest, but with an exhausted sort of resignation he knew there was no avoiding it. This was why the forest had been so lenient.

The hut seemed to move as he approached, as if it were breathing. He passed a gate with skulls perched on the narrow fence. He paused and eyed them—some were far too fresh for his liking—before continuing through a small garden of what he was fairly certain were fingers embedded in the dirt—he didn't really want to investigate *that* further—until he knocked on the door.

It swung open on its own into darkness. He closed his eyes, almost wishing he didn't know what was coming. He shook his head. Better to face this with dignity.

"*Czijow,* Pelageya," he called, stepping inside. "How are you always exactly where I don't want you to be?"

"I was rather enjoying watching you turning in circles in the forest."

He was in her sitting room—the one from the tower in Grazyk?—but different. The skulls weren't all fleshless here, and something bubbled thickly in a cauldron on her fire. The witch looked old; her white curls tied back and her face lined with wrinkles. She glanced over her shoulder at Malachiasz before turning to the fire.

"Oh, you bring a vile taste in with you, shut the door."

Was it too late to leave? The door shut before he could touch it. Well, that answered that.

"Just you?" Her face screwed up. "Sit down, boy. You and I have a great deal to discuss."

That wasn't what Malachiasz wanted at all. "Not like you to want anything to do with me," he noted, sitting regardless. They never got along, he and the witch. He turned to magic for answers, and she refused to give him any, and he hated her for it. He was volatile and rattled the order of the world, and she hated him for that.

"You bring death with you, no, no, worse than that. Something else." Her head tilted as she considered. "What *have* you done?"

He opened his mouth, unsure how to answer, but she waved a hand. Filling a bowl with something from the cauldron, she offered it to him.

"Soup?"

A whimper broke from his chest. He was so *hungry*. He didn't have the restraint to not desperately grab the bowl from her hands. She watched him as he ignored the searing heat and drank down the thick stew.

"Ah, I thought so," she said softly.

The bowl was empty, and still he felt hollow. Ravenous. It clawed at him from the inside. He tasted iron in his mouth, blood and flesh and *need*.

The bowl clattered to the floor. Malachiasz pulled at his hair and, pressing the heels of his palms to his forehead, let out a long breath through his teeth. This wasn't what he was, was it?

"Your true nature finally come to light," Pelageya said. "I did think that you might escape it, beat what you are, but we all succumb to ourselves eventually."

He curled over his knees, tears spilling past his hands as he shoved his palms against his eyes. "What did you *do to me*?" It *hurt* and beside the hurt was the knowledge that nothing he could do would sate the hunger. That the gnawing at the core of him that he had always carefully fed so very slowly to keep it at bay had finally become enough of a beast to ravage him.

"Ah, child . . . I did nothing." She picked up the bowl and filled it again, crouching in front of him. "This won't really help with *that*, but it will ease the mortal hunger. I feel the touch of that shin bone on you and I can guess what happened there. Not what I expected, I thought she would use it on . . . someone else, but it takes a lot to die and be alive again, doesn't it?"

Malachiasz lifted his head slowly. He wiped the back of his

shaking hand over his eyes before taking the bowl carefully. "Why does this feel suspiciously like you're helping me?" he asked, trying to keep from devouring the second bowl as quickly as the first.

Pelageya leaned back, glancing at the relics in his hair. "This wouldn't be the first time."

Quiet settled over them as he ate, almost painfully slowly this time. And she was right, it didn't help, but the tremors eased when the bowl was empty.

"What is this?" he asked.

"You know, *sterevyani bolen,* you've always known. You've been keeping it quiet your whole life, feeding it magic and progress and promising that one day you'll get there. One day things won't be *quite so bad.*"

It was what he had always held close. That someday he might know a life that wasn't pain and disaster and the constant ache of hunger. He closed his eyes briefly, knuckling the bridge of his nose.

"You made it easy for him." Pelageya's eyes tracked through Malachiasz as if she wasn't seeing him. "To grasp the pieces of your soul, the little you had left, and crush them. Little godling, little chaos god, little boy so far from home. Chyrnog didn't even have to try. You've given up. You gave whole pieces to me, after all."

Malachiasz flinched.

"But does it matter? You want a total freedom from the gods, and yet, what are *you*?"

"Not a god," he said, his voice hoarse.

"No and no and no and yes. Yes, my boy. Both and everything and nothing all at once. How much will you consume before you are done? How much will you destroy?"

"I only want peace," he whispered.

"Do you lie to yourself, too? I'm surprised."

He had a name, at least, to tie to the god. It was meaningless to him. He vaguely remembered Katya telling Nadya about Chyrnog, but he hadn't been paying attention. He had been watching the way the forest light played against the pale strands of Nadya's hair. Gold and honey and snow.

"Are you actually here or am I dying, and this is how I'm continually punished?"

Pelageya laughed. "I'm as real as you."

"Just making sure."

"Why are you here?" she asked, finally settling herself in a chair across from him. "You've never wanted my help before; I hardly believe you'll start now."

He frowned. "I'm here because your hut showed up before me? I don't understand."

"It doesn't show itself to people who don't already want it."

Did he want it? He wanted help, but not from an antagonistic Kalyazi witch. "I don't think you'd want to help me, all things considered," he replied. Chyrnog didn't exactly seem like the best of news.

"How have you come this far and not yet realized that my will and my desires are my own and not tied to any fanatical sense of place or purpose? You could stand to think a little less about your country and a little more about the fact that thirteen—no—fifteen eyes just opened on your skin at once."

"It's rude to point that out," he said primly.

Pelageya perked up suddenly. "More visitors?" she grumbled. "I need more heads for the fence to keep them away. Can I have yours?"

"No." Malachiasz tried not to panic. Who else could be here? He realized that he didn't know where in the forest he even was, and it was likely that they were close enough to a Kalyazi village that the witch got wanderers all the time. Still, he should probably hide.

"Oh, stay where you are," she said, waving a hand at him. "I've been wanting to speak to you together for a long time and now I finally can!"

Malachiasz didn't like the sound of that *at all* and he prepared to flee. He almost relaxed when the door opened to the figure of a girl, tall, face weather-worn and exhausted. He couldn't make out the words that she and the witch exchanged, but she stormed away in a rage. Another figure was shoved inside.

Shit.

"*Shit,*" Serefin said as he stared at Malachiasz over Pelageya's shoulder.

Serefin Meleski stood there, tall and pale and looking like he had been dragged through hell and back. His brown hair was messy and too long, his left eye covered with a bandage that wrapped over half his face, the other half raked with painful cuts. A weird jolt struck at the thought that this infuriating idiot prince—*king*—was his brother. Older brother. He had an older brother.

He had an older brother who stabbed him in the chest and left him to die on a mountain.

Pelageya clapped her hands together with glee, suddenly appearing the same age as them. "Well, won't *this* be fun!"

10

SEREFIN

MELESKI

*Something has gone wrong. The gods speak, sometimes,
not like before, something has changed. I'm gathering
accounts, trying to place the pieces together but . . .
Something is missing. Something was erased.*

—Passage from the personal journals
of Innokentiy Tamarkin

When Serefin died and then was no longer dead, the concept
of death never really changed for him. People still died. The
particularities of his circumstances didn't shift the world on
its axis for him because it was so entirely bizarre that he
didn't think it could possibly happen to anyone else. Death
was death was death.

But there Malachiasz was, looking as bad as Serefin felt.

His long black hair was a tangled, wild mess. He was
wearing his military jacket over the shredded tatters of the
tunic he'd died in—Serefin's stomach turned at the blood-
stain on his chest. If Serefin's hands hadn't been tied he

might have tried to run in the opposite direction, but they were, and he didn't particularly want to land face-first in Pelageya's finger garden, so he remained where he was, frozen in shock.

When Olya had started talking more about her plans, Serefin had guessed who they were being taken to. She didn't seem thrilled that Pelageya wanted nothing to do with her and only wanted to speak to the Tranavian she had prisoner.

Malachiasz is alive.

He kept bouncing off the thought, rejecting it, letting it come back so he could consider it, and throw it away again. He had killed his brother and he had to live with the regret of what he had done. There were no second chances.

Except Malachiasz was *alive*.

If he was alive, he would want revenge. Before Serefin could back away, Pelageya grabbed him, cut the rope on his wrists, and shoved him into the room. The door closed behind him with a resounding thud.

Serefin swallowed hard. "I have a question," he said, voice strained.

Malachiasz was tense as a bowstring and Serefin did not want to consider those claws going through his chest. It would hurt very badly and take him a terribly long time to die.

How long did it take Malachiasz to die?

"Yes?" Pelageya asked.

"How can you be here if you're in Tranavia?"

A strange whining hiss of air broke from Malachiasz's chest. He leaned back in his chair. Serefin was relieved that he didn't immediately run him through.

Pelageya laughed. "How did your friend Velyos take you across the continent in a heartbeat? A lot can be done with magic."

"My entire body still hurts from that nonsense," Serefin replied, his eye not breaking from Malachiasz's gaze. He needed Malachiasz to say something, even if it would destroy Serefin, because he still couldn't believe that his brother was in front of him and alive and *he hadn't wanted to kill him, he hadn't wanted to do it.*

"What did you do to your eye?" Pelageya asked.

Serefin pressed a hand over the bandage, self-conscious. "I took care of the god problem," he murmured.

"But did you?"

Serefin froze, breath catching. How could she know? Yes, Velyos still spoke to him, but the other one didn't, and that one scared Serefin the most. He tentatively sat down, casting Malachiasz a sidelong glance, waiting for him to . . . he didn't know. Stab him, honestly.

Pelageya closed her eyes, fingers tapping against the deer skull on the side table. The sound bored into his head, *tap tap tap*. "Not right, not good, not at all as planned."

"We can't follow some divine nonsense plan if we don't know about it," Malachiasz pointed out. Serefin relaxed slightly at the sound of his voice.

"Shut up, stupid boy," Pelageya snapped.

Malachiasz's body tensed, a curtain falling over his expression.

"The eye," Pelageya said to Serefin. "The eye! Where is it?"

"Blood and bone, I don't know! I ripped it out of my face and left it on top of the mountain where I left *him*." He gestured at Malachiasz.

Pelageya nodded slowly. "That explains why you both stink of death."

"People don't come back from the dead," Serefin said plaintively.

"Yet you both have. Two Tranavians taken by gods you rebel against. What irony."

"I'm not—" Malachiasz started, but Pelageya interrupted him.

"And now what? What do you plan to do, *sterevyani bolen*? *Koshto bovilgy*? All that power chained up. I know what he wants—do you?"

Malachiasz scowled petulantly. Serefin wasn't sure he'd ever seen Malachiasz admit he didn't know something, and he clearly didn't want to start for Pelageya. He shook his head quickly.

"A god of entropy. Ancient, mad—"

"Weakened."

"Maybe so. But how long until he regains his strength? And you will help him, I think, because you feel the same urge to consume, to devour and destroy. Even before they made you what you are— before you made yourself so much worse, it was always there—the hunger, the desire for chaos."

Malachiasz closed his eyes.

"So many have woken up. Little *bovilgy,* flocking to the wake left behind by the death of one so old and powerful. Will you consume them?"

He opened his eyes, frowning at her. *"Bòwycz?"*

Serefin was equally confused by the word she was using.

Pelageya's gaze flicked between Serefin and Malachiasz. She sighed. "Tell me what you know of magic as it stands now, after the cracks and the crumbling."

"No." Serefin said emphatically as Malachiasz brightened considerably.

"Well—"

"No." Serefin cut him off. "Don't play this game."

Malachiasz shot him a withering look. "What broke?" he asked Pelageya. "It's connected, yes?"

The witch nodded slightly. Her eyes fluttered shut. "Fractured, yes. A boundary snapped—you snapped it—and now we see how each crack breaks another piece. How magic sparks to life in those who never should have touched it. What will the world look like when you cannot box such power into two neat little avenues? How much will atrophy when power spreads?"

Malachiasz's eyes were bright with almost manic delight, but he had the decency to appear mildly concerned.

"So much magic with such little control. What will that spell? You, a new creature, *bovilgy* of chaos. That Kalyazi girl, a nightmare waiting to happen." She waved a hand at Serefin. "And you have not escaped unscathed, though total divinity, I think, does not suit you."

"Great," Serefin muttered.

He glanced at Malachiasz. The Black Vulture curtain had fallen fast; he sat curled in on himself, small. A pale, young boy who had been shown how truly monstrous he was. Serefin wasn't sure if pity was the correct emotion, but he felt it in that moment.

"You took care of the god problem, so you say, but he still speaks to you, does he not?" she said to Serefin.

He nodded.

"Do you know what you did?" Pelageya asked. "In the forest that takes and takes and takes? The same forest we are in, in fact, but it fed so fully that it rests, temporarily, waiting for when it will hunger again."

"I—I set Velyos free," Serefin replied. He didn't understand what that meant. Or know anything about these Kalyazi gods. He hadn't wanted to see it into reality, but he hadn't been strong enough to fight them off. He wasn't strong enough for much of anything. Maybe it would be better if he never went back to Tranavia. If he let the throne go to whoever fought for it the hardest because he would never be good enough for it.

"Yes, the little Kalyazi nightmare started it, and you finished it."

"I don't understand what that means."

"No, you wouldn't. Tranavian boys, you prod and you bite, and you lash out at the world, but you don't know, you don't know anything at all."

"But you *do*. What about those fractured prophecies you kept spouting at us?"

"Oh, you've long past broken those. Foretelling or prophecies are never set in stone. They are mere suggestions of how the world might turn if each piece lines up properly, they never account for a boy willing to murder his brother, or a boy willing to murder a god."

Serefin flinched. Malachiasz didn't.

"It wasn't me," Serefin whispered.

"I'm not the one you need to convince of that, little king," Pelageya replied.

Serefin did not look at Malachiasz. *How is he alive?*

Dealing with Pelageya always left him more rattled and confused than before, and without any answers. He just wanted to understand what he had done.

"What happens now?"

"It depends what you want this world to be when it all comes crashing down. If you are willing to put down your vendettas for the sake of something different, or if you are dead set upon the path you walk. If you are willing to work with the Kalyazi, or insist on destroying them."

Malachiasz's expression was carefully blank in a way Serefin knew was dangerous.

What did Serefin want? To disappear back to Tranavia and leave the Kalyazi to whatever became of them from the fallen gods, really. He wanted to do what he did best and run away from his problems. He was *very* good at it.

But it was time for Serefin Meleski to stop running. It was time for him to be the king that he absolutely wasn't good enough to be.

"And if I wanted to stop these gods I set free?"

Pelageya smiled slightly, her gaze moving to Malachiasz. His chin rested in his hands and he looked thoughtful.

"I don't think I have a choice," he said, a tremor in his voice. This was Malachiasz when truly terrified, not pretending to be scared for the sake of an image he couldn't uphold any longer.

"No, you don't. But will you interfere with your brother's goal, or will your plans align?"

"What about—" Serefin started.

"I don't know," Pelageya said. "I don't know where she fits in this any longer. I thought her a witch waiting to happen, but not a witch, not a cleric, not a, well, who knows. I can no longer see her threads. I only see yours."

Serefin couldn't help his gaze trailing to Malachiasz, who had paled considerably before his expression hardened.

"She's done enough," he muttered.

Pelageya tilted her head. "Yes, she has, hasn't she? But haven't you, as well?"

He didn't respond.

"Nothing rests on the edge of a knife any longer. You've tipped the balance. Velyos remains, but where have the rest gone? Where do you suppose Zvezdan is? Why would he remain in Kalyazin when the shallows run deep in Tranavia?"

Serefin swallowed. "Nothing will stay here."

"I have tried to tell you. Again and again and again. The girl, the monster, the prince, the queen. There were four then and four now and you've destroyed your roles so utterly but there must still be four, always four. The world has scattered into chaos after the birth of a god of chaos and there is no way to pick up the pieces, but you can try, oh, you can try. Fail, succeed, what will become of us all?"

"God?" Malachiasz asked.

"Are you a boy or a monster or a god?"

He shook his head. "I don't know," he said, voice soft.

"No. Of course not. As if it isn't all the same thing."

He rubbed at the scars on his forearms absently. "I'm so hungry," he whispered.

Pelageya regarded him almost sadly. "He's going to grow stronger. He's going to consume them all. You'll get your wish. You'll topple that divine empire. Will you help him?" she asked Serefin suddenly.

"H-help Malachiasz?" Serefin asked, startled.

She nodded blithely. "Is your enemy not Kalyazin and their gods? Did they not rip magic away from you? Will you not respond to the affront with vengeance?"

Yes and yes and yes. *This would never end.*

He hadn't wanted to kill Malachiasz. He deserved any kind of vengeance that Malachiasz might exact upon him, expected it, even. There was no way he would let what had happened go without retaliation. That was all they were. That was all they would ever do to each other. That was the cycle they belonged in.

"Yes," he finally answered. He would help Malachiasz. Whatever that meant.

Pelageya blinked as if that wasn't the answer she was expecting. Malachiasz said nothing, only frowned at the floor for a long moment.

"You don't know what you're saying," he said at last.

Serefin didn't. But he had lost his power and his kingdom and working with the Black Vulture would be the only way for them to pull through.

"What are the gods going to do?" Serefin asked. He needed that question answered before he could push forward. "I thought they couldn't directly interact with the world. That's why Velyos acted the way he did."

Pelageya wordlessly gestured to Malachiasz, who was looking rather ill. "You don't think about them the right way. Is *he* aware of the chaos that trails his wake? Does he know, actively, what he does to the world by mere existence? Of course not. Such is the way of divinity and gods. You have been in that forest. You know it is moving outside its borders. The world will flood with the horrors of Tachilvnik. The gods of the depths will bring out what lies beneath the dark water. Is this what you want? Do you want to face a war against things so much older than you? This is what the world hurtles toward with each passing day."

"The birds," Serefin murmured.

"Hm?"

"On our journey . . . The birds were screaming. The trees chewed up with decay. It was horrible."

"The horrors did not have far to go. But they will stretch, reaching until they overtake everything. Your country will not be spared because your country already faces horrors of its own."

"*Oh,*" Malachiasz breathed.

"The Vultures have not rested in the absence of their Black Vulture. And absent you have been. When was the last they heard from you? Did the ripples of your death spread like dark water? Who would claim your mantle?"

Malachiasz seemed to recede in on himself, a deep frown on his face. Absently he sliced his forearm on the edge of an iron claw. Blood welled up, trickling down his pale skin. Could he still use blood magic? He had no spell book that Serefin could see, so this was something else. Were the Vultures above what had happened? That would be fitting, in line with everything else he knew about them.

"I can pull their threads in my hands still," Malachiasz said, his voice distant. "So, no, no new leader, not in any rightful capacity. A new Black Vulture is chosen by killing the old. It's a cycle."

"Rebirth," Pelageya said. "A cycle you have broken. You retain your power, but your cult is left to scramble in your wake, and where will they look next?"

Malachiasz closed his eyes, letting out a slow breath. "Grazyk."

A cold sweat prickled at Serefin's skin. If the Vultures had swarmed the capital and taken it as their own, he wasn't sure what he could do, even with Malachiasz. He didn't trust him to help get his throne back from another Vulture. Malachiasz would take it for himself.

"Fascinating, isn't it, how things fall apart in your absence? Two boys so important to the turning of the world. And you have spent your days in enemy lands and what do you have to show for it?"

"Do we go home?" Serefin asked Pelageya, desperately.

"Do you? What a choice that lies before you. You won't get out of this alive if you do not work together. And, yes, you have tasted death—it lies heavy on you both—but it is all too ready to take you again."

"What happened when I killed that goddess?" Malachiasz asked suddenly.

"It was what Velyos wanted, for Marzenya to die," Serefin said before Pelageya could answer.

"It was, wasn't it? How does it feel, to know that every one of your actions has been nudged forward by a being other than you? How little control over yourselves you have had, even when you thought you were acting in your interests."

"She had to die," Malachiasz snapped.

"Did she?"

He opened his mouth and closed it. Slowly he said, "She was going to kill Nadya."

"Ah. We return to the girl."

"Not anymore."

"Oh, you don't escape so easily. Her role is . . ." Pelageya trailed off. She blinked fast, rattled. She did not finish her thought.

Serefin didn't like the idea of anything rattling Pelageya.

"Oh," Pelageya whispered. "Many spinning parts, fractured spines under the weight of terrible choices." Her voice got louder and grew frantic. "Dead gods awake, live gods dead, magic and blood and a devouring so great it will consume the world and drown us all in shadows. Something has shifted. Someone has woken, agreed to something, decided a path, but darkness . . . eternal, still. Take in your mouth the ashes of divine consequence."

Malachiasz's eyes were wide, his face deathly pale. "What?" His voice cracked.

A frenetic energy built in the room. The flames in the fireplace started to glow with a sickly green light. "There was divine justice and divine providence and paths to walk and you—you *children*— tore them down. A curse, a doom, a blackened stain on each and every one of you who have touched the darkness and swallowed the light. This isn't a matter of stopping anything," she whispered. "You can't stop it. What are you? A boy, a child, *bovilgy*, small and fragile under his thumb."

"I told you, he's weakened," Malachiasz said, sounding desperate.

Serefin did not want to be here.

"Weakened?" Pelageya cried. "Even weak he is still the doom of the world. Who set him free, who let him out?" Her eyes focused in on Serefin. "It was you. The eye. The eye! *Where is it?*"

"Witch, it isn't in my face, how should I know?"

She turned to Malachiasz, who flinched suddenly, his fingers curling into a fist. "You have it," she hissed.

A dread horror began to pool at the pit of Serefin's stomach.

Malachiasz's eyebrows tugged down, pulling at the tattoos on his forehead. He slowly uncurled the fingers of his left hand and embedded in the center of his palm was an eye, blue as midnight, with stars scattered through it. "Oh," he said very softly, looking ill himself.

"How is that possible?" Serefin asked.

Malachiasz shook his head wordlessly.

"A devouring," Pelageya murmured. "Oh, no, oh, this is worse than I imagined. This is worse than I dreamed. What have you done? What have the both of you done?"

"Do you . . ." Malachiasz poked at the eye with a finger.

Serefin was dangerously close to losing the contents of his stomach.

"Do you want it back?"

Serefin stood, and without another word left the hut and promptly threw up.

NADEZHDA

LAPTEVA

Under the darkest water, the deepest water, are buried old things that Zvezdan has brought unto himself. A hoard of foul magic.

—The Books of Innokentiy

Nadya was used to isolation. She was used to Kalyazin's mountains and forests and tiny, worn villages. But as they traveled farther west, they passed through entire cities, and her daily life became populated by prying eyes. She was instructed to keep her hand gloved at all times, even when the *boyar* pushed hospitality on Katya and shoved them into bathhouses.

"Don't take it off," Katya would mutter. "You'll be on a pyre in ten minutes."

So Nadya kept her hand carefully tucked away. Katya was shockingly cavalier about the whole situation, though Nadya had finally worked a plan out of the girl, vague as it might be. The world thought she was the cleric. And that was how it would stay. She wished she knew the truth. She almost wished she could speak to Pelageya about it. Instead she would hope whoever she found in Komyazalov could be trusted not to immediately set her on fire.

They were in the city of Voczi Dovorik, nestled in a wide gap, a break in the woods. It was only a few more days of travel to Komyazalov, but Katya was reluctant to leave.

It seemed they all had problems going home.

The *boyar* had been more than willing to open their homes to the *tsarevna* during their journey, but Nadya had seen no shortage of uncomfortable looks leveled at Parijahan and Rashid, and outright hostility toward Ostyia.

They were wandering aimlessly through the city. Nadya couldn't take being cooped up in the *boyar*'s extravagant home. She needed to be outside. She was angling to the edge of the city, and Ostyia was content to follow. They had crossed through the marketplace, a sad state of affairs. The winter was choking the country, starving it. Voczi Dovorik was in a marginally better place—the marketplace was still functioning and Nadya had seen a few outlanders from the north selling their wares and their furs. The city lived, but for how long?

"You know, I always wanted to see your cities, but I thought it was going to be at the other end of a torch."

They were speaking in Kalyazi, and Ostyia wasn't the best at the language, but she managed. Her accent was terrible. She got side glances every time she spoke.

"You genuinely thought Tranavia would get this far into Kalyazin?"

Ostyia shrugged. "Hold to your idle dreams to survive at war."

"Ostyia, you're going to make it home."

"You are distressingly optimistic for someone who can't drag her head out of her own depression most days."

"Distressing optimism is all I have left."

Ostyia didn't respond, perhaps to spare Nadya from her inevitable agreement. Nadya was just glad Ostyia had stopped threatening her. It wasn't her fault Serefin had gone into that forest.

Nadya tried her hardest to ignore that people moved out of her way as she passed. She ignored the reverent whispers. People talking about the gods and the girl who could speak to them. She missed the time when those words were true.

The melt and freeze of the snow had muddied the roads into wide permanent ruts from the wheels of wagons. Old snow weighed heavy on the roofs of buildings. Most were made of wood in the sector they wandered through. Stone buildings were few and reserved for the very rich up the hill. People passed them, tired and cold, fur collars and hats tucked low. For Nadya, it was too many people and she ached to find some solitude.

She was tempted by the nearby church, but she didn't want to drag Ostyia into one against her will.

"I don't care where you go," Ostyia said when she mentioned it offhand. "I wanted to be away from that *boyar*. He wouldn't stop staring. If we don't leave soon, I'm certain he's going to murder me in my sleep. He doesn't even know that I'm a blood mage! Only that I'm Tranavian."

"Isn't that enough?"

Ostyia shot Nadya an incredulous look as she veered their path south to where the church sat outside the city. She'd found that a little odd, but Katya had explained it was the last remnant of the village that the city had sprung from, and as the city had grown past the church, it had remained at the bottom of a hill with a graveyard to tend.

"Ostyia, if you had known I was Kalyazi when I showed up in Grazyk, you would have killed me on the spot. No questions asked."

Ostyia looked thoughtful but didn't argue; they knew their roots.

The church was old, wooden, and underkept, with peeling paint and worm-eaten boards. It was smaller than she had expected, considering the size of the city. It spoke of old things, old times, forgotten and left in the dust. It made Nadya immeasurably sad;

even with all she knew and had broken, the thought of the church being left behind as the world hurtled on was heartbreaking. A tear slipped down her cheek, and she roughly wiped it away.

Ostyia let out a small huff as they went inside.

"You're not the only person who's lost someone," Ostyia said, her voice far gentler than Nadya deserved.

"I've lost *everything*," Nadya snapped.

She pushed past Ostyia, through the tired nave and into the sanctuary. It was small and worn like the outside. No benches— one was expected to stand throughout a service and most churches had not yet decided to give their people respite. The sanctuary at the monastery where Nadya had taken Malachiasz had had benches, which, Nadya supposed, was rather modern of them.

She stood in the silence, wishing she could relish it instead of hurting so much, before Ostyia followed after her.

"You haven't lost everything," Ostyia continued. "You're still here, more than can be said for many others. And, yes, it hurts, and, yes, you want to give up. But you can't. You're the only one of us left with magic—"

"Katya—"

"Is about as good as a hedgewitch. She has a lot going for her, but magic is not one of those things," Ostyia replied.

Nadya frowned. "You don't understand—"

"No, Nadya, *you* don't understand. You've had it rough, I won't deny that, but I've spent the past three years of my life on a battle-field losing everyone I love day after day after day. You don't know what it's like to be faced with a choice—save the friend you've grown to love or protect your prince. It's not a choice. I always chose Serefin. I will always choose Serefin."

Nadya faltered. Ostyia had struck her as untouchable, but in the dim light of the church, the older girl's haphazard haircut suddenly didn't seem so cavalier and Nadya saw the desperation behind it. The exhaustion that cut her features looked bone deep.

"He's fine," Nadya said quietly.

"You don't need to lie to me," Ostyia replied. "But you also don't get to tell yourself that as an excuse to do nothing because surely he'll fix this problem."

"Serefin doesn't have a reputation for fixing problems."

Ostyia laughed, making Nadya smile. It had been so long that the movement felt foreign on her face.

"I suppose not," Ostyia agreed. "He'll get there one day. He has to, he's the king."

Nadya made a noncommittal noise.

"But . . ." Ostyia trailed off, staring up at the icons on the walls. "You've ruined us. He has no magic, either."

Nadya didn't even flinch. It was the truth. She had broken the world.

"I can't have the weight of the entire world on my shoulders," Nadya whispered.

"You should have considered that before you shattered it," Ostyia pointed out.

Nadya *did* flinch at that.

"I expected more from you after what you did in Grazyk."

If Nadya could go back to being the girl in Grazyk, full of righteous fury and untempered curiosity and the ability to hold them both instead of this unending, overwhelming grief, she would in a heartbeat. She would strip back all she had done and find another way to prove herself to Marzenya. Tell Malachiasz the truth instead of playing his game against him. But life was a series of bad choices made in desperation, and there was no going back.

"I did what I had to," Nadya said softly. "It wasn't enough."

Ostyia considered that. "When I was young, my family presented me with a choice that wasn't a choice, as was the way of noble families in Tranavia."

Nadya wondered if they should be talking so openly about Tranavia here, but Katya had been very loud and obvious about the "Tranavian prisoner" she had taken captive, so they would only have to yell for Katya to come crashing in with her title and protection if they needed it.

"My parents only had me, which isn't ideal when you need one child to go to war and one child for the court. They assumed I would choose court life, because why would I go to the front at only sixteen if they were telling me that I didn't have to? But Serefin was being forced to the front, and my parents were working under the assumption that I hadn't heard yet, and that if I had, he wouldn't be enough to sway me to certain doom." Ostyia smiled slightly. "I made my inclinations obvious *very young*."

Nadya snorted softly.

"In the end, it wasn't about loyalty, leaving. Said inclinations, as they are, frustrate my parents because they close doors that good Tranavian nobility want to remain open. If I wanted to live my life, then war it was, and I could only hope I'd last at least a few years."

Nadya frowned, not entirely sure why Ostyia was telling her this.

"I don't want anyone else to be presented with the same choice I was: stay home and pretend you're something you're not for the sake of an old Tranavian name, or go to war, and probably die quite terribly, because at least no one there will care that you've no interest in men."

"Would it have mattered if you weren't a *slavhka*?" Nadya asked.

"No. It's old court ideals. Bloodlines and children and whatever."

Nadya made a thoughtful noise. The door to the sanctuary opened, and a young man approached the altar, but made no indication that he noticed the two girls in the room, so Nadya ignored him.

"I don't want to leave the world doomed to a very different kind of war," Ostyia said. "And that's the path we're hurtling down."

"Because of me."

Ostyia did not disagree. And Nadya knew she was right and that she and Rashid could both be right. It wasn't her duty to fix every problem in the world, but it was up to her to try to mend some of her mistakes.

"Instead of contemplating the doom of the world by old gods, could we instead return to you talking about your childhood? That was much more palatable."

The young man stiffened slightly but didn't turn. Soon the entire city would be whispering about the old gods.

Ostyia laughed. "Absolutely not. War was awful. Court was worse. Except for that *Rawalyk*. I did quite like the drawing of every pretty, powerful girl into Grazyk, that was a *very* good idea."

"I was too scared out of my mind to truly appreciate it."

"Is your taste in girls as awful as your taste in boys?"

Nadya wrinkled her nose. "Almost guaranteed."

The door opened, the young man almost fleeing the room when Katya sauntered inside.

"Viktor!" she called, sounding delighted in a specific way that Nadya had come to learn meant the other person was about to be wildly uncomfortable and Katya was going to enjoy it immensely. "I didn't know you had left Komyazalov!"

"Yeah," Ostyia said softly, watching Katya, "I have awful taste, too."

"That's . . . bad," Ostyia said.

It was a massive understatement.

"Oh, is it? I wasn't sure. I wanted you to confirm it for me," Katya drawled.

Nadya rolled her eyes.

The *tsarevna* had led them outside to the graveyard. Half of the graves appeared fine, perfectly well tended. The other half were ravaged. As if the bodies had been hastily dug up—or had clawed their way out.

Nadya ran a finger along a grave marker. It came away black with mold. She glanced over her shoulder to where the swamps lurked in the distance. Katya followed her gaze.

"The priest says it's gotten closer," she said.

"The whole swamp?" Nadya couldn't hide the skepticism from her voice.

Katya only nodded.

"How, pray tell, does that happen?"

"Don't be willfully dense, dear, it doesn't suit you," Katya replied absently.

Nadya sighed.

"You're the one who had that Vulture break a wall that has been in place for centuries."

The last thing Nadya needed was a reminder of yet another thing that was her fault. She tightened her fist. Ostyia caught her eye and shook her head slightly.

"He would have done that even if Nadya hadn't asked," Ostyia pointed out.

"Even so," Katya said with a frown.

"Even so," Ostyia agreed. "It did happen. So, where do we think the bodies are?"

"And where *is* the priest?" Nadya asked.

She moved closer to inspect one of the empty graves. Her first guess was proving to be spectacularly incorrect. Something had clearly clawed its way out of this.

Serefin came back from the dead, now this? Death was Marzenya's domain, what happened when the goddess who tended it was gone? Apparently, death did not hold so tight a grip.

Nadya almost missed Katya shifting on her feet uncomfortably. She looked back over her shoulder at the *tsarevna*, who was avoiding her gaze.

"The priest?" she repeated.

"Did not wish to speak with you," Katya replied.

Nadya blinked. "What?"

"Apparently since you got here, the icons have been weeping." There were a few crumpled pieces of paper in Katya's fist.

A chill dragged down Nadya's spine. She hadn't noticed anything amiss in the sanctuary.

Katya didn't make eye contact, instead crouching to inspect another grave. "I've been gathering reports in each city and village we pass through and they're all like this. Icons weeping—usually tears but not always. In Gazhden'viya the statues dedicated to Veceslav, Bozidarka, Myesta, and Alena were found to be crying tears of blood, which is novel. Marzenya's statue has begun to erode."

A sick feeling settled at the pit of Nadya's stomach.

"I have more," Katya said, sitting back on her heels and glancing up at Nadya.

"Tell me," she whispered.

"The ancient poplar tree that has protected the city of Czezechni for centuries caught fire. The bodies of an entire sect of monks in the Voltek hills were found dead with absolutely no way to tell how they died. The farmers in the land around the Yevesh'tiri lakes have reported that something in the largest of the lakes has drowned all their livestock."

Each report hit Nadya like a blow. "And the winter," she whispered.

"And the winter," Katya agreed. "One thing has followed in your footsteps, though, and that is the tears of the icons." She eyed Nadya's corrupted hand, hidden by a long kidskin glove that had been far too expensive, but which Katya had paid for anyway. "I thought you were a cleric; I'm beginning to wonder."

"I was," Nadya said softly. "I *am*." But she was something else, too. There was more Katya wasn't telling her—so much more, she suspected, and she didn't know how much her heart could take.

"The Vultures have moved to the front," Katya continued. "You did something to blood magic, yes, but it didn't have the desired effect. They weren't touched."

But it was gone—wiped out, the knowledge as if it had never existed in the first place. Nadya looked at Ostyia, who appeared to be chewing that over.

"The Vultures are made of magic," she said. "They're more than blood mages. To take magic away from them would be to unravel them."

"Then why didn't they unravel?" Katya asked.

"Malachiasz would have known," Nadya murmured. She didn't

realize she'd said it aloud until she turned to see the other girls staring at her. She shrugged.

"I warned you about speaking of him," Katya said.

"No one in Kalyazin knows what his damn name was," Nadya snapped. "It doesn't matter." Żywia might know. Nadya didn't want her anywhere near Katya, but it was worth an attempt. "What do you have?"

Katya glanced at the papers in her hands. "Leaflets from the church. Seems the age of magic is over. The time of the cleric has ended. All we can do is turn toward the church for guidance."

Nadya swallowed. She should have expected this. "I'm going back into the church," Nadya said. "I'll catch up with you both later."

Katya nodded curtly. Ostyia almost looked torn at leaving her, but ultimately, she went with Katya.

All right. One of you talk to me, I don't care who.

Nadya pushed her way into the sanctuary. It was empty and the air stifled, the light was . . . dimmer.

The icons were crying tears of blood.

12

MALACHIASZ CZECHOWICZ

I hear whispers in the night. I thought it my dreams,
nothing more, but they've grown so insistent and the
things they say . . . is there truth to them? Is there truth
to what Odeta has said? Are we fighting for a lie?
—Fragment from the personal journals
of Celestyna Privalova

When Serefin returned, his skin was so gray it was almost green. He wordlessly sat back down. Pelageya had spent Serefin's absence muttering nonsense to herself and glaring at Malachiasz as if she would kill him on the spot if able. It was a rather unnerving shift in atmosphere.

"Oh," Serefin said. "It's gone."

Malachiasz rubbed at his palm. "They do that. It'll be back. There's no real pattern to it."

Serefin looked like he was going to throw up again.

"Get out, both of you," Pelageya said. "I need to think. To plan. Don't give me that," she snapped at Serefin. "If I need you, I'll find you. You have bigger problems to worry about. I'm not the only one who knows what has woken up, and that witchling outside has some rather unpleasant company."

Very suddenly her hut was gone and Malachiasz and Serefin were left abandoned in a darkened clearing. Serefin scrambled to his feet, putting significant distance between them. Malachiasz considered that before he tilted over, landing face-first in the grass, and was very still.

The only sound in the clearing was the occasional rustling of branches in the wind.

"I expected you to be more upset," Serefin said.

Was Malachiasz upset? Yes, very. It hadn't been fair of Serefin to stab Malachiasz right as he finally started to remember all that had been wrenched away. It hadn't been very fair to stab him in the heart at all, come to think of it.

But he was alive. And whatever he was being led to do, he wouldn't want to go about it alone. Everything was very confusing and very loud and he was used to every emotion he had being too much and too loud but now it all felt even *worse*. And his fury didn't manifest as destruction—it never had—so the idea of lashing out at Serefin rang hollow. He considered his usual defense—planning Serefin's downfall somehow—and tucked the thought away. Later, revenge might be necessary since he had no idea what Serefin was willing to do anymore and murdering Malachiasz was apparently an option.

"Please don't stab me again," Malachiasz said, more to the dirt than Serefin.

He heard Serefin sigh, and the sound of him sitting down heavily near Malachiasz's head.

"I . . ." Serefin hesitated. "I'd only just rationalized that I was willing to mourn you."

Malachiasz rolled onto his back. He wasn't in a survivable situation, so Serefin would probably fight that internal battle once more.

"I don't think there's anything I can say that will fix this."

"No," Malachiasz agreed absently. He was hungry again.

Serefin leaned back on his hands, tilting his gaze up at the canopy of branches. "I'm relieved you're alive, if that counts for anything."

"You sound surprised."

"Well, I don't particularly like you."

"The feeling is mutual."

Something flickered on Serefin's face. "I did once, though, a long time ago. All I can say is I'm sorry."

Malachiasz squinted up at him, taking in the full extent of the damage to Serefin's face. He looked . . . bad. His face was covered with long, scabbing gashes, the bandage over his left eye promising a mess of an eye socket underneath. His hair was long enough that he wore it tied back, and exhaustion shadowed his features.

"The *slavhki* are going to have quite the time with you," he said.

Serefin smiled slightly. "Kacper has been avoiding telling me how bad it is, which suggests very."

"I have a Vulture in my order with as many scars as you and she got in a fight with three *leshy* at once."

Noises rang out abruptly, the sound of something crashing through the woods at an alarming speed. Serefin jumped to his feet. Malachiasz merely sat up. He had the power of a god rattling through his bones, he wasn't particularly worried about anything this forest spat out.

Although one furious Tranavian *was* a bit alarming. He scrambled away from a blade that went spinning for his face.

"Kacper!" Serefin cried.

The other boy was absolutely not stopping. Malachiasz bolted to the other side of the clearing, afraid that if he was forced to fight back, things would go very badly for Kacper. He didn't want to give Serefin another reason to kill him. Malachiasz lifted his hands. "Call off your general, please. This really isn't the time."

Serefin blocked Kacper from throwing himself on Malachiasz. There was a beat of silence; Malachiasz could see the strain in

Serefin's arms as he held the other boy back. Finally, Kacper re-laxed, his head dropping to Serefin's shoulder.

"I'm not a general," Kacper muttered.

Serefin blinked. "You're not?"

"Lieutenant," Kacper said.

"No . . ."

Kacper was nodding.

"But Ostyia is a general."

"You promoted Ostyia but didn't promote me."

"That can't be right."

"You were very drunk when you promoted Ostyia."

Serefin paused. "That . . . sounds right."

Why is this happening, Malachiasz thought wearily. He started picking at a spot of decay on a tree. That didn't seem good. In fact, the closer he looked at the state of the clearing, the more *wrong* he saw. The ground was scattered with the bodies of dead birds. Tiny bones were strewn everywhere. The air had been strangely quiet since Pelageya left, he realized, especially strange for somewhere so deep in the forest. Even with all the noise they were making, they should be hearing *something.*

"Well, would you like to be promoted?" Serefin asked.

Kacper considered that.

"I'm going back into the forest," Malachiasz announced. "I think my chances are better there."

"Wait, Malachiasz," Serefin started, right as Kacper said very quietly, "I would like to be promoted."

Malachiasz lifted his eyebrows at Serefin. "Is this not where we part? Before either of us do more stabbing, or, throat cutting, as it were."

He hadn't expected the flicker in Serefin's expression. The moment where the other boy looked utterly *lost* because . . . why? Malachiasz was leaving?

"You need help, Malachiasz."

"I don't. Especially not from you." Malachiasz turned to leave.

He didn't like not knowing where he was. This forest was a maze and already he could feel it trying to feast on his bones.

He also realized the god had been suspiciously quiet for a long time, and silence was not absence.

Is this not what you want? My compliance? he thought sarcastically.

"*Is this you complying? Strange, that's not how it appears to me.*" It was a knife dragged through his brain, needles underneath his fingernails. Every time the voice spoke it brought unimaginable pain that Malachiasz was forced to press through.

Are you why I feel like this?

"*It's merely your nature. You mortals are so very good at hiding from your true natures, but they always catch up eventually.*"

Malachiasz didn't understand what was happening to him.

"*And that's what ultimately matters to you, isn't it?*" Chyrnog's voice sounded curious. "*Not what has happened to you, truly, but to understand it?*"

Of course that's what matters, he snapped. That was the only thing that had ever mattered.

Something else was moving heavily through the trees. Malachiasz shivered, magic itching underneath his skin. There were no guarantees that he could maintain control if he fell into the other parts of himself. He'd avoided knowing how much magic had been lost to him because testing those waters might mean he would drown.

"We've got to go," Serefin said suddenly, grabbing Malachiasz's arm.

Malachiasz flinched but didn't fight as Serefin dragged him out of the clearing and into the woods.

"Wait, he's coming with us?" Kacper cried.

"I can't keep an eye on him if I let him go, can I?" Serefin called over his shoulder. There was a smile in his voice that baffled Malachiasz.

"We don't even know who we're running from," Malachiasz said.

"Not something I intend to find out!" Serefin replied, before slamming face-first into someone, his grip on Malachiasz falling away. Malachiasz skidded to a stop, underbrush flying underneath his boots.

The tall figure was hooded, features hidden in shadow, uncannily familiar in a way that Malachiasz couldn't place—until—

A spike of iron driven through a pale palm. Nadya's. His claws punching clear through her hands because she was giving him *power* and it was so much darker than he ever could have guessed. Except no, not that instance, a different one. But that hadn't been real, he had written it off as the forest toying with him when he was alone. He *had* been alone, hadn't he?

Who are they?

"Did you think I had no disciples in this world?"

A tight circle of hooded figures had closed in around them. Malachiasz glanced at Serefin, who seemed to catch what Malachiasz was about to do, his eye widening.

"Wait, Malachiasz—"

The taste of copper bloomed in his mouth. His vision shifted, sharper, *more,* as dozens of eyes blinked open and closed on his skin. Iron claws grew out of bloody nail beds, his teeth sharpening in his mouth. He stopped there—he tried to stop there.

Taszni nem Malachiasz.

Don't fall too far.

Don't lose the fragments that make you human.

"Boy, you lost those long ago."

Malachiasz struck.

He was infinitely faster than Chyrnog's acolytes, infinitely more powerful. But he was tired. He was hungry. He was wrapped around the will of a being so much older than him and even as he moved, claws shredding through black robes and teeth tearing through flesh, it wasn't enough.

Chyrnog did not want him to fight. Chyrnog wanted submission. Suddenly his body was no longer under his control. He was slammed to the ground hard enough to rattle his bones, sharp teeth cutting through his lower lip. He spat blood onto the boot of one of the acolytes.

"Now, now, none of that." The voice was calm and smooth, lilting and deceptively gentle. "We don't want to break you or your companions." Someone knelt down in front of Malachiasz, tilting his chin up with a gloved hand. "What a creature." They straightened.

He regretted wasting the blood in his mouth on a shoe. Everything was moving too fast and too slow and he couldn't seem to form words.

"Knock them out. We have a long way to go and I don't want them fighting."

Malachiasz tried to struggle but his body wouldn't *listen. What is happening to me?*

"You have made a great many assumptions about what I will allow, but it never occurred to you how this arrangement truly worked. You are nothing. Mere flesh, a worm, nothing but a vessel for me to enact my will, and my will is destruction, consumption. You can fight, or you can be compliant, none of it matters. I will win. I always win. And you need some nudging in the right direction. My acolytes have captured one who has awakened, and I need you to destroy it. Aren't you hungry?"

He was starving.

13

NADEZHDA LAPTEVA

The rivers of Kalyazin were drawn by Ljubica's fingernails as she raked them through the ground from her grief.

—The Books of Innokentiy

Nadya had spoken with many gods during her life. Other children at the monastery had their imaginary friends—imaginary siblings, imaginary family—but Nadya had the voices in her head that spoke to her of the world. It had been Marzenya over all the rest. A sheltering hand over a girl born at the heart of chaos. She whispered of magic, of war, and she whispered, again and again, how much she loved the girl that she had chosen. The girl whose hair had all the color leached out from the touch of the gods. The girl who sat and listened and held magic in her palms. The girl who dreamed of war.

Would love have smothered her so? Or asked the girl to tear out her heart and offer it, broken and bloody, for a possible fragment of forgiveness? To choose between her goddess and the friends she had made, the boy she had loved. Would love have asked that she lose everything to gain nothing?

Nadya did not understand love.

The sanctuary was empty, and no one would disturb her. No Tranavian, no Kalyazi *boyar* looking for gossip. It was here, in a place where the atmosphere was tainted and unholy, that she would make her next move. She went to the icons on the walls, touching the tears that tracked down Svoyatova Celestyna Samonova's cheeks. She wasn't surprised when her fingers came away covered in blood.

What is happening?

She didn't know who she expected to answer her. No one, ultimately. Ljubica, perhaps. The only one who had spoken with her since the mountaintop. But Ljubica was a fallen god, and Nadya desperately wanted to speak to one of the gods she always had known.

I know you hear me. I know Marzenya was lying. What she didn't understand was *why?* Nadya could have done so much more with the truth—was *doing* exactly what Marzenya wished as it was. Until the end.

Saving Malachiasz had been the only thing that mattered, even though she had known, absolutely, what he would do with her magic. She gave him the power to do what she could not. Marzenya's fingers were poised at the back of her skull, prepared for destruction, and she would never have been able to step away from her goddesses's touch. Marzenya had been ready to kill her. A lifetime of devotion, and for what? A lifetime of manipulation.

She took the icon off the wall and moved to the center of the sanctuary, sitting down and pulling the glove off her hand. Corrupted flesh and too sharp fingernails and there, in the center where a scar spiraled around her palm, an eye blinked open.

Nadya swallowed hard, flexing her hand, waiting for the eye in her palm to close and disappear, but it didn't.

She had thought the eyes, the constant shifts in Malachiasz's body, were because of what he had become during the ritual.

A chaos god, slipping through the cracks of mortality. But this meant she hadn't been totally right. *Divinity twists mortality.* That made sense; it explained the way her skin had cracked and fissured, stained and twisted. The scar on Malachiasz's palm had healed because so much of him was already tainted by divinity. It didn't need to react the same way. But what was happening to her was growing more pronounced. Would the corruption—blessing?—spread further, or had it stopped in its tracks? It hadn't moved since she had torn herself into pieces and put herself back together. Obliteration and coherence. She tasted blood and spat, wiping her mouth with the back of her hand.

She touched the skin near the eye. It didn't hurt anymore but it did feel strange. She carefully curled her fingers closed. Would this not have happened to her had she not shed her blood for power in Grazyk, or was this inevitable?

Nadya wet the tips of her fingers with blood from the icon.

"Ignore me, fine. I will force your attention upon me." She pulled Malachiasz's spell book out of her bag.

She had read most of it in the past few weeks, deciphering his almost incoherent handwriting. Even on the pages with carefully constructed spells she'd found scattered sketches. It was a part of him that she had overlooked until it was too late, his constant frenetic need for creation. Regardless, he carefully denoted on each spell page which were experimental and which he had thoroughly tested. There were pages upon pages of contemplations on divinity, experimental spells tucked in between. Alongside investigations of greatness were spells of unspeakable horror. The depths of his capacity for cruelty were greater than she had imagined. He had been truly dangerous, but she couldn't help thinking—as she flipped through his labor of passion—that he could create wonders as well as nightmares. He had been complicated, more beautiful and terrible than anyone had known, and the world was better and worse for his passing.

But she found what she wanted within those pages. The knowledge of blood magic might be gone, but she could read the spells he had constructed, somehow. She wondered what it was she had done. There were exceptions that suggested she had been prodded in a more specific direction than a broad stroke of wiping out blood magic. Marzenya had some bigger plan that included Nadya in a way that she could not escape.

Or there was power in blood that could never truly be wiped away.

She crossed her legs and rested the book open on the floor before her. Using her bloody fingertips, she carefully copied a spell onto the floor in front of her. It didn't totally make sense. It felt fragmented, so even within her something had shaped around the destruction of blood magic, but it would serve the purpose she required.

"I know you're listening," she said aloud. "I can tell, I *feel* it. I will force you to hear me. I don't care who, but one of you will speak to me." *I am more than a cleric and I will not be ignored any longer.*

She yanked a *voryen* from her belt and very carefully cut the back of her corrupted hand. Corrupted or . . . *divine?*

Regardless, it bled all the same. *Spilling the blood is the hard part. Using it is easy.*

Desecrating this holy place with heretical magic was easy. If this world was going to be saved from destruction, this is what she had to do.

The spell caught. Nadya's head snapped back, her spine arching. Something pressed against her, a weight, a presence, and her vision blanked out—nothing but white.

"You are persistent."

She did not know this voice. One of the fallen, then. There was a twinge of disappointment at being ignored by her pantheon, but she would speak to whoever answered her.

I've been called worse.

She was no longer in the small sanctuary and snow fell in this place. Her feet were bare and bloody footprints trailed behind her. Funny, how blood always followed her dealings with the gods.

Where am I?

"Not where you belong; not where mortals tread. Who are you?"

That is a very good question.

"But you didn't answer."

No. You first.

Amusement hung in the air. She was very close to witnessing a god and there was no preparing for it, not truly. She came to the edge of a lake, and there was no making it any less terrifying when he was in front of her.

Something churned within the dark water. Moving closer, ever closer, until a soaking, wriggling tentacle came curling up onto the shore near Nadya's feet. And more, dozens, as a hulking figure hauled itself out of the water. Almost human in shape, but not quite, churning with tentacles that did not stop moving, seeking, searching. His eyes were covered in dirty rags. Barnacles clung to his skin and hung from dripping pieces of scraggly hair.

A smile stretched, punctuated by broken teeth. "Zvezdan. And you still stand."

"I still stand."

"Not mad yet?"

"No more than usual, I should say."

"Interesting."

That *should* have been her fate. Her brain was rationalizing Zvezdan's form. Just as it had flickered over Malachiasz and only took in the pieces that made sense, protecting her from everything that simply *did not*. She curled her fingers over the eye in her palm, wishing she had her glove in this place.

"Not even my drowned priests have survived this," Zvezdan contemplated.

Nadya had no interest in this god's—fallen god, but a god all the same?—priests. How long had he been locked away? Had his priests continued on in his absence? Well, maybe she had *some* questions about being devoted to a god that no longer existed.

Though Zvezdan had not died, merely been locked away for centuries. There was no hope for her with Marzenya.

She was aware of the god watching her intently, somehow, even if his eyes were covered—though she suspected there were no eyes underneath.

"Are you the one that set us free?" he asked.

She had moved closer to the edge of the water, almost letting the waves lap at her bare toes. "No," she said, voice soft. "What are you planning to do with your freedom?"

"There is much to tend to. Many have fallen to heresy in my absence. Many have forgotten the terrors of the deep. I intend to make them remember."

Nadya's eyes narrowed. She did not take her gaze away from the water. "Not revenge for being locked away? Why were you locked away to begin with?"

The water splashed as Zvezdan shifted, his tentacles in constant movement. "Who would I revenge myself on? It is so much easier to enact my will on this world than the other, so I shall."

"Are the others of the same mind? Those who were locked away?"

"Ask them yourself. I'm sure they'll come when you call, little cleric, the glimmer of something we have never before tasted is too strong within you to resist." He was very near. "What are you?" he asked, sounding curious.

She could smell the rot of his breath, feel the strange ice of his presence. She did not move.

She had no answer for this question that kept being asked of her.

What kind of power did a fallen god have? They wanted to consume her, what could she do in return? She who had taken the power of the gods her entire life, who had held more than any mortal ever should have been able to withstand, who yearned in its absence in a way no human ever should.

She stretched out the fingers of her left hand, the eye blinking open.

Then she slammed her palm against Zvezdan's forehead. He froze, every part of him going still, air choking in the back of his throat. Did he need to breathe, she wondered? Did gods need air in their lungs?

Her vision went white and she saw the ocean of dark water, dark power. She could dip her hand into the water, she could take whatever she wished.

It could go in reverse. The gods could give her power, but she could also *take it*. She didn't know what needed to be done yet. But how much power would she need to do it?

She knelt at the edge of the black water and drank deep.

The shadows on her skin were up to her shoulder. Had it been wise, what she had done to Zvezdan? Almost definitely not, but that hadn't stopped her. Not much could.

"We can't leave, not yet," Katya said, dropping a full bottle of wine onto the table and sitting.

Nadya rolled her eyes. Katya was so much like Serefin sometimes, it was uncanny.

"Why not?" Nadya asked. She felt jittery and strange; the light had hurt her eyes when she'd left the sanctuary. At least they were no longer in the *boyar*'s home. Nadya could relax. The inn was more crowded than she would like, but the fire roared hot in the pit and the lingering chill from the magic she had done began to leave her bones.

"We have to figure out what's happening with those empty graves."

Rashid, who had been about to sit down next to Nadya, frowned slightly and straightened. "On second thought, I don't think this is a conversation I want to be involved in. Let me live in my sweet, grave-less ignorance."

"A whole bunch of graves in the cemetery are empty," Ostyia said.

"See, now you've ruined everything." Rashid gave an exasperated sigh and sat.

Nadya peered at his plate. "They have herring here?"

"You are not allowed to eat off my plate, you absolute monster."

"Old monastery habits die hard," Nadya said, taking a piece of bread and herring off his plate when he wasn't looking. He pretended he didn't notice.

Rashid's forearm rested beside her. He didn't have any tattoos—that she knew of—but it looked like vines had been painted on his skin, cut through with strange gashes that didn't appear to be healing. Katya and Ostyia were discussing the empty graves, and Nadya half-listened as she took Rashid's wrist and tugged his arm over. He followed her gaze and grimaced.

"What is this?" she asked.

"I don't know."

Parijahan joined them, saw the strange markings Nadya and Rashid were inspecting, and her eyes widened.

"No . . ." she whispered.

Rashid glanced down the table; Katya and Ostyia weren't paying any attention to them. "She knows, it's fine."

Parijahan let out a breath through her teeth. "Not here."

Nadya traced the vines on his arm, frown deepening. She didn't know what kind of magic would do this except . . . she shivered, thinking about her arm. Divinity and corruption; all the same. She met Rashid's gaze and the worry in it stabbed her through the chest. He had been running from this his whole life and it had finally caught up to him.

She took his hand and squeezed. "We'll make it."

"I can't believe you took my food when I told you not to," he replied.

She grinned and he immediately brightened.

"You're right, we will. Somehow."

Katya tapped the tabletop. "Back on task."

"When did it start?" Nadya asked. If they weren't going to move until this problem was solved, she might as well try to fix it.

"I think you know," Katya replied dryly.

"A handful of weeks ago," came a new voice as a thin boy with gently curling blond hair sat across from Nadya. It was the boy from the church—what had Katya said his name was? Viktor.

"Where have you been?" Katya asked.

"Doing my job. I moved out here for a reason, you know," Viktor replied.

He was about Katya's age, maybe a few years older. His clothes were fine, with his *kosovortka* embellished at the hem and collar. His coat was trimmed with fur so hearty it had to be bear. He wore his hair half tied, long, past his shoulders. A *boyar,* though Nadya should have expected that from someone Katya knew.

"No one has seen anything aside from an old woman who is known to have a habit of raving."

"No one has *said* they've seen anything," Ostyia replied.

Viktor immediately tensed at Ostyia's heavily accented Kalyazi. Katya shrugged at his quizzical expression.

"What, you don't have a Tranavian prisoner you cart around?"

Nadya expected Ostyia to snap but she only rolled her lone blue eye. *She really is in the same mess I was in last year.* Escape impossible and thus settling into the inevitable. A survival tactic, and one that Nadya didn't want to see someone else using.

"Ostyia has a point," Nadya said. Kalyazi were a superstitious bunch and catching a glimpse of a neighbor who had passed away wouldn't necessarily be a noteworthy occasion. They might have gone home and left food in their bathhouses and at their ovens, muttering about the spirits being a little stronger than normal, but think nothing more of it. "If there hasn't been anything malevolent from the corpses, who's to say they would be reported?"

Viktor lifted an eyebrow.

"Has there been an uptick of people attending church?"

"That's a question for the priest," Viktor replied.

"Ah, well, apparently a lost cause for me."

"Why is that? And what is your name?"

"Nadya, and—"

"Nadezhda is too humble," Katya cut in. "It's not every day someone meets our famed cleric."

There was a glint of recognition in Viktor's blue eyes. That and something Nadya knew all too well. People always wanted an easy ear to the gods. And the gods had never really cared to hear petty grievances.

"It's not that we don't care, *but why would I want to hear it second-hand? It makes me feel like they don't want my help."

Nadya didn't jolt at the voice even though she didn't recognize it. *Another* fallen god?

And you are?

"Ah, you don't know? Pity. Has everyone forgotten me? A shame."

Nadya tuned back into the conversation at the table but found it flowing steadily without her. Parijahan cast her a knowing glance and purposefully redirected Viktor's attention away from Nadya.

It wasn't obvious when the gods were talking to her, Nadya knew that much. But maybe Parijahan knew her well enough to sense when Nadya wasn't wholly present. It was a nice thought, that someone might know her like that. She never thought she would have that again.

You never answered my question, Nadya pointed out.

"I was hoping you would reach the proper conclusion on your own, but I suppose that's expecting far too much from a mortal. My name is Zlatana."

It's only polite that I ask what your domain is.

"Is? You are decidedly charming. I dwell in the dark and shallow waters, the marshes. I whisper to the creatures of the dark and they listen to me."

What interesting timing that you show up now.

"Oh? Is it?"

"Are there swamplands near here?" Nadya asked suddenly, and everyone fell silent. She had no idea where she had broken into the conversation. "Sorry," she said. "I had a thought."

"Apparently," Viktor said wryly. "Yes, there are swamps about a mile south of here."

Katya rested her chin in her hands. "What are you thinking, *kovoishka?*"

"Serefin set a fallen goddess of the swamp free and now any place near a swamp is going to face particular difficulties."

Ostyia let out a short laugh. "That's all of Tranavia, then."

Nadya met her gaze and shrugged. Ostyia's face paled as she

realized the gravity of the situation, that Tranavia was not safe from these fallen gods. They no longer had the veil of magic that Malachiasz had strengthened protecting them; they were vulnerable, those heretics—

Nadya had never considered *why*. Even after getting to know the Tranavians, she had never stopped to think why these people were so abhorred beyond how they spilled blood over parchment. Almost like there never was any real reason.

"What should we do?" Viktor asked Katya.

Katya didn't answer, her green eyes were on Nadya, uncomfortably sharp.

Nadya picked at her glove. "We should go to the swamps tonight."

14

SEREFIN
MELESKI

Lev made a breakthrough, somehow, but everything he writes is nonsense. Innokentiy is at a loss. I think Sofka has lost her mind. We're doomed.
— Passage from the personal journals
of Milyena Shishova

Serefin couldn't shake the feeling when he woke that he was *very* far from the clearing and Pelageya's hut. His head pounded like nails were being driven behind his eye sockets.

It was dark. One dim torch on the wall had to be sufficient as he took in his surroundings. He couldn't tell where he was. Was he alone? Blood and bone, he hoped not. He felt around, fingers catching on a *lot* of hair. Malachiasz. He shoved hard on his shoulder.

"Wake up, you scrawny disaster," he hissed.

If Malachiasz was down here, hopefully Kacper was as well. He kicked Malachiasz for good measure, and he groaned in response, finally stirring.

Serefin choked back the urge to cut his hand for magic. There was only disappointment there. He did have the stars, though. If he reached, he could touch them, in that place outside his awareness, the place where *other* magic dwelled. It was easy this time, natural.

"That's what happens when you're godstouched," Velyos noted.

Divine magic. It was growing harder to push back against what he had become. He cast out a handful of stars. The room lit up.

Malachiasz groaned again, softer, curling in on himself. Then his whole body convulsed, suddenly shifting wildly out of control. Serefin frantically scanned the room, finding Kacper in the opposite corner, unconscious. Torn, he hesitated. But there was little he could do for Malachiasz except let him ride out the seizing of chaos. Serefin started toward Kacper, his legs almost giving out. He shuffled over before crumpling to the floor, gently shaking Kacper's shoulder, panic gripping him when there was no immediate response.

"Kacper," he whispered. He kissed Kacper's temple. Pressed his fingers against his neck. There was a pulse, he was breathing.

Serefin leaned back on his heels, hoping desperately that this wasn't magic. He glanced over his shoulder at where his brother— *blood and bone, his brother was alive*—convulsed on the floor. He let out a breath and kissed Kacper's forehead before returning to Malachiasz, unsure what he could do.

It was hard to watch. Serefin had seen this in the mountains, his loss of control, the god that Malachiasz had become overpowering his mortality. It was cracking bones and tearing skin and teeth and claws and horror. Bile rose in the back of his throat and he choked it down.

Abruptly there was light from high above and Serefin realized they were in a cellar, the steps very far away. A door slammed closed and the light disappeared. A few seconds later a far-off torch flickered.

Serefin wanted to restrain Malachiasz somehow, keep him from tearing through his own cheek with razor teeth, but he couldn't get close enough.

What happened to you? This was more than eyes and tremors, and Serefin felt a twinge of unexpected sympathy. At least Serefin's divine troubles had only manifested in losing an eye. It seemed like a paltry trade, watching this.

Footsteps were coming closer and Serefin tensed as a hooded figure lit by a torch appeared next to him.

"Interesting," they murmured at Malachiasz. Their head moved, taking in Serefin. "Who is he to you?"

Months ago, he would have said no one, the Black Vulture, a monster, nothing more. Now he wasn't sure how to reconcile what it meant—this shifting of meaning between him and a boy he hadn't liked since he was a child.

"My brother," Serefin finally said. "Where are we?"

"Oh, I'm sure you have many questions. And I do apologize for—" they waved a hand at the cellar. "All of this. You had to be purified before entering the temple."

Serefin didn't like the sound of that at all. "Excuse me?"

"You weren't conscious for it. *He* appears to be reacting rather badly to it."

The shifting had slowed to the shivers and cracks that Serefin was fairly certain were Malachiasz's new normal. Eyes and mouths and teeth. His breath was shallow, eyes flickering open but strangely glassy, unseeing. Like something held him and wanted the last word. His spine arched, head cracking back on the hard ground, before he was let go and relaxed. He groaned softly, sitting up very slowly before burying his face in his hands. When he lifted his head, his eyes were onyx black.

Serefin startled, scrambling back. The figure did not move. Malachiasz eyed them, head tilting, the black fall of his hair a separate kind of darkness in this place.

This was going to end badly. Serefin had seen enough of the Vultures to know when they weren't entirely *there,* and Malachiasz had the look about him that he didn't particularly care for feeling human.

"I have to say," Serefin said. "It doesn't seem like you have the proper materials to handle someone like him."

Malachiasz struck. He moved faster than Serefin had thought possible.

The figure didn't move at all. His hood was knocked back, revealing the strange, twitchy boy from Olya's party. That explained how they were found. The boy was now seemingly stoic in the face of certain death.

Malachiasz slammed into a barrier of magic.

He dropped to a crouch, barely fazed. Serefin watched the boy; he hadn't seen him reach for anything to cast magic with, could he use it inherently? Impossible.

Well, not entirely impossible. Serefin could do *something* without his spell book, and Malachiasz was the same. But they had become something more than blood mages, and the rules had warped around them. It was disconcerting. Rules of the universe weren't made to be broken and Malachiasz had broken a great number.

"Don't worry," the boy said. "We were given ways to keep someone like him contained."

Serefin's eye narrowed.

Malachiasz held out his palm, fingertips fluttering against the magic. A smile tugged at the side of his mouth. Blood trickled out of the corner of his eye. He slammed his palm against the wall of magic, and it shattered.

The boy stepped back, surprised.

"Like I said," Serefin said, taking another step away. "I'm not sure you realize what you're up against."

The boy cast a harried glance at Serefin when he spoke. A mistake. Malachiasz shot forward, claws slamming into the boy's chest. He choked, blood dripping from his lips. Serefin winced.

"Tried to warn you."

Malachiasz yanked his hand away, dropping the boy.

Then he turned on Serefin. As Serefin ducked away, a breath too slow, and was grazed by Malachiasz's razor claws, he realized the last thing he wanted was to be around his brother when his most primal instincts were all he listened to, including the drive for vengeance.

"Malachiasz, I need you to snap out of this," Serefin said. He lifted his hands, pleading, aware this was a hopeless attempt.

Malachiasz shivered at the sound of his name, something in him recognizing it, but it wasn't enough. They weren't evenly matched, not like this.

Suddenly Malachiasz jolted, an odd expression passing over his face. Chains wrapped around his torso and wrists, moving of their own accord, and he fell to his knees.

The boy stood behind Malachiasz with a wry smile on his face, blood all over his chin and chest where he'd been stabbed. He *should* be dead.

He let out a pained breath through his teeth. "I told you. We have ways of keeping him contained."

"Malachiasz?" Serefin ignored the boy.

Malachiasz's onyx eyes flickered before the black leaked away to a pale, almost colorless blue. He frowned, straining against the chains, before sitting back on his heels, looking perplexed.

"Do you remember what happens when you're like that?" Serefin asked curiously. He had always wanted to ask.

"Sometimes," Malachiasz said, his voice sounded scratchy and wrong. He cleared his throat, which devolved into a fit of coughing. He spat out a mouthful of blood. "Do remember this one."

"Oh, so how you nearly killed me."

Malachiasz tried to shrug but the chains were weighing his arms down enough that he barely managed it. He tilted his head back at the boy.

"I suspect you have questions," the boy said brightly.

Kacper took that moment to finally stir awake. Serefin tried his hardest not to make a fuss but played his hand by pulling Kacper to him and kissing him like he was drowning.

"My head feels terrible," Kacper said when Serefin broke away and the boy started chaining him up as well.

"You and all the rest of us," Malachiasz muttered.

Kacper glared, as if he had forgotten Malachiasz was around and was being suddenly and unpleasantly reminded.

The boy moved on to chaining Kacper, almost apologetically. "Until I know you can be trusted, this is the way things have to be," he said.

Serefin and Kacper exchanged a glance. Malachiasz was gazing up at the ceiling.

"This is a cult," he murmured.

The boy finished with Kacper's chains and took a step back. Without another word, he returned to the stairs and left them in the dark once more.

Serefin tossed out a few stars.

"What a parlor trick," Malachiasz said, a touch more derisively than necessary.

Serefin thought of what the stars had done to the Vulture that had attacked him in that inn but kept it to himself. Let the Black Vulture underestimate him.

"What was that?" Serefin asked flatly.

Malachiasz rolled his eyes. "What do you want me to say?"

"'Sorry for nearly murdering you, Serefin,' would be a real good start."

"It'd be a lie."

"And you're so above that."

That got a smile out of Malachiasz, which was unnerving.

"How did that boy survive being stabbed?" Serefin asked.

"Now *that* is a good question."

Serefin had forgotten how profoundly condescending Malachiasz was.

"If the internal bleeding hadn't gotten him, the poison absolutely should've," he continued.

"You poison your claws?" Serefin said. It was supposed to be a question, but the idea was so ridiculous yet completely unsurprising that he didn't know what he was expecting the answer to be.

"You don't want to know the particulars of why the Vultures are the way we are," Malachiasz replied.

Serefin didn't, in fact, want that. "Never mind."

"Truly, I hate him," said Kacper.

Malachiasz grinned brightly before an odd expression flickered across his face and he pitched over, coughing. It was mildly pathetic. After a few moments he straightened with some effort.

"Where are we?" Serefin asked.

"How would I know? You ask so many questions." He couldn't wipe off the blood that had smeared across his chin and every time he spoke there was a glimmer of teeth sharper than was natural.

"You know something."

Malachiasz inclined his head. "Whoever they are, they follow the god that has me."

"*Oh,*" Serefin breathed.

Kacper shot him a questioning glance. Of course. *Of course* that was how Malachiasz was alive. This wouldn't be like with Velyos. Because Velyos was, ultimately, a being of mischief but nothing so destructive.

"That boy is too much trouble," Velyos noted.

Who is it? Serefin asked.

"You know. You dealt with him and walked away alive, which is more than most—more than anyone—can say. That's how he knew it was possible, you see. The blood is the same. If the elder brother could look upon one as old and twisted and wrong as he, then the younger, who is so much worse, so much madder, could as well, and the younger was the one he truly wanted."

Chyrnog. Serefin's stomach churned. "He's why I lost my eye," he said softly.

"This is *your* fault?" Malachiasz asked incredulously. Like he couldn't believe that Serefin was capable of anything, let alone something that had touched him.

Serefin opened his mouth and closed it. Yes. Yes and no and yes. He shrugged helplessly. "I—I didn't mean—"

Serefin was interrupted by the door slamming open. Malachiasz tensed, curling inward, like he was poising to strike, though Serefin didn't think he could do much while chained.

Serefin had set an old god free. And the god had taken the most powerful person alive who didn't have a shred of a conscience. If the world was to fall, it was very much Serefin's fault.

15

MALACHIASZ CZECHOWICZ

They cut off Svoyatovi Dimitry Teterev's ears, burned out his eyes, cut out his tongue, but still that did not stop him, nothing could stop him, and he brought down the city of Kowat alone.

—Vasiliev's Book of Saints

The boy returned with an extremely tall woman whom Malachiasz thought was potentially the cult's leader, until she hauled him to his feet to stand before the boy.

"If you are expecting me to be scared and incoherent, I am sorry to disappoint," Malachiasz said.

A smile pulled at the boy's mouth. He had feathery black hair and golden skin, the high features of someone from the Kalyazi north. One of his pupils was the wrong shape—a horizontal slit of black within brown. He lifted a hand to tuck a lock of hair behind his ear, two of his fingers as well as a chunk of his ear missing.

"My expectations are low, I assure you."

"Even better!"

He was hoping to get a better read on this boy who had survived his claws, but he got no reaction and a shiver of anxiety itched at his hands; he picked at a hangnail on his middle finger behind his back.

"Are you sure this is the one?" the woman asked. "The other has a godstouched eye."

Serefin jolted, as if trying to cover his eye but forgetting his arms were tied. Malachiasz knew what the woman was not saying. He stifled a sigh.

"You want a show," he said flatly.

It was a constant effort, holding the roiling chaos at bay, and thus a release to let his body succumb instead. He closed his eyes—though he saw through every other damn eye that opened on his skin, a veritable assault on his fragile senses. No limbs this time, odd since that had happened during his episode on the floor earlier. He supposed there was no predicting chaos. After what felt sufficient, he carefully pulled everything back, smothering it down, knowing that every time his shields fell it was a little bit harder to put them back up.

He opened his eyes, watching as the boy's pupils dilated, a hitch of breath at his throat. The boy's pulse quickened in a beat so fast that Malachiasz could almost see it against his skin.

"What's your name?" he asked, like he was leading this conversation.

The boy's eyes narrowed, but after a pause, he allowed, "Ruslan Yedemsky."

Malachiasz liked that moment of surrender. When someone handed him their name, not realizing what they were giving him. So few realized the power held in their names, especially not Kalyazi.

Serefin frowned slightly, his face pale, sweat beading on his skin. He needed to get that eye treated or it was going to kill him. Malachiasz was surprised to find he didn't want that; he wanted Serefin alive.

"You have the blood of gods underneath your fingernails," Ruslan observed.

"And yours."

Ruslan's fingers kept tugging at a ring on his finger—a bulky thing that Malachiasz suspected held a relic. Malachiasz caught a flash of an ugly open wound on his palm. A wound made by a spike of iron being driven through flesh.

Had that happened? Who was this boy? A flash of something passed over Ruslan's face. Malachiasz couldn't quite decipher it. Interesting.

"What did you mean by purified?" Serefin asked.

Ruslan cast him a glance. "I wanted to be certain I'd found what I was searching for."

"Me? I'm flattered," Malachiasz said. "What do you want?" he asked, though he knew. Someone had awakened, whatever that meant, and this cult wanted Malachiasz to kill them.

He would address that particular moral quandary later, he decided, because he still didn't know if he was going to aid this god or fight him. If Serefin could rip himself free, he certainly could.

"I allowed the boy to go," Chyrnog said. *"You will not be so lucky."*

Malachiasz shuddered.

Ruslan didn't deign to answer Malachiasz's question. "Let's bring our guest upstairs," he said.

"What about the other two?" the woman asked.

Ruslan peered at Serefin and Kacper, focusing in on Serefin, eyes running over his features.

"Brothers, you said? We'll keep you both as incentive for this one to cooperate. Also," he tipped Serefin's chin up, "we can use you."

"Can't say I'll be much use," Serefin said. "He and I are deeply estranged."

They were taken up the stairs. The windows cast light down the bleak hall in jagged knives. Malachiasz had the vaguest feeling that it was a torture chamber. He trembled, his heart beating too fast in his chest.

Ruslan pulled him down a different hallway.

"Well, that answers one question," he said. "Chyrnog's priests and prophets cannot be touched by the light lest it burn them."

"I'm not a priest or a prophet," Malachiasz snapped.

"Yet still blessed."

It wasn't a blessing. Malachiasz didn't even know how to twist this into something he could use. He stumbled as a hunger pang struck him. He hissed out a breath through his teeth, suddenly dizzy.

"Has the god told you to keep me chained up, then?" he asked instead, ignoring the jittery feeling in his chest. He was going to pass out. "Doesn't it make more sense that you would be delighted to find someone like me?"

"We've been waiting for Chyrnog for a very long time," Ruslan said. "It's unexpected, you see, for him to choose a Tranavian."

"A heretic, you mean? It's fine, I don't mind." The word never had any true bite to it, and Nadya had used it against him enough that he had almost grown fond of the term.

Ruslan frowned slightly, as if unsure what to make of him. Good, he wanted the boy unstable. To wonder if maybe Malachiasz wasn't so bad after all, maybe he really did have Chyrnog's best interests at heart.

He didn't, of course. Only his and Tranavia's. And Tranavia above all else.

Though wasn't that what had gotten him into this whole mess? He should have been more tactful, *careful*. He shouldn't have given Nadya such an easy way to destroy everything. He should have questioned her intentions. He hadn't expected her to be so adept at lying.

He had been willfully foolish. Because of course she wasn't still the scared, naive girl from Kalyazin that he had manipulated. If she had been, he never would have . . . well, he wouldn't have cared so much. It was *because* she was clever and cunning and absolutely ruthless that he was so damn fond of her. She was far more trouble than she was worth.

But he'd liked the trouble.

He held back a sigh, pushing her from his mind.

The building they were in was large, a fortress of some sort. Malachiasz couldn't quite figure out the structure of it, but this wasn't a church, it was too big.

They were taken into an open, airy space. A vast tree, dark and brittle looking, sat in the center of the immense room. Clearly dead, its branches dry and thin as they raked up to the top of the ceiling.

Interesting.

Malachiasz's attention lit on a single white flower that had blossomed on one of the branches. Benign enough, but when his vision split, the flower was crawling with worms. Chained to the tree was a young man, only a few years older than Malachiasz. There was something wrong with him. It took Malachiasz a heartbeat to realize that he wasn't chained at all.

Serefin let out a soft, distressed sound.

The tree had grown into and around the man, roots digging into flesh, flesh becoming root. His eyes were closed.

Malachiasz was struck with a very particular kind of hunger.

"Good, you know what you must do."

Ruslan stepped toward the man in the tree, tipping his chin up. His eyes did not open.

"He was one of ours, once," he said, sounding sad. "We noticed something was wrong a year ago but thought little of it. His daily life had been unaffected. But a few weeks ago, something broke within the world."

The wall he'd torn through. Tranavia's magic stripped away. The death of Nadya's goddess. So much had changed. Pelageya had said things were waking up. What had Chyrnog called them? *Awakened ones.*

Malachiasz swallowed hard, his mouth flooding with saliva.

"What is his name?" he asked.

Ruslan lifted an eyebrow. "Ivan."

He was very, very hungry.

"You know what you must do."

16

NADEZHDA

LAPTEVA

Zlatana and Omunitsa have always had a bitter rivalry. Sisters, once, but sisters no more.
—Codex of the Divine 866:73

Nadya pulled her hood over her hair and lightly regretted the suggestion that they come here. It was so cold—how long would they survive this? Maybe they didn't even have to worry about the fallen gods, the winter would kill them first.

"It's too quiet," Katya grumbled.

They should have been able to hear frogs, bugs, birds, *anything*. But everything was silent.

"What are we looking for?" Viktor asked.

Nadya had been surprised he'd wanted to go with them, but he had offered not only to join, but to give a particularly good excuse to the *boyar* they were staying with as to what they were doing during the night.

She didn't know how to explain what it was they were about to do, however. She wasn't entirely sure herself.

"What do you know about the goddess Zlatana?" she asked.

Katya frowned, shrugging. "I only know the name. She's one of the fallen, but that's all."

Unfortunate. Nadya could have used more information. "What about Zvezdan?"

Viktor's eyes widened and he shot a rather accusatory look at Katya. "You said she was a cleric."

"She is."

"I am," Nadya said.

"Those aren't our gods."

They were once, Nadya thought. What had happened to cast them out, truly? Ultimately, it didn't matter. Zlatana was doing something detrimental here and she was proof that all the fallen gods would act in kind.

"That seems a tad judgmental. We don't all want the same things." Nadya immediately recognized the thin, reedy voice.

Velyos.

"Hello, little bird."

Don't call me that.

She moved a few steps away from the others, sensing an involved conversation.

If you don't all want the same things, what do you want?

"Oh, I got what I wanted."

Why is this the first I've heard from you?

"I have my own little mortal to watch over."

Serefin.

"The charming Tranavian boy, yes!"

Nadya clambered over a fallen log, making sure she didn't trample any snakes on the other side.

Is he alive?

"Yes."

Velyos offered no extra information about Serefin and Nadya didn't ask. That was enough. She could tell Ostyia, and it would make her feel better.

Nadya could ask the obvious question—what was Velyos doing

here? But that didn't particularly interest her. What she wanted to know was something vastly more specific.

If you're free now, does that mean the other gods are accessible to you?

Velyos paused. A hesitation that meant she was going to be let down very gently with her next question.

You all exist in the same realm, no?

"What are you asking, child?"

I'm only curious about the others, that's all. It doesn't matter. You don't have to answer my questions. I don't expect you to.

"You are curious because they do not speak to you."

Obviously. Where was Serefin, why wasn't he with him? Did she truly care? He had killed Malachiasz so easily.

Like you killed Malachiasz so easily, she reminded herself.

If you're here, you may as well help, she said to Velyos.

"Well, I certainly don't need to give you power. You have enough of that of your own."

Where is Zlatana? Nearby?

"Near enough. Are you going to stop her?"

She simply wanted to know what Zlatana was planning; what they needed to be ready for in the city. Was she going to unleash those corpses on the world? Was she collecting them for a specific purpose? Nadya wanted answers. She couldn't say what Viktor and Katya were hoping to get from this excursion.

Parijahan had declined to come, and after thoughtful consideration Rashid had elected to stay with her. Ostyia had also stayed behind. Something about too much divine nonsense. Nadya couldn't help but agree.

"You have the scent of salt and power on you," Velyos observed. "What have you been up to?"

That's none of your business.

"The world has grown so much larger without Marzenya, yes?"

Don't speak her name.

"Why do you mourn, daughter of death? She is a goddess of cycles."

Nadya gasped, her chest fluttering uncomfortably as Velyos left. Her steps faltered. Katya grabbed her arm, holding her steady.

"What happened?" she asked, voice low.

"Divine nonsense," Nadya said.

Katya fingered her necklace of teeth. Nadya's eyes narrowed. Katya had a bracelet with the icons of saints carved into it, and countless other minor relics. The girl could cast magic through drugs and dreaming, but what kind of power was that next to what Nadya could do even without the gods?

Or with them. She thought of the power she'd stolen, from Zvezdan, from Malachiasz. Was that all she did? Use the power of others because she didn't truly have her own? But that wasn't true; she almost wished it was. It would be an easier truth to deal with.

The ache in her chest that was the missing and the guilt and the absence and the absolute wrong that was Marzenya's death was still too real and too raw and it clashed too horribly with the agony of losing Malachiasz and—

Nadya slammed face-first into something hard. Katya bumped into her from behind.

"Why did you stop?" Viktor asked, a few paces back.

Nadya pressed her hands against a solid slab of magic. She frowned, tugging the glove off her hand. It was too dark for anyone to see what was wrong with her skin, the eye in her palm. She tapped her fingers against raw power.

"It's like the wall in Dozvlatovya," Katya observed.

"Similar," Nadya said. She pressed at it with power. Dark well. Dark water. *Daughter of death.* "Not so old, not by far. This was placed recently, and not by the divine."

"Blood magic?" Viktor asked.

Nadya probed a little deeper. No. This wasn't blood magic. She didn't want to spark an inquisition, but she knew this magic. She felt it each time Pelageya took her into her home. Earth, deep and heavy.

"Witch magic," she said softly.

Viktor tensed. He was standing a little too close to Nadya. She could smell the incense on his clothes. She shifted away slightly, fingering her prayer beads.

"What is that supposed to mean?"

"It means you have swamp witches, *moy gorlovky*," she replied dryly.

He cast her a sidelong glance. She scratched her fingernails against the magic, tugging on the threads of power she had taken from Zvezdan. It would be easy to pull this apart.

"Hold on," Katya said, her hand gripping Nadya's wrist. "Will you be letting anything out if you do this?"

Nadya frowned. "I don't know," she replied. "Sometimes you have to act."

"I won't have you setting off another *event*," Katya warned. Her tone bit at Nadya.

So much had gone wrong and for what, because Nadya had lost her connection to the gods and wanted it back. She had been selfish. Leading Malachiasz to his doom with the promise of forgiveness. Sending Serefin into the dark instead of helping him, when she was one of the only people who could.

Who would still be alive if not for her?

"Katya, I cannot promise nothing will happen. But this wall was made to keep people *out,* not hold people in."

"I thought we were here because of a goddess."

"All gods have their acolytes," Nadya replied. "Even ones who have been lost to us for centuries." The fallen gods probably had the most zealous followers. Who else would so fervently believe that a god who had not spoken in centuries would come back?

What did Velyos mean? A goddess of cycles? Marzenya was the goddess of winter. In the spring, her statues were burned to end the season and bring on the next. At the end of fall those statues would return as Marzenya's domain returned to the land. Those were natural cycles; what had happened to her was not natural.

Nadya shook it from her mind as Katya let go and took a step back.

"Do what you must," she said.

Nadya tugged at the threads of power holding the wall in place and pulled. There was a rush of stagnant air as the wall fell.

"Should we be getting a priest?" Viktor asked amiably as they stepped past a body half submerged in the muck.

"We have Nadya," Katya said.

"I don't think that's the same."

Nadya stooped to inspect the closest body. It had been well preserved by the swamp. This wasn't one of the corpses from the city. These had been here much longer. She frowned. There were a lot of bodies scattered around them.

"Katyusha, *melunishna*, I forgot you threw the absolute best parties in Komyazalov."

"Shut up, Viktor," Katya said.

"Well, *kovoishka*?" he asked, completely undeterred.

"I'm thinking . . ." Nadya said, leaning back on her heels. "I don't like this."

"What were you saying about acolytes?"

"That's what I'm worried about."

They could go farther and run straight into whatever it was that had decided it needed all these bodies. But they would have to go into the water, and that would risk alerting an *utopnik*. She had seen the glint of one's eyes earlier. They were nearby and watching.

"I wish I knew how this magic worked," Nadya said softly. She thumbed one of the beads on her necklace, not really expecting any responses from Omunitsa.

"You're persistent."

Nadya froze. She choked on her next breath. Katya moved toward her, alarmed, but she waved her off.

It's you.

"It's me," Omunitsa said flatly. *"You want something."*

Why are you talking to me?

"It doesn't matter. Mortal surprise and whatever human emotion you want to charge into this. Tell me what you want."

Nadya reeled. Had something happened? What had taken them from forced, deliberate silence to talking to her? Or was Omunitsa breaking the rules? She was like that. Nadya didn't interact with her much, but she knew what the goddess of the waters was like. She was protective of her territory.

Zlatana is making you nervous, isn't she?

"I don't appreciate your assumptions, child."

But Nadya knew her gods were threatened by the fallen, and Zlatana's domain was the swamps, one Omunitsa had taken for herself.

Are there witches nearby?

"Swamp hags, yes."

Nadya shuddered. She relayed that to Katya, who paled and fingered the hilt of her sword.

Would asking for power be a step too far?

"You don't need power from me." Omunitsa sounded snide.

What did that mean?

Stay close, please, Nadya said instead of arguing.

There was grumpy acknowledgment. She would be thrilled by this turn of events if it didn't also terrify her.

"What are we dealing with?" Viktor asked.

Nadya prodded Omunitsa for a little more information, which she conceded reluctantly. "They've been feeding off these corpses for a while, but found it wasn't enough when their goddess started speaking again."

"And they turned to the city," Katya said.

Nadya nodded. "Pulled corpses from the graveyard to feed."

"What do they plan to do?" Viktor asked. He sounded nervous. But Nadya expected that of anyone rational when suddenly confronted with corpse-stealing witches.

Nadya stood slowly. "We need to go back." She couldn't fight the witches from within their domain, she wasn't strong enough. "We should barricade the city."

Katya lifted her eyebrows. "You think they're going to attack?"

"I told you the war is the least of our concerns," Nadya said, her voice hushed. "For Voczi Dovorik that's even more true. Zlatana isn't content with the size of her domain. She wants more. Her acolytes will be all too willing to comply with her demands."

"And she wants to reach past the swamp's borders?" Viktor asked.

"She wants the swamp to swallow the city alive."

17

SEREFIN

MELESKI

The curls of his tentacles within the dark ocean creep
ever closer to the surface and when Zvezdan finally
breaks, the world will drown in saltwater.
—The Books of Innokentiy

The silence was unnerving.

The cult left them in the odd chapel room, unlocking Kacper and Serefin's chains, but not Malachiasz's, and locking the door behind them. Malachiasz immediately darted to the shadows. His skin was ashen and sweat beaded at his temples.

Kacper looked ill. "Where is this going?" he asked sotto voce.

"I don't know," Serefin replied. The man on—in?—the tree hadn't moved, but Serefin could feel power radiating off him in cool waves.

Kacper glanced to where Malachiasz was curled in the corner, his eyes locked on the man. "And what's wrong with him?"

"Everything. I'm going to try to help him."

"Bad idea," Kacper said.

"I know."

"He tried to have you killed." Kacper's gaze fell to the scar along Serefin's neck. "Not tried," he muttered.

"And I murdered him for it. We're even."

"That's not how this works *at all*."

"We're pretty far outside the realm of knowing how this works, I'd say."

Kacper scowled. Serefin kissed his cheek.

"We're here *because* of him," he grumbled. "He doesn't deserve your help."

Serefin let out a breath of a laugh. "He absolutely doesn't. But who does?"

Kacper rolled his eyes.

Serefin moved over to Malachiasz, who did not stir as he sat down next to him.

"Can you hear it?" Malachiasz asked in a toneless drone.

Serefin tensed. "No."

"The singing. He's singing."

There was no singing. There was nothing but the soft sound of chains as Kacper carefully shed his and sat down, leaning against the opposite wall.

What's wrong with him? Serefin asked Velyos.

"The awakened one will drive him mad."

What? What does that mean?

"The need, the call. Chyrnog is entropy; he consumes. Power, flesh, it's all the same."

"I'm going to hurt him," Malachiasz said, his voice small. His pale eyes were glassy with tears.

"That doesn't seem like something that would particularly bother you," Serefin replied.

Malachiasz swallowed hard. "You'd think not, huh?"

Serefin's eye narrowed. What did this cult really want with Malachiasz?

"It's so loud, how do you not hear it?"

"I can't hear anything."

What is he going to do? he asked Velyos frantically. *What is about to break?*

"I shouldn't be here," Malachiasz whispered. "I'm not strong enough to stop this. I thought I could fight him, but I can't. I'm— I'm so hungry."

"*Everything,*" Velyos said simply.

NADEZHDA

LAPTEVA

A drop of rain fell against Nadya's cheek and a part of her was surprised to find only water, not blood.

The city rallied quickly, thanks to the *tsarevna*. The *boyar* couldn't exactly tell her no, especially when she had the cleric to wave around as proof of something wrong. But Nadya couldn't shake the feeling this was all a distraction from something bigger.

Nadya kept her concerns to herself. For once, she wanted to leave this battle to the soldiers who were trained for it, even if it wouldn't be that easy. She knew what was expected of her. She was the good little soldier to be used for mass destruction whenever Kalyazin wished it. That was her fate.

It took everything in her not to turn and walk away.

Darkness fell quickly, blanketing the world, smothering. How clear it was that this was magic-borne and unnatural. Even as torches were lit along the wall, facing the swamps, it wasn't enough. Nothing would be enough.

"Tell me what's about to happen," Katya said as she came up beside Nadya on the wall.

"Zlatana was banished and she wants her domain returned," Nadya said.

"Using swamp witches."

Nadya nodded.

"They should be easily dealt with."

"Possibly, if we didn't also have an army of corpses to contend with," Nadya pointed out.

Rashid arrived in time to hear this and made a small noise of distress. "I had been so hoping the corpses weren't going to be involved."

"No such luck," Nadya said. "What happens if they can't be cut down without magic?"

Katya shot her a sidelong look. "Then it will be good we have you."

Zvezdan's power still hot within her, Nadya wondered what would come of her spilling her own blood—how much power could she gather? It wasn't worth the risk, not in Kalyazin, but the idea was tempting.

Deep in the swamps something screamed.

Rashid shifted on his feet next to Nadya.

"Where's Parj?" she asked.

"On the other side of the wall with Ostyia."

Another scream. Soul-wrenching and wailing, it tore jagged edges into the night. There was a movement at the border of the swamps. She caught power in her palms, hot light spilling through her fingers.

"Why are we here, Nadya?" Rashid asked, his voice pitched low.

She gazed into his terror-stricken eyes, and whispered, "I don't know."

MALACHIASZ

CZECHOWICZ

It was beautiful, eternal, transient, unending unending *unending* and if he did not stop the singing, he would die.

It was flipping itself back and starting over and it was driving him mad. Or maybe when he had woken up in the snow, careful, quiet, the life slowly returning to his limbs, his mind had not come with the rest. Maybe this was normal. So cold. So *hungry*.

And the singing, *the singing*, it was taking him apart. He knew this feeling. It was the forest as it had shredded Malachiasz's mind and tried its hardest to consume the parts that remained. But he hadn't been consumed—he *had* been consumed. He would consume.

It was distant. Everything was distant. He was on his feet and halfway across the room. Very far off he heard Serefin trying to get him to come back. But all that mattered was the person in the tree. All that mattered was tasting the power tearing them apart.

Malachiasz needed it. It *belonged* to him. It would be so easy. There were only the roots of the tree and the worm-eaten flowers and the thrum of power. He needed to stop the singing. If he didn't, the singing was going to kill him. His mouth flooded with saliva, teeth sharpening to iron nails.

Fingers grasped at his sleeve. He shrugged them off.

He rested at the edge of a precipice. He could hear his name and tried to reach for it. If he lost his name, there would be no coming back. He squeezed his eyes shut. He had no control; he'd never had control. He wasn't strong enough to fight back. He didn't want to.

He wanted the singing to stop. He wanted to taste the poison of power.

SEREFIN

MELESKI

At the end of everything, Serefin would remember that he had tried. He had done all he thought possible, but nothing reached his brother's ears. He was dimly aware of Kacper pulling him back, and he let him, not wanting to be near what was to come.

Malachiasz had shrugged off the chains binding him and was at the tree. There was nothing human in the way Malachiasz moved. A monster preparing to strike, tension coiled in every line of his body.

Ivan's eyes opened. Malachiasz grabbed his head, claws digging into his skin, and kissed him, hard.

There was blood. So much blood. Serefin couldn't tell where it was coming from. Kacper made a low moan, turning and pressing his face against Serefin's neck.

But Serefin did not look away. When Malachiasz slit the man's throat with his teeth, Serefin did not blink. When he did exactly what a god of entropy would wish of him, Serefin made himself watch. Someone needed to bear witness to this desecration.

It's not Malachiasz, he thought.

But he wasn't entirely certain that was true.

NADEZHDA

LAPTEVA

The number of corpses that crawled out of the swamps overwhelmed them. They didn't have an army to protect the city, and an army was what emerged from the darkness. Rashid had let out a horrified breath and Nadya had gripped her *voryens* a little tighter.

After, it all fell apart so quickly.

The corpses swarmed the city walls, keeping the soldiers distracted as the swamp witches struck. Nadya had been in battle before. Her hands had been stained with enemy blood. She had fought *Vultures* and survived. But this was different. Something here was at work against the Kalyazi, against *her*.

She and Rashid left the walls on Katya's order to take care of the witches or get somewhere safe. The latter was hardly an option, so go after the witches who had breached the city walls they would.

They were in an alleyway, the dirt road muddy and thick beneath their boots as it rained. Vines sprouted, abrupt and sharp with thorns, from the walls, cutting off their path.

Fire. She needed fire. But Krsnik would never respond to one of her prayers again.

So she pulled it from herself, and hoped it would not kill her.

There was a bewildering feeling of being torn apart, of having her insides rearranged. With a spark, her hands went up in flames.

Rashid, hacking at the vines with his sword, stepped back so Nadya could plunge her hands into the tangle of thorns. They hissed in protest, the rain diminishing her efforts, but she pressed harder, focusing, until the vines became an inferno.

She glanced at Rashid and backtracked through the alley. The witch at work would make herself known soon.

As the noises of battle flared through the night, Nadya realized quickly that she was being toyed with. A chasm would open in the streets before her and Rashid, only to close behind them. They would go down an alley to find it swarming with rats. Everywhere they turned was something else, some magic, and no witch behind it.

The city had become a maze and they were trapped inside.

The sounds of a skirmish came from a few buildings down, and Nadya, frustrated, chased after it. She plunged face-first into darkness.

The rain was gone. The lights from the torches, gone. The screams and shouts and clash of iron, gone. An unreality so all-consuming that Nadya faltered.

A laugh rang, soft and playful, at the shell of her ear. She lashed out, blade catching on nothing.

Nadya closed her eyes, tried to slow the pounding of her heart in her throat, tried to reach for *something* within the nothing.

There was a shift. Nadya wavered on her feet, dizzy from a rush of power that was not hers and that was not the unreality around her. She shook her head. She knew this. She had shoved it away, forgotten, let it rot from disuse. Yet power flooded through the tether, impossible to ignore.

It couldn't be.

He's alive.

Someone was calling her name. She turned, trying to find the voice because it sounded like Rashid and where had he gone?

She could feel Malachiasz, near enough to touch. She didn't want to press farther—there was no time, something brushed against her arm and pain flared all the way down to her hand. He was so terribly cold, panicked and scared and—and—

Nadya drew away, her stomach turning. She needed to press through the darkness, pull light from somewhere, and soon, but she didn't know how to mold the amorphous threads of power into what she needed. Fire was easier, she turned to that instead, her palms sparking.

Another glancing brush, this time across her stomach. She doubled over in pain, warmth blooming across her middle. A laugh. A whisper of words she couldn't understand and another flare of pain.

She was too warm and too cold all at once. A starburst of pain struck her back and she staggered. Something jagged and iron protruded from her chest. Distracting—she needed to focus on—she needed—

Nadya stumbled. The unreality fell and the sound of violence was deafening around her, until it wasn't. Everything was tunneling back into darkness. She blinked hard and tried to focus, but it hurt, everything hurt. Someone was screaming her name, but she couldn't—there wasn't—

Her knees hit the ground. She was very cold. It was very dark. And the rain looked like blood.

MALACHIASZ

CZECHOWICZ

Copper and iron and ashes. He had tasted power before; had tasted divinity, madness.

He had come to think that he could play this game the same as the gods. He had taken that kind of power into himself and survived. He had killed one of them. He would be feared.

He was in over his head and he was going to drown.

This was older, darker, and much more powerful. This was the roots of the trees buried deep within the earth. This was the depths of the water that had never been touched by mortals. This was the space between the stars that cascaded eternally and wound its way back to itself.

Malachiasz was only a boy.

He choked on blood and power. He lost his name and his control and everything that kept him *Malachiasz* and there was no one to pull him back.

The man hadn't fought. He had been too numb with power he wasn't used to touching. It had been so very easy.

His entire body shook with magic.

And if this was what Chyrnog wanted of Malachiasz, he could not parse whether he felt horror or exultation. Whether this was the power he had been searching for his whole life and *finally* had, or if it was too far, too much, not worth everything he would be destroying in the process.

(But what did he even want with this power? It wasn't his to use and he knew that—he did—but it tasted so good and he had wanted it for so long.)

He didn't care about the horror. The blood staining his teeth. The flesh underneath his fingernails. He knew that he should. He knew that he *needed to*.

He wasn't strong enough to fight Chyrnog's will, so why not enjoy it?

Then something snapped. Malachiasz was jerked back into the semblance of consciousness. Two words, devastating, lonely, repeating again and again and again through his mind:

She's gone.

18

SEREFIN

MELESKI

*A tongue of deceit, a spirit of mischief, a desire to foster
chaos, these are the things that make up Velyos.*
—The Books of Innokentiy

It was a full day before Malachiasz's seizures stopped. Serefin kept wiping blood from his remaining eye and brushing
away moths, keeping his distance from Malachiasz's chaos
and wishing there was something he could do. He understood the helplessness of losing everything when a god decided their will was more important than yours.

The Kalyazi boy returned, eyeing what remained at the
foot of the tree with a slight, feral smile. He pushed a stack
of blankets into Serefin's hands with an unfathomable look
toward Malachiasz before leaving, locking the door behind
him with a resounding clank.

When Malachiasz's seizures quieted to trembling, Serefin carefully draped a blanket over his thin frame before returning to the safety of the other side of the room. Kacper

sat there, bleakly staring at the tree with a moth-eaten blanket around his shoulders.

"We're going to regret this," Kacper said.

"You say that as if I'm not already regretting it," Serefin replied, sitting next to him and tugging the blanket over his shoulders. He held his arms out, frowning.

Kacper glanced at him, lifting his eyebrows.

"Nothing," Serefin said. "Just noticing what all this trauma has done to me." He had never been a particularly imposing person, but he had grown rather slight. He couldn't remember the last time he had eaten an actual meal.

Kacper's expression wrenched. "How long until he turns on us?"

"Neither of us has anything that god wants."

"That implies Malachiasz had nothing to do with what happened."

Serefin hesitated. Malachiasz was ruthless enough to comply with what Chyrnog wanted. Malachiasz was enough to *take* like that. Especially when it came to power.

He let the silence go on until Kacper sighed.

"He's a liability."

"Kacper, we can't handle what we'll find when we return to Tranavia."

Malachiasz could still use magic. Whatever was making blood magic inaccessible didn't seem to reach him.

"You'll have to deal with the Vultures."

Malachiasz was standing before them, skin pallid, a hollowness to his expression that Serefin couldn't quite work out. He faltered, slumping down to the floor, the blanket clutched around his shoulders. It was difficult to watch him for more than a few seconds at a time as his body twisted.

"How are you?" Serefin asked, feeling strangely charitable. Malachiasz just looked so miserable.

"Remember when Elżbieta fed us mushrooms that turned out to be poisonous? I feel a little like that."

"You remember that?"

Malachiasz shuddered through a shift. "I . . . get pieces sometimes."

"You were sick for a week. Threw up on *everything,* including the cat."

"I don't remember a cat."

"Piotr. Father hated him. He was a stable cat with an attitude. I kept bringing him into the palace, much to the dismay of everyone around me."

Malachiasz smiled wanly.

"What *was* that?" Kacper asked, voice hard, clearly unimpressed by their filial bonding.

"The destruction of an . . . awakened one," Malachiasz said, pitching over and landing on his side. "I've decided having more power is a bad thing."

"Oh, you've *finally* decided this?" Serefin asked.

He nodded, burying his face in the crook of his elbow.

"But that will change the second you feel better, huh?"

"Probably," he mumbled.

Kacper rolled his eyes. "We don't know what these cultists want now that Malachiasz did as they asked. We don't know that we can get out of here to make it *back* to Tranavia. We don't even know where we are!"

Malachiasz tilted his face toward them and opened one eye. "Is he always like this?" he asked Serefin.

"Oh, yes," Serefin replied warmly, ignoring the all-suffering look Kacper was giving him. "I'd be dead many times over if he wasn't."

Malachiasz responded with a sound of disbelief before hiding from the dim light of the torches once more. Dawn was starting to break through the grimy windows, but it was too early to do much good.

"And what does that *mean,* the destruction of an awakened one?" Kacper continued.

Malachiasz sat up with a groan, cradling his head with long, pale fingers before slowly dropping his hands. He stared at the tree, the fingers of his right hand pressing hard against the scar on his left palm. Serefin frowned as he noticed the metallic sheen of Malachiasz's claws digging into his own skin.

"I don't know," Malachiasz whispered, standing shakily. "He tasted like ashes. Divinity tastes like copper and ashes. He had . . . power."

"Well, you did make it so we couldn't ask him any helpful questions," Kacper pointed out.

Malachiasz was nonplussed. Serefin shouldn't be surprised that he wasn't horrified by what he had done. How much worse had he done during his reign as the Black Vulture?

"It's a question we'll need to answer, in any case," he said absently. "If magic isn't like what we thought, if it can appear in someone who previously could not use it . . . that changes things. That changes *everything*."

Malachiasz's gaze fell to Kacper's hip. "May I see your spell book?"

Serefin glared at Kacper. He shouldn't have been wearing it when they were captured by the Kalyazi. It was too dangerous. Kacper bit his lower lip.

He unclipped the belt and held it out, hesitating right before Malachiasz took it.

Malachiasz's expression softened. "I wouldn't ask if it weren't important."

Kacper relinquished the book and Malachiasz, with a gentleness that Serefin had rarely seen in him, cracked it open. He flipped through the spells, a frown creasing the tattoos on his forehead.

"Can you read them?" Kacper asked, hopefully.

Malachiasz stopped on a page, inspecting it further. He squeezed his eyes shut, swaying as if overcome with dizziness. "Not entirely. I don't know what Nadya did. I don't know how to fix it."

"*Nadya* did this?" Kacper asked, and Malachiasz flinched at the sound of her name.

"Yes," Malachiasz said, his voice small. He cleared his throat. "But if blood magic had truly been eradicated, I wouldn't be here. There's too much of it in me. The Vultures are made of it, and I can still feel them, faintly. Our link is supposed to sever when a Black Vulture dies, but I don't think I stayed dead long enough. If they try to appoint a new Black Vulture, they'll fail. They're mine."

"So, you can have them stand down."

Malachiasz nodded slowly.

They were no longer chained, but still prisoners. Malachiasz handed Kacper his spell book and lowered himself to the floor. He curled up, looking young and frail, before dragging the blanket over his head and appearing to attempt sleep.

"They're going to make him do that again," Serefin said with a frown.

"To what end?" Kacper asked.

That was what Serefin didn't understand. What did Chyrnog want? Destruction? Something more cosmic that they couldn't fathom? Serefin considered the temple Velyos had taken him to, the arms reaching for him; that feeling of morbid inevitability.

"This is hopeless." Serefin sighed. "Chyrnog was always going to latch onto Malachiasz's soul. There was no stopping any of this."

"Don't have one," Malachiasz mumbled.

"I'm sorry?" Kacper asked.

Serefin tilted his head, alarmed. He straightened his leg and nudged Malachiasz with the toe of his boot. "What did you just say?"

He groaned softly. "I want to sleep."

"Tell me what you said."

He opened one eye. "I gave Pelageya the pieces. I don't know what she did with them."

"Why would you *do that*?" Serefin cried.

Malachiasz sat up, slowly, a defeated slump to his shoulders. The terrifying, calculating Black Vulture wasn't home anymore and he had left the broken boy in his place.

"It was the only thing I had left to give," he said, blankly. "The ritual wasn't enough—I miscalculated, and I needed one more piece, but I didn't know who else to turn to. I don't know what she did with it."

"If you hadn't done that, would we be dealing with this old god?" Kacper asked, starting to sound desperate.

Malachiasz shrugged listlessly.

"He had me, for a time," Serefin said.

"But you got rid of him," Malachiasz pointed out.

Serefin touched the skin under his left eye socket. So he had.

Kacper rested his chin in his hands. "If you could get it back, would you be able to break free from him?"

"Oh yes, I'll go *find my soul*, I'm sure that will be easy," Malachiasz said spitefully.

But Kacper had a point.

"We'll talk more about this later," Serefin said slowly, needing to think. The concept of a soul was tricky in Tranavian culture, souls were so tied up with Kalyazi theology that Tranavians didn't really think about them much. Their concept of the afterlife was different, quieter, a rebirth and a renewal; it didn't weigh so heavily on the idea of a soul. For Malachiasz to have involved himself with the Kalyazi witch was out of character.

"Did it work?"

Malachiasz looked thoughtful, his fingers tugging on a piece of bone threaded through his hair. "I suppose so. The eyes started not long after, though that's a guess. I was barely lucid after the cathedral. Then I went . . . somewhere else on that Kalyazi mountain, and I don't think I would have had I not gone to Pelageya." He sighed. "I don't know. I thought I could fight him. I don't think I can."

Couldn't, or didn't want to? Malachiasz had always made it perfectly clear that there were no lines he was not willing to cross, nothing too horrific for him to not consider and see into reality. Serefin wouldn't fool himself about his brother; he was a monster to his core. He wanted to believe that Malachiasz could be something better, could claw his way back to human—at least a little— but he didn't know if he *could* believe that.

Malachiasz was eyeing a patch of light streaming in through the windows. He carefully moved to a corner that almost definitely wouldn't see any light.

"Sleep," Serefin said, not wanting to know. "Our problems will be here in the morning."

"That is *not* the comforting Kalyazi version of that saying," Malachiasz mumbled as he curled up.

"Well, no." It was dawn now.

"Ugh, Tranavians."

Serefin smiled at that.

They were either forgotten the next day or deliberately abandoned to think on what had happened in the eerie sanctuary. Either way, Serefin was hungry and bored. He tipped back until he was lying down, draping an arm over his eye. His head hurt, a pulse right behind his left eye socket. He let out a breath as Kacper rolled on top of him.

"You're moping," he observed.

"I'm not, though I'd deserve it if I were. My head hurts, is all."

Malachiasz let out an irritated huff, getting up and wandering away. Kacper lifted his head, watching him.

"We're making your brother uncomfortable," he observed.

Serefin tilted back to see where Malachiasz eyed the tree, avoiding the mess but tense all the same.

"No, it's not that."

Kacper frowned. His one hand was close to Serefin's head, his fingers twining through Serefin's hair.

"I find it difficult to believe that Malachiasz would be so limiting."

"Blood and bone," Malachiasz muttered. "Stop." He returned and sat down nearby, closing his eyes when shifts rippled through his body, coughing into the crook of his elbow. "I don't care what you two do." His mouth twitched. "And, no, I'm not."

Kacper rested his chin on Serefin's sternum, relaxing against him. "Please tell me you have sordid Vulture tales."

Serefin lifted his eyebrows at the unexpected shift in Kacper's attitude toward Malachiasz. Kacper glanced at him, shrugging lightly as if to say, well, we're stuck with him, might as well make the best of it.

Malachiasz drew his knees up to his chest, wrapping his arms around them. "It's the Vultures, it's all sordid." He also seemed puzzled by the lack of cool disdain from Kacper, who breathed out a laugh. "There was one when I was younger, Łukasz," Malachiasz continued. "He was brilliant, but things changed when I took the throne."

"Thrones'll do that," Serefin said.

Malachiasz snorted softly. "And now . . ." he trailed off.

"Did you know what Nadya was planning?"

He shook his head. "I naively thought she was telling the truth. That she wanted her power back. It was such a Tranavian senti-ment, I should have expected that she wanted something else."

"You were also baiting her," Kacper pointed out.

"I saw an opportunity."

"Would you have killed that goddess if Nadya hadn't . . ." Sere-fin trailed off. If she hadn't stripped them of their power. If they hadn't gone from three of the most powerful blood mages in Tra-navia to three boys, broken and in an enemy country.

"I don't know," Malachiasz said, softly.

Serefin suspected that, yes, he would have. Very little could stop Malachiasz once he decided on a course of action, and the instant he realized where Nadya was going, he had made his decision.

Kacper was idly running his fingers along the shell of Serefin's ear. They caught on the bandage and his expression twisted. He rolled off Serefin and Serefin was sadder for the loss of his warmth.

"I want to see how your eye is holding up," he said, straightening. "Does your head still hurt?"

"Only a little."

"Told you. Moping."

Serefin chose to ignore that, letting Kacper carefully unwrap the bandages from his head. Malachiasz moved closer, curious, and paled.

"You're a mess."

"A mouth just opened on your neck so, really, speak for yourself."

Kacper shook his head. "I can't believe we didn't realize you were brothers," he muttered. "You're both insufferable."

Serefin met Malachiasz's gaze over Kacper's shoulder. There was a world of conflict in the other boy's expression.

"I don't think this needs to be wrapped," Kacper continued. "The swelling is almost gone, but it's impressively bruised. I'll leave the stitch in, but we'll see how it does without the bandage."

Kacper kissed Serefin's cheek and shifted away, and Serefin leaned back on his hands. Malachiasz was mercilessly picking at his cuticles to avoid looking at him.

"How long have you known?" Malachiasz asked.

"I thought we were cousins, though I hadn't seen you in a long time—that I realized, anyway. I learned that wasn't quite the case a few months after that night in the cathedral."

Malachiasz frowned. "Do we keep this a secret?"

"There'll be rumors enough in Grazyk if we're ever seen in the same place," Serefin said.

Kacper nodded, gaze shifting between them. "You definitely appear related in a way that even the denser *slavhki* will eventually notice."

"But I'm so handsome," Serefin whined.

"I am *so sorry* to be the one to tell you this, truly the words are acid on my tongue, but he is, too," Kacper replied solemnly.

Serefin clutched his chest. Malachiasz grinned.

They had fallen into an uneasy sleep when Olya was shoved inside. She did not enter quietly, and the cultists did not stay to listen to her stream of curses. The door slammed shut behind her.

Olya stared at the tree in the center of the room, her eyes wide. Serefin watched her. He was the only one who had woken, surprisingly.

The girl took a tentative step into the light. There was a significant amount of blood on her arms, like she had been bled a great deal by the cultists. She was gazing at the tree with something close to reverence. Her face went ashen as she noticed the blood on the white bark.

"You don't want to know what happened here," Serefin said.

She whirled on him. He got up, carefully extricating himself from Kacper, and crossed the room. He caught the tension in the Vulture's shoulders as he passed. He was awake, then, listening.

"You," she said flatly.

He waved. "Your twitchy friend is involved in a cult. I've been there." Serefin gestured at Malachiasz. "So, in a way, this is all your fault."

A flicker of fear passed over her face before she shuttered it away. A slight tremor remained in her lower lip. She was younger than he thought—maybe Nadya's age, or younger.

"As if you would have left a pair of defenseless Kalyazi alone in Tranavia."

"A fair point," he allowed. "I've killed my share of wandering Kalyazi."

Her hand reached for a *voryen* that she did not have. She winced, blood trickling down her arm. It was such a normal sight for Serefin, he almost didn't register the deep alarm on her face. She looked to the tree again.

"It's Svoyatova Varvara Brezhneva's tree. A sacred, sacrifical space."

Serefin lifted his eyebrows but said nothing.

"Not *her* tree, of course, but an ancient rite. Where are we?"

Serefin wished he knew. "Guests of a cult of a very old god."

Olya flinched. "And the desecration?"

"Better you not ask. What did they do?" He nodded to the cuts. She hesitated, distrust in her gaze. But she was in the same mess as the rest of them, so he wasn't going to be particularly un-charitable about the whole kidnapping thing.

"In case you haven't noticed," he continued, "the cultists are Kalyazi, so it's not like you have a better option with them. Wor-shipping an old god makes them heretics too, no? But why would you care about that? Aren't you a witch?"

She lifted her chin defiantly. He lifted his hands.

"I have nothing against witches."

"You can be a witch and hold to the faith," she said.

"Literally everything in my understanding of your Kalyazi reli-gion says that you can't, actually."

"Not if you listen to the church," Olya replied.

"Apostasy, all right, I don't care one way or the other, frankly."

"They said they were testing me," she said, words rapid. "I don't know for what."

Malachiasz shifted. Of course *that* got his attention.

"You're predictable," he said to Malachiasz when the other boy stood and stepped past him, stopping just shy of the patch of light Olya was standing in.

"And you're useless," he replied, but he faltered when he turned to the girl. "I—I'd like to see the cuts. I have a sense of what they might be looking for, but could you step out of the light?"

"Why?"

Malachiasz appraised her. She was tall. Not quite so tall as him, but enough that she only had to tilt her head slightly to meet his gaze with fire in her dark eyes.

Serefin didn't know why they were still fighting these people. Yes, their religious intolerance, and the so-called heresy of the Tranavians and their blood magic, but . . . when he thought of Nadya—zealous and sharp and so very tired—or Katya—bossy and irreverent—he thought there might be a chance between these two kingdoms.

Except Nadya had taken away Tranavia's foundation. Kalyazin would always see his magic as horrific, and he would never be will-ing to give it up, not even if forced.

Malachiasz opened his mouth and hesitated. "It's too difficult to explain," he eventually said, shoving his hand into the light. His flesh began to sizzle.

Olya let out a horrified gasp. Serefin reacted fast, grabbing Malachiasz's wrist and pulling his hand back into the shadows. The commotion finally woke Kacper. Malachiasz's hand was an angry, scalded red and Serefin dropped his wrist, staring at him in horror. He only shrugged.

"Chyrnog," he said, as if it were simple.

Malachiasz was hiding something. Fear or anxiety or desperation, whatever it was, he was trying to force it away. Serefin understood Malachiasz well enough to know that there was no way he was handling this well. He was merely putting on a damn good show. That's what he did. He lied. He pretended. He made everyone believe everything was perfectly fine. And when people lowered their guards—he stabbed them in the back.

Though Serefin supposed he was the one who had stabbed Malachiasz, so he wasn't much better.

"Please, step out of the light," Malachiasz said, intent on Olya.

Serefin watched her eyes track over the Vulture. A ripple of eyes opened on his skin and horror flickered across her face. But she stepped into the shadows.

Malachiasz quietly asked for permission before taking the girl's arm and inspecting the cuts that were scattered across her flesh. He spoke softly, his questions disarming as he asked about the methods the cultists had used to draw her blood.

"There are a lot of people trying to discover new avenues for magic," Malachiasz said, after she had finally answered. "It's changing, spreading out like the roots of a tree." He nodded to the pale, bloody tree and Olya grimaced. "Were you trained?"

She shook her head. "I taught myself what I know."

"Hedge witch?"

She nodded.

"Do you use blood in your magic?"

She shifted on her feet. "Sometimes," she said softly.

"Was that how it started?"

She hesitated, before nodding.

"Interesting," he said. The door opened. He immediately tensed, curling in on himself, as if he had been struck.

"Well," Ruslan said, "you survived! It seems we have a great deal to discuss."

19

NADEZHDA

LAPTEVA

Out beyond the safety of village walls dwell the witches
of the swamps whose magic can confound and corrupt.
—The Letters of Włodzimierz

Her footsteps were bloody against the fallen snow. It was too bright, and shielding her eyes did no good. She wasn't alone, but all she could see was a blinding white.

"Hello, child," someone said. Nadya had never heard this voice, yet she recognized it. "It has taken a long time to get you to a point where you could hear me."

She closed her eyes, searching. "Am I dead?"

"Yes."

She blinked rapidly, a sudden onslaught of tears forcing her eyes open. Her knees went watery, but she remained standing. This fate had been waiting to catch up to her for so long. No clerics surpassed what they were meant for; all ended in an early death. Nadya was no different; why should she escape something no one else ever had? But she wasn't ready. There was so much that could be saved still.

And what she'd felt as she'd fallen . . . Maybe it was fitting. He had lived and she had died. A particular twist of irony. They had squandered any chance at happiness by spending their short time alive trying their hardest to tear each other down.

"That's it, then?"

Whoever she was speaking to laughed. Nadya's vision grew sharper, like she was seeing *more*. Something itched at her forehead.

There were two of them. Similar, yet different, and impossible to look at for more than a second at a time. Light and dark and the agony of eternity twisting them beyond reason, beyond coherence. Were horns sprouting from the one's head? Antlers from the other? Neither or both? She couldn't tell. And while she *saw* them, the instant their features changed she forgot what they had been before. Transience in continuity.

Alena and Myesta. Goddesses who did not speak to mortals, ever. So why were they talking to Nadya?

"You can hear the rest, but you couldn't hear us. Not yet," Myesta said. "Your mortal mind is not attuned to the particular torment of our voices. Too old, you see. But it could be."

"You brought me here?" Nadya asked.

"That blade did not have to meet your flesh. Veceslav watches still, and this all makes him so upset. He's soft."

"Iron must be tested," Nadya said.

"Your iron was tested a long time ago."

"And its measure found wanting."

"Was that the conclusion?" Alena asked. She had granted power to Nadya in the past, unlike Myesta, but Nadya had never heard her voice. It wasn't what she expected. It was lighter, musical, yet with a dangerous sharpness.

Nadya shrugged hopelessly. "That was Marzenya's conclusion."

If the goddesses had faces to track, she would've sworn they exchanged the equivalent of a dry glance.

"I thought that was what everyone else thought, too," Nadya continued. "Because no one talks to me anymore."

"You don't want to listen." Myesta shrugged. "And, for a time, you were unable. That Vulture is trouble. But Marzenya was afraid of you. I think we have a lot to talk about, don't you?"

Nadya frowned and sat at the feet of the goddesses. "Why tell me now?"

"You weren't ready before. You would have balked at the well of magic, at what you are, at what you could be. You may still, but things have changed. Your enemy is so much greater than a country of heretics," Myesta said. "Marzenya wanted to keep you quiet, small, and that worked for her, for a time. She knew what you were capable of and how it could shake the world to its very foundation if you decided to go against her."

"But I did what she asked. I chose her."

"Did you?"

Did she?

"You don't seem particularly troubled by her death," Nadya noted.

"We die. Sometimes our deaths are quiet; sometimes not," Alena said. "Marzenya is a goddess of rebirth. She'll find her way back to us in time."

A terrifying thought.

"Sometimes those of us we thought were dead come rising to the surface. The oldest of us, long since turned away from the world, deciding they want a piece of it once more."

Nadya frowned. "The fallen gods?"

"An annoyance. Peloyin and Marzenya cast them out for a reason," Myesta said, waving a hand.

"I never knew about Peloyin," Nadya said. He had never spoken to her.

Again, that weird feeling of the goddesses exchanging a glance. Sometimes they had limbs—almost human—but mostly not. Nadya saw every animal in creation shifting within their depths.

"No, we speak of older than even them."

"Chyrnog?"

"The world eater," Myesta said, a musing hum. "He's not the only one, but he *is* the one who has claimed a mortal and thus can move against your world."

"Why are you telling me if I'm dead?"

Alena laughed. "I forgot how dense mortals are."

Nadya had forgotten how circuitous talking to gods could be.

"Marzenya was afraid of you because you and the world eater are made from the same stuff," Myesta said blandly, as if giving Nadya a benign piece of information she already knew.

Nadya suspected that if she wasn't already dead, she would feel like the world was falling out from underneath her.

"A mortal child born with the blood of the gods. Her power twisted down and carefully molded so that it was only used when Marzenya would allow it."

"What *am I*?"

Alena shrugged—if it were possible for her to shrug. "You are an enigma. A problem. A child. You are not the first to be born this way, there have been other clerics like you, but those never set their power free. The others never spilled their divine blood for magic."

There was no distaste in her words. Like the goddess cared little for the heresies of the Tranavians. Nadya had thought all the gods cared *so much* about blood magic and it being an abomination. Even here, dead, her hand was monstrous.

"Why are you telling me this?" Nadya whispered.

"Because if entropy is not stopped, there will be nothing left. We can fight him in our realm, but he will merely call upon his siblings, as old and terrible as he, and we will be lost. If our world falls, so too will yours. If your world falls, we will not last long after."

How was Nadya supposed to stop an old god? She hadn't been able to stop Serefin from setting a fallen god free. *She* had set a fallen god free from his prison, starting it all. She wasn't the one to save the world. She was the one to ruin it.

"Daughter of death, you have come so far," Myesta said. "You may fail at this."

"Also, I'm dead."

That was ignored.

"But why not give you the chance? You cannot do this alone; you will need help. Luckily, there are plenty of you mortals running around, blood tainted with the divine."

Nadya frowned. "But what about everything else? The war? Tranavia?"

"Do you think I care about Tranavia and their mistakes? Do you think I care what the Akolans do with the blood they spill across the sands? Do you think I care what the Gentle Hands do to the mages of Česke Zin and Rumenovać? What those people do with our bones? You mortals and your magic are your own problems. It is all insignificant," Alena snapped.

"Then why did Marzenya care so much? And the other gods?"

"Because we act in reflection," Myesta said simply. As if it were obvious.

Her answer left Nadya unmoored and reeling. But it didn't matter; she could not change how Kalyazin saw the gods, how Tranavia saw them. To Kalyazin, they were a comfort, their priests and churches stable footholds in a world of chaos. But Tranavians saw it all as stifling. Forcing them to see would change nothing, just as showing Kalyazin that the gods they worshipped were as monstrous as the abominations the Tranavians called the Vultures would change nothing.

She buried her face in her hands. She wasn't ready to go. This was all useless, merely information in hindsight; all that she had been unable to unearth on her own. A reminder of her failures.

It was silly to think the goddesses couldn't hear her thoughts.

"Failures, certainly," Alena said. "But that's what we expect of mortals. It's the failures that make it all so infinitely fascinating."

"The rest of the gods would disagree with you," Nadya muttered.

"They're young yet. Their ideals are still being formed."

"If Chyrnog has his way, your world will be devoured," Myesta said, returning to the task at hand. "It's as simple as that. He has been waiting a very long time for this. Waiting a long time to de-vour Alena."

"But he isn't the only old god?"

She gave what could almost be read as a shrug. "There were others. They faded, died, went away. There were others far more terrible, and there were those full of light. None of them matter."

"Because Chyrnog is the current problem?" Nadya asked.

"Precisely."

Nadya swallowed. "Or, whoever is left deals with him, I guess."

Myesta laughed and Nadya cringed. It wasn't a pleasant sound. The goddess moved, fingers brushing against Nadya's forehead. Exquisite pain.

"Will that be a blessing or a curse?" Alena asked, lightly disap-proving.

"Likely both," Myesta replied.

If they said more, Nadya didn't hear it. Everything fell into a heavy, crushing black around her.

interlude ii

PARIJAHAN

SIROOSI

Parijahan would never forget the deadened expression on Rashid's face when he brought Nadya's body in from the rain. The cleric looked young and fragile in his arms. She was so small as he gently placed her on a bed in the *boyar*'s house, carefully pushing her hair away from her face.

Biting her lip to keep the rush of grief from overwhelming her, Parijahan did her best to lock it away. To place it on the shelf next to Malachiasz's death. She couldn't take this.

They couldn't *both* be gone.

The *tsarevna* followed Rashid into the room, but when he stepped away from the bed, dark eyes glassy with tears, she clearly wanted to flee. She touched Nadya's forehead, closed her eyes with fingertips that were achingly gentle, and left the room in a hurry.

It had happened quickly; she had fallen quietly. Parijahan had watched it from a distance, unable to stop it, and it was too much like watching Malachiasz fall when she was still struggling up the mountain. The blade a careful caress that had slipped from a woman's hands into Nadya's back. Nadya had been gone by the time she had crossed the muddy square.

Nadya had survived so much. She'd seemed so impervious.

Parijahan moved to Rashid, who was staring, unseeing, at Nadya. She wrapped her arms around his waist, resting her forehead against the back of his neck.

It's time to tell the truth.

"No more of this. No more death."

"Parj . . ."

"You never asked what I was doing the night we left Akola. All this time, all these years, you've never asked what we were running from. What my family would want returned to them so badly. What makes it impossible for me to go home."

She had asked him to go, and he had. She'd asked that he follow her into Kalyazin, and he had. He had watched her gather a group of misfits and renegades around her and never asked what she was doing. He would listen to her tell Taraneh's story and know she was giving a partial truth, but never asked what she was hiding.

"I never told you," she continued. "For foolish, petty reasons. I never told Nadya for similar reasons. And I should have."

"No more secrets. We'll talk later," Nadya had said before going with Katya to defend the city. And now it was too late. Her arms tightened around Rashid.

"Too many secrets. Too much death."

"They're trying to get you back," he said.

"I'd just lost Taraneh and I was scared and confused. Arman was never coming back. He had gone to the mages in the sands and I knew what that meant. I knew what you were capable of."

Rashid tensed.

"It was so impossible, living in that palace, listening to talk of how to handle the problem in the west."

What a benign way to talk about what amounted to attempting to eradicate his people, she thought blandly.

"And conversations about the north . . . Did you ever hear how they spoke of these countries? They were barbarians, mad, and this was the problem with power. This was why Akola kept their mages locked away."

It would have been his fate. The mages in the Travash only had a few years at court before they were imprisoned. Chained under locks made unbreakable by some long dead mage of the past. Only drawn out for death and pain before being swept back into the dark, out of sight, out of mind.

"They spoke of you constantly. The little indentured servant from Yanzin Zadar who had power. Do you remember being tested?"

He was quiet for a long time before a very soft, "Yes."

She swallowed, overcome with tears. "Rashid, I'm sorry I didn't trust you."

He pulled out of her arms, turning to face her. "What do you mean? What did you do?"

She closed her eyes. "It's what I didn't do. I don't know how the missives kept finding me. How they *knew*. They kept begging me to return, but begging turned into threats, and the threats became something much darker and I—I . . . it was you. I know what not going back to Akola means for me, but it's more than being the *prasīt*, it's—it's far more in line with all this divine nonsense. And I'm sorry, but Rashid—" she reached out and took his wrist, pushing his sleeve back. She ran her fingers along his forearm, down the vine markings.

Suddenly flowers were blooming from his skin. He choked on a breath. She hated doing this to him, she knew how much he didn't want to use his power.

"I knew what bringing you here would do because I'm like you. I knew the stars in our blood would burst in this land of gods and power. In Akola, it was only magic on sand, but here it's different. The gods that walk these lands are not our gods. They are much worse. They're greedy and they *want*, and our foolish friends have set them free."

She closed her eyes. "In the forest, I chose to stay here, knowing what that would mean. We're going to be burned up by all of this and it's my fault. Without Nadya . . . we're doomed."

The flowers growing from his skin were white and crimson and shot through with purple. They would be beautiful if they weren't so terrible.

He would have a thousand questions. She didn't know how she would answer them all; she had been holding this close for too long. Malachiasz knew a piece of it. That she had magic, a kind unlike the power used in Kalyazin or Tranavia. But Malachiasz had died and taken that truth with him.

Rashid didn't get the chance to ask any questions. Nadya's voice, small and tired, jolted them both.

"I'm going to need to hear all of that again, but in Kalyazi," she said.

The world dropped out from underneath Parijahan and Rashid's hands held her up as her knees gave out.

Nadya lifted a hand very slowly, her eyes still closed, her eyebrows furrowed. "*Gods,* I feel . . . well, like I was dead. Give me a second for my limbs to work."

Parijahan struggled out of his arms, moving to kneel at the side of the bed. She reached out, very carefully, and touched Nadya's hand.

Her eyes opened at the touch. Her skin was like ice. A moth appeared and settled in her white-blond hair.

How was she back?

Nadya groaned, closing her eyes again and pressing her hands against them. There was a long beat of silence.

"Right, then, now I can say that dying is extremely unpleasant, in case you were wondering."

20

MALACHIASZ

CZECHOWICZ

It started with a finger. A paltry trade for magic. Took it clean, he did, right off, little pain. Didn't blink when he took another. My hand was missed, but it was the left one anyway. Walking got tricky when he took the leg. Let him take whatever he wishes.

—Fragment of a journal entry from
an anonymous worshipper of Chyrnog

Malachiasz felt better after sleeping, suspiciously so. That he had slept at all was suspicious. He hadn't slept much in months.

"Astonishing how different things are when you comply with me," Chyrnog said.

Malachiasz didn't respond. There was a lot he was trying not to consider. How it had felt to slide his teeth across that boy's throat. To kiss him. How much he did not want to *remember* what he had done. Each time he thought he had fallen as far as possible, he proved it untrue.

But what haunted him most was the chill when, somewhere, the girl with hair like snow had been struck down forever. Her death was an ocean he would drown in. Better for her to be alive for him to quietly hate from afar.

Let him live with the denial.

"Were you expecting something other than my survival?" Malachiasz asked amiably.

Ruslan smiled slightly, tilting his head. Malachiasz was better, sharper, stronger, and those things were bad news for these people.

"You wanted me to destroy the boy, no? I hope that was your intent because it's certainly what happened." He gestured vaguely at the tree and straightened to his full height. "We have things to discuss, you and I," he said, smiling. The barest flinch, nearly invisible, as Ruslan got a good look at his teeth. "Just the two of us," Malachiasz continued, stepping around the square of light and closer to him, away from his brother. It was strange, thinking of Serefin that way, but . . . right.

"Wait, what?" Serefin sounded distressed.

Malachiasz glanced at him, holding back a sigh. He'd *hoped* Serefin would have figured out his game by now.

"I'm the vessel for their god reborn," he said, flatly. "They don't really need to talk to you."

Trust me, he thought, knowing Serefin wouldn't. He had no reason to. What had Malachiasz done except consistently undermine his power and ignore his authority?

"Only talk?" Serefin asked cautiously. He glanced at Kacper, whose fists were clenched. For all he knew Malachiasz was intending to go off with these cultists and leave him to die. Malachiasz had found people played their parts so honestly when they were truly desperate.

"Well, if we come to an understanding during our chat, that wouldn't be so bad," Malachiasz replied with a shrug.

Except this time the deception didn't feel particularly good. He discovered, with some measure of surprise, that he didn't want Serefin to think he was betraying him. He'd committed a horrific act and Serefin had treated him with kindness after. He didn't deserve that. As much as he hated what Chyrnog had made him do, he'd relished it all the same; he was too much a monster to fight Chyrnog's appeal to his basest instincts.

A wounded look flickered over Serefin's face. Malachiasz bit his lip.

"Malachiasz, don't you dare," Serefin said, his voice dangerously soft.

Ruslan held the door open, glancing over his shoulder to see if Malachiasz was following. He did, feeling wretched the whole way.

"How long have you been waiting for his return?" Malachiasz asked, unable to keep the curiosity out of his voice. He folded his hands behind his back as he trailed after Ruslan.

They were in a stone church, potentially a monastery, but Malachiasz wasn't entirely certain. It had a similar feeling to the one Malachiasz had been to with Nadya, though this was exceedingly colder. Empty and hostile. He carefully stepped around sunlight spilling in through window slits, though it couldn't always be avoided and at times he was forced to grit his teeth and press on. He gathered Ruslan had taken him on this route purposefully.

"The order has stood since the beginning of time," he replied.

"A nonanswer. That's fine, it's worthless information anyway."

He took a step back in expectation of Ruslan whirling on him. Ruslan moved closer, holding a blade to Malachiasz's jaw. Interesting. He wanted magic. His skin didn't react to the blade, he noted with relief. Not a relic, then. He could survive any number of blade wounds—outside decapitation, the only true way to kill a Vulture—but not a relic, as had been discovered so painfully.

"Don't press your luck," Ruslan hissed.

He'd had plenty of practice thinking quickly with a blade at his throat thanks to Nadya. He had plenty of practice pressing his luck, too.

How much control over me do you have, truly? he ventured to Chyrnog. He didn't want a demonstration, but he had a theory and quite liked the idea of testing it.

"You are mine," Chyrnog replied.

That doesn't answer my question. Whatever. Malachiasz had picked up enough nonsensical religious jargon from Nadya to hold his own.

Reluctantly he let a thread of control go—his shifts roiled faster and more chaotically when he gave in—bracing himself for the kaleidoscoping of his vision as it shattered and reformed only to shatter again.

"I am the voice of your god made flesh," he said, dropping his voice and speaking through teeth of iron. "My genesis is irrelevant. I don't *need* you or your order if you choose to treat me without the respect I am due. *I* am entropy. *I* am chaos. You will bend to my will or I will see you in the same pieces of flesh and marrow that are left of your last acolyte. What makes you think you can chain me, bind me, break me, and drag me like a fool through your halls of light?"

He had Ruslan's jaw in his hand, turning to slam him against the wall before he had the chance to blink.

"Think very carefully about how you have chosen to go about this and how you are planning to proceed," he said softly. "We could be allies. You could have glory at my ascension as I rip apart the heavens and take it all for Chyrnog. Or I could kill you right here."

A shift of muscle under his fingertips as Ruslan swallowed. Malachiasz smiled ever so slightly. This was a game he played very well.

"But how long until it no longer is a game?" Chyrnog contemplated. *"Do you think I chose you without reason? That I had not been biding my time, waiting for you? I spent eons tempting Velyos to be in my thrall. To have him finally take a vessel and to lead that vessel to you."*

Malachiasz refused to believe that what was happening here was predetermined. It brought up *far* too many questions that he simply was not willing to contemplate.

"I will let you continue pretending, but, oh, just wait until the day it is no longer a pretense."

Malachiasz dropped Ruslan, eyeing him dispassionately.

"Have we come to more of an understanding?" he asked, pulling everything back and carefully folding it up, his voice cheerful.

Ruslan looked up at him from underneath dark eyelashes. Was that hatred or respect in his eyes? Veneration? Malachiasz would take any of the three. They could all be molded into zealotry.

The other boy grinned, blood staining his teeth. "Yes," he said. "I think we have."

"Please," Malachiasz replied, gesturing. "Lead on. And keep it to back hallways, if you will, my skin is sensitive."

He was led to a study that seemed to double as a library. Though he knew that the majority of these texts were religious in nature and thus ridiculous, he couldn't shake the itch of desire the sight brought him.

He missed this.

He missed being left alone to his study and his books and his paintings. He missed living without the weight of desperation and the feeling of his time running out clinging to his chest. He missed his idle dreams of holing up in his study with Nadya and showing her what could be accomplished if they worked together with their equally enigmatic magic.

He missed Nadya.

She's in a better place. The thought was poison. If Kalyazi beliefs about the afterlife were to be trusted, the thought was true. If it were Tranavian, well, things got a bit trickier. She deserved peace. But he wished he could have seen her one last time.

Did he?

He didn't know.

Maybe idealistic hindsight was all he had to keep himself from going mad with grief. He couldn't really think about it. The knowledge was very distant, unreal. The longer he avoided that snapped tether, the longer he could pretend. He had to deal with this god and this cult when all he truly wanted to do was break down and shatter into pieces.

Ruslan was talking, and he hadn't been paying attention. He was out of practice. Even when he had been lying to Nadya, he hadn't been, not really. He'd hid pieces of the truth from her but found it near impossible to hide everything else. She brought out the anxious, messy parts of him that he tried his very hardest to conceal from the world.

He had to stop thinking about her.

"Come again?" he asked, tone flat.

Ruslan moved to the desk, sitting behind it. Malachiasz remained standing. He wasn't going to sit before the boy like a student being tested. He moved to a bookshelf behind his chair. Ruslan tensed. He was resistant, which was curious. Had he thought that he might be Chyrnog's vessel? Had the god ever spoken to his followers?

"Why would I speak to maggots?"

I'm sure they would appreciate knowing you think of them thus, Malachiasz returned. Though he didn't think they would particularly care. It took a certain type to be dedicated to a dead entropy god, he figured.

"I'm sure you have questions," Ruslan said.

"Why, because I'm Tranavian?" Malachiasz replied. But he *did* have questions. What he knew about the Kalyazi gods from his years of study had never lined up with what Nadya had told him; though Nadya seemed to be working off dubious information at best for someone who could literally talk to them. "Don't bother with the base pantheon. Too tedious. I understand all of that. If you have more, give me more, go deeper."

Ruslan lifted an eyebrow, a smile tugging at his lips. "You mean the old gods."

Oh *good.* Chyrnog had friends.

"There is much of the world we don't understand," Ruslan said. "Much has been destroyed in this ceaseless war. A wealth of knowledge burned because it dances too close to what one mortal council decided is heresy."

Malachiasz turned, leaning back against the bookshelf.

"Worship of the fallen gods is heresy. Worship of the old gods is worse."

"But aren't they all your gods?" That was what Malachiasz didn't understand. This line drawing between deities. "Or is it rather about where they came from?"

"Do we know the genesis of the gods?" Ruslan asked, raising his brows.

Malachiasz thought of the pages upon pages of spells in his study in Grazyk. Of draining the blood from so many veins. Of it pouring from Serefin's throat as he died and gave Malachiasz a key element to so many interlocking pieces of power. About the copper taste as he'd drunk it.

He did not remember much after that.

"I should say it's easier to guess at the current pantheon," Malachiasz said, treading carefully.

"And *that* is why we welcome Chyrnog's return. One of the ancient powers. A true god. No ascension. No time before consciousness. He has always been, and we have always been made to be ground under his heel."

Malachiasz made a thoughtful noise.

Ruslan's expression darkened. He gazed over Malachiasz's shoulder at the bookshelf. "There was a war," he murmured. "Not here, but there, yet it spilled over all the same."

"How does a god of entropy lose a war?"

Ruslan's eyes narrowed. Malachiasz was being obvious, but he hadn't shown himself resistant to Chyrnog's will in front of this boy, so there was little risk.

"When the divine war spilled over, there were mortals drawn into the battles. Old clerics turned saints. Our magic always comes from the gods, but not always from *sanctioned* divine sources." His hand ghosted over the ring on his index finger. It was absolutely a relic.

"Why do you have the girl, then?" Malachiasz asked, distracted.

Ruslan waved a hand. "Olya? Because Olya went from being a terrible witch to one with actual power in a matter of months and I want to know how."

Idly, Malachiasz considered how he had killed the goddess of magic. How there had already been new avenues of magic springing forth, but with her death and Nadya's meddling, something had broken and all the rules they had lived by and fought for were ashes. Their new reality was one where magic was not so carefully bound—how would they survive it?

Well, he supposed they wouldn't, if Chyrnog had his way.

"Apologies for the diversion, about the clerics?"

Ruslan didn't seem perturbed. "There were four, Innokentiy Tamarkin, Milyena Shishova, Lev Milekhin, and Sofka Greshneva." He got up, raking both hands through his hair, leaving it standing on end as he nudged Malachiasz out of the way, reaching for a thin volume on the bookshelf. He handed it to Malachiasz, something feverish in his gaze. "*The Books of Innokentiy* are all we really have that tells us anything about what happened. Four clerics who, by some means or another, lost contact with their patron gods. There are more volumes, but they've been lost. One of my order is chasing rumors of more in Komyazalov, but nothing yet. They were the ones who turned the tide against Chyrnog. They were the ones who accomplished the impossible."

Malachiasz opened the book and skimmed through the pages. "Well, we won't have to worry about that now, will we? We no longer live in the time of the clerics."

Ruslan grinned. "Exactly."

Ruslan was a fanatic driven by the desire to understand the past, but he had cracked, fissuring so that he could only look back. Everything would be made right if it were made to be like it had been before it all went wrong.

"Of course," the boy said, "telling you this voids your brother's life."

Fear jolted down Malachiasz's spine. "What?"

Ruslan's fingers danced across the ring on his finger. "Did you not feel it? I suppose not. You wouldn't, if you were truly Chyrnog's vessel. You wouldn't be able to feel his power on you. But I know now that you are as you say, but I also know that your brother disobeyed Chyrnog's will, and for that he must die. It's fine. I won't make you watch. Unless you want to?" He glanced over his shoulder at Malachiasz, lifting a dark eyebrow.

Malachiasz realized with a startling clarity that he did *not* want Serefin to die. He had lived for so long with the idea that he was wholly unwanted, that there was no family, that he had come from the Vultures and there was never anything else for him. Finding that there was *someone,* even if that someone was Serefin, it meant something. And he was not willing to use Serefin as a sacrifice for his own pride.

"I'm doing what you want," Malachiasz said. "Leave him."

Ruslan chuckled. "Absolutely not." The ring on his finger glowed with a sickly light.

21

NADEZHDA LAPTEVA

When a battlefield was flooded, Svoyatova Nyura Zlobina, a cleric of Omunitsa, molded the water to drown an army.

—Vasiliev's Book of Saints

It was like surfacing from underneath an icy river. Nadya couldn't get warm no matter how hard she tried, even when a mug of near-boiling tea was pressed into her hands. Her back hurt—she was quite done with being stabbed. And Parijahan's, and then Rashid's, embrace, warm as they were, couldn't quite chase the cold from her bones.

Katya had entered the room, taken one look at Nadya, and sighed, relief rippling across her taut shoulders. "You are far too much trouble."

"So I've been told." Nadya sat at the edge of the bed, a blanket snug around her shoulders. Lying down was too much like death.

"What happened?"

Nadya felt different, lighter, like something had been taken away from her. Had something else taken its place? "The gods are speaking to me again."

Katya lifted an eyebrow. "What changed?"

"Chyrnog woke up."

Katya's face paled and she immediately sat down on a nearby chair. "Oh."

"We have to stop him, bind him. It's the only way."

Katya opened her mouth, only to press her lips tight and shake her head. Nadya didn't know how, either. That was their next step. Maybe Komyazalov would work out. If any place had that kind of esoteric knowledge, it would be the capital of Kalyazin.

The *tsarevna* tugged on a dark curl. "All right," she said very softly. "I'll talk to Viktor. Make sure the city is still standing, though it seems like we fought off the witches."

"Zlatana will still devour the city," Zvezdan said.

No hard feelings about earlier, then?

"I'm curious to see what you plan on doing."

Are any of you aligned with Chyrnog?

"Aligned would be a simple description of a complicated relationship. Zlatana has always been fond of him, as has Cvjetko."

What of Velyos?

"Velyos does what he likes, when he likes, with whomever he likes."

That sounded right. Nadya gestured beside her and Parijahan sighed and sat down. "What were you planning with Malachiasz?"

Parijahan flinched.

Nadya didn't want to touch the thread but she knew that desperation, that hunger. Why hadn't that magic broken when he died? The implication that it could have survived was troubling.

Would she look for him? If she survived this, if he did? If their paths weren't set in opposition to each other, which she had a bad feeling they were?

No, she decided. Whatever they had was over. She couldn't hope for anything more, not after what he had done. Not after what she had done, either.

"What aren't you telling me, Parj? I got pieces but my Paalmideshi isn't very good yet." She had been trying to learn with Parijahan, but it was slow going. The language didn't have much in common with Kalyazi like Tranavian did and Nadya wasn't grasping it as easily.

"A great deal," she said, falsely cheerful. "And . . . and it's not that I didn't trust you or Rashid. I just . . ." She buried her face in her hands.

"Maybe start at the beginning?" Nadya suggested.

"I can't exactly lay out Akola's history in succinct terms," Parijahan replied sarcastically. She glanced at Nadya, considering. "But you do know more about the technicalities of magic than you let on."

Nadya smiled wanly. "And that's what this is about?"

Parijahan scooted back on the bed so she could draw her knees up to her chest. "That's what everything is about. The changes in magic have been happening for far longer than the night in the Grazyk. I remember eavesdropping on a meeting between my brother, Arman, and a group of mages from the southern dunes. They were talking about how the stars were changing, which is . . . impossible."

"I didn't know you had a brother."

"He left to join the mages. He's long gone." There was pain in her voice, wrapped in a careful shroud. She didn't talk about this; she never talked about this. Nadya could understand that.

"You have magic, don't you?" That would explain Parijahan's fear. It would explain why she would hide it and tell no one, surrounded as she was by people consistently ruining the world because of magic. Nadya looked to Rashid. "You *both* do."

Parijahan chewed on her lower lip. Rashid lifted an eyebrow.

"It's complicated," Parijahan said. "I don't have *magic* in the way that you and Malachiasz and Rashid do. But I was born under a bleeding star. So, there's something. And being a mage in Akola isn't like it is here or in Tranavia. In Tranavia, it's banal. Here, it's revered."

"*Well,*" Nadya said.

Parijahan waved a hand. "In former Paalmidesh, you're a tool.

A weapon. In Rashnit, you're cursed. In Tahbni, you're akin to a god."

"And in Yanzin Zadar?" Nadya asked.

"You hide it away in hopes that you won't get sold to a Travash in a different part of the country," Rashid said softly.

Ah. That also explained a great deal.

"You didn't come to Kalyazin to avenge your sister, then," Nadya said.

Parijahan's steely gray gaze was firmly locked with Rashid's. "No, not entirely," she said softly. "There's research happening in Akola. Research to get further with magic, do more, and my family would not be a Travash left in the dark."

Rashid's face had gone gray.

"I'll never know if Arman went to the mages willingly. But—" Parijahan broke off, swallowing hard. "He told me what our Travash mages were doing to him. 'Asking of him,' they always put it, so politely, but he didn't have a choice."

Nadya felt dizzy. "That makes it a bit surprising you were so close with Malachiasz, considering."

Parijahan shrugged, not denying it. But they had both looked away, fully knowing what Malachiasz had done to other people in his pursuit of power.

"The court mages were going to take Rashid. I never would have seen him again. It was selfish. My family kept me hidden away because of the stars I was born under. There was a chamber underneath the throne, below the council room, and they would put me in there, lock me up in the dark, so I could influence decisions to be made in their favor. Because things *happen* around me. Sometimes good, sometimes bad. I can't control it, ultimately a very useless kind of magic. In Akola, they talk about how the gods of the North are vicious and mad and so wrapped up in this war that they don't notice mortals the way the Akolan gods do."

"What are the Akolan gods like?" Nadya asked, trying to wrap her mind around locking a child in the dark so that the power she had no control over might work. Was it worse than isolating a child in the mountains to prepare her for war? She supposed not.

"It's hard to explain. What I've witnessed here isn't similar. They care about the collective, while you have gods who attach to individuals. But I thought that by coming here, I would be safe. I wasn't attached so the gods here wouldn't care."

Nadya could see where this was going. "And then you ran into me."

Parijahan shrugged. "I was curious. And I did want revenge. To make Tranavia suffer."

"Do you still?"

"I don't know."

Nadya could relate. "What changed?"

"My family wants me back. My father is dying, so the Travasha have to bid for the throne. I'm next in line for the Siroosi household, and with my influence . . ."

"Oh," Nadya said softly.

Parijahan nodded. "I wanted Malachiasz to help me get out of it, as it were. But he wanted me to go back and tell them I was abdicating. I don't think he understood that the second I cross the border into Akola, that's it. I'm there until I die."

Rashid sighed. "Would that be so bad?"

Parijahan tilted her head back, releasing an uneasy breath. "That's what I had such a hard time explaining to Malachiasz. I don't *want* the Travash. Give it to someone who wants it, who wants to rule. I don't. I've never wanted it."

"What *do* you want?"

Parijahan glanced at Rashid.

"I care about Akola, I do. I don't want to rule it. But I do want to *help*. And I don't think I can help there until what is happening here has settled. Everything is about to spill over in Akola. When my father dies there won't be a careful process to choose the next ruling Travash. We're on the verge of a civil war."

Nadya lifted an eyebrow at Rashid and he groaned. He held out his forearm and she watched as flowers burst from his skin. She sighed.

"And you still don't know what you can do? Have you talked to Ostyia yet?"

"There hasn't been time, what with you dying and all," he replied.

Nadya winced.

"You have different gods, though, because there are so many gods spread out so far," she said, and her voice wavered a little at offering knowledge she was confident in when she was confident in so little these days. "That's one of the dangers we deal with now, that these fallen gods might decide it would be more beneficial to latch onto someplace already being watched over by a different god. Cause a war."

"But who knows, what has happened here might very well be happening there, too," Parijahan said.

Nadya closed her eyes. "Is there more?" She didn't know if she could take much more.

"A bit, but later. You've been through a lot."

"We all have."

"Yes, well, not all of us have literally died on top of it."

Who knew I would one day have so much in common with two Tranavians? Nadya rubbed her face with her hands. "There's no time to rest," she said quietly.

This was going to spiral out of control faster than they were ready for. She doubted the attack on the city was the only one of its kind happening in Kalyazin. There would be more, in other places less prepared. More forests would stretch past their borders and devour, more monsters would come out of their darkened corners to consume.

She didn't know how to stop an old god. She didn't know what Myesta and Alena had given her. She didn't know, still, what she was, though she was on the cusp of answers. It was terrifying, it was thrilling.

She had *died*.

Nadya moved to stand, only to be gently shoved back down by Parijahan.

"No," she said. "This nightmare will still be spinning when you wake up. *Rest*." Her palm pressed against the side of Nadya's face and she leaned into its warmth. Rashid slipped out of the room.

"Everything . . . hurts," Nadya murmured.

"That's how life is," Parijahan said. She kissed the top of her head. "Nadya, I am so glad you're all right."

"Bit of an overstatement, I think."

"You're alive. That's enough."

There was no staying to aid with the aftermath. Nadya refused to even stay long enough to heal. They didn't have time to waste. Things had become all the more desperate now that they knew what they were up against. To the capital they went.

"Let me know if you need to rest and I'll get Katya to stop," Ostyia said to Nadya, moving her horse up next to hers. She glanced sidelong at Nadya. "I cannot believe I'm about to say this, but I'm glad you're alive."

"Ostyia, *what*."

"I know!"

She laughed and it hurt. "Serefin is all right," she said. "I meant to tell you earlier, but there was no time, and then, well . . ."

Ostyia closed her eye, letting out a soft breath. "How do you know?"

"I spoke with Velyos. I guess he's still hanging around Serefin, but he assured me that he's alive, at the very least."

"Does that mean all the nonsense on the mountain was in vain?"

It was impossible to say.

"Do you know if Kacper . . . ?"

Nadya shook her head. Ostyia bit her lip.

"Knowing Serefin is alive helps. Thank you. I know you probably have . . . fraught feelings about him."

Nadya and Serefin had become something close to friends during the time she'd spent in Grazyk and she did not know how to put to words what he was to her now. She had led Malachiasz to that mountain knowing it would tear him apart. She had saved him knowing it would lead to his destruction. That Serefin had been the one to land the final blow was a painful shock, but wasn't it inevitable?

"I wish he hadn't done it, but I understand why he did. I want this war to be over. I'm tired of fighting. What we have to fight now is far worse than a century-long squabble that is, ultimately, wildly petty and has broken so much. I get the impression that you feel the same, else you would have killed Katya the first second you had the chance."

Katya, who was clearly listening, glanced over her shoulder and winked at them. Ostyia's face immediately flamed. Nadya grinned.

"That's a political disaster."

"I don't want to hear it from the girl who was involved with the Black Vulture."

Nadya laughed.

She almost touched the thread tying them together. It was easy to ignore, easier than when it had first appeared. It had unraveled; there was little left still hanging on. What if she was wrong? He had died in her arms and there was no coming back from death.

Except she had. And Serefin had.

"Did you know about Serefin and Malachiasz?" she asked.

A flicker of distaste passed over Ostyia's face. "I knew. He's a bastard."

"Well, yes."

Ostyia laughed. "No, literally. They're half-brothers. Malachiasz isn't legitimate, which, honestly, if he hadn't been so . . ." She trailed off.

"Terrible?"

"Evil. It wouldn't have been a problem for Serefin. He has no claim to the throne."

Nadya gave a soft huff. What could they have been in a different world? Maybe not so broken, maybe so much worse.

"Serefin would have been sentimental about it and that would've been a mistake. I don't like Malachiasz, to be clear. He's bad for Tranavia and bad for the Vultures, and I know how you feel about him, but I knew him when we were children, and he has always been poisonous."

Nadya pursed her lips.

"Serefin cared, though, because that's who Serefin is."

"He still murdered him."

"Serefin knows what's best for Tranavia."

Nadya rolled her eyes. Ultimately, though, she didn't know what Malachiasz had meant to Tranavia; what he had done as the Black Vulture outside of tormenting her people. Maybe Ostyia was right. Maybe it didn't matter; maybe that was over.

Or maybe he's alive. But the thought was only stressful because Nadya didn't know for certain, and she couldn't check. If she pulled on the threads that bound them, he would know. And if he was alive, well, she didn't want that. If he was dead, it wouldn't matter because dead was dead.

Her heart ached—everything ached—and she wasn't sure if she was allowed to hope for him to be alive, or she was only allowed to mourn him in death. Because she knew. She knew what he was and what he had done. She had his spell book. His cruelty was unfathomable.

"What does it matter, that they were brothers?" Ostyia asked.

Nadya was quiet, unsure if it was for her to share Malachiasz's truth.

"He cared," Nadya said softly, "so much about the family that he didn't know. He wanted so desperately to know them. I wish he'd had the chance."

There was a flicker across Ostyia's face. A heartbeat of doubt, sympathy. She wiped it away. She glanced up at where Katya rode. The *tsarevna* wasn't listening anymore and probably hadn't been since they'd started talking about Malachiasz.

She wasn't naive about the doubts she had drawn up in the *tsarevna* because of how she felt about Malachiasz. But if he was alive, he wasn't returning to her, so Nadya's misstep in falling in love with him would eventually become nothing more than that. A mistake.

It sounded easy. It didn't account for how she would suddenly realize she wanted to tell him something, only to remember he would never again shoot her a soft half-smile as he listened to her talk. She missed the quiet intensity he brought when he was arguing with her about utter trivialities. She had loved their arguments. He had, too.

She had to move on. This half-formed knowledge—this quiet secret that maybe he wasn't dead—had to remain just that. For her to keep close to her heart but never set free. A caged bird.

She had fallen in love the wrong way with the wrong person. That was that. She had learned her lesson. She did not understand love.

22

SEREFIN MELESKI

The only cleric to ever be taken to the Salt Mines and survive was Svoyatovi Lukyan Starodubtsev. When he returned his eyes never stopped bleeding.
—Vasiliev's Book of Saints

It wasn't another betrayal. It couldn't be. Malachiasz, the night before, shaking and sick, hadn't been an act. Malachiasz with his face shuttered and his eyes cold as he'd left them had surely been an act. But Serefin wasn't certain and the odds were hardly in his favor. Like everything else it could be both. Malachiasz willfully leaving them behind, but oh, he'd feel bad about it.

Kacper had grumbled, tetchy, "I guess we'll wait and see what your damn brother has done," with the bite of an oncoming argument.

His damn brother, as it were, *had* betrayed them. Serefin was bewildered to find that it stung. It should be expected from Malachiasz. He *was* expecting it. But, apparently, a part of him had been hoping to be wrong.

Even without magic, Serefin was sensitive to the power around him. He could feel it moving through Olya, through the tree in the center of the room, under his feet. It was like all the air being sucked out of the room, the moment it was gone. One heartbeat and the world tipped upside down.

Olya staggered as if dizzy. She didn't speak, a raw noise scraping from her throat before she collapsed, blood leaking from her nose and mouth.

Kacper jumped to his feet. He had enough time to turn to Serefin, a spark of panic in his dark eyes, before the corner of his eye started bleeding. Serefin blinked, puzzled. Blood mages had a tendency to break blood vessels in their eyes or get nosebleeds, but he had never seen Kacper use enough power to get to that point. Serefin was opening his mouth to say something when it felt like a boulder was dropped on his head.

It was a clearing, it was an altar, it was a door. All-consuming shadows. Vast and black and deep. Crawling, churning, seething. Again, in this place. Again, the terror chewing at his chest, making its home in his bones. Again again *again.*

Serefin had torn out an eye rather than go through this again but here it was and here he was and there was no escape as the door opened before him. Maggots, snakes, a thousand hands grasping for him. Too many finding their mark, too many long fingers taking him apart and sequestering his pieces. He thought he had escaped. The severing, the *snap,* the moment where he had lost so much but gained—what? A fraction of coherence that was already cracking? His father's son. Just another mad Tranavian king. Someone to forge a path of blood and steel and keep the world roiling in the chaos that fit it so well.

Before he had his power, the will to fight, but that was gone, and Serefin simply wasn't strong enough. He couldn't fight off entropy. Not again.

There was blood filling his mouth, the copper tang bitter, and he tried to spit it out, but there was only more to take its place. He could feel it dripping down his face, wet and slick like when he'd torn out his eye—so much blood.

How would he be destroyed? A quiet annihilation was too sweet for Serefin—he had tried to deny Chyrnog's will. Torn apart by the thousands of grasping hands? Scattered into the wind like ash? Crushed under the earth like his near fate in the forest? How many times had death brushed her pale fingers over Serefin's throat? He could not keep escaping it. There had to be an end. This was the moment where everything finally ceased.

Silence.

At last.

If he was dead his head shouldn't hurt *this* badly. Serefin groaned, turning and spitting out a mouthful of blood.

"Oh, very nice, thank you for that."

Right onto Malachiasz's boots.

Adrenaline surged with anger and left Serefin with enough energy to . . . sit up, not jump to his feet and punch Malachiasz hard like he wanted to. He was going to be sick.

"Don't throw up on my shoes. Kacper is fine, before you panic. There was a lot of blood, but he doesn't seem injured. The witch . . ." he broke off. Serefin looked over at where he crouched back on his heels nearby. His expression was distant. "Well, she's alive."

Serefin didn't like that. *"To raszitak?"* He was unable to keep the venom from his voice.

Malachiasz straightened, hurt flickering over his face. *"Uwaczem ty,"* he snapped. He wandered over to inspect the tree, turning his back on Serefin.

Saved? He scrubbed his hands over his face, pausing when he lowered them. His hands were covered with blood.

He worked his way to his feet, checking on Kacper. He seemed intact, just unconscious. He made his way over to Olya and stopped short.

Her hands were gone.

He was actually sick this time.

"Entropy," Malachiasz said shortly, not turning away from the tree. "She'll live."

It was like they had been sawed off at the wrist. Serefin swore, scanning the room for something to bind them. But they weren't bleeding—the wounds were dry like they had happened some time ago.

"Don't be cruel," he murmured.

Malachiasz shot him an incredulous look over his shoulder. He ignored it, shredding the last blanket and using his teeth to tear it into strips. He carefully bound her wrists.

"He struck her hardest," Malachiasz said, turning to eye the un-conscious girl. "Likely because she was the one with magic of her own. Losing blood magic saved you."

"Who?"

"Chyrnog."

Serefin tightened the bandages and dreaded the moment the Kalyazi girl woke. "You have to tell me what's going on."

Malachiasz's hand touching the tree looked twisted and wrong, his iron claws digging into the tree's flesh. Eyes flickered open on his cheek—in odd colors, pale and bleeding, dark and void-like—and disappeared.

"I was going to fight it," he said softly. "There's nothing that scares me more than the thought of losing myself completely, and if this god has his way, I will. But . . ."

Serefin didn't like that this statement had a hinge point.

"There's no point in fighting. Let the world burn. We tried to fix it—"

"*Sznecz.*"

"It didn't work. Nothing is ever going to work."

"You tried extremes, Malachiasz," Serefin said.

"I could say you did as well," he replied, a hand pressing against his chest.

Serefin grimaced. "It was Chyrnog," he said. "I—I couldn't stop him."

"I want to say that makes me feel better, but you were traveling with *Voldah Gorovni.*"

He sighed. "Katya was a chance encounter. I used what I had to keep her from slaughtering me."

"Do your intentions matter when the end point was you murdering me?"

"Did your intentions matter when you convinced my father to kill me?" He touched the scar at his neck.

Malachiasz smiled slightly. Something strange flickered across his face. "Wait. He's not—"

"No," Serefin said, anticipating the question. "Klarysa, resident invalid whose machinations are an enigma, has the honor of being our mother. I don't know who your father is."

"Oh," Malachiasz said softly. "I remember pieces of her but pieces of someone else, too."

"Sylwia, probably. Klarysa's sister. She was pretending to be your mother when we were children."

Malachiasz frowned. He hadn't looked at Serefin once the whole conversation.

"What are you planning, Malachiasz?"

"I never tell," he said softly. "Ever. Not once. I didn't tell Żywia. I didn't tell Parijahan or Rashid. I didn't tell . . ." he paused, then added, resolutely, "Nadezhda."

"To your detriment, I should say."

"I don't know what to do. I can't see a way out. I don't think there's any hope for us left. We've used it all up."

"You're going to let this old god have his way," Serefin said flatly.

"This old god wants to destroy Kalyazin's divine empire," Malachiasz said.

"You're still on that?"

Malachiasz finally looked over at Serefin, his expression frantic. "Serefin, there's nothing else. They're going to destroy us if they're not stopped. You know that. You were so desperate to get out from underneath Velyos' thumb—"

"It's not what I expected of you."

"You don't know me."

It was a simple statement, and maybe Malachiasz hadn't meant for it to be cutting. It was the truth, an obvious one. The only things they really knew about each other were their betrayals.

Serefin absently brushed a moth off the shoulder of his jacket. He wished he had his damn sleeves, but Katya had cut them off. "I suppose not."

Did he want to know Malachiasz? He suspected the actual boy was only seen in the flashes that happened when he was around Nadya.

"It's convenient," Malachiasz said softly, "for you to blame killing me on Chyrnog."

"If you want us to be enemies, fine. I can leave you to your fate. I can go home and do my very level best to dissolve the Vultures. You can burn this world down, but I'll take everything you have left and burn it right down, too."

Malachiasz closed his eyes, sighing. He leaned back against the tree. A rippling shiver cut through him.

"No, I don't want that."

"It doesn't seem that way."

Malachiasz slid down until he was sitting at the base of the tree.

"What happened?" Serefin asked.

The tiniest crease pulled at the tattoos on Malachiasz's forehead. "I thought I was getting somewhere. Then that boy set his magic on you all. He tried to kill you because you struggled against Chyrnog."

"I don't think he succeeded, and I've been dead before," Serefin said dubiously. "And then?"

"Then?" Malachiasz asked, puzzled. "Oh. I knocked him out and came back to neutralize Chyrnog's power."

"You can do that?"

Malachiasz grimaced. He carefully rolled back his sleeve, revealing a network of gashes, as if every cut Malachiasz had ever made across his forearm had reopened. Serefin winced.

"Chyrnog has particular ways of showing his disapproval." He tilted his head. "And his favor. The boy lost another finger using that power on you three."

"Wait—does that mean we're not locked in here?"

Malachiasz did not respond. Serefin wanted to scream.

"You left the cult leader unconscious somewhere else in the building and we're *not escaping*?"

"To go where? Do what?"

"Home! Survive?"

Serefin spun in a frustrated circle before sitting down in front of Malachiasz. They couldn't leave with Kacper unconscious and he didn't know if he was willing to abandon the Kalyazi girl, damn his sentimentality. He kept his distance from the tree. The memory of being dragged into the earth and roots growing over his body was a little too close for comfort.

"Fine," he spat. "You clearly have a plan. Let's plan."

"What?"

"We are, somehow, against our better judgment, in this together."

"I can plan nothing without Chyrnog knowing."

"And?"

Malachiasz scrubbed his hands across his face. "What if he makes me turn on you?"

"We'll burn that bridge when we get there, and it sounded suspiciously like you wouldn't enjoy that."

Malachiasz waved a hand dismissively.

"What happened when you . . ." Serefin faltered. ". . . killed the boy?"

Malachiasz looked down at his hands. They were trembling. Serefin wondered if they ever stilled.

"I finally found what I've been searching for," Malachiasz whispered. "It's been so long, wanting something that feels right, and it was like it was finally there."

"And that's it? That's what you want? Was there power? I'm trying to understand."

"I don't know. Yes, there was power, of course there was."

Serefin simply couldn't shake the feeling that working with the cultists, doing what Chyrnog wanted, wasn't the right choice. They needed to be stopping Chyrnog, not aiding him.

"Malachiasz, when this god topples Kalyazin's divine empire, he'll turn on us next. You know he won't stop. It will all be ash. This isn't something you can manipulate to your advantage. This is bigger than that."

"I can't stop him," Malachiasz whispered. He dropped his head into his hands. "I don't think I want to."

A chaos storm in the shape of a boy waiting to claw the world to pieces. Serefin didn't know how to stop *him* and he had a bad feeling that he was going to need to.

"I refuse to believe you have no plan."

Malachiasz was quiet before the tension in his shoulders retracted a fraction. "Play the cult's game for now. Tear them apart when they show weakness."

This didn't make Serefin feel any better.

23

NADEZHDA LAPTEVA

Marzenya knows the taste of blood.
—The Letters of Włodzimierz

Komyazalov was a city built on a swamp.

Nadya hadn't known that when they were discussing Zlatana and her swamp hags. It explained why Viktor had come with them, and Nadya still couldn't decide how she felt about the *boyar*. He reminded her of the *slavhka* she had interacted with in Grazyk: shortsighted, strangely out of touch, and hopelessly obnoxious.

"Built on the bones of a lot of people," Parijahan had muttered, safely out of Katya's earshot, when they were approaching the city.

The bridge leading in was massive, able to hold multiple carriages and carts riding abreast, the swamp lurking just beneath. It made Nadya nervous, like the swamp was waiting to suck the city back under. How far was Zlatana's

reach? How would she take to having her swamps desecrated this way?

But it would only be one more disaster in a series of oncoming storms. *Little fatalities all in a row,* Katya would mutter. It wouldn't be one thing but many at once that they would be hopeless to stop.

But she didn't have time to dwell. Katya had led them into the city and Nadya was already overwhelmed by the noise.

"How is this *worse* than Grazyk?" she asked Parijahan.

Parijahan appeared sympathetic. Nadya was aware that she always showed how sheltered she was any time they traveled somewhere larger than a village.

Vibrant wooden buildings lined the wide road. There were so many *people,* and from places in Kalyazin that Nadya could barely fathom. They passed a group outfitted in striking kaftans. The men's were embroidered with wolves, and the women wore colorful scarves over their hair, not like the ones Nadya had; these were of finer, soft-looking silks.

Katya made a noise as her gaze followed Nadya's. "Chelnyans. From the west. They don't usually venture this far east. A lot of religious differences."

Nadya raised her eyebrows. Katya returned the look with a shrug.

"Maybe they worship the same gods under different names. To the Church, do you think it matters?"

Nadya's eyes drank in everything around her. Zhariks, from the south, with coins sewed to their hats and around their necks. Men in jewel-toned coats with eagles on their shoulders from the north. It was a stark reminder how little Nadya knew about her own country. There was so much more to the land and its people. So many who lived their lives without the war painting everything red. Maybe they didn't care how the war ended. Maybe Katya was right, their gods were hers under different names.

She wouldn't know. She was only ever given the information that would push her in the direction of the Church's agenda. And Alena had said the gods worked in reflection.

It was a troubling thought. Some things were too big and too weird, and some questions were meant to go unanswered. What if all of this was truly a chaos of their own making?

A group of people on the finest horses Nadya had ever seen went riding past and Katya tensed.

"Aecii," she murmured. "Interesting."

Nadya knew there was trouble brewing there. At least she knew *one* thing.

She was rattled further when they made it to a large stone wall, and she realized what they had ridden through wasn't even the city proper. It was unfathomable to Nadya. All those people and animals, foul smells meeting the occasional scent of fresh bread in the air.

"I will get too many questions if I show up with all of you," Katya said. The palace was in sight, a massive sprawling structure with high onion domes. "Nadya, you come with me. Viktor, do me yet another favor?"

"My household can survive a few guests," Viktor replied, clearly anticipating her question. "It's hardly a favor, Katya."

Katya tapped Ostyia's arm. "Stay out of sight. I'd rather not explain you at all if I can help it."

Ostyia frowned. "If I knew what was good for me, I'd escape."

"And miss out on my exquisite company? You wouldn't."

Ostyia rolled her eye, all-suffering, when Katya leaned over and kissed her cheek, but she was smiling when she went off with Viktor.

Parijahan very clearly did not want to be split up from Nadya, but Katya wouldn't hear any arguments.

"Considering the current state of your country, the last thing I need are missives from a Travash showing up at the palace asking after you," Katya explained. Parijahan eventually went after Viktor in a huff, Rashid in tow.

"We're staying in the palace?" Nadya squeaked as she hurried after Katya.

"Obviously," the *tsarevna* replied over one shoulder.

Why couldn't Nadya stay with Viktor, too? She'd had enough of palaces. Too big, too crowded, too easy for Nadya to get lost in.

Like the rest of the city, it was made of wood, but it was so much bigger than anything Nadya had ever seen before. It sprawled in a way that not even the palace in Grazyk had, and was so much more joyful painted in bright colors, with high arches and tall domes.

Nadya realized she had stopped and was staring, and Katya was halfway across the courtyard. She ran after her in time to see her bowled over by two wildly excited, lean, thin-faced dogs. Nadya couldn't tell if they were saying hello or trying to eat her. She decided to keep her distance until one of them broke off and went tearing toward her.

"He wants to say hello!" Katya called, now on the ground at the receiving end of the other dog's frantic tongue.

Nadya tentatively patted the dog, who was practically vibrating. When the dog gave an earnest whine, she laughed and sat down to let the beast say hello as it wanted.

"That's Barhat, and this is Groznyi."

Nadya frowned. "Terrible?"

"He's the worst!" Katya said happily, ruffling the dog's fur. "All right, leave her alone," she said, hauling Barhat away from Nadya. "I'm sure you boys aren't supposed to be in the courtyard anyway."

"*Vashnya Delich'niy,* we were not expecting you!" A tall woman with a severe demeanor and a long blond braid was approaching from across the courtyard. Her *letnik* was the richest Nadya had ever seen. A deep burgundy with embroidery down the front and cuffed with fur. Her *kokoshnik* was simple, but Nadya had a feeling that was only because it was for day-to-day wear. No jewels were encrusted in the headdress, but the cream fabric was intricately embroidered with crimson thread.

Nadya got to her feet, grateful when one of the dogs moved over to her again and she could use him as a shield. Katya glanced at Nadya's hand—safely gloved—and a glimmer of relief crossed her features.

Nadya wasn't about to get herself put on a pyre her first day in the capital. Wait until the third or fourth day, at least.

"Iryna, *dozleyena*," Katya called. She squinted against the sun glaring off the pale stones of the courtyard. "I meant to send a message, but I lost my company somewhere in the eastern provinces."

Nadya experienced a blistering memory of Malachiasz sheepishly telling a Tranavian soldier he'd lost his company in the mountains. She shook it off.

The woman lifted an eyebrow. "I'm sure you did. Your father isn't here."

Something flickered on Katya's face. Something Nadya didn't wholly recognize but which reminded her of the look Serefin would get anytime his father was mentioned.

"He's not?" A beat of uncertainty that Nadya had never heard from Katya before.

"He went to Torvishk. He should return in a few weeks."

Katya sighed. "The springs?"

The woman nodded.

"How is he?"

"Not a conversation for the courtyard, and you know it."

Katya fell quiet before continuing. "Ah, Iryna. This—" She hesitated almost imperceptibly. "—is Nadezhda."

The woman nodded dismissively. Nadya lifted her chin, refusing to shrink inside herself. She knew what this woman was seeing. Her tunic was torn at the collar, the crimson belt around her waist dirty. Her coat was open to the cold and she wore no headscarf, her hair instead in its usual braid crown, messy strands coming loose—they had been riding all day. She was worn down, defeated, bruises yellowing across her skin. She was small and broken and nothing like the girl meant to save a country from the war burning through it.

Then her brain caught up. Katya hadn't given the woman her full name. Iryna had no idea who she was. She blinked, but Katya had already barreled on ahead.

"Nadya, this is Iryna Chernikova, she makes sure everything around here doesn't burn to the ground around our ears."

"To put it exceptionally simply," Iryna said. She inclined her head slightly to Nadya. "Well, come with me."

Nadya, bewildered that she didn't want to know more than her name, followed her into the palace.

Where she was promptly bowled over.

"Naden'ka!"

It took Nadya's brain no time to realize who had slammed into her, smelling of incense and apples, or for tears to flood her eyes, as they both crashed to the ground.

"Oh, gods, Annushka." She wrapped her arms tightly around the priestess, burying her face against the other girl's neck. "I never thought I would see you again."

Anna leaned back, tears in her dark eyes. She touched Nadya's hair, her face, took her hands. "You made it. I never thought—we heard what you did but then everything went dark and I thought—I thought you were gone." She grabbed Nadya and pulled her into another embrace. "I've missed you so much."

"I've missed you, too," Nadya said softly, voice trembling. This was going to be the thing that finally broke her, because the thrill of finding Anna was immediately crushed by the knowledge that she would have to tell her *everything*. It had gone so terribly with Kostya, she couldn't imagine it would go well with Anna.

"Oh, you're probably exhausted, I should let you find your rooms."

Nadya reluctantly let Anna go. Anna stood up and held her hands out to her, hauling her to her feet. She frowned at the glove on Nadya's left hand—there wasn't one on her right—but said nothing.

Her hair was covered in a headscarf, iron temple rings on either side. Anna took a long look at her and Nadya waited for her expression to falter, for her to note her weary gaze, but Anna only smiled and pressed her forehead to Nadya's.

"I want to hear everything."

"Annushka—"

"Even the bad, Nadya. I—well, a lot has been happening and I think none of it will come as a surprise."

Nadya shook her head.

"I thought so."

"Oh! Parijahan and Rashid are here! I don't know where, they went off with a *boyar* we traveled with, but they'd probably like to see you."

Anna grinned. "I'd like that!" Curiosity filled her eyes. "What about—"

"A long story," Nadya said. "He's . . ."

Katya cleared her throat. "No."

Nadya rolled her eyes.

"Have some tact, Nadezhda," was her reply.

Anna laughed softly. "We'll talk. I promise."

Suddenly the prospect didn't fill her with dread like it had with Kostya. Nadya missed him so much. She'd treasured the times when things had been better between them. When Malachiasz had been elsewhere and she and Kostya could talk without tension. But Malachiasz would inevitably return and Kostya would darken.

It seemed obvious now, why he had been so upset. He had wanted something that Nadya hadn't. And she had turned away and fallen in love with a monster.

She clutched Anna's hands. "Come with me?" Nadya asked.

"Of course."

Katya, who had come up beside them with Iryna while they were still on the ground, gave a very put out sigh.

"Oh, and this is Katya. She's the *tsarevna.*"

"*Dozleyena, Vashnya Delich'niy,*" Anna said.

Always swayed by a pretty face, Katya grinned. "Anna, right?"

"Yes."

"Lovely to meet you. My apologies, but we have been on the road for a very long time. I want a glass of wine and to sleep in a real bed."

"Will you need me?" Nadya asked.

They were still in the entranceway and Nadya hadn't truly taken it in. She had noticed the lush carpets, but now she saw the many icons hanging on the walls, and fear gripped her heart. What if they started crying like the others?

"Honestly? I'm going to bed. If you want to also go to bed, I can ensure no one bothers you."

The thought of sleeping in a real bed was so sweet that Nadya almost broke down right there. The last stretch of their journey had been particularly miserable. She nodded emphatically. "Please."

"Iryna, you heard her."

"I'll make sure you aren't disturbed," Iryna said, sounding amused. "I'll have food brought to your rooms, as well."

Katya took her energetic dogs and disappeared into the halls of the palace. Nadya tried to keep her bearings but was lost almost immediately.

Iryna led Nadya to rooms that weren't quite as spacious as her rooms in Grazyk had been, though still lush enough to be over-whelming. The woman took her leave, and Anna kicked the door closed.

There was a sitting room with a bedroom attached to it. The stone floor was covered with furs to keep away the chill, and the chairs were upholstered with a dark blue brocade. There was no art adorning the walls or the ceilings, but Nadya found comfort in the relative simplicity. She missed her cell at the monastery.

Nadya dropped her pack. It spilled open, Malachiasz's spell book falling out. Anna lifted an eyebrow, picking it up.

"Oh, that's—"

"I know what it is," Anna said, flipping through it. "I've seen it before."

Nadya said nothing, letting Anna page through the book. She found some of Malachiasz's sketches, her eyebrows tugging down.

"Why do you have this?" she finally asked. She held it out to Nadya, who took it, hugging it to her chest.

"He's dead."

She expected a reaction like she'd gotten from Katya, but Anna only looked sad.

"Oh," she said softly. "I . . . gods, he was awful, but I know you saw something in him that I didn't. I'm sorry."

"He might be alive," Nadya continued. "He died in my arms, but I . . . everything is confusing and complicated."

Anna blinked. "What?"

"It's . . . well—I mean, death isn't transient, it's permanent, but it hasn't been for . . ." she trailed off. "Serefin, Malachiasz, and me."

Anna waited for her to continue, puzzled.

"We all died. We all came back."

"You *died*? Naden'ka, what? And, wait, the prince?"

"He's the king now," Nadya replied quietly. "I—" she paused. "A lot happened the night we killed the king. After, I was trapped in Grazyk, but Serefin made sure nothing happened to me. When the *slavhki* figured out who I was, he got me out of the city. He could have had me hanged and saved himself a world of trouble, but he didn't. With him on the throne, I—I don't know—I think there's a chance."

He'd killed Malachiasz, but she found everything she'd told Ostyia was true. She didn't hate him for it. If anything, she understood what he had done.

Anna lifted her eyebrows. She moved to a chair and sat down. Weariness deep in her bones, Nadya collapsed into the chair next to Anna.

"Malachiasz was the Black Vulture—"

"*No.*" Anna paled. "I *punched* him," she whispered. "He didn't even retaliate, he fled."

"That's how he was." He hadn't retaliated because no one had expected him to. Anytime he could be Malachiasz and not the boy with the weight of an ancient cult on his fragile shoulders, he took it.

Anna shook her head. "This is going to be a lot, isn't it? Do you want to rest first?"

Nadya drew her legs up onto the chair, wrapping her arms

around them. She had Malachiasz's spell book wedged between her heart and her knees. She shouldn't have it out in the open, but she couldn't let go.

There were no halting pauses and hesitant moments where she had to gather her thoughts. Instead, she pulled the glove off her hand and told Anna everything.

24

MALACHIASZ CZECHOWICZ

He tells me how he will make this world anew. How sweet the goddess of the sun will taste. He takes a bit more from me each time. We cannot be stopped. There's no one to stop us.

—Passage from an anonymous account
of a worshipper of Chyrnog

Tranavia would burn if Chyrnog had his will, devoured right alongside Kalyazin. Malachiasz couldn't stop this, it was hopeless. Chyrnog had him in all the ways that mattered. With each awakened one devoured, he would only grow stronger.

But Malachiasz would grow stronger, too. He liked to think the god was underestimating him like everyone else did.

He had considered leaving Serefin after Ruslan struck. It had taken no effort to take down Chyrnog's priest and leave him unconscious in the study. He'd considered killing him, but the thought of Chyrnog's retaliation stayed his hand. Killing him wouldn't have stopped the spell he'd set into motion anyway. Malachiasz should have run, but he'd returned to the sanctuary with its marble floors and cracked walls and watched as something unmade the witch.

He was in so far over his head.

He still had the book Ruslan had shown him, slipped into his pocket with the hope that the boy wouldn't notice its absence. He wasn't planning on giving it back.

Ruslan had recovered fast and entered the sanctuary, looking perturbed that his attempt to kill everyone had failed.

"Did I make my point?" he asked Malachiasz pleasantly. He was cradling his bloody hand, another finger gone.

Olya hadn't yet woken and Malachiasz was dreading when she did. He swallowed, fully understanding what it was Chyrnog could do. If he had hesitated, the witch would have been destroyed, and his brother and his lieutenant would have been next.

Ruslan had made his point.

"What now?" he'd asked, ignoring the despairing look Serefin gave him.

Malachiasz never did have to worry about the witch's reaction to losing her hands. Ruslan had his cultists remove her from the sanctuary, sadness in his expression. Malachiasz couldn't parse if it was genuine.

"I considered us friends, when I traveled with her band," he said. "I suppose not anymore. Ah, well, the things one does for their god."

"What will happen to her?" Malachiasz asked.

Ruslan frowned. "She wasn't supposed to be caught in that, but it was Chyrnog's will. I'll have her returned to her village."

Where she'll have to live with no hands. Malachiasz bit back the comment. Plenty of people lost limbs at the front and returned home to live without pieces that had seemed so necessary once. There were a few Vultures with complicated hooks for hands or braces strapped to the stumps of legs that worked just as well. That wasn't relevant. What mattered was she never should have been put in this position. Ruslan never should have been able to use Chyrnog's power. Chyrnog never should have woken up.

"Another awakened one has been found. You're coming with me," Ruslan said.

And because Malachiasz didn't want to risk Ruslan turning on Serefin, he agreed and tried not to think about what he would be forced to do.

Apparently the second awakened one was close. They would travel by night to avoid the sun. Malachiasz hated it.

Snow piled up so high that it was difficult to walk. They were so far from civilization that the roads weren't tamped down by the feet of travelers. They had left behind the dark forest for wide, dead, untouched plains.

"How does it work?" Malachiasz asked.

"What?" Ruslan cast a wide-eyed glance up at him.

Ruslan had done some complicated magic that Serefin had complained about the entire walk, claiming it felt like being chained up.

He folded his hands behind his back. "The magic." He wished he had his spell book. He wanted to take note of these strange divergences of power, but also Ruslan had a fascinating face and he wanted to put it to paper. And there were so many sketches of Nadya folded in those pages and he wanted desperately to cling to her memory.

A fracture, another piece crushed, another loss. She was clever and strong, and her power skirted the edges of what Chyrnog's power tasted like. How could she have been cut down? What had happened?

What if . . . ? But no. His death would not have been enough to force her hand. She would have moved on without him, been fine. She had practically plunged the knife into his chest herself. She was stronger than he would ever be. She wasn't sentimental like him.

Ruslan was talking and Malachiasz tried to focus as the boy explained the same scenario Nadya had described when using her divine magic. *Interesting.*

If Ruslan was able to channel Chyrnog's power, then why did they need Malachiasz at all?

He didn't wait for the god to chime in. He knew the answer.

All these different roads for power where there had been only two. What did that mean? Change was inevitable, but some things were fixed. What had pushed this one into being?

"Are you so arrogant as to believe it was you?" Chyrnog asked.

I rather am, though I doubt that's the case, Malachiasz returned. He had sent out a shockwave through the world when he had pressed past the mortal limits of power. Nadya had sent out another when she'd torn blood magic away. And there had been a third when Serefin had dealt with his eye. Tiny ripples of chaos that he, as the minor god of chaos, had caused, all creating a far larger catastrophe.

He picked up on it first, the sound of hoofbeats in the distance. Seconds later Serefin glanced to him, lifting an eyebrow. Did they tell Ruslan who had fallen silent, intent on their destination and another violent death? Malachiasz shook his head slightly.

They were in Kalyazin. There was no way this would end well for any of them.

Ruslan didn't notice until the pounding was loud enough that it could no longer be ignored and they could not hope to outrun whoever was approaching. Serefin grinned. "Let's trade one captor for another."

Ruslan reached for his ring. Malachiasz snapped his hand out, lightning fast, and caught his wrist, yanking his arm away.

"None of that," he said softly, smiling wryly at the boy's glare.

"I talked my way out of the *tsarevna* murdering me, I'll risk the army," Serefin said.

"You're an idiot," Malachiasz replied.

Serefin shrugged.

Neither of them ran, though. Malachiasz recognized the uniforms. The army it was. They let the soldiers come, let themselves be surrounded. Serefin barked out a laugh when one of the soldiers dismounted.

"Milomir! What a pleasant surprise!"

Malachiasz vaguely recognized the boy from their time with the *tsarevna*. Dark hair and eyes and the saddest resting face Malachiasz had ever seen. The dour boy shot Serefin a weary look and did not give the order for his soldiers to lift their spears.

"*Ona Delich'niya* has had a tracking spell on you for weeks," he said, sounding deeply bored. Malachiasz got the sense he always sounded like that.

"Oh, really?" Serefin asked, patting at his jacket as if searching for something lost in a pocket. "I had no idea. Where is she, then?"

"Komyazalov. Where you'll be going."

Serefin's pallor went white as a sheet. "What?"

Malachiasz shifted uncomfortably. Komyazalov meant the *tsar*. Could Serefin hold his own? With no magic?

"*Vashne Cholevistne,* I would ask that you come without a fight," Milomir said deferentially to Serefin. "But if you protest, I will take you by force."

Kacper's hand reached out, catching Serefin's. His knuckles tightened. Serefin's demeanor transformed. His chin lifted, the uncertainty gone. He nodded once.

"We travel at night," he said. "My brother cannot tolerate the sun."

Malachiasz did not have a name for the feeling that bloomed in his chest at hearing Serefin acknowledge him as his brother.

Milomir nodded, frowning. Malachiasz closed his eyes briefly.

This will not last. I will simply find another for you to devour. I will be made stronger. You cannot hide. There are so many waking up.

A sinking feeling overcame him. How long did he have?

"The *tsarevna* won't have us slaughtered the moment we reach Komyazalov?" Serefin asked.

"As far as I'm aware, she has no plans of that sort," Milomir said.

Serefin looked at Malachiasz, something careful and closed in his expression that Malachiasz recognized. This could very well doom them. This could very well doom *Tranavia*.

But Tranavia was already doomed. His Vultures would reach for power without him to hold them back. They weren't content to remain in the mines and study magic the way he was. It was simply who they were. He could get his order back under control if only he could be there. He could hold the threads of magic, but . . .

He hesitated, puzzled. They felt closer than the last time he had tugged at the strings.

Finally, Malachiasz nodded. A flicker of relief passed over Serefin's face.

"Let's not waste any more of the dark, then," Serefin said. "Also, put a spear to that boy's heart, please."

Milomir lifted an eyebrow but waved to one of his soldiers. A blade was immediately at Ruslan's chest.

The cultist's eyes were wide. Malachiasz could almost taste the salt from the sweat beading at his temples. He could hear the rapid fluttering of his heart.

"I—I—please. Let me go."

"Oh, *absolutely* not," Serefin said pleasantly.

Malachiasz took a step closer, placing a hand on the boy's shoulder and tugging him back to whisper in his ear. "The ring."

"No."

Malachiasz let his iron claws grow out of his nail beds until they were pressing into Ruslan's shirt, the tiniest bit of pressure away from piercing his flesh.

"Don't make me say please," Malachiasz murmured. "You won't like it."

Ruslan's fingers grasped at his ring before tugging it off and handing it to Malachiasz.

"Thank you," Malachiasz said. "We could be friends, you and I. But if you ever put a spell like that on my brother again, I'll take you apart, piece by piece, and eat your heart."

He let the boy go, shoving him forward a little so the blade at his chest cut him just a bit.

"Very good," Serefin said.

"You're making the right decision," Milomir said to Serefin, voice low.

"Almost certainly not, but we'll see, won't we?" Serefin returned, easily.

The company was small, and they clearly hadn't anticipated Ruslan. Milomir wearily had a few of his soldiers double on their horses, which promised to slow them all down.

"But if we're riding at night we'll have to go slowly anyway," he said morosely. "I don't like the screams I've been hearing, even when we're far from the forests."

Chyrnog settled, a tense thread of anger prevalent, in the back of Malachiasz's mind. He could feel the god's hunger—he was *hungry,* too—and knew Chyrnog had been betting on the meal that Ruslan was promising, even so close on the heels of the last one. Entropy, hunger, all those things were eternal, and one meal alone would have hardly sated him, even for a day.

"Well, this was unexpected," Serefin said to him as Milomir rearranged his light company.

Malachiasz was starting to feel anxious and twitchy, the hunger gnawing at him in a way that was hard to ignore. Serefin noticed.

"You wouldn't be driven to . . ." Serefin paused, glancing at the Kalyazi.

"I don't know!"

"Malachiasz."

"I have the barest thread of control, Serefin. He is much older and much stronger than anything we have faced, and each destruction will only make him more powerful."

"You said you *wanted* to do that."

"I don't know what I fucking want," Malachiasz snapped.

It wasn't simple anymore. He didn't know what he was fighting for, if he had anything left to fight for. Nadya had betrayed him and was gone. What was the point of living and fighting for a world that didn't have her in it?

Serefin sighed. He raked a hand through his hair, pushing it out of his face.

"Well, I suppose we'll see what Komyazalov brings."

"Each day we spend away from Tranavia . . ."

"I know, Malachiasz. But we have a Kalyazi problem that I don't think can be solved with Tranavian solutions."

25

Will the world remember what we have done—if we
survive this? Will any of this matter, in the end?
—Fragment from the personal journals
of Innokentiy Tamarkin

He had watched his brother fall apart before, but this was
something else. Deeper, somehow. Malachiasz was cracking. He was snappish—Serefin had to tread carefully or risk
getting his head ripped off—and he seemed . . . *sad.* Hopeless. Serefin didn't want to make assumptions because, as
he was so readily reminded, he didn't *know* Malachiasz, but
it just didn't feel like the Malachiasz he *did* know.

They were being watched carefully, but after making it
clear that he was coming willingly, the Kalyazi soldiers didn't
seem too concerned about transferring the Tranavian king
across the countryside.

"Here," Malachiasz said. A black silk eye patch landed in

Serefin's lap. "One of the soldiers gave this to me for you. Your face could scare children."

"Aw," Serefin said, picking up the eye patch. "How nice."

"It's not that bad," Kacper protested. He turned to Serefin. "It's not that bad."

Serefin tilted his head to Kacper so he could tie the patch on. He started to gather his hair back as well.

"I suppose it makes you look less related," Kacper mused. "Your hair isn't helping, though."

Malachiasz, who had been halfway through tying his own hair back, wordlessly dropped his hands. The easy back and forth between the three of them was *almost* nice. Kacper was resigned that Malachiasz was with them regardless, and Malachiasz wasn't being willfully hostile. Serefin only hoped they could maintain their fragile alliance.

Things were mostly calm as their journey progressed. They slept through the day and passed through a world shrouded in darkness, screams and cries echoing off the plains. The dark made for what would have been exceptionally dull traveling if not for the sounds happening outside the rim of the torchlight. Serefin rode next to Milomir, if only to appease him that Serefin wasn't going to bolt.

"I'm not going to ask about that brother of yours," Milomir said.

"Good."

"Katya will kill him if you bring him into the city."

Serefin glanced over at Malachiasz at his other side. He looked pensive and withdrawn, idly shredding his fingernails as he gazed blankly into the dark.

"Is not bringing him into the city an option? She doesn't have to know he's alive."

"Why would I aid in harboring a war criminal?"

"Fair," Serefin said with a sigh.

Milomir ran a hand through his dark hair. He was a handsome fellow, if a little too morose for Serefin's tastes.

"Have you been tracking us since the mountains?" he asked,

changing the subject to one the Kalyazi might find remotely palatable.

"More or less."

"How?"

Milomir withdrew a small disc of metal from his coat pocket. He handed it to Serefin. It was hot. Serefin had never seen anything like it before.

"How on earth did you use this?"

"Not easily, especially when you seemingly fell off the map."

Serefin wasn't sure if he 'fell off the map' in Pelageya's hut, or the cultists' temple. He handed the disc to Malachiasz, who took it with a slight frown and turned it over between his pale fingers. Serefin had no idea what it was made of, but maybe Malachiasz might. What did the *tsarevna* have of his that allowed her to keep tabs on him?

He wanted to know more. Were there more cultic sects like the one they had encountered, or was it a condensed problem? As religiously devout as Kalyazin pretended to be, he'd discovered a lot of darkness lurking underneath the golden veneer.

"Why is our favorite *tsarevna* so desperate to find me? Or am I a political prisoner? If that's the case, I think I *will* make an escape attempt," Serefin said.

"Thank you for warning me."

"No problem."

"I cannot begin to understand how the *tsarevna*'s mind works, but I suspect it's difficult to get anything done with the king of Tranavia wandering the Kalyazi countryside."

"Oh, her intentions are noble, then."

Milomir lifted an eyebrow.

"Ah, fine, I'll tell her to her face."

Milomir almost looked like he was going to laugh, which Serefin didn't think was even possible.

A ripple shuddered through the shallow fields. The frost below their feet seemed to crack, and Serefin frowned, shifting in his saddle. A presence blanketed over them. Ruslan straightened, his head lifting. Malachiasz let out an odd, rasping whine. Serefin glanced at him. His eyes were murky, blood beginning to rim one. His nose started bleeding and he touched it with gentle, absent fingertips.

Foreboding curled in the pit of Serefin's stomach, ice cold.

Malachiasz's body jolted hard, once, before he fell out of his saddle.

He wasn't Malachiasz anymore.

Shit. Serefin's dismount was rocky, everything was *off* since losing his eye. He landed on the dirt with a hard thud. He ignored the cries of alarm from the Kalyazi soldiers and the spears pointed at his chest. He smacked a nearby horse's flank, startling it off, grabbing a soldier's dagger from his waist as he passed. It wouldn't do him any good, but he needed *something.* He missed his magic. Moths blew out in a cloud around him as Milomir tried to regain order while Malachiasz changed.

Damn it, what happened? He was fine.

"Hardly," Velyos replied. *"He has no control of his own."*

How was I able to break away from Chyrnog, yet he can't?

"You have your soul, and you gave up a piece of yourself as a distraction. Besides, Chyrnog didn't really want you. He wanted that Vulture."

Malachiasz had been dismissive of his missing soul, but what if that was what they needed? Did Serefin want to help fix Malachiasz? Or was he merely waiting to destroy him? For his hand to be forced into moving against his brother a second time? Stopping Chyrnog meant stopping Malachiasz.

Except . . . he couldn't destroy him again, not like that.

Iron spikes, dripping with blood, pressed out of Malachiasz's skin, through his clothes. A mouthful of iron nails for teeth, his eyes onyx black. Serefin realized dimly that he had never seen Malachiasz this way, only the in-between states where he had a thread of control. Heavy black wings tore through the back of his coat, black horns spiraling into his hair. Blood trickled from the corners of his eyes and mouth. And there were so many eyes.

Milomir moved his horse in front of Serefin, spear leveled at Malachiasz. Serefin blew out an irritated breath. Malachiasz snapped the spear in half with his bare hands, pulling Milomir off his horse. Serefin scrambled past panicked hooves, grabbing the back of Malachiasz's coat and yanking him off Milomir right before he struck. He was immediately slammed to the ground.

"You bloody idiot, you're making it difficult to want to help you," Serefin grunted through clenched teeth.

He wedged his legs underneath Malachiasz, flinging him off. Malachiasz landed on his feet, moving to strike.

A Kalyazi soldier got in between them and Serefin didn't have time to scream out a warning. They had to stay back, they couldn't fight a Vulture, much less what Malachiasz was: roiling, churning horror.

He saw blood in a wet spray, and the soldier fell in front of him. Malachiasz's head tilted, and he swallowed hard.

Oh, no. Serefin vaulted over the dead soldier, slamming into Malachiasz before he could do something there would be no explaining to the Kalyazi. He ground one knee down on Malachiasz's chest, the dagger at his throat, aware that it would do nothing to stop him, but it might give him pause.

"Malachiasz, I need you to snap out of this. I'm trying my hardest to protect you and I don't know how much farther I can take it."

A low growl spread from Malachiasz's chest. Serefin slammed his elbow down across the other boy's face.

"I'm not your precious cleric. I'm not going to bring you out of this gently." He struck his elbow across Malachiasz's face again, the hiss of pain cutting through Malachiasz's teeth the only spare indication that he felt anything. "*You* sold your fucking soul for a scrap of power. *You* killed a god and made this bad situation worse. If the Kalyazi want to hang you, I can't stop them, Malachiasz."

Malachiasz's expression shifted. His eyes cleared to a strange grayish murk.

"Serefin."

"*Czijow*, brother of mine."

Malachiasz squirmed, dislodging his arm and pressing the strange disc of metal against Serefin's chest.

"Let me go," he whispered. "You have to trust me."

Serefin's hand closed around the disc. Milomir hadn't asked for it back and it was hot in his hands. He could figure out how to make it work. He let out a breath in resignation.

"Trust me," Malachiasz repeated.

"You bastard," Serefin muttered. He hit him again, less hard this time, for good measure.

Malachiasz's eyes flickered to onyx and he bared his teeth at Serefin, spitting out a mouthful of blood and throwing him off. He kicked Serefin hard in the ribs and was gone, using those powerful black wings to escape into the distance.

Serefin lay on the ground as things settled around him. He pressed his hand against his eye and swore softly. Someone nudged him with the toe of their boot, and he opened his eye to see Kacper. He held out his hand for Serefin, sympathetic. Serefin let Kacper haul him to his feet.

"I don't want to end up on a battlefield with him on the other side," Serefin said.

Kacper nodded.

"Might be inevitable," Serefin continued, eyeing the spot where Malachiasz had disappeared.

He had chosen to trust his brother. He hoped he wouldn't regret it. Serefin touched the metal disc as it cooled underneath his fingers, Malachiasz drawing farther away. Malachiasz wouldn't have given him the means to find him if he didn't want to be found.

Serefin braced himself as he turned around. One soldier was dead and any goodwill from the Kalyazi gone. Milomir's face was ashen.

"We ride harder now," he said simply.

"I suppose that answers those questions I had before," Serefin said weakly. He got no response but glares.

"What about Timur?" a soldier asked.

"We'll stay here until morning," Milomir said. "We bury him. We remember why we're fighting." He leveled a glare at Serefin. "And who."

Serefin had to fight the urge to reach for Kacper's hand.

They were sequestered off and guarded as the Kalyazi made camp and buried the dead soldier. Kacper sat heavily on the ground next to Serefin, who had taken off the eye patch and was massaging his eye socket.

Ruslan was shoved over to them. Serefin didn't have the energy to confront him. His side hurt from where Malachiasz had kicked him, absolutely harder than necessary, but he hadn't needed to give that third elbow to the face. He tilted back onto the ground and pressed his hand over his eye. Kacper's fingers twined between his, thumb gently rubbing circles on his wrist.

The journey to Komyazalov was going to be miserable.

26

NADEZHDA

LAPTEVA

Svoyatova Yulka Lokteva was led by a Vulture into their foul Salt Mines, hoping to sway just one. No one saw her again.

—Vasiliev's Book of Saints

It wasn't complete understanding. There was fear, confusion, bewilderment. Ultimately, though, there was quiet. Nadya didn't cry as she told her story, she didn't know if she could. She was far past feeling.

Anna had taken off her headscarf as the story went on. Her straight black hair had been chopped off just above her collarbones. She ran a hand through it before taking Nadya's hand between hers, fingers tracking over the stained skin, the claws of her fingernails.

"Oh, Naden'ka," she said, voice soft.

"It's me," Nadya said blankly. "I don't know what I am, but . . ." She drew her hand back, flexing her fingers. An eye opened on the center of her palm. Anna gasped. Nadya swiftly pulled her glove back on.

"Does the *tsarevna* know?"

"Yes. But no one else can. The Matriarch *cannot* know. If she never learns I was here, it would be for the best."

Anna nodded. "Those in the Church talk in whispers. There are omens everywhere. Signs of the end. Icons crying—"

"Mm," Nadya assented. She dragged her chair to the doorway, standing on it to take the icon over the door off the wall. She carried it to Anna, her chair scraping behind her. It was Svoyatovi Viktoria Kholodova, and her icon was weeping tears of blood.

Anna reached for the icon, horror flickering over her face.

"The fallen gods have risen, and we cannot look to our gods for help," Nadya said. "We're on our own."

"Not only the fallen gods," Anna said.

Nadya straightened. She took the icon from Anna, setting it on the side table. Dread was a feeling that had settled deep in her bones, almost ordinary, but it spiked at Anna's words.

Nadya pressed out tentatively, slowly, searching for what she had been ignoring since the mountains. The thing that had bled all the color out of the world and was eating at the trees like black decay. She couldn't live from day to day with that feeling, even though it existed at the edges of her awareness.

A hunger that wanted to devour the world. To feed and feed and feed until there was nothing left. That would bleed out the sun and plunge the world in darkness.

"There have been whispers," Anna continued, "of his followers rising out of the shadows. There are . . . people with magic, power, but not like yours, and not like blood magic. It's something else, different, and those people have two fates before them: be captured by the Church or be Chyrnog's followers."

Nadya's eyes opened. Anna's expression was gray.

"People who . . . wake with magic. They're called the Quiet Sinners. I—the Church—I . . ." Anna closed her eyes. "They are executed. Quickly. Better for them to die in sin than be taken by Chyrnog's followers."

"To what end? Why do Chyrnog's followers want them?"

Anna shook her head. "I don't know. But the way their power manifests is . . . strange."

Nadya thought of flowers sprouting from Rashid's arms. He already had magic but what if the flowers were something else? He'd said that was new.

The bleakness in Anna's voice was telling, though. It sounded like her friend had found the same disillusionment that had struck Nadya.

"The church leaders are frightened," Anna said. "This isn't a threat they know how to face because it's the thing we were supposed to be staying with our faith. If we remained faithful, magic would never become tainted. Haven't we done right by the gods? Haven't we fought this war for them? What have we done wrong that they allow one who would destroy the world to rise? There were prophecies, once, about how the end of the world would come, but they were never like this. The end of the world in the Divine Codex is nothing like this. What did we do?"

Nadya stared at her friend, the blood draining from her face. It was *her*. She had set this into motion.

And she couldn't let anyone know.

It was presumptuous, and she'd received an odd look when she'd flagged down a servant and asked, but the next morning Katya flounced into Nadya's rooms dressed in leggings and a fine crimson *kosovortka*. Her black hair was in unbrushed wild curls and one of her dogs was with her, Nadya had no idea which, though it was much calmer this time, curling up at the foot of Katya's chair as she sat down.

"You've avoided talking to me since the mountains, so I assume this is important," Katya said.

There was another knock on Nadya's door. She frowned.

"Oh, I had Nina fetch us some tea, that's all."

Nadya let in the girl, who set the tray of cups and samovar on the table and departed.

"Seems a little light for you," she noted.

"The sun just came up," Katya replied. "Give me a few hours before I get into my cups."

"You are much like Serefin in that way."

Katya lifted an eyebrow. She sighed and tilted her head.

"He was at the front far longer than me, and at a much younger age. I was mostly kept from harm, but I did a few months out there, and what you see . . . never really goes away. The drinking dulls the memories, some."

"Do you like him?"

Katya took a moment to consider. "I'm fond of Serefin."

"But you *like* Ostyia." Nadya wasn't one to tease Katya, so it came out of nowhere, and Katya *blushed*.

"This is absolutely not why you called me here at the crack of dawn," she said, her voice strained.

"I need someone to talk to who will know about this," Nadya said with a sigh, tugging off her glove. She showed Katya the eye at the center.

Katya's face paled. "The Matriarch—"

"Not the Matriarch."

The *tsarevna* took a long sip of her tea, eyeing Nadya's hand. It was quiet in the room for a long time. Nadya could hear the palace slowly coming to life outside her window. Katya stared up at the ceiling, clearly puzzling through things.

"Gods. He was right, wasn't he?"

"I have found Malachiasz did not make a habit of being wrong."

Katya tapped the arm of her chair.

"Katya. I know we don't see eye to eye. You find me suspicious. Though, frankly, me traveling with the Black Vulture was about as weird as you traveling with the King of Tranavia. I'm not the cleric that was promised, and for that, I'm sorry, but this is bigger than the war and you know it."

"It's not that I find you suspicious, darling, it's that you're so damn stubborn and unwilling to work with me," Katya said, with the light drawl of someone avoiding Nadya's point. "And I don't think you're going to turn Kalyazin over to the Tranavians you love so much; you certainly proved your loyalties on that mountain."

Nadya flinched. "Anna told me about the Quiet Sinners."

Katya groaned.

"Katya . . ."

"I'm not going to defend the Church."

"I know. Just, please, tell Viktor to keep an eye on Rashid."

Nadya didn't miss the way the *tsarevna*'s eyes widened. "Oh." She was quiet before continuing. "Viktor isn't nearly as devout as he wanted you to believe. He'll be trustworthy."

Trustworthy. That was what this was now. They had to figure out who they could trust. Because it wasn't the Church she had once loved so much. If they knew what she was, they would kill her.

"How did you learn about the fallen gods? And the old gods? I know you know, Katya. What the decay means, what the forests moving past their borders means. It's all going to end. *Everything* is going to end. Who can we talk to?"

"Pelageya."

"Someone *else*," Nadya groaned. "We don't have the time to hunt her down." Nadya picked the icon up off the table and handed it to Katya, who took it with a frown. "How long until the other icons in this palace are the same? The longer I'm here, the more likely it is to happen, and then no number of lies will hide what I am."

"You're a monster," Katya whispered. She wasn't leveling an accusation; it was a statement of the truth.

"It depends how you look at it, I suppose."

"But you didn't set the old god free."

"No, but *someone did.* I don't know if it was Serefin, or Mala-chiasz, or someone else entirely."

"Even the old gods cannot work without a vessel."

"How do we know he doesn't have one? The cultists, the sects dedicated to these gods, how do we know that he hasn't claimed one of them? Or someone who has had power awakened in them? *Katya.* I need to know what I am. I cannot stop him if I don't get answers."

"I don't know if you can stop him at all."

27

MALACHIASZ CZECHOWICZ

Don't wake him up. Don't wake him up. Don't wake him up. Don't wake him up. Don't wake him up. Don't wake him up. Don't wake him up. Don't wake him up.
—Passage from the personal journals of Innokentiy Tamarkin

He hadn't meant to lose control. Well, he had. He had and he hadn't. A well-timed admonishment by Chyrnog gave him the means to escape. He had quickly figured out the rudimentary Kalyazi tracking spell—Serefin could find him if he needed to, and he had a plan.

No. No, he didn't. He didn't have a plan. He needed help. Help that his brother couldn't give him, not yet. No one could. He had gotten himself into this mess and he had to get himself out of it.

Except he still didn't know if he wanted to get out of it, only that he found the idea of enacting the will of a god so detestable that he would rather fight back on spite alone.

When Nadya had leveled the—entirely true at the time—accusation that he would always choose his Vultures and Tranavia over her, it had shifted something in him. He could choose his order and his country, but it meant nothing if he never chose her, too. And she was dead.

His face hurt. Serefin was uncomfortably strong in a way that Malachiasz sensed meant he was always holding back, but he had *tried*. No one ever tried to get Malachiasz back when his control snapped. He'd had a lifetime of other Vultures telling him to embrace the part of him that he had no control over. But other Vultures didn't have the problems he did. Other Vultures were perfectly capable of maintaining control. He had always been different. He was too volatile.

Thus, everyone ignored him as he fell apart. Until Nadya, descending into hell to throttle him back to himself. Until Serefin, weight on his chest and elbow against his face trying his level best to get him to snap back to himself.

"You can run from them; do you think it so easy to run from me?"

He ignored Chyrnog. The god was weak. As long as Malachiasz stayed away from any other awakened ones, he would remain so.

"You think it is that easy? You think you'll be able to stay away? You underestimate how many have woken. How few I need to consume before I can shatter you."

But until then, you need me. What happens when you've consumed all you need? What happens after you feed off their power?

He didn't know why he was asking when he knew. The end of the sun. The end of everything.

Malachiasz didn't want to end everything. End a few dynasties, destroy a few empires, sure, but burn the world to ash? He refused to be a king of charred bones and ashes. Chyrnog didn't respond, which was good. He didn't really want to talk to him.

It felt like giving up, turning to the witch.

"You should be able to fix this yourself. Do you expect me to clean up all your messes for you?"

It was going about as well as Malachiasz had expected.

"What's happening to me?" he asked, deciding that he would take the high road and not bite back even though he *desperately* wanted to. He missed Nadya.

It had happened very suddenly, finding Pelageya's strange hut. Then he'd struggled to get past the gate, and he had a feeling the witch was toying with him simply because she could. He didn't have time for her nonsense.

Malachiasz had stepped into her sitting room, noting it was more erratic than the last time. Bones piled in corners, the furs covering the floors matted with blood. Something other than herbs hung from the ceiling, something that Malachiasz didn't really want to investigate.

"Each moment of surrender binds you closer to him. Little by little he becomes more *you* and you become *him*."

"I don't want that," Malachiasz said quickly.

"Don't you? Haven't you always been driven by the pursuit of power? Now you can have it. You and he are already so alike; it's why he chose you."

"I destroyed one of them. The . . . whatever you called them."

"*Bovilgy?*" Pelageya arched an eyebrow. "You're well on your way to destroying the world, then."

"That's not what I *want*," he groaned.

"No?"

He threw himself down in a chair and dropped his head into his hands. "No."

She made a vaguely disbelieving sound. "And what about your vast plans for destroying gods? It all leads into itself, you realize. It's a snake devouring its own tail, eternally linked. You cannot have one without the other. You cannot have the destruction of one without the destruction of all. I know, I know, you've been burned by this fire you toy with and now you panic because you don't know how to keep it from spreading."

Malachiasz closed his eyes. He'd known coming here would mean being berated by Pelageya, but he hated it all the same.

"I can't fix this, can I?" His eyes flickered open to stare at her.

"Can you?"

He sighed.

"How much further must I lead you by the hand, *Chelvyanik Sterevyani*? How much longer until you realize the pieces you need are before you, if only you looked for them?"

Malachiasz toyed with the bones in his hair, unwrapping one and rolling it between his fingers. Her head tilted, a slow smile spreading across her mouth.

"What did you do with it?"

"With what?" she asked innocently.

He didn't want to *say it* and he hated that she was making him. Hated that she was forcing him to acknowledge his mistake, that he was at her mercy.

"I gave you the last pieces—"

"Of?"

"My soul," he ground out through his teeth. "What did you do with them?"

Her onyx black eyes regarded him for a long, drawn out moment. "What did I tell you, when I took it?"

"Is this a test?"

She shrugged.

He didn't know. He couldn't remember *most* things, but especially not a conversation that he'd had when he was not wholly there.

"What a thing to throw away so frivolously. Was it worth it?"

"It was at the time."

"Ah, what a thing, hindsight."

"Pelageya, what do you want from me? Why are you doing this?"

"Have you ever once admitted you were wrong?" she asked, pointing the knife right back at him. Talking to her was like running in circles.

"Is *that* what you want? You want me to admit I was wrong?" he asked incredulously.

"It's very difficult for you."

He leaned back in his chair and eyed her. It was very rare that he *was* wrong, about anything. But he knew he had made mistakes. He had done things he shouldn't have in his reckless pursuit of fixing *something*.

"I shouldn't have given you that power over me," he said with a shrug. "It was . . . not well thought out."

"Not very good and not a true admittance, but I suppose it will do. Are you strong enough, I wonder? Will you ask for the help you will need or take the burden on your own shoulders and surely fail?"

He frowned.

"I don't have the pieces anymore, dear boy. You'll have to get them yourself and I doubt you'll enjoy what will be asked of you."

"Spare me, I haven't liked any of this. Whatever is required of me will be nothing new."

Pelageya smiled at that, which was rather alarming.

"You're going to spin me around in circles and push me out the door and expect me to stop the destruction of the world when I don't know how," he said wearily.

Pelageya stood. Malachiasz tensed, ready to bolt.

"This world has been turning for so very long. There have always been people like you in it, ones who reach too far. People who want to change and burn and ruin and save the world. What do you think that gets them? Nothing and nothing and nothing. What do you think makes you so different that you can succeed where all who came before have failed? Why are you special? Why should you, a boy who sold the only pieces of humanity he had left for a few paltry shreds of power, be given a second chance? I may care little for the lines drawn between the Kalyazi and Tranavians, but I *am* Kalyazi, boy, and I do know what you've done to the people of this country."

"So, you would rather I die for my transgressions?"

"Do you think you can stay the course? Do you want to?"

"I want to try," he said quietly.

She stared at him. He fidgeted. He didn't like being *seen*. He was a monster. He had eyes opening on his skin. He was aware of his own horror. But even before this, even when he was a boy among the Vultures, he didn't like being known, standing out. It had changed some, when he'd realized how much he could affect if he took Łucja off the throne, and it had changed when he realized how good he was at getting people to listen when *he* was on that throne. But his quiet anxiety never went away. It lingered, torn open anytime he found himself under Nadya's quietly focused gaze. She had always seen so much of him—too much. Even at the beginning, when he was doing his best to hide things, he could never shake the feeling that she was seeing it all anyway. That she had known he was trying to manipulate her and yet did it all anyway.

"Will that be enough, I wonder?" she mused.

It had to be.

"He knows you're here, of course. There's no hiding from him. And you're right, with a few fragments of your shattered soul you *might* bind him back into the earth, but you cannot do it alone, and my time of telling you what you need to hear is over. I gave you warnings. I gave that brother of yours and that cleric warnings. You all ignored them."

Malachiasz's eyes narrowed. "What did you do with it?"

"Hid it away. Can't say I remember where."

"Of course not." Malachiasz tilted his head back with a groan as Pelageya started digging through the ephemera in her cluttered hut.

"It's not *here* here, souls are too messy, they demand too much. I like to put them out of sight, out of mind. Yes, yes, somewhere else, a different place than here. You need four, you know. I told one of you this, a lifetime ago, but I can't remember which." She counted on her fingers to herself. "Yes, four, there were four before and there have to be four now."

Before . . . That was it. This god had been locked away once; he could be locked away again. His hand brushed the book in his pocket.

"Was it not the other gods who locked away Chyrnog?" he asked.

"Other gods? No, no, a fairy tale, a story, the truth forgotten.

They can't touch the mortal world without a mortal to work through. This has not changed."

"But if I kill like Chyrnog wants me to . . ."

"Then, yes, it would be the endpoint of that particular disaster." Malachiasz shivered.

"You would be destroyed. He would become you, and you him. It's already started."

He picked up a skull from the table beside his chair. He couldn't tell what it was, some kind of small animal. He turned it in his fingers.

"Who are you, Pelageya?"

He didn't expect her to respond, let alone answer. He was surprised when she winked at him.

"No one important."

That left something to be desired.

"Maybe if you gather those you need, you'll be able to accomplish this."

"But what about—"

"The soul business? Well, maybe they can help with that, too."

Malachiasz was quiet. Who were the other three? "Is one of them my brother?"

Pelageya grinned. "You better get a move on."

28

SEREFIN

MELESKI

When she sang, stars fell from Svoyatova Evgenia
Grafova's eyes and lips.

—Vasiliev's Book of Saints

"We have to talk about this."

Serefin squinted up at where Kacper stood, the setting
sun at his back. They had camped for the evening and he and
the others were back under guard. He glanced pointedly at
a nearby soldier.

The soldier who wasn't remotely paying attention. Kacper
dryly returned the look. Serefin sighed.

"Very well, sit down at least."

Serefin leaned on his hands as Kacper sat. He knew where
this was headed. "Are you going to undermine my decision?"
he asked.

Kacper blanched, clearly remembering the argument he'd
had with Ostyia that had spiraled much further out of control
than any of them could have known.

"I'm worried the decision that you're making is going to get you killed. Is that a problem? We have *no protection*. We have nothing as leverage. There is literally nothing stopping the *tsar* from killing you—covertly or otherwise—if you do this."

Serefin nodded mildly, but said nothing, sensing Kacper wasn't finished.

"It was uncanny, the situation with Yekaterina, but not something that we can assume will ever be replicated. They have no reason for keeping you alive. No reason for courting talks of a peace treaty since the last I heard the front isn't going so great for us because our magic is *gone*."

Serefin flinched. How many had died that day? Or had a ceasefire been called as the Tranavians were forced to regroup? It was killing him, the not knowing.

"I've thought about all of this, Kacper."

"Then what are you doing?"

He straightened and reached out to take Kacper's hands. Kacper softened, as if forgetting that he was supposed to be upset with Serefin.

"I'm not saying that you need to go along with everything I do. You're not my underling, I want us to be equals."

"*Sznecz.*"

Serefin rolled his eye. "All right, fine, as much as we can be considering the circumstances."

"You *are* the king."

"But that's exactly what I'm saying."

Serefin glanced over. The soldier had wandered farther away. Milomir eyed them from afar but didn't seem inclined to come closer. They had established that they weren't going anywhere—and weren't going to fight back—so the Kalyazi hadn't taken drastic measures. He thought they should be taking drastic measures against Ruslan, but they hadn't so far. He couldn't shake the feeling that bringing the boy into the capital would be bad news for them all.

"Kacper, I know how I've acted in the past. Half of Tranavia thinks I don't want this."

"More than half."

"Not helping," he said. "I do, though. I didn't, that's fair, but I do now and I'm doing my best and sometimes I'm going to make decisions that seem off-the-wall and foolhardy and you'll have to trust me."

Kacper managed to appear both heartened and distressed. Serefin sighed ruefully.

"Can I at least know why you think this will work? Or are you asking for complete and total blind acceptance?" Kacper asked.

"Rude."

Kacper glanced at Serefin's left eye and winced. "Sorry."

Serefin waved him off. "No. Obviously not. I just . . ."

"I'm not going to undermine you in public, if that's what you're worried about. I've been to court, Serefin, I know how this works. But I *am* going to ask you to explain yourself in private."

"This is hardly private, Kacper."

"You know what I mean, don't be difficult."

"All I know how to be is difficult."

"*That* is very true. Regardless, I'll trust you—of course I trust you—but I want you to trust *me* enough to tell me what you're planning."

There was one fatal flaw with that perfectly reasonable sentiment. "And if I don't have a plan?"

"Serefin."

"Great talk!"

Kacper groaned.

"They're listening, you know," Serefin pointed out.

Kacper didn't bother glancing over his shoulder. "I know."

"Talking of plans at all will make them nervous."

"It does," Milomir called.

"Eavesdropping is rude!" Serefin called back.

Kacper was giving him a *look,* and he knew why. They were effectively prisoners. Kacper was right. There was nothing in place that would stop the *tsar* from executing Serefin the second he stepped into Komyazalov. He should be worried. He should be *terrified.*

But he . . . wasn't.

Was it sheer exhaustion? Was it something else? It certainly wasn't hope. But Katya—outside of carving open his chest—had never really given any indications of hostility toward Serefin. She had been honest that if it were up to her, she would have drawn up a peace treaty, damn what their respective courts had to say. But it wasn't up to her. It was up to her father.

And the *tsar* was a variable he did not know how to plan for. He knew surprisingly little about Yulian Vodyanov. He'd known more about Katya, all things considered. She was the one that he might meet on a battlefield. He knew only that Yulian was deeply devout, to the point where he would never bend to heretics. That worried him, but such a deeply devout man *had* ended up with a daughter like Katya, so maybe there was hope for the world yet.

There weren't many wartime stories about the current *tsar*. He was more content to hole himself up with his priests in his church than focus on what was happening at the front.

"It's not that I have a plan and it's not that I trust them," Serefin said, his voice soft. "It's that if we go there and they kill me, so what? We're going to die. It's no longer a chance, it's inevitable."

"Because of your brother."

"Because of Chyrnog," Serefin clarified, though Kacper didn't seem to appreciate it. He was still holding Kacper's hands and he didn't want to let them go, ever.

Ruslan was off whispering with one of the soldiers, which concerned Serefin. How persuasive could Ruslan be? He reminded Serefin of Malachiasz, but without the anxious earnestness that Malachiasz used to win people over so effortlessly. Ruslan was more obviously conniving.

What would happen if he convinced these soldiers that an ancient god had awoken and needed worship? What could he twist them into doing?

Serefin really wished Malachiasz hadn't left. Milomir had contemplated sending someone after him until Serefin pointed out that Malachiasz could kill literally everyone in the company without much thought or effort. He'd received a poisonous look in return—it was, admittedly, a little on the callous side—and Milomir had decided to let him go. Serefin hoped it wasn't to their detriment.

He wanted to trust Malachiasz so badly.

Kacper had been quietly toying with his fingers. "Thank you," he said softly.

Serefin tilted his head. "For giving you no answers to your questions and telling you we were doomed instead of reassuring you?"

Kacper shrugged. "You let me in. You don't do that, usually."

It hurt to hear that and realize Kacper was absolutely right. He didn't *try* to be like this. He didn't know how to *not* be like this.

"Oh," he said, his voice small.

Kacper squeezed his hand. "It's not like it's a surprise."

Serefin frowned.

"You've spent a good part of your life watching everyone around you die."

"You have, too."

"I don't have anyone dropping the weight of a country on my shoulders. Actually, literally no one cares what I do with my life, which is very freeing."

"I care," Serefin murmured.

Kacper grinned.

The rest of the journey was uneventful. The screams across the fields that came from nowhere and everywhere at once, benign. More than once Milomir had to send soldiers out to kill . . . something. They always returned haggard and traumatized. The monsters of Kalyazin were no longer sleeping.

But it went quickly. Too quickly. He had never truly had to be a king and now everything hung in the balance and there was nothing to do but press forward. To Komyazalov. To the heart of his enemies.

interlude iii

RASHID

KHAJOUTI

Either Viktor was fabulously wealthy, or Kalyazi *boyar* could afford more than one home. Rashid suspected the former. And he did not like it here one bit.

There was something deeply wrong with the air in Komyazalov. Not like in Grazyk . . . or maybe, possibly, *exactly* like in Grazyk.

Rashid had never believed Nadya when she'd insisted the Kalyazi did not experiment with magic like the Tranavians. The *tsarevna* was proof enough that Nadya had been drastically misinformed.

He flopped onto a chair in Viktor's sitting room while Parijahan tossed a log onto the fire before someone could scold her. The servants didn't like when the two Akolans did everyday tasks. Parijahan should have been used to it thanks to her position in Akola, but she liked being self-sufficient. Meanwhile Viktor kept getting dragged away by a seemingly constant stream of people requiring his attention.

Parijahan watched him leave for what was possibly the fourth time before she said, "Why would anyone *want* that?"

"Money to not starve," Rashid said softly.

Her expression twisted, like it always did at the reminder that she'd always had everything, and he had been effectively sold into her household as a boy. It wasn't slavery, but it was close.

"I don't like it here," he said.

"No," Parijahan replied, eyeing the fire. "I don't, either. And I don't like Nadya being on her own."

"If anyone can handle herself, it's Nadya," Ostyia said from where she was sitting on a lush rug, her back to a chair. Parijahan stepped over her to get to the chair. Ostyia was idly leafing through her spell book. "Also, she's supposed to be on her way here. Viktor gave me a very panicked message from her that said something about being eaten by dogs and getting lost in a maze of icons."

"So, she's doing fine?"

Ostyia shrugged.

"Even if she can handle herself," Parijahan said, "she didn't want to come here."

Ostyia tilted her head back to shoot Parijahan a quizzical look.

Nadya appeared soon after, ushered in by one of Viktor's servants and very frazzled by it. She yanked her scarf off the second the servant left, leaving her white-blond hair messy. She collapsed facedown on the rug next to Ostyia. She mumbled something unintelligible.

"What was that, darling?" Ostyia asked.

She flipped onto her back. "We're in over our heads."

"True enough."

"Katya didn't tell anyone who I am, though, so I live another day."

Rashid's arms were itchy under his sleeves. The flowers came and went on their own now. It was wildly inconvenient. But Nadya *had* suggested he talk to Ostyia about it . . . He rubbed at them absently.

Parijahan climbed back over her to sit on the arm of the chair Rashid was in. He leaned his head against her side.

Nadya continued staring fixedly at the ceiling.

"I hate feeling like this," he whispered.

"I know," she replied, weaving a hand through his hair.

Maybe if he hadn't buried his power so deep, it wouldn't have clawed its way to the surface, tearing him apart in its wake. Maybe they could still be in Akola and everything would be all right.

But that wasn't true. He'd known, the night Parijahan had stolen into his rooms and shaken him awake, whispering that they had to go, how she was going to get revenge and they *had to leave,* what he was getting into. He hadn't realized she was saving him. He hadn't thought he was important at all.

"Don't you ever want to go back?" he asked.

She sighed, tilting her head against his. "Sometimes. I don't think it would feel like home anymore, though."

"No?"

She made a thoughtful noise. "Only if you were there, but if you ever go back . . ."

Locked away. Burned out.

"Magic doesn't work that way here," he said with a frown. "Why is it like that in Akola?"

Ostyia's head perked up. "Stop whispering when I'm trying to eavesdrop."

"Is it eavesdropping when you're in the same room?" Parijahan asked.

"Was it supposed to be a secret, that the two of you have magic?" she asked. "I've known for months."

Parijahan's eyes widened and Rashid swallowed thickly, shivering as everything in him went cold. Nadya finally sat up, leaning back against the chair.

"What?" Parijahan asked, voice strained.

Ostyia tilted her head.

"How did you know?"

"You hide it well, but it's my job to make sure that no one with particularly strong magic is around Serefin that I don't know about."

"So, you deemed us harmless."

"You weren't going to be a threat on his life, from what I could gather. It's nebulous"—she waved a hand—"imperfect. I figured that if you never used or spoke of it, you didn't want anyone to know, so I kept it to myself. I can't say I'm not curious, though. We don't see many Akolan mages."

Rashid scowled. He wasn't entirely pleased at being referred to as harmless. "Because there aren't many Akolan mages," he said. "They burn out."

Ostyia frowned slightly. "What does that mean?"

Nadya straightened with interest.

Rashid glanced between the two of them, mages both. "They're tools. When the Travash have used them to their full extent, they die."

Ostyia glanced at Nadya. "Can that happen to clerics?"

"The gods only give the amount of magic a cleric can handle," Nadya said. "Though we can always reach for more . . ." She winced. "But it's a channel, and the gods can stop the flow of power. I don't think clerics generally die because of magic."

Ostyia nodded. "If, say, Kacper were to cast from my spell book, he would probably get a headache and the spells would fail. I couldn't cast from Serefin's spell book, he's stronger than both of us. I don't think there's a blood mage alive who could cast from Malachiasz's spell book."

The sickly expression that passed over Nadya's face did not escape Rashid's notice.

"There's a reason we buy our spell books with the spells already written. The writers construct the spells to control the flow of power so you don't try to cast one that will, well, kill you."

"So, it's not that the concept is unfamiliar, it's that we have different words for it," Nadya said.

"We have different ways to handle it, yes. We try to avoid it. But magic can still kill you if you overextend yourself. Do you know what it is you can do?" Ostyia asked him.

Rashid hesitated and shook his head. "She influences things." He pointed at Parijahan, who scowled at him.

"In a good way?" Ostyia asked.

"It's rather hard to determine," Parijahan said.

"Do you think you were counteracting the Black Vulture's madness?"

Rashid lifted an eyebrow. Nadya looked like a brick had been dropped on her head.

"Everything truly bad with him happened when I wasn't around," she said. "But it's impossible to know."

"It would be interesting to test," Ostyia said thoughtfully.

Parijahan rolled her eyes. "Every damn Tranavian is the same."

Rashid snorted softly, though he didn't disagree with Ostyia. He supposed this was the reason that Nadya had suggested he talk to her. Ostyia was never as loud about her magic as the other Tranavians, but Rashid knew she was particularly adept.

"What about you?" she asked Rashid.

"I would like to test the perimeters," he said slowly. "Carefully, because I don't know how it will truly manifest."

Ostyia nodded. She gazed down at her book for a long moment, something sad in her blue eye. Nadya reached out and took her hand.

"I'm sorry," she whispered.

It was hardly something that could be apologized for, and she seemed aware of that.

Rashid rolled his sleeves back. He moved to sit across from Ostyia on the floor.

"But you can't remember how magic works," he said uncertainly.

"Blood magic. And it's not that I can't remember. It's . . . it's like the path has been ruined."

Parijahan slid down into Rashid's chair. "Magic works in different avenues."

"And the one I know isn't viable anymore. It could be a matter of finding a different branch—I have an affinity for magic, but in Tranavia no other way of using it matters."

"Do you know other ways?"

She shrugged. "I was taught by an old Vulture who found whispers of Akolan and Aecii magic fascinating. Who was constantly paying exorbitant sums to have books from Rumenovać smuggled across the borders. It's all out there. But in Kalyazin, everything else is heresy, and in Tranavia, well, why use anything else when we know how far you can take blood magic if you're really trying? We have the Vultures; we have proof of how far you can grasp. Maybe other countries have their Vultures as well."

It was impossible to know. The war had locked these two countries together so long that any hope of learning without bloodshed had been lost.

Ostyia closed her spell book. "I doubt Viktor will appreciate us doing this here, but if you'd like, we can see what it is you have hiding away."

Rashid glanced at Parijahan. He couldn't help it. It was his decision to make, but he had walked this road with her for so long that he wanted to make sure she was ready for whatever this meant.

Her expression was carefully blank, but she slipped. He saw the fear cut through her that she did her very best to shutter away.

"I'll hardly stop you," Parijahan said. "I knew this day would come. I just . . . I worry you'll attract attention that we don't want."

Ostyia tucked a black lock behind her ear and adjusted her eye patch. "We're out of time for that way of thinking," she said. "Don't act as if we haven't all seen Nadya"—she gestured—"scrambling because her and those damn boys did something too big for any of us to stop. Do you truly think Akola would send people out here when the threat of cosmic annihilation is on the horizon?"

"You underestimate how far Akola is willing to go for resources that they think belong to them."

"But which part of Akola?" Ostyia returned. "You're from different territories, I can tell by your accents. And I can't say I'm afraid of Tehran."

Rashid had always thought Ostyia was more astute than she led everyone to believe, but he was still surprised she was aware of his and Parijahan's differences. It was . . . rare someone from the north ever noticed. It stood to reason, though. She was the king's right hand. Her games of flirting with girls and caring very little about the world were only a mask to keep people from suspecting everything she saw.

"Paalmidesh," Parijahan replied with a slight frown. "He's from Yanzin Zadar."

Ostyia's eyebrows lifted. *"Really?"*

"Frankly, I'm shocked that our particular tensions have made it all the way up here."

"We share enough of a border with Akola that we aren't going to ignore when one part of the country moves against the other," Ostyia pointed out. "Besides, what are you worried about? It would take them a good year to get this far west."

Parijahan did not look reassured. Ostyia turned back to Rashid.

"Close your eyes," she ordered.

Rashid sighed and let them flutter shut.

"All right, we need to do this gently. I don't want to blow up this snotty *boyar*'s—well, actually, who gives a shit if we do. Let's go."

29

NADEZHDA LAPTEVA

Zlatek blanketed a battlefield with his silence and the horror was profound.

—Codex of the Divine 44:867

Nadya slowly braided her hair. She wanted to make a good impression. She wasn't planning to speak to the Matriarch—she knew where that would leave her—but she *was* going to the cathedral to dig through the library, and she wanted to at least look nice as she snuck underneath the Church's noses.

It was like planning for a war where anyone could be the enemy and they could attack at any time, Katya had complained. But there were answers to be found in Komyazalov and Nadya intended to find them. She needed to figure out who the woman was that had given Kostya the pendant trapping Velyos and warned him about her. Gods, what would be different if she hadn't bled on that damn amulet? If she had seen out the mission to assassinate the king as she was supposed to?

But that plan had been thought up by a boy desperately search-ing for power, and even if she hadn't used Velyos' power, Mala-chiasz still would have had his way.

Though he wouldn't have had a reason to go to the one spot where killing a god would be possible without Nadya . . .

This was pointless. She needed to stop. She dropped her hands halfway through braiding her hair and tilted her head back.

She was missing something. There were too many pieces, too many variables. Where had Serefin gone? What had happened to him? All she knew was he was alive and Velyos was with him, which meant Serefin hadn't really succeeded at what he'd set out to do. Funny how they were all such miserable failures in their own ways.

They had sent out messages to the front—Katya using her strange, weak saints' power to speak to another *Voldah Gorovni*—but Serefin was nowhere to be found.

Nadya wondered if he had given up like he'd always clearly de-sired to. She had been present for his coronation and it had been the only glimmering second where she had thought that maybe he could be a king. Since, he'd only proven himself to be a boy who drank too much and ran away from his problems.

It would mean the war wouldn't end. No one in that damned court in Grazyk wanted that. They didn't care about the stripped land, death's hand at the front, the children that were sent to war and came home shattered—if they came home at all.

Nadya had expressed her worries to Katya, but she was as cava-lier as ever. She suspected the *tsarevna* was terrified by the thought of Serefin either dead or abdicating his throne. He was the only hope for a peace treaty.

A peace treaty he will never sign after what you did, Nadya thought, staring up at the high wooden ceiling. Listening to Marzenya had been a mistake. Stripping away blood magic had been a mistake. Even if they did find Serefin, it would only create more problems.

She knew the darkness the king of Tranavia hid. He and his brother were more alike than anyone realized. Serefin would turn to revenge far faster than he would sign a treaty after Nadya had harmed them so grievously.

Nadya lost her balance and wavered, her hip bumping into the dresser she stood in front of, knocking a hairbrush to the ground. She sighed heavily.

Besides, Serefin had surprised her before. Maybe he'd surprise her again. She missed that ridiculous boy. She regretted, so much, what she had done to him.

"The Tranavians deserved it." The voice jolted her, and it took her a moment to parse who she was hearing. Kazimiera. A goddess who had spoken to her very little even *before* everything.

Where have you been? Nadya asked.

"Around. Watching. Recording. The others were so mad at you. Then no one could reach you. Then the Death Goddess told us we weren't allowed to talk to you. That you had sinned and needed to be punished. That you were no longer holy, but that's silly. You always were and never were."

Nadya took a shaky step back and slowly sat down, closing her eyes. She had known that the first time the gods had stopped talking to her was because of that damn veil. It cut her access off, made all the more powerful by Malachiasz's careful, pointed refinement. He had never admitted using magic on her without her knowledge, but she knew he had.

But the rest . . . The forced isolation. She didn't want to believe that of Marzenya, even though she knew it was true. She could remember the cold touch of her goddess's fingers over her skin, the bruises that had bloomed, the cuts splitting open her flesh from being near her.

Never and always holy.

Because of what I am? Nadya asked.

"Of course," Kazimiera replied. *"I wrote it all down."*

The gods keep records?

"Not like you're thinking."

Do the Tranavians deserve this war, truly? What have they done that we have not returned in kind?

Kazimiera was quiet.

You don't control the country south of us. The gods are so fickle with their borders. Why not relinquish Tranavia completely and leave them to this fate they've chosen?

"There were wars," Kazimiera said. "Up here, not down there. Many of us died and did not return. So many lost. The west was ripped from us by other gods and no one wanted to see more people lost when Tranavia began dabbling in heresy."

Nadya frowned. So much of what she had learned suddenly lined up. That the gods may have been mortal once, long before mortal record. It explained why Akola had different gods, why Kalyazin had not turned its eyes to the west, though it might, one day.

What did you mean, both holy and not?

"Marzenya never told you?"

Marzenya never told me anything.

A knock at the door sounded, and Nadya shot to her feet, the connection snapping.

"Shit," she said quietly, patting her messy hair. She headed to the door.

Anna was on the other side. She stared, looking Nadya up and down. "Are you all right?"

"No. I mean, yes. Yes, I'm fine. Give me a minute?"

Nadya worked fast, braiding her hair and pinning it to the back of her head. She scrambled for her glove, tucking it underneath the sleeve of her dress. So much for presentable. She was rattled.

The gods spoke as if their deaths were common, but what had happened to Marzenya was a first. The gods killed *each other* but no mortal had ever . . .

Well, Malachiasz had been a god, hadn't he? A chaos god. Usually those were struck down by the other gods, but not this time.

"You have—" Anna reached out and rubbed at a spot on Nadya's cheek. "Sorry."

Nadya shot her a weary smile.

"Maybe wear a glove on your other hand, too? It's conspicuous and someone might ask."

"You think I should lie about it?" It would be lying by omission and Nadya could hardly believe her deeply pious priestess friend would encourage that kind of sin.

"Of course," Anna said, her voice low.

Nadya shook her head. "Two would be harder to explain. With one I can make up a story that will sound plausible enough."

Anna didn't look convinced, but only said, "Be careful."

"Annushka, it sounds suspiciously like you mistrust the Church."

Anna flushed. "It's strange here. Nothing like the monastery at all. I've missed you . . ." She fell silent with a distant frown.

They met up with Parijahan near the cathedral. She was bored and wanted to help, complaining Rashid and Ostyia spent all their time trying to figure out his magic. The Akolan girl was wearing a nondescript gray kaftan, Akolan in style but not enough to stand out.

Nadya would never forget the day she had seen the sprawling black cathedral in Grazyk, and a similar fear flooded her as Anna led her to the steps of this one.

It wasn't nearly as ominous as the one in Grazyk. It hadn't been defaced and half destroyed and painted black. This was, if anything, the opposite in every way. It towered, certainly, but the arches were squat and vibrant, colorful onion domes topping its highest points. Gold shone off some domes, while others were painted bright blues and reds that glowed in contrast to the red toned brick of the cathedral.

But there was something about it that made Nadya uneasy, that made her hand itch and her shoulder ache. That made her forehead hurt as if a headache were forming right between her eyes.

She paused and Anna cast her a worried glance over one shoulder.

"If I go in and the icons start weeping . . ." Nadya trailed off, unable to contemplate any further.

Anna's face paled. "Do you think that will happen?"

"If not now, it will within a few days," Parijahan said, answering for her with a grimace.

Anna grabbed Nadya's hand. "They won't know it's you. The world is falling apart."

"Katya knows it's me."

"And *Ona Delich'niya* won't tell the Matriarch, right?"

Nadya hesitated but nodded. She could trust Katya. She had to.

Anna's expression was scarily resolute. Nadya remembered when Anna's complete trust in her had frightened her. She'd thought it was because of her connection with the gods. For Kostya, the connection had played a larger role than she had realized, but with Anna, maybe it was just Nadya. Maybe she wanted to keep Nadya safe simply so Nadya was safe. She trusted *Nadya*.

Nadya had never thought she would get that kind of trust from a Kalyazi. Tears welled in her eyes.

"Naden'ka?"

"I'm fine." She scrubbed the back of her hand over her eyes. "Sorry. I'm fine. I'm ready."

She tugged out of Anna's grip and toward the church. Carvings of holy script lined the vast wooden doors. There were no statues of saints but plenty of mentions in the text carved into the stones. Nadya pushed open the doors and stepped inside.

As she passed the threshold, she was struck by the weight of something vast. A shifting. A click into place. Something groaning awake that had been still for a long time.

She hated this feeling, how normal it was becoming for her. She braced herself as divinity and magic and darkness crashed down onto her shoulders and all she could do was wait out the storm.

This church was old, older than the city, as old as the swamp Komyazalov was built on. This church was a stone altar, blood pooling in the cracks. This church was a dagger made of bone piercing flesh, wet with blood. This church was sacrifice and sanctity and darkness, violence, death.

Something slumbered beneath this church.

Something that stirred at Nadya's presence.

"Naden'ka?"

Anna's fingers slid through hers again, jolting her. She was standing in the foyer, staring at the high ceiling. Icons lined the walls, crowded so thick there was no space between them. So many saints. So many martyrs. So many dead. It was too colorful and too loud. Every inch of the interior was painted with icons and lined with gold. The colors were beautiful. They were agony.

"Give me a second," Nadya said, her voice strained. It was all so heavy. She was feeling something she never would have were she only a cleric. It was innate within her, calling down to the darkness. A well of churning water. A storm in girl's flesh.

She might get answers here, after all.

"What's happening?"

Nadya shook her head. Heard Anna's little gasp, surely meaning nothing good. She must control this; she heard footsteps on the tiled floor—she noted absently that they made a mosaic—and she had only moments before an acolyte asked if they needed help.

Anna's hands were on her shoulders, turning her away. Before she knew it, Anna had wrapped a scarf around her hair and was firmly tying a headband around her forehead. The temple rings on the band were heavy. She closed her eyes, something tearing through her, pain making her hiss through her teeth. Something inside *her* was changing.

"*Dozleyena,*" Anna said cheerfully. "My apologies, my friend has been in the forests a long time and has forgotten how civilized folk dress."

Nadya swallowed, opening her eyes. Anna squeezed her hand.

Her insides were twisting even as she turned to the boy. Five years or so younger than Nadya, he was approaching without caution. He had messy brown hair and dark eyes. He greeted Anna and asked her business, then blinked.

"Oh, apologies, Sister Vadimovna, I didn't recognize you. Do you need any help?" He glanced curiously at Nadya and Parijahan.

"No, thank you, Andrei, we're just going to the library."

He smiled. "Sister Belovicha was asking where you'd run off to, but I told her you were taking a walk in the forest. I know how you enjoy a walk."

Anna looked disconcerted, but then smiled, all relief. "Thank you for that, as well."

Nadya was glad they weren't going into the sanctuary. She wasn't sure she wanted to know what would happen there if the foyer was enough to turn her inside out.

Anna's hand was clammy against Nadya's, but she didn't let go as the boy turned and led them through an eastern corridor and into a vast library. Nadya let out a long breath, something unlatching from her heart. She had moved out of sight of whatever had her.

The library was enormous. Multiple levels with rickety ladders attaching them together and an ornate spiral staircase in the center that led up to the second level, housing books all the way to the vaulted ceiling.

"How do you even reach those?" Nadya asked Andrei. Books on questionable topics would definitely be found at unreachable heights.

"Ladders and hooks. I can help if you let me know what you're searching for!" he chirped.

Nadya opened her mouth but Anna replied before she was able.

"That's all right, Andrei! It's lineage work, very boring."

He looked disappointed. "Well, let me know if you need anything," he said before bounding away.

Nadya took in the room, overwhelmed. "Where do we start?"

Anna chewed on her lower lip. "By avoiding the head librarian and praying we come upon something quickly."

"Ah, just like home."

Anna grinned. For a moment, Nadya forgot that they were at the heart of Kalyazin and the world was falling down around them.

"Well," Parijahan said, staring wide-eyed, before heading for the stairs. "What I wouldn't give to have our reticent academic here."

"He would find what we're looking for in a matter of seconds and then be wildly condescending about it for months," Nadya replied. "We'll be fine without him. Just . . . look for apocrypha."

interlude iv

RASHID

KHAJOUTI

"I know a little of Akolan magic," Ostyia said, "but explain to me how it's manifested in your family line. Magic isn't generally hereditary, but it can be."

It was a difficult question, one Rashid was glad Ostyia asked after Parijahan had left to meet Nadya. The things she had been keeping from him weighed too heavy between them.

"Is it for you?"

She nodded. "A family business."

"My grandfather and uncle had magic. If my parents had it, I never knew."

"What did that mean for them, though?" Ostyia asked.

They were in Viktor's sitting room, and Rashid had Ostyia's spell book in his lap while she paced in front of the fireplace.

But he didn't really know what his uncle could do—he was gone before Rashid could know him. His grandfather had dealt in minor prophecies.

Ostyia made a frustrated sound. "That won't help us. Seer magic is easy to figure out. You'd be having weird dreams and it would be a matter of accessing them consciously. That's not what's going on. The flowers are *weird*. Can you manifest power?"

"I can manifest weird flowers."

She snorted softly. "It should be, well, there are many metaphors for how it can feel. A thread, a river, a song, a simple feeling of something *different* off in a cornered part of your brain. For people with power like, well, Malachiasz, it would be a storm. Do you have that?"

"What's it like for you?"

"A blade—sharp on all sides—and if I reach for it the wrong way, it can cut me. It's always there. Even now, the magic hasn't gone anywhere."

"If you had ignored it, what would have happened?"

"Repression is dangerous."

He shrugged, closing his eyes. The thread metaphor made the most sense, and there was something there that he had been avoiding. A place within himself he'd always forced away. He reached for it and pulled, feeling the bright spark of long ignored power.

When he opened his eyes, his breath caught. There was a pile of flowers in his lap. Ostyia's eyes narrowed. She leaned down and picked one up. It was red, the petals curling outward.

"I've never seen anything like this," she murmured. "I wonder . . ."

Ostyia spun a *szitelka* between her fingers. She unsheathed it in one fast motion and slashed her forearm. He didn't react, used to Tranavians openly cutting themselves for little reason. She fluidly dropped to the ground in front of him and held out her bleeding arm.

"Heal that."

"What?"

She lifted her eyebrows.

"Even I know how rare healing magic is."

"Incredibly so. Blood magic can't do it. From what I understand, there have only been a handful of Kalyazi clerics who have been healers. Magic can do strange and wonderful things, but there are tempers on it and healing is one of them."

Rashid laughed. "You can sidestep right into Kalyazi theology with that."

"It's all different ideologies explaining the same inexplicable conundrums. Nadya has used healing magic, yes?"

"Nadya can commune with the Kalyazi goddess of health, so yes. How do Tranavians handle wounds?"

"Medicine. Plants and science. How you would, yes? Nadya said you're the one patching everyone up in your mad little band."

He nodded. He had seen Nadya and Malachiasz survive impossible things and the only explanation he'd had was that their particular magics were keeping them alive against all odds. But if what Ostyia was suggesting was true, he might have had a hand in it.

"Blood magic is, well, messy. It's very easy for it to go sideways. We're destructive; we're not healers," she said with a slightly wistful smile.

"I feel like you and I are dancing around something."

"If you can heal this, you have something every one of these blasted countries wants," Ostyia said seriously. "And it would explain why Parijahan has been dancing around things, as well."

He inhaled sharply.

"And it might mean you can do a whole lot more."

But it didn't explain everything. "Nadya broke Malachiasz's jaw once and he was talking within hours."

"The Vultures heal remarkably fast. The Vultures are, for all intents and purposes, indestructible."

"Why hasn't Tranavia figured out that magic for everyone then?"

She stared. "We have. It's the Vultures. It's what's done to them that makes them that way."

Oh. The torture. Metal and bone. Skin and salt and darkness. Malachiasz never talked about it except obliquely; had claimed he couldn't remember in a way that suggested every torment at the hands of his cult was always vividly present.

He slowly reached over, taking her pale forearm in his hands. He glanced up. Her eye was trained very intently on his face. He reached into that dormant, slumbering part of himself and yanked. His hands grew hot and he carefully placed one over the cut. A small, black flower sprouted between his fingertips.

When he pulled his hand away, the cut was healed.

Ostyia let out a short laugh. "Rashid, I think we have a lot more to figure out."

He nodded. "You know something?"

"Hm?" They were both staring at her healed forearm with the same kind of hopeless awe.

"This is much better than discovering that I'm very good at, I don't know, blowing people up."

She looked up at him sadly. "But all the more dangerous for you."

30

NADEZHDA
LAPTEVA

*Peloyin ruled the gods with a hand that was not
benevolent.*

—The Books of Innokentiy

It wasn't an *entirely* useless venture, the library. Now Nadya
had more names of more old gods to worry about: Rohzlav,
Nyrokosha, Valyashreva, Morokosh, and Chyrnog. A delightful prospect, to know that even stopping one might mean
there were merely more on the horizon. That they were
considered the purest of the gods. The oldest. A few thrown
out during the last divine war. Some buried under the earth,
bound in chains, waiting to be set free. Some killed, but, as
Nadya read, nothing divine stays dead for long.

They returned to the palace, finding Katya, who extricated herself from a pack of *boyar* when they stumbled
upon her in a wide hall and promptly ferried them into
her rooms. Her dogs were fast at her heels. She looked ill

and had a piece of paper clutched in her hand that she thrust at Nadya.

Nadya took it, her heart falling as she read. It was a long and angry screed about *her*. Again, how Kalyazin could no longer look to their clerics to save them. That she was in bed with the Vultures— her face heated—and only ever a false cleric.

A mad girl hearing the voices of devils, not our gods. A girl, deluded and broken.

A screed to turn to the Church, the only thing that would save them. That the heretics were being fought back but would return in their murderous quest for Kalyazi blood.

"What is it?" Anna asked. Nadya shifted the paper slightly so Anna could read. She paled. *"Nadya."*

"I know," Nadya snapped.

"It has the Church's seal on it," Katya said flatly.

"I know. How did they find out about him?" Nadya asked.

Katya shrugged. "You were traveling openly through Kalyazin. Didn't you stop at a monastery?"

Nadya felt the blood drain from her face. "And that's it?"

Katya chewed on her lip. "Together with everything else, yes. I've been accosted by too many *boyar*, here from their territories because of what's happening out there."

The monster attacks, the strange things happening with religious iconography, it was all going to spiral steadily into chaos until the final arresting moment when Chyrnog struck.

Nadya blinked back tears. She could feel the dark thing from before pushing at her thoughts. Maybe the propaganda was right.

Just a girl who talks with monsters.

What dwelled here, beneath the city, that recognized her? What dwelled in the swamps?

"You didn't know about these?" Parijahan asked Anna.

Anna shook her head vehemently. "I knew the Church had sent out edicts. And I—I knew there were whispers about the cleric, but—Nadya, please."

Nadya sat down heavily. All her irrational fears had come horribly true.

"A few *boyar* brought me others. As well as my father's favorite pet, a holy man named Dimitry." Distaste colored her voice. "They've been circulating for a while now," Katya said softly. "They want someone to blame."

There was a knock at the door and Katya called for them to enter. A servant came in, handing Katya a slip of paper. A slow smile broke across her face as she read.

"Go find Viktor Artamonov. Tell him I need to speak to the girl with one eye, then send her to the eastern courtyard."

Nadya perked up at that.

Katya clapped her hands together. "New crisis! We've got to hide a king before word gets out and I've got a real mess on my hands." Abruptly she got up and left the room.

Silence stretched out, Nadya, Parijahan, and Anna staring at each other in shock.

"What?" Nadya said incredulously, her mind reeling. "Katya, *what*?" She ran after her.

Katya walked swiftly through the palace and into a wing that Nadya hadn't seen yet. She would get lost if she didn't keep up. Eventually they spilled out into a back courtyard inaccessible from the outside.

A small company of Kalyazi soldiers waited there. Among them Nadya recognized Milomir.

It was deeply weird, to be *searching* for him. After what he'd done, after everything. But nevertheless, she pressed past the others to where the king of Tranavia stood.

It had only been a few months, but the gashes on his face had healed to scars and were more plentiful, and he wore an eye patch. His brown hair was tied back, making him look more like Malachiasz than Nadya remembered. It was silly they hadn't known they were brothers. The two had the same knife-sharp cheekbones and ice-pale eyes—though Serefin's single eye was a dark pupilless blue now. He tensed when he saw her, hand reaching reflexively for a spell book he didn't have.

Before she realized what she was doing, she slammed into him. He let out a startled breath before he laughed, returning the embrace.

"I didn't know we were friends like this," Serefin said.

She buried her face against the furs on his collar. She hadn't either, frankly. But she couldn't fault him for what had happened on that mountain. "You're an idiot."

"True." She felt him kiss the side of her head.

"I didn't realize we were friends like this," Nadya said wryly.

"Nadya, I can't stand you." He was quiet before murmuring, "I'm sorry."

Her arms tightened around his neck. Then she leaned back, taking his face between her hands. She ran her thumb down a scar the length of his face and touched the eye patch.

"It's bad, huh?" he asked.

"What happened?" The scars on his face were uncomfortably spaced, like they were made with human fingernails.

"I got Chyrnog out."

It hit her all at once that he wasn't wearing the eye patch because of his notoriously bad vision. "Oh," she whispered.

He shrugged. "It wasn't doing much for me anyway."

She glanced over her shoulder at Katya. "I have a good sense of who's responsible for you being here."

"The one and only. I'm hoping to make an escape attempt before her father knows. Do you think it will work?"

"I love the thought of the king of Tranavia bolting in the night to avoid an uncomfortable meeting."

"That was the exact reason I left Tranavia, what are you talking about? I want to discuss *terms* and *treaties* and it will be awful."

Something grasped Nadya's insides. "Really?"

Serefin was eyeing the activity around them as the soldiers started to disperse. "Hm?"

"Serefin, a peace treaty?"

He hesitated. "If he'll agree. I'm led to believe he won't. And it could take . . . years for it to be finalized."

"But you're going to try?" She grabbed his hand fiercely.

He lifted his eyebrows at her. She didn't drop his hand.

"I'm going to try."

She threw her arms around him.

"All right, you've expended your quota. Enough with the hugs," he said with a laugh.

"You like it. You like anyone who'll remind you that you're just Serefin."

He went very still against her before hugging her back. Warm and tight and earnest.

"I still can't stand you."

"The feeling is mutual."

He stepped back, finally meeting Katya's gaze. "You," he said.

"Me!" She grinned. She turned to Milomir. "How did you get into the city?"

"Covertly," Milomir assured her. "I don't think we were seen, but there are no guarantees."

"No, we should assume someone saw, it's safer that way. There's no real way to keep this from getting out."

"Serefin!"

Serefin was promptly bowled over by a short girl with a bad haircut.

"Blood and bone, your *face*!" Ostyia said, her arms around Serefin's neck.

Serefin's expression wearied briefly, but he grinned, hugging her. "I was so worried."

"About me?" Ostyia asked.

"Shut up."

She left him to throw herself at Kacper, also knocking him over. Nadya eyed a wiry boy with black hair and a twitchy look to him, still under guard.

"Who's he?" she asked Milomir.

He shifted uncomfortably. "It's hard to explain. Also," he glanced at Serefin, "we had the brother, but lost him."

"*What?*" Katya's voice cracked hard over the single word.

Nadya's vision tunneled and she wavered on her feet, dizzy. She'd *known*, but she'd convinced herself it wasn't true.

"You weren't supposed to tell her that!" Serefin complained.

Milomir scowled. Katya's fist was clenched so hard her knuckles were white.

"I thought you killed him," she ground out through her teeth.

"I did."

One eyebrow arched.

Serefin almost seemed to smile. "He's resilient. Runs in the family."

It struck Nadya very suddenly, what had happened, what she had been missing. She closed her eyes. The conversation continued on around her. When she opened them, Serefin was watching.

"Chyrnog," she said softly.

Katya let out a disbelieving huff. "That's *impossible*."

Serefin frowned and pointed at the slash of scar tissue around his neck.

Katya conceded the point with a sigh. They couldn't really act like the gods weren't willing to claim Tranavians.

"We need to figure out what to do with them," Milomir said quietly to Katya.

"My father isn't in the city, so we have some time."

Serefin sighed, looking very put out. He glanced at Nadya after Katya pulled Milomir away to discuss the other prisoner.

"I was going to tell you," he said softly.

"I knew," she replied. "I thought I was imagining it but . . . I knew."

"You sound unsure."

"I *am* unsure."

He nodded. "Explains your greeting, though. I was *certain* you were going to stab me."

"Was . . . how is . . ." No, she couldn't do this. There had to be an end, it had to be over.

Serefin eyed her, clearly debating his answer. "He's not well, but he's alive."

That had to be enough. She couldn't ask for more.

"How do *you* feel about it?" she asked.

Serefin looked thoughtful. Something about him had changed. She saw a king standing before her, the weariness of lifetimes on his shoulders. A conscious choice had been made to stop running.

"I'm relieved," he said simply. "Chyrnog was in control when it happened, and the regret would have killed me."

She tilted her head, curious. His gaze strayed to Katya and his expression shifted.

"We can talk later, best not discuss him around the *tsarevna*. I didn't want her to know he was alive but hopefully her attention can be diverted. We have enough to worry about as it is."

Nadya agreed. She met Anna's gaze from where she stood across the courtyard looking dazed. Nadya let out a breath and turned to Serefin. One of his scars tugged his lips into a permanent sneer. It fit the picture she'd had of the bloodthirsty prince. It didn't fit the boy she actually knew.

"You should be upset with me," she said.

His hand strayed to his empty waist again. "I should, yes."

"Are you?"

"Are you asking if I'm waiting to put a blade in *your* heart?"

"More or less."

Serefin shrugged. "I should."

"You should."

"Was that your intent all along? To destroy Tranavia like this?"

"No." She had meant to strike a blow, yes. If she had known what Marzenya was planning, would she have done it, still? She liked to think she wouldn't have, if only because she knew the true ramifications of taking away blood magic. Their magic used in everyday life wasn't harming anyone, and without it, they might not survive. It was no longer as simple as ending a war.

"Why should I believe you, when you've lied to me for as long as you have?"

"Why should I believe that you didn't intend to kill your brother?"

Serefin grinned. "Now there's a conundrum."

"I don't think we can trade atrocities and call it even," Nadya said dubiously.

"No? Well, of course I'm mad at you. And now you have to work with me to stop this before we don't have countries left to bicker with each other. Your punishment is dealing with *me*."

Truly, that would be a trial. Nadya nodded slowly. "Another thing."

Serefin lifted an eyebrow.

Nadya glanced over her shoulder. Anna was staring at Serefin, her face chalky and pale. Serefin followed Nadya's gaze, his expression faltering. She didn't expect him to recognize Anna from the day he attacked the monastery. She couldn't remember the faces she had struck down in battle, as much as they probably deserved it.

"I grew up with her," she said, her voice soft. "She was there, that day, she was with me in the tunnels."

"Ah," Serefin said tonelessly.

Nadya did not expect Serefin to step past her and approach Anna. The priestess froze, eyes widening as she readied to bolt.

She followed Serefin, watching as he inclined his head to Anna, a bow no king should make, and said something very soft that she couldn't quite catch.

Anna's expression cleared some. "That doesn't fix anything," she snapped.

"No," Serefin said. "There's no fixing anything that has happened on the battlefield. All we have is what we choose moving forward, and I am weary of war."

Katya turned from where she was talking with Milomir, looking Serefin over appraisingly.

"Nothing I say will bring back the lives I've taken," Serefin continued. "But I was dragged across this entire country by your cleric and your *tsarevna* and . . . whatever he is," he said, waving at Milomir, who made an affronted noise, "and all I saw was a country as tired and broken as my own. As seeded with monsters, as ravaged. You don't have to forgive me, I don't expect that, but I wanted to extend all I have to give at this point."

Nadya exchanged a glance with Katya, whose eyebrows were raised. She was clearly thinking the same thing. When had the drunkard princeling decided to become a king? Maybe when he realized, like the rest of them, that they were fighting a war that none of them believed in anymore.

Nadya had spent so long fighting for a cause that had given her nothing in the end. The choice she made on the mountaintop had been the wrong one, and she could only hope it could turn things toward some kind of healing in the future.

But that likely wasn't meant to be.

It was early afternoon, yet the sky had begun to grow viciously dark around them. Nadya frowned. Serefin turned, meeting Kacper's gaze. He looked just as bewildered.

"Serefin?" Nadya said idly as dark acrid clouds roiled above them, a slow build until it became clear they were going to blot out the sky.

"Hm?"

"What did you bring with you?"

"Well, that's the thing. I don't know anymore," he replied. He took a metal disc out, turning it in his fingers. "Huh, not him, though he's not as far away as I expected. This is something else." Milomir made a strangled sound and Serefin held the disc close to his chest.

Nadya tried to pretend she didn't know who he was talking about.

Katya swore loudly. "*Vashny Koroshvik,* I hate you."

Serefin grinned at her. "I wish this was my fault!" He dropped his pack and pulled his spell book out, holding out his other hand to Nadya.

She frowned dubiously but handed him a *voryen,* ignoring Katya's protests. Serefin sliced the back of his forearm and bled onto his open spell book.

Nothing happened.

"In case you were concerned," he said.

Kacper rolled his eyes.

Serefin turned to the dark-haired boy. "Is this you?"

"Your brother took my ring," he snapped, but the way he watched the sky gave Nadya pause.

"Oh, so he did. Can you survive another claw to the chest without it?"

The boy's hand ghosted over his chest, his face paling.

"Then, Rusya—"

"Don't call me that."

"—I suggest you help us however you can."

Thunder cracked ominously and with it something pierced directly down Nadya's spine.

"Ah, damn," she said tonelessly. "Serefin, if we're friends now, could you do me a favor?"

"Depends on the favor," Serefin replied. "Don't know if we're friends like that."

"Fair. Well, I'm about to pass out. Don't let me break my head on the cobblestones."

"Oh, I can manage that."

31

MALACHIASZ
CZECHOWICZ

*So close, so close. All it would take is a few more bites, a
few steps closer to ascension, I can feel it, I can taste it.*
—Fragment of a journal entry from
an anonymous worshipper of Chyrnog

"You think it will be as easy as that?"

Malachiasz faltered, tripping and landing hard in the
dirt. He hadn't been walking long; he needed to be careful
this far into Kalyazin.

He spat out a mouthful of dirt and dragged himself up,
smiling through the grit. Chyrnog was anxious because
Malachiasz had something. It was impossible, too big too
much too hard to put the pieces back together, but he had
something. The four, the book, what he would need to bind
Chyrnog back into the earth.

It was dark. It had to be, he couldn't stand the light.
Destroy the sun and the pain will end. The thought was sly
and insidious and very much his. Or not? He and Chyrnog

would be the same, one day. Shape the world instead of changing for it. How many times had this world beaten him into an image that fit its shape better? Why should he submit again when this was his chance to finally take everything he had been working toward for himself? Why save a world that deserved to burn? Or, in this case, fade painfully into cold dark nothingness.

He was at the edges of a forest, a frozen river at his side. His breath ghosted out before him in the freezing air, his fingers stiff beneath thin gloves. His hunger had him in an iron grip, tugging in a direction he did not wish to go.

"You think I can do nothing without you? Boy, do not overestimate your importance. I am not the god you ended. Do not think I have not already started what will cause your downfall if you fight."

Anything can be killed, Malachiasz returned. *I killed death.*

"Marzenya wished to have what I have."

Panic fluttered in Malachiasz's chest.

"How long can you ignore your hunger, child? How long can you pretend it's not eating you from the inside out?"

Malachiasz swallowed, mouth flooding with saliva. No. Not this again.

"You make it so easy. Your fighting is a game. You yearn to know what would happen if you kept going, pushed farther, let go."

No.

"You lie so easily. A lie all the same."

Malachiasz coughed, choking on blood. He spat. Wiped it from his eyes and nose. There was nothing he could do as his control slipped away and chaos took over.

He wasn't always conscious when this happened. Usually he hid until it was over and then investigated the damage he had wrought. This time was different. Chyrnog wanted him to bear witness, to see what he was, what he would do underneath the god's sway.

He couldn't close his eyes against it. He couldn't stop it.

There was a village nearby, someone awakened. Not a soldier, not a cultist, not someone who had chosen this life of horrors. Someone who had simply woken up at the end of the world and discovered something had changed. Someone who had never touched magic, and only ever heard the fables of saints.

Once upon a time, Svoyatovi Igor slew a dragon with three heads and stole its scales to make armor that could not be broken by spear or sword.

Delizvik dela Svoyatova Kataryn threaded the stars through her hair and danced in the woods and kissed a god.

Delizvik dela.

Once upon a time, magic was a thing nestled under the roots of trees and in the sky and it could be taken so easily as whispering a prayer.

How did he know this?

He shouldn't know this.

Nadya leaning her head against his shoulder and reading fanciful stories of the saints aloud to keep the darkness of the forest at bay. Her voice gentle and rhythmic, the ice in it melted in the warmth of the fire. Somehow, the stories had remained.

Once upon a time, there was a boy who had helped break magic free from its prison. But with it, entropy had escaped. And one would devour the other until only darkness was left.

The end.

That was why the Kalyazi had hidden their magic away, kept it sacred, safe. Worried so deeply when their neighbors pressed too far. Let worry turn fear to hatred to war. They knew what could happen. Would Tranavia have pressed so far without the war? He didn't know. But Malachiasz had seen the way the war dictated the use of magic. In the darkness of the Salt Mines. In the salt poured down his throat, the iron in his bones, the blood, the blood, the blood.

It was too late to stop.

And here, there was a woman, alone. She lived apart from her village. There had always been whispers of witchcraft, but nothing that required an inquisition. Malachiasz tried to stop himself, so desperately, but he had no control, he had nothing.

"You fight as if you care," Chyrnog noted. *"You fight as if you haven't slaughtered thousands of innocents."*

Malachiasz couldn't argue. He knew what he had done. But that was different, this was different.

No, it wasn't.

But he didn't have a choice and he couldn't look away. As much as he wanted quiet oblivion and to forget the promise of her blood in his mouth, the screams and the thrill of power, in the end what got him was the singing. It was constant and needling, burrowing deep into his bones until he wanted to scratch off his skin to dig it out. And so, he gave in.

There was something in their blood that thrummed against Malachiasz's skin and he wanted more, so much more than would ever sate him. What could he do if he let go? Where would this end?

In darkness at the end of everything. He knew those answers.

How long would Chyrnog only set him on random innocents? How long until he was set on . . .

Serefin, godstouched and powerful. How long until Chyrnog decided he wanted that strange power of stars and moths and forests that Serefin quietly maintained? Serefin had fought the god off in a way Malachiasz could not. How long until Chyrnog wanted revenge?

At least Nadya was gone. That was one particular horror he would never have to face.

He still couldn't wake up. He couldn't come back. He sat in a pool of blood on the dirt floor of the woman's tiny hut and he listened to the voices in the distance as the village was awoken by the sound of her screaming.

SEREFIN

MELESKI

Serefin caught Nadya as she fell. She was too light, like her bones were made of air. He let out a breath, casting another glance up at the darkening sky.

"Well, *tsarevna*?" he asked.

Katya's face was pale. "I—I know this feeling."

Serefin did, too. He spat a mouthful of blood over his shoulder. It was like the air was pressurized. There was so much magic in the air, he could taste it.

"They wouldn't dare," she whispered.

Serefin adjusted Nadya in his arms. Her eyes fluttered wildly underneath thin lids. Suddenly her whole body stiffened.

"Shit," Serefin said, dropping to one knee and gently resting Nadya on the stones of the courtyard. Kacper was fast at his side.

"This is not unlike what happened with you," Kacper said.

"Yes, but Nadya's supposed to be able to handle all this divine nonsense," Serefin replied.

The Kalyazi girl knelt down by Nadya, looking distraught. Parijahan whispered something to Katya before taking off out of the courtyard.

"Call Eugeni," Katya barked to Milomir. "I have no idea how many soldiers we have in the city, but I want them ready. Is Danulka around, or any of my order? I need them, all of them."

Serefin rested Nadya's head in his lap so she wouldn't hurt herself.

"Serefin?" Katya snapped.

"I'm busy," he replied. Katya wrenched his head to the side and crouched next to him.

"Can I trust you?"

He stared at her for a heartbeat before looking to the sky. "Katya, darling, I'm not going to use your distraction by our impending demise as a chance to take over your capital, if that's what you're asking."

"That's exactly what I'm asking. Did you order this?"

"I didn't. I don't think he did either, but I—I don't know."

"You trust him that much?"

Serefin hesitated. He shouldn't trust him at all. But he genuinely believed this was not Malachiasz. "I do."

Katya glanced at Nadya, her face paling. "What is she?"

The strange stain on Nadya's hand had spread, swirling across her collarbone and up the side of her face. An eye opened at her forehead, then her eyes popped open, milky white and unseeing. Her spine arched as her body convulsed.

"I have no idea," he murmured. "But she's the best chance we have."

Her and Malachiasz, he added silently.

Katya hesitated for another moment before she ran off.

Serefin exchanged a glance with Kacper. Once, this would have been the opportunity of a lifetime. The Kalyazi had left the three most powerful Tranavians in the courtyard of their palace, unguarded.

But they no longer had magic, and all Serefin wanted to do was keep Nadya safe and survive the disaster about to strike.

"It's the Vultures, isn't it?" Ostyia asked, sounding uncertain.

Serefin grimaced, nodding.

"But . . ." Ostyia trailed off.

"Malachiasz said he could get control back, but he had to be in Tranavia to do it," Kacper said, voice low. "And he's not here. That means this is about something else."

Serefin looked over at him. "Ruminski." He hesitated. Ruslan was still staring at the sky, rapturous. Serefin jerked his chin toward him.

Kacper scowled.

Nadya's skin was hot to the touch. The moths around Serefin fluttered in a panicked frenzy, feeding off his anxiety. He hated feeling useless.

"Why?" Ostyia asked.

Serefin closed his eye. "Take one throne, then the other. Also, who's to say they don't know where I am? Two birds. One stone."

Ostyia swore.

"It could be simpler than that, but—" Serefin cut off as a choked scream broke through Nadya's clenched teeth.

"Has this been happening to her?" he asked Ostyia, who knelt across from him.

She shook her head. "Everything has been weird, off. She's been acting strange, but nothing like this."

He didn't know what being on that mountain would have done to someone like her. He glanced at Ostyia.

"Should I help her?"

Ostyia tilted her head. Anna let out a sharp breath. Serefin ignored the Kalyazi girl.

"You've been with them for months. I'm asking you."

"Serefin, yes, obviously. What kind of question is that?"

It was the kind that needed to be asked. No, he wasn't going to do something drastic while Katya wasn't there, and yes, he had been relieved to see Nadya, but she had still stripped Tranavia of blood magic, made them weak—he couldn't simply forget it.

But Ostyia had always been a little more bloodthirsty, and slower to forgive, than him. If Kacper was his voice of reason, Ostyia was the one who pushed him. That she didn't think Nadya deserved this fate was a relief.

Serefin only had one idea and it wasn't a very good one. He cast out a handful of stars, plucking one out of the air. In one swift movement he pressed the white-hot light between her lips and hoped he wasn't making a mistake.

A crash sounded, terrifyingly close. Ostyia tensed, ready to fight.

"I'll be back," Kacper said, his lips brushing against Serefin's cheek.

"Wait." Serefin caught Kacper's sleeve, tugging him back and kissing him hard. "Where are you going?"

"I'll be useless against Vultures. I'm going to find Katya; I can help there."

Serefin nodded. "Be careful."

"Always am!" Kacper replied cheerfully before he took off.

Blood trickled from Nadya's eyes, but she'd stopped shaking. Serefin couldn't tell if that was a good sign. The fingers of her corrupted hand fluttered uselessly at her side.

Suddenly she coughed. Ostyia shot to her feet and away as Nadya rolled off Serefin's lap and retched. She sat up and leaned back on her heels, wiping blood off her face.

"Welcome back," Serefin said. "We're about to be slaughtered by Vultures."

Nadya laughed so hard she looked like she was going to have another fit. Ostyia exchanged a glance with Serefin. Nadya spat out a mouthful of blood and swore.

"There's an old god underneath the church," she said simply.

It took Serefin a moment to process that. "You, what—how do you know?"

The eye on her forehead had closed, but the strange, inky black was still swirled up her neck and jaw. "I spoke to her. Some things make sense now."

Serefin waited. Anna cleared her throat.

"The darkness in the old gods is in me, too."

32

NADEZHDA LAPTEVA

Without Alena there would be no warmth, there would be no light. There would only be Nyrokosha's realm and the suffocating dark.

—Codex of the Divine 835:99

How much longer could she run from the truth? Ignore the pieces she had been given by Pelageya, Marzenya, Malachiasz, Ljubica? Everyone telling her the exact same thing that she was too damn stubborn to listen to because it was impossible. Except it wasn't.

All she knew was that Nyrokosha, the elder goddess locked beneath Komyazalov's cathedral, had pulled her under. To whisper and prod and remind Nadya how she was different. To tell her that Nadya should be helping her, helping Chyrnog, helping the ones who only wished to not be caged.

How were they caged, though? Nadya hadn't had a chance to ask before Serefin yanked her back, but she'd left

knowing one thing with certainty: she was made from the same stuff as the imprisoned old gods.

"*Hold tight to your mortality, it's the one thing you do not want to lose,*" Ljubica reminded her brightly. The same words she'd spoken on top of the mountain and now Nadya understood *why.* Why it was so important, why so much could be lost if she fell.

"We don't really have time for that world-shattering revelation," Serefin said, staring at her. He picked up his *szitelki* from the ground and threaded it back onto his belt, standing. "Can you fight?"

She nodded. She had magic, if that's what he was asking.

"Should we," he paused, faltering, "keep this between us?"

Nadya glanced at Anna. "Katya definitely has suspicions, but I don't think they go this far."

Serefin pulled her to her feet. He rested a hand on her head, fingers pressing lightly into her hair. "Are you all right?" he asked carefully.

"Serefin, I don't know." She looked down at her hand, the skin fissured and *wrong.* She hated the not knowing.

The sky was unfathomably dark, and it was starting to rain blood. Of course it was blood. It was the end of the world and they had run out of time. Except . . . The end wouldn't be loud but quiet. The sun's soft death and a world embraced by darkness. That was what Chyrnog wanted. That was what Chyrnog would have. This wasn't him.

The boy—what had Serefin so mockingly called him? Rusya? Ruslan, then—was staring at Nadya with a curiosity that made her uncomfortable.

Nyrokosha's voice had been cool and gentle as it tore Nadya apart. Pulling her into pieces, discovering what they were, debating whether to put her back together. She had woken in front of a vast cathedral like the one that morning, but different, wrong. It was warped, like only some of it was there and other parts were somewhere else. Bodies were impaled on the points of domes, hanging from the edges, clinging to the grips of stone gargoyles. Something acrid grew between the stones.

She had been here before. Chyrnog's stone temple. The thousand hands, reaching. So small, insignificant, yet there was a feeling of kinship she could not shake off before the unnamable horror that could crush her so easily. An ocean of black water. She walked up the steps and through the door and found total and all-consuming darkness.

So, she stopped, waited, until there was a point of light to walk toward. She didn't want to know what she would find, but she pressed forward anyway. Until she found the churning well of blood and realized that all these pieces had meant something. Nothing worked in isolation. All the familiar, all the uncanny, it was connected. There was no stepping around it, and she knew better than to go into it, and so she waited some more, until the walls of the sanctuary melted around her, the icons turning into rivulets of blood that ran into the well, faster and deeper, until Nadya stood before a chasm with no end, lined with gold and splitting the sanctuary in two. Screams echoed from below, digging deep into her skull.

She stood at the edge of a prison for gods. After a heartbeat, she sat, kicking her feet out into the open air.

"There you are, daughter of death." The voice swelled up from the darkness, lighter than Nadya had expected, softer. *"You have been gone from me for so long."*

Nadya tilted her head.

"Who are you?" she asked.

"Nyrokosha. You know me. You've always known me. I have a thousand names and a thousand faces even as I am chained. You have spent a long time with Marzenya's hand shadowing your eyes, covering your mouth, your ears, so you would not see or hear or know. She was mine once, too. They were all mine, once. But she took another path and you hide from what you were born to be."

There had always been a question mark hanging over her, but it had never been one she had thought much about. She was one of many orphans, so it had seemed silly before, to wonder about her parents. But she couldn't help but think of them here. Where *had* she come from, really? Was this all random? Was she a product of chance and divinity, formed from pieces of different worlds, never fitting into any of them?

"You will let me out, child of darkness, daughter of death. You're chained by mortality, but you could break free. Embrace the divinity in your blood."

Nadya rested her fingertips against the golden floor that cracked off into nothing. Something skittered past. She froze, drawing her legs up as spiders began to race up the edges of the chasm, spewing over the top and into the church. None of them touched her, dashing close only to veer off at the last second. She hurried to her feet when she heard something else, something bigger, coming up from that endless darkness.

"It's what you were made for," Nyrokosha screamed, her voice suddenly losing its softness. *"Freeing me. Freeing all of us."*

Then Nadya was pulled back into the world where she stood beside the boy she had once planned to kill, the sky going black around them.

"Nadya?"

She realized Serefin had been trying to catch her attention for a while. He looked worried. Blood from the sky dripped down his face, matting in his hair.

Nadya tugged her *voryens* from her belt. She closed her eyes, calling on that well of dark water, the blackened core of her, the parts made to set old gods free. Could she resist them? How long did she have until they unmade her?

Flame shot down the edge of one blade, something black and poisonous dripped down the other. She opened her eyes and glanced at Anna.

"Go inside. Stay inside. Please, I can't lose you."

"I can fight," Anna snapped.

"Not against these." She lifted onto her toes and kissed Anna's forehead.

The other girl looked torn, but swiftly disappeared into the palace.

Nadya grinned at Serefin. "What are you waiting for?" she asked, before she took off, out of the courtyard and into the city. He followed, swearing behind her.

She pushed past people huddled in panicked clusters, snapping at them to go inside, go anywhere, why were they standing in *blood rain*, didn't they know what this meant?

Something pierced through her, a strike against her head, pain flared white hot behind her eyes. Oh. Not only the Vultures. There was a god.

She didn't know which. One of the fallen, presumably. Who had she not spoken to? Cvjetko, in his strange, nebulous position. She had never been told what he held power over.

"Oh, you didn't know?" Kazimiera chirped. *"He's the storm that comes in three. He's horrors and teeth. He's mortality's worst nightmare."*

Kaz, I gotta be honest. This is not helping.

Kazimiera laughed.

Would the Vultures really ally themselves with a god if Malachiasz was not there to guide them?

"The beasts of Tranavia are wounded, bloodthirsty. Their world is crumbling, and they lash out. Their king has died, and they cannot crown a new one, and they know not why. Not all are so angry, though. They don't all want this."

Żywia. If she was here . . . If Nadya could find her, they might have a chance. She ducked through alleys, through muddy streets made worse by the mess from the sky, searching. She was at the gates to the lower city when a form landed in front of her, hunched and lanky.

An iron mask covered the Vulture's entire face. Their claws were already out.

"You're very fast for someone who was unconscious not that long ago," Serefin said, sliding to a stop next to Nadya. Somewhere along the way he'd found a sword.

"I didn't know you knew how to fight with one of those," she returned, taking a step back as the Vulture advanced.

"Darling, I can fight with anything. I'm very good," he replied.

The Vultures appeared more intent on Serefin than her. What was going *on*?

The Vulture struck as another slammed into Serefin. Nadya immediately lost track of him as her focus narrowed to herself and the Vulture. She caught its strike with her *voryen,* landing her foot against its chest and shoving. She sliced her *voryens* across each other and magic flared, bursting out in a strange, acrid mess that splashed onto the Vulture, searing into the light armor it wore. The smell of burning flesh met her nostrils. She tried her hardest to tune out the screams, turning on another Vulture.

There were . . . a lot of them. Too many, and Serefin and Ostyia had no blood magic. The Vultures weren't using magic either, not like when Nadya had fought them in the past. They were relying on teeth and claws and some power that seemed to thread in between, whatever it was that had been tortured into them. Her back pressed against Serefin's as the Vultures knocked her into him.

"I'm going to be so put out if I die in *Komyazalov,*" Serefin said.

Before Nadya could respond something tore through the lines that were threatening to overwhelm them. There were two, neither wearing masks. Nadya recognized Żywia, but it took longer for her brain to put together who the second was.

Żaneta.

Serefin stared at her, narrowly avoiding death by impalement.

She looked so much better than when Nadya had seen her last. A monster, but not shattered. She shot them a sharp-toothed smile, winked at Serefin, then turned on the other Vultures.

"What's happening?" Serefin asked.

"Your old girlfriend is saving you."

"That bodes badly for me, I think," he said, sounding dazed.

Nadya snorted softly, shoving him toward a Vulture who was distracted by Żaneta.

It wasn't quick work. It was messy and bloody. There were more Vultures than Nadya thought were in the order, and they didn't have the magic that let them shift through physical blows. Hitting a Vulture in the throat with a *voryen* knocked them down like it would any mortal.

Nadya didn't think any Vultures were dead, but their crumpled bodies soon littered the ground. There was a moment of silence, a fleeting calm. Żywia turned to grin at Nadya, her white teeth like knives.

"I told them not to, but no one listens to me! The Black Vulture's Hand, still, but no one listens!" she said. Her tangles of black hair were tied back and coated with blood. Her onyx eyes slowly shifted to blue. She let out a breath, kneeling down next to an unconscious Vulture and checking their pulse. "Idiots. If Malachiasz were alive—"

"He is," Serefin said shortly.

Żywia's head shot up.

"How did you not know?" Serefin asked. "I thought you were connected?"

"That *bastard*," Żywia snapped, straightening. "I'm going to kill him. Is he here? He shut off the connection himself, then."

"No, he did die," Serefin said. "He said the threads were too weak when he came back."

Żywia shook her head in disbelief. "*Liar*. He didn't want us to know."

"He's not here," Serefin said. "But we have other problems to worry about."

"What about the god?" Nadya asked.

Żywia frowned. "What? No, the Vultures came for him." She nodded at Serefin.

Oh gods, she really didn't know.

"Cvjetko, he's here, somewhere."

"You can't fight a *god*," Serefin began, stopping when Nadya stared at him. "Listen."

"Serefin, really."

He was avoiding making eye contact with Żaneta, who appeared like she could be convinced quite easily into strangling him. Her wiry cloud of dark curls was limp and heavy with blood. She stepped closer. He tensed.

"*Czijow,*" he said, very, very quietly.

Żaneta clasped his head between her hands. "Bloody idiot, that's what you are."

"Yes."

She tilted his head back, wincing at the scar that ran along his throat. "I did that?"

"You shoved me down the stairs, actually, and *then* my throat was slit."

"I guess you got your revenge."

Serefin sighed. "That was not my choice, Żaneta."

"Too late for apologies," she said, but she tugged him closer and kissed his forehead. Her nose wrinkled. "Gross."

"I am covered in blood, why would you do that?"

"Ugh." She wiped at her mouth. "Nasty."

"I'm glad you're *you* again," he said softly. "I *am* sorry."

"This is wildly sentimental," Żywia interrupted. "Very cute."

Nadya turned to her. She pointed blankly to the road, which wound down over the vast bridge to the city beyond where a massive beast rampaged. A god in the flesh. She put her hand on Żywia's arm when she started to move.

"You should get out of here. There are *Voldah Gorovni* around."

Żywia shot her a grin. "And miss all the fun? Hardly."

33

MALACHIASZ CZECHOWICZ

Every head of Cvjetko is at odds with the other.
—The Books of Innokentiy

Chyrnog held Malachiasz in a grip so tight it felt as if his ribs were being crushed. He wanted to close his eyes. But instead he was forced to quietly wait as the village stirred, as the torches burning in the distance grew closer, as they prepared to face a monster.

Don't do this. Let him flee into the darkness and have that be the end of it.

"*Every death gives me strength,*" Chyrnog replied, sounding amused.

They're nothing. You get nothing from them.

"*Simple fool, I get everything.*"

I'm only one person. I can still be overpowered.

Chyrnog did not deign to respond. Because it didn't matter. However many they set after Malachiasz, it would never be enough. He was an army in and unto itself.

He was too dangerous to live.

This would destroy him. The blood and the rending and the devastation. But it didn't take long. They were mere mortals and Malachiasz was something so much more and so much worse. He didn't know how many he cut through in the darkness. For each that fell, there was another wielding a rusty scythe. They tried, valiantly, but they weren't enough. They would never be enough.

It was over before it truly began. Chyrnog let him go like a bored dog dropping a toy. He wanted to die. He needed to be stopped and he didn't know that he could stop himself. He wasn't strong enough.

This was his fault. So many things would not be shattered if only he had . . . stopped. Stopped when Izak asked for the power of a god. Stopped when he had run—the single moment where he had made the right choice.

He didn't know how he was supposed to break out of this. How he was supposed to find the fragments of his soul that he had bartered away.

His respite did not last. Panic bore down on his chest, so fast and heavy that it took him a moment to realize it wasn't his own. He filtered through the threads of magic he had flowing and realized it was one he hadn't drawn on in some time.

What were his Vultures doing?

What had they *done*?

They were closer than he would have guessed; he had traveled farther than he thought. He was very close to Komyazalov. His Vultures were in Komyazalov?

Damn. He worked his way to his feet. He was covered with blood and surrounded by corpses. He closed his eyes as dizziness threatened to overtake him. None of these people deserved this fate.

He needed to move, to stop his Vultures before they died on the walls of Komyazalov. He didn't know who was behind this—Rozá must have finally worked up the courage to fight against him. He'd kept his thread of power over them closed even as it had woken up alongside him. There was only so much he could focus on and Chyrnog was a more important issue.

Malachiasz reached for the threads that bound him to his Vultures. He'd told Serefin he needed to be in Tranavia to fix the fraying threads, and that was mostly true. In the Salt Mines his power over them would be at its highest, but desperation could force his hand to do great things. He threw his power into the threads and felt the trembles of those who had taken advantage of his absence.

He had to stop them. His Vultures were powerful, but this . . . whatever they were up against, was madness. But he was so tired. He wanted to sleep, only for a few minutes. Just a few. He lowered himself to the blood-slick floor of the hut and knew only darkness.

NADEZHDA

LAPTEVA

Nadya had to close her eyes against the crushing wave of *despair* that swept over her as she stood before the fallen god. The feeling of inevitability, of being so so small and utterly helpless. She took in a deep breath, Serefin close and Żywia at her side.

Żywia doubled over, holding her head. "Oh," she gasped. "Malachiasz is *angry.*"

Nadya swallowed her heart down from where it leapt into her throat. She had other things to worry about.

He had the look of a dragon, Cvejtko. *Well,* Nadya considered, *a dragon with three heads: a lion, a bear, and a wolf.* He was horrifying to behold, but in a different way than the other fallen gods. Her brain glanced away from true comprehension, but it wanted so badly to rationalize. A shivering of horror—a thousand eyes—then gone. A shiver of razor teeth and screaming, gaping mouths, then gone. She staggered under the weight of *knowing.*

Żywia shook off whatever Malachiasz was doing and slammed into the god, all teeth and claws and wild black hair.

What's the plan here? Nadya asked. *How did the Vultures convince you to come here?*

"Convince me?" Cvjetko sounded like three voices speaking at once. It was profoundly unsettling and immediately gave Nadya a headache. *"Convince me? Hardly. All I had to do was whisper, to nudge, to convince these beasts this was what they desired."*

Serefin cast her a concerned glance before he very gently put his hands on her shoulders and pressed her to the ground. He crouched in front of her. Here, in the shadows of a burning building, they were momentarily safe.

Serefin opened his mouth but Nadya put her hand over his lips. His expression wearied as she shushed him absently.

"Let me talk to him," she whispered.

"You don't have much time," Serefin said, staying with her. She almost told him to go. The Vultures who weren't trying to kill *him* would need his help. But he was solid and strong and his hands on her shoulders were a grounding weight she would need. She wanted him there.

Why come here? she asked. *What could we possibly have that's of use to someone like you?*

"Who are you, little bird?" One of Cvjetko's heads began searching for her.

She didn't even blink. He wasn't the first god who had used the nickname for her, he wouldn't be the last.

Daughter of darkness, daughter of death, she replied, suddenly realizing why the god was there. It was deceptively simple. *You want to free Nyrokosha.* It explained why the goddess had stirred, sensing freedom at hand. If Nadya wouldn't free her, someone else would.

"You are clever! How novel! You smell different than the others, why is that?"

How condescending.

She wasn't willing to set the goddess free. Not when they already had to stop Chyrnog. They couldn't survive both. Why was this fallen god concerned with the fate of an old god when the others weren't? Old alliances coming out to play?

She got to her feet. She needed to stop Cvjetko before he freed Nyrokosha. Serefin scrambled after her.

"What are you planning?"

"To kill a god," she said flatly.

"But—"

"Use a god to kill a god." Nadya plunged herself fully into the dark water.

SEREFIN

MELESKI

Serefin stumbled back as Nadya ripped away some shield over her power. She was practically incandescent with magic. Her eyes, already dark, went shadowy, and her skin threaded with power like molten iron.

Żaneta thudded to the ground next to him, eyeing the cleric as she spat out blood. Nadya held out a hand, a bundle of discarded spears coming to hover next to her.

"That girl almost won the *Rawalyk*," Żaneta observed blandly. "I suppose she would have made a visually impressive queen."

"Żaneta, I've missed you," Serefin replied.

"Ah, my idiot prince, I have not been conscious enough to miss you. Do we help?"

Cvjetko slammed a clawed paw down where Nadya was standing as she deftly stepped away, flicking her fingers and slamming a spear up into the hinge of his shoulder. The bear head roared. Serefin couldn't move past the feeling of utter helplessness. This would crush them all.

"I think we're more likely to get in her way." He saw Katya near-ing them and remembered her necklace of teeth. "Shift back," he said, voice low.

Żaneta cast him a sidelong glance. "What?"

"The *tsarevna* is a Vulture hunter."

Her eyes widened. Her claws were gone in the next instant, onyx eyes clearing to brown. Her teeth looked a little sharper than normal, but that could be explained away. She was Żaneta again, and though Katya would certainly know how a Tranavian got into her capital, Serefin hoped she would be distracted enough to let Żaneta go without notice.

The Vultures had been stopped by whatever Malachiasz had done, but this god, oh, this god was more than any of them were able to stop.

NADEZHDA

LAPTEVA

It was too much. It didn't matter that Nadya was a creature of strange divinity, that she harbored power stolen from so many sources. Malachiasz, Marzenya, Zvezdan, who else would she take from before she finally had enough?

I suppose I could steal from this one, she considered, the thought strangely idle as she narrowly avoided the sharp teeth of the wolf's jaws. Claws raked close to her flesh, each one large enough to tear her into pieces on its own.

She had walked the limits of her capabilities before. She could only press so far until she became no more than charred bones. She was still mortal.

"You could . . . not be, you know." So many voices were speaking up and she had no idea who this was.

She shoved a spear into Cvjetko's chest, rolling out of the way as a foot slammed down. Too close. She wasn't fast enough.

"It would be so easy to take and take until you left this behind. Until there was nothing left. You were made to be one of us. All you have to do is keep going. Take his power. See what you become."

Nadya had three spears left and there was so much blood pouring down Cvjetko's strange body. She struck again; another blow landed.

He batted her away like a gnat and she slammed into a building hard enough that something cracked, all the wind knocked out of her. She lay on the ground, frantic heartbeats passing where there was no air in her lungs. A beat, another, another.

"Pathetic. You could be so much more."

A gasping breath. She struggled to her feet, flinging out her power and finding the last two spears. Two more.

Cvjetko slammed her into the wall again. She was going to die. All that power and it would never be enough.

"All you have to do is reach a little further . . ."

She didn't want to die like this. She gave in, pressing harder—

And grasped both spears with her power, slamming them up into the jaws of the lion and the bear. Blood rained down from the beast and she could *feel* the magic escaping the god as he crumpled inward, a supernova, a dead star. She could feed on it, let it carry her out of this pain.

All she had to do was reach.

SEREFIN

MELESKI

As the death of a god yanked all the air away from the night, Serefin ran to pull a shivering Nadya away from the wreckage. Blood dripped from her mouth. Her eyes opened, pure white, her skin so hot he thought it was going to burn him.

Then she went limp.

Everything was quiet, eerie. Serefin's arms trembled as he held Nadya, because he didn't think they were going to make it. Because he was trying his very hardest to not take in the absolute devastation around them.

Żywia raked her hair back with a weary hand and turned toward where Serefin stood across the road. Or what was left of the road.

She stopped, her gaze meeting Serefin's, and his stomach dropped. Her eyes weren't seeing him, her expression lightly puzzled. The front of her shirt canted out in the strangest way, and Serefin realized the tip of a blade protruded from her chest.

"Wait," he said. He would have dropped Nadya if she hadn't woken up struggling. He set her on her feet, and she gasped.

"No!" She ran toward the Vulture girl as she fell.

The *tsarevna* stood behind her, face impassive. Serefin recognized the pale blade in her hands with intimate familiarity. He had forced it through his brother's chest.

Serefin's hand absently patted for the metal disc and nearly dropped it when his fingers burned. Malachiasz was *here*.

And Katya had killed his right hand.

34

MALACHIASZ CZECHOWICZ

He takes and he takes and I can feel myself unraveling and I'm so hungry, but the power he gives in return is worth the hunger. The ability to bypass every law of magic made by the gods is worth every piece of flesh he takes.

—Passage from the journal entry of
an anonymous worshipper of Chyrnog

When Żywia's thread snapped, a hundred thousand memories threatened to bury Malachiasz underneath their weight.

A scared young girl, crying, curled up next to him in the Salt Mines. Her name had been ripped from her, and when they went to give it back, it was gone. He had his name, but she couldn't find hers.

"Am I going to be a monster forever?" she'd whispered.

"No," he'd said while wrapping his shredded knee, trying to decide what wound to deal with after. "Choose your own name. Keep it for yourself and they can never take it away."

The girl who had stayed with him when the order deemed him useless.

The only one he'd trusted when he realized he was going to take down Łucja. That he was going to take the mantle and change everything.

She hadn't tried to convince him not to. She'd tilted her head, her black curls falling to one side as she regarded him with her dark blue eyes, before shrugging. *"It's your head she'll take, not mine."*

The Vultures liked to tease—torment them—because in another life they could have been mistaken for siblings, and for Malachiasz, that's what Żywia was.

What did Malachiasz have left?

Nothing and nothing and nothing.

He slammed into the wreckage, into the road where her body fell, knocking someone away. She was still breathing, shallow, pained, almost gone.

He *knew* the taste of power that seeped from the wound in her back and he was going to burn down this world until every relic that could do this to his Vultures was destroyed.

"Żyw," he whispered, barely managing to pull himself back enough to talk. He cradled her head, stroking the bloody hair away from her face.

Her eyes opened at the sound of his voice, hazy and confused. "Malachiasz? *Fuck.* You're a little late."

He touched her cheek where something wet had splashed. Oh, it was him, he was crying. Everything he'd ever had was being taken, piece by piece.

Someone reached out across from him, and he lashed out. He barely had control, and no one was going to touch Żywia.

Undeterred, a small hand, the skin stained and claws curling from the nail beds, lightly touched the bloodstained spot on Żywia's chest. Malachiasz frowned, looking up, and his world was shattered and remade in the same painful breath.

She was dead. He knew what he'd felt.

Her pale hair was stained to rust, and there was mud and more blood smeared across her face. He'd thought he would never see those warm brown eyes again. This couldn't be happening. This was Chyrnog. All of this was Chyrnog and he would wake up and be in that damned forest. None of this was real.

Żywia's breaths grew more labored. He couldn't lose her, not *her too.*

"Malachiasz," Nadya said. "I don't know if you can hear me . . . if you're *you*. Malachiasz, how do you kill a Vulture, truly?"

He couldn't tell *Nadya* that. Nadya was a cleric. The enemy.

"Cut off their head," he said, so quietly that she probably wouldn't hear him.

He heard a thoughtful sound, felt magic in the small space between them. Like a fire in the heart of a blizzard. An ocean of roiling, churning, dark water. Narrowing down, focusing to a singular point, one open wound.

Żywia stopped breathing.

"Wait," he said, strangled, gathering her in his arms. "Wait, Żyw—"

"*Let her go.*" Not aloud. Through the bond of magic created when she'd stolen his power. "*I make no promises. But . . .*"

He met Nadya's gaze. He couldn't find his way out of the chaos.

NADEZHDA

LAPTEVA

He was *alive*. He'd almost ripped out Nadya's throat before and now the only friend Malachiasz had ever had for so long was probably gone and his eyes were dark and so much of him swirled with chaos. If he lashed out again, she didn't know that she could fight it.

He'd killed her goddess.

But she'd killed a god, too.

And she didn't know what the feeling in her chest *was*. She thought her heart was going to beat so fast it might explode. Nadya couldn't tell if he recognized her. Recognized his name. If he had regressed so far back, there was no saving him.

Chyrnog had him. If she had any doubts, they were gone with a glance. Shivering chaos he could not control, entropic decay picking at his edges in the strangest way. It wasn't there when you looked straight at him, but Nadya could see it out the corner of her eye. There was a strange, jittery twitch to him. Eyes and eyes and mouths at his skin. His lower lip was shredded from his too-sharp teeth.

He tensed, prepared to strike, and froze. A spear point rested at the base of her neck. They were surrounded. Ever so slowly, his eyes began to clear, until they were pale blue, and swimming with tears.

"*Dozleyena*, Malachiasz," she whispered.

"*Nadya.*" There was so much in his voice that she did not understand. What had happened to him?

She had to fight to keep her hands still. She wanted to touch him. He was so close, and it had been so long, and she was so angry with him, but he was *alive,* and he was *here* and—

He was in Komyazalov.

They were going to die.

His gaze flicked over her shoulder, eyes narrowing.

"Well." Nadya didn't know that voice. An odd, puzzled expression flitted across Malachiasz's face. "No one informed me our *kovoishka* was in the city."

Nadya slowly leaned back on her heels, the spear point giving just enough to not impale her. Malachiasz reached toward her, fingers brushing her jaw. He winced as one of the spear points made its home in his flesh.

The spot he'd touched was on fire. She didn't move. Katya stood nearby, disappointment on her face.

"*I can't protect you when it comes to him,*" the *tsarevna* had warned her.

She hadn't thought it would really be an issue, frankly.

"Someone knows what happened here." The Matriarch. Magdalena. It had to be. "Though some of it is fairly obvious. *Dozleyena, Vashny Koroshvik.*"

Serefin was still here. *Shit.*

"But the rest, I'm not sure about." Magdalena moved closer, tipping the blade of a sword under Malachiasz's chin. "I have heard much of you, *Chelvyanik Sterevyani.*"

Nadya expected the curtain of the Black Vulture to fall over Malachiasz's expression, but it remained broken and vulnerable.

Magdalena eyed him before turning her attention to Nadya. "And what are you, truly? The cleric to save us, they all said, but I knew the truth. Your mother burned like the witch she was, and my only regret was I didn't kill her when we were children."

Wait.

What?

Malachiasz inched his hand forward until it was covering hers, fingers twining into the spaces. She couldn't—she didn't—this wasn't—

Nadya swallowed hard. For an instant, she regretted turning away from the power Cvjetko had left for her to take. She regretted clinging to her mortality. She didn't want to hear about the mother she had never known.

She bowed her head, the spear point digging into her skin. Gods, wouldn't it be easy. Take out the damned cleric and the Black Vulture in one fell swoop. Nadya held back the tears threatening to overtake her. She clutched Malachiasz's hand.

Magdalena made a disgusted sound. She started to bark out an order, but someone cleared their throat.

"Mother Fedoseyeva, please," Katya said, softer than normal. "Let me." She stepped closer to Malachiasz, shoving her fingers into his hair and wrenching his head back, ignoring the spear point that dug into his spine and his whimper of pain. "I've been waiting for the chance to pry his teeth out myself."

There was silence as the Matriarch deliberated. "Your father will return after hearing what has happened. You may keep them in your prisons until then." She considered further. "Take those Tranavians and the king as well. I don't want them causing any more trouble."

Distantly, Nadya heard Serefin's exasperated huff. She went cold as Malachiasz was torn away. Her eyes fluttered closed. Too much magic had swirled through her. He was alive and she was going to lose him again and there was nothing she could do.

35

SEREFIN
MELESKI

*The gods are greedy, they take and they fight and what
is left but for those in the world to suffer their mistakes.*
—The Books of Innokentiy

"We went from 'things could be worse, but we're managing'
to 'things literally could not be worse' in, what, four hours?
Five? Is that a new record for us?"

Serefin tipped over until his head was in Kacper's lap.
Kacper did not let that deter him from telling Serefin quite
concisely how screwed they were.

"Who was the terrifying church lady? It sounded like
she knew Nadya *and* her mother, which, I didn't realize we
even knew who Nadya's mother was."

"We don't," Ostyia said quietly.

"We don't! Great! Do we know anything?"

"Kacper," Serefin said.

"Because it seems to me like we've been thrown in the

314 EMILY A. DUNCAN

Komyazalov prisons and the *tsar* is coming back and we're all going to get our heads cut off!"

"Kacper, *shut up!*" Nadya groaned from somewhere nearby.

Well, at least they were in the same cell block. Easier to round them up for execution, he supposed. He sighed, fiddling with the patch over his eye. His head hurt.

"Don't mess with that," Ostyia said, gently pulling his hand away. "It's going to act up and you have to push through until you don't notice it."

He looked up at her. She smiled sadly at him.

"Sorry that we have this in common, now," she said.

"We match!" Serefin replied.

"Blood and bone, I missed you."

At least Kacper had calmed down enough to bide his time by rubbing his thumb in slow circles against the spot just behind Serefin's ear. The tiniest comfort. He sat up, sliding his hand behind Kacper's head, tugging him closer until their foreheads pressed together.

"I'm not letting us be executed in Komyazalov," he said, voice soft. "We can die literally anywhere else."

Kacper wheezed out an anxious laugh. Serefin kissed him, a gentle press of his mouth. It was hard to not keep going. To not kiss him harder, to let his desperation take over. He had to stay calm.

The longer they let Malachiasz rot in a cell with Chyrnog churning inside him, the more danger they were in. Serefin hoped Katya understood that. He trusted the *tsarevna* about as far as he could throw her—and she was very tall so he couldn't imagine it was far, honestly—but things would have been worse if that church leader had taken them. Katya had been manipulating the situation back into her control.

But Katya had killed Żywia, which was wildly unnecessary as she had been *helping them*. And—fuck.

Serefin stood up so fast that Kacper jumped. "Where's Żaneta?" he asked, trying to keep the panic from his voice and failing.

Kacper shot him a wounded look. Oh, no, he wasn't—he couldn't be—was he jealous? Did he think Serefin wanted the girl who had betrayed him? Who did he think he was, Nadya?

"Don't be silly," he murmured. "If the *tsarevna* got her hands on Żaneta, she's dead, and Ruminski would—"

"Don't you *dare* speak of my father."

Relief spread through Serefin.

"You're so bloody loud, shut up. Let me sleep until my execution, please."

"No one is getting executed," Serefin muttered.

Nadya and Ostyia made near identical noises of disbelief. He'd forgotten for a fleeting second that Ostyia had spent the past few months with Nadya. This was a nightmare.

The cell they were locked in was cramped. A heavy wooden door, one lone window cut into the center with bars over it. He could see another door across the hall. Nadya must be there. Żaneta's voice had carried from the same general direction. Where was Malachiasz?

"I doubt we're going to have useful conversation like this," Nadya said, sounding weary. "We have about ten minutes before the next guard rotation comes through and they tell us to shut up."

"That will sound familiar," Kacper said.

"Do we know where Malachiasz ended up?" he asked amiably.

"Oh, he's here," Nadya said, her voice gentle. "He's unconscious."

Serefin considered the space of the cells. "Be careful if he starts having seizures."

"Of course he does that now," Nadya muttered.

"Why didn't they separate us?" Kacper asked.

"Ostyia's dramatic paramour is trying to be helpful while she also betrays us," Nadya said.

"Nadya, I'm going to kill you," Ostyia said.

Ah, he'd wondered if that had progressed in his absence. He glanced at Ostyia and she shrugged.

"Please."

Nadya was right, though. Katya knew they couldn't remain trapped; they would run out of time.

"Everyone shut up." Katya threw open both cell doors in one impressively fluid motion. "No, you can't go anywhere. Yes, the Church wants the executions of, well, all of you. I am holding onto the situation by the barest tips of my fingers and my father will return in a matter of days."

Katya peered into the cell where Malachiasz was, his head in Nadya's lap where she sat with her back to the wall.

"Would this end if we killed him?" she asked Nadya.

"Chyrnog would find another vessel. We didn't try killing Serefin when Velyos had him, did we?"

"Velyos is harmless by comparison."

"That's rude."

Where have you been?

"You had the situation in hand. Cvjetko was never going to last long in this bold new world anyway."

Serefin moved into the doorway. Nadya's edges looked shivery and strange, like she wasn't totally in the same realm of reality.

"Are you all right?" he asked her.

She closed her eyes. "No. I want to know what the Matriarch was talking about."

"Magdalena's told everyone you're a heretic and a witch and going to be burned," Katya said. "And considering the display earlier, public opinion was easily swayed."

Nadya sighed.

"I have questions myself. What are you?"

"I don't know."

Katya tilted her head.

"I don't know," Nadya repeated.

"I can't shake the feeling that we need to be stopping *you* as well."

"Well, we're going to be executed," Serefin pointed out.

"Do you truly think I'm going to allow that?"

"Katya, it's very hard to tell if you want to help us or not. You didn't have to kill that Vulture."

Katya lifted her chin. "Yes. I did. I would kill him too at the first chance."

He sighed. There would be no cracking that layer of zealotry.

She rubbed a hand over her face. "I only have a few more minutes; I'm not supposed to be down here. Ugh, you all are the worst things that ever happened to me."

"Going to take that as a compliment." Ostyia smiled.

Katya shot her a *very* dry look.

"Stay calm. There must be a way out of this."

Serefin exchanged a glance with Nadya. What did she know that he didn't? Did she know about the awakened ones? About what Chyrnog wanted Malachiasz to do?

He straightened with alarm. "Move Malachiasz out of that cell."

Katya frowned. Nadya made a small noise, curling around Malachiasz protectively.

"No, Nadya, you don't want to be in that space with him if he wakes, he's not—" Footsteps echoed in the distance. "I can't explain, there's no time. Katya—"

"Already doing it," Katya said.

Kacper ducked out to help her haul one lanky blood mage farther down, Nadya protesting the whole way.

"Shut up and get back in your cells, I'll return soon." Katya slammed the doors closed and disappeared down the hall. A guard patrol came through moments later.

"What the *hell*, Serefin?" Nadya cried when they were gone.

"I don't know how to put it more elegantly than he'd *eat you*, Nadya."

There was a beat of silence.

"*What?*"

"Oh, so we're not talking like in a fun—"

"Żaneta, thank you for your contribution, but I'm going to have to ask you to not." Serefin rested his forehead against the wall. "He doesn't have control. Chyrnog has him, well, *consuming* beings with a lot of magic and you're almost definitely included."

"What about you?"

"I've been informed I am 'something else' and thus not yet on the menu."

Nadya sighed.

There was nothing more to do. Time passed. One day, less, more, who knew. Malachiasz woke up but only gave Serefin a few terse words before descending into silence. Serefin didn't press. He was allowed to mourn. He heard Nadya whispering to him, but he mostly ignored her, too.

"Is Katya waiting for her father?" Kacper muttered at one point, and the thought terrified Serefin.

But when soldiers came and took Nadya, Serefin realized something might have gone very wrong with Katya's plans.

interlude v

"You can't just lock me in my room and tell me I'm being a bad *tsarevna*," Katya said, frustrated.

"The Matriarch warned you not to go into the dungeons," Iryna said with the same calm indifference she did everything else.

There was no time for this. An entire city sector had been razed and they were still trying to determine how many lives had been lost. Throwing the king of Tranavia in a jail cell and planning his execution wasn't the thing to be doing.

"They were all *helping*," Katya argued.

"They brought the Vultures into our city," a low prince, Kirill Balakin, said. "That's an act of war."

Katya was surrounded by *boyar* and low nobility. She was going to scream. She whirled on Kirill. "We're at war with them already," she snapped. "What are we supposed to do?

Continued retaliation? Don't you think it's a *little weird* that the Vultures came to assassinate the Tranavian king?"

Made all the weirder by the Black Vulture showing up. Katya thought of the propaganda crumpled in her pocket and was so overwhelmed she was going to crumble into dust right there. She had to get her friends out before the Matriarch made her next move. And they *were* her friends, damn them. She didn't trust Nadya, and she had to be careful with Serefin because of who he was, and, well, Malachiasz didn't count because she hated him and wished he had remained dead, but she was aware that the truly pressing problems wouldn't remotely be fixed unless she had all three.

Her life had been so much easier when she had no friends.

A soft-spoken *nize'ravta tayzhirefta*, Zinaida Nekrasova, approached Katya. The general handed Katya a folded missive, her dark eyebrows arched. Judging by the seal, this was a military note. Katya scanned it quickly before pocketing, giving Zinaida a brief nod.

How had the Tranavians moved an army into Kalyazin when they had no blood magic? Something must have gone wrong at the front. Someone had become complacent. But Katya had no time to worry about it because there was talk of a pyre and she knew exactly who it was for.

She extricated herself from the group as elegantly as she could, fleeing the room. She found Anna in the halls.

"You," she said, grabbing the girl's arm. "Are you ready to commit grand disobedience against the Church?"

"No," Anna said. "Wait. Is Nadya all right?"

"She is not."

"Oh, then yes."

Katya couldn't help but laugh. She needed to find the Akolans. She could only hope they were still with Viktor.

"What was that? What happened?"

"We were attacked by a fallen god," Katya replied, "who was using Tranavia's Vultures to a dubious end. It rather seems as if they were trying to assassinate Serefin. It's all deeply convoluted. Nadya was a bit too forward, and now the Matriarch knows our dear friend is more monster than anything else. Adding insult to injury, the damn Black Vulture is back."

"Wait—Malachiasz?"

"You know him, too?"

Katya ducked around servants and *boyar,* never letting go of the priestess's arm.

"He gets around."

"Apparently."

She pushed through the guards at the palace gates, ignoring their protests. She wasn't supposed to leave. Did they think another fallen god was going to drop out of the sky? Hardly.

Gods, this was a mess. She hadn't anticipated things to go smoothly when she brought her pack of miserable disasters to Komyazalov, but this was worse than she'd expected. Before she had been confident that she could convince her father to hear Serefin out. Now she knew that would not be the case. Her father was too devout and trusted Magdalena far too much. While Katya had expected the Matriarch to be a slight point of difficulty, she hadn't expected an *enemy.* She should have. How many conversations had she had with Nadya about the things the Church had withheld? She had been honest about her worries and Katya had brushed her off.

Had they known this whole time what Nadya was? Magdalena certainly made it sound like they had. But how? She'd grown up a world away in a monastery.

Katya pounded on Viktor's door, pushing past a servant. Viktor stepped into the main hall, looking flustered.

"I don't have time," she said, holding up a hand. "Are the Akolans here?"

"Of course. Katya, love, what's going on?"

"A mess. Parj! I need your help!"

Parijahan poked her head out of the sitting room, followed by Rashid. Katya explained as quickly as she could. Parijahan had been in a different part of the city during the attack, she hadn't seen the hatred in the Matriarch's eyes. They *must* beat her to Nadya.

Parijahan's expression was wan. "I thought you had it handled!"

"Yes, well, not this time."

Noticing Anna hovering at a distance, Rashid waved. Anna's face broke out in a grin. Katya did not have time to consider that, either.

"We need to get them out and fast."

Parijahan glanced at Rashid, a slow smile flickering on her face. "Well," she said. "Ostyia and Rashid spent some time recently figuring out just what good Akolan magic can do."

What? Katya frowned.

"They're all together?" Rashid asked.

"In the same block, not the same room. We had to isolate the Black Vulture at the king's request."

"Malachiasz is here?"

"Why are we surprised?" Katya said wearily. "More importantly, you have magic? Do you want to be the distraction, then?" she asked Parijahan.

The Akolan girl grinned. "I would love to."

"I'll help," Anna said.

Katya looked to Rashid. "Let me raid Viktor's cabinets for the ingredients I'll need. I'm going with you."

He nodded, flipping a dagger between long brown fingers. He was entirely relaxed for someone who had unlocked his own magic that day.

"Well, then, time to make ourselves enemies of the Church."

36

NADEZHDA

LAPTEVA

Blood pooled at every point her hands touched.
—Anonymous account written
about Celestyna Privalova

Every part of Nadya was in agony and all she wanted was to hear Malachiasz's voice. Żaneta was in the other corner, eyes closed. Tentatively, Nadya tugged on the fragile thread of magic that bound her to him.

She felt him jolt.

You don't have to talk to me if you don't want to, she said. *I understand. I just . . .*

"Are you all right?"

Me? She almost laughed. *I have some broken ribs, I think. And apparently I'm mad and have never heard the gods. I've been better.*

"Nadezhda . . ."

She wished she could see him, touch him. She wished he was closer.

I'm sorry. About everything. I never got the chance to tell you. It was a mistake.

He was quiet. It wasn't hard to picture him sitting against the wall, head tilted back, cuticles picked at and bleeding.

"*When I woke up, I thought it would be better if you never knew I was alive. Better to let it have ended on the mountain.*"

She hugged herself tightly. His words dug into her heart. She deserved it.

"*And you're not mad, towy dżimyka. Any more than I am.*"

Not a comforting metric.

"*What we've done to each other isn't as simple as words can fix.*"

No, it's not.

It didn't feel real, talking to him. He was going to be ripped away again and she would return to that cold unfathomable blank of living past his death.

"*Nadya?*"

I'm here.

"*Don't go,*" he said, his voice sounding so very small. "*I'm scared. I don't think there's any way out of this. We've used up all our chances.*"

Her heart broke anew for the monster boy who had been beaten down by so much.

I've missed you.

"*Honestly, once I got past the frustration of being betrayed so thoroughly, I had to admit, I liked your style. It was very well done.*"

She couldn't tell if she was going to laugh or cry. *I learned from the best.*

"*That you did. I missed you too, towy dżimyka.*"

They were interrupted by the clank of her cell doors opening. She didn't have time to shut off the bond before she was roughly yanked out, Malachiasz's panic flashing through her. They knew where this would end.

She wasn't going to come back from this.

Nadya was dropped before the Matriarch in a new cell, a small, pathetic, broken girl.

The woman was younger than Nadya was expecting. In her forties, no older. Her hair was covered but a few strands had worked free, pale hair paired with dark eyes and eyebrows. A sick feeling settled deep in the pit of Nadya's stomach.

Magdalena crouched before her, tilting her chin up with cool fingers, appraising.

"There's no *time* for this," Nadya said, yanking her head away. "Chyrnog is free and Nyrokosha will be soon and we need to *stop it*. If you truly cared about Kalyazin you would help me."

Magdalena gave a harsh laugh. "But it's *your* mess. If only we had drowned you in the river like I suggested," she paused. "Your mother was my sister, you know. A priestess here, in Komyazalov. A *witch*. It was so much easier to root them out back then. Though you've made it easy to make your heresy known."

What?

"I have only ever done what the gods wished of me," Nadya said, failing to keep her voice steady at the lie. She had set off this dark chain of terror, and she knew it. But why didn't Magdalena want her to prevent what was to come?

"Half the city razed and abominations in the streets and you believe that you have done the gods' will? Oh child, the gods would not deign to speak to you. Look at the horrors you've wrought heeding the whispers of madness."

No. Nadya had spoken to Alena and Myesta and the oldest gods in their pantheon. She had stolen power from Zvezdan and Velyos. She had walked with Marzenya. She had fallen for a boy turned god. *She* was divine.

"We do not listen to a mad woman's ravings and call it divine doctrine," Magdalena said. "We burn out those who have committed heresy. You should know, Nadezhda, it was the one thing you were meant to do and failed at so utterly."

But that wasn't what the gods wanted. Marzenya had, sure. But as they'd slowly returned to her, she'd found the righteous fury against the Tranavians had tempered as the risk of Chyrnog grew greater. The gods acted in reflection.

"I knew you would never be what we would need to burn out the heretics," Magdalena continued. "My sister tried to run, to hide you. Her mistake was in returning after she left you at that monastery. But now you will die as you deserve, and the Church will hold the power it was always meant to have."

Nadya had known she would find no answers here, but the confirmation stung, regardless.

"You will destroy everything if you see that into reality," Nadya said.

"I don't need to listen to a girl who has thrown her lot in with the Vultures," Magdalena said, straightening. She opened the door of the cell, gesturing to the guards outside. "Is it ready?"

It was over.

"Wait! What was her name? My mother," Nadya asked.

Magdalena turned. She eyed Nadya for a long time. "Lilya," she finally said. "You look like her. Shame you fell for the dark like her, too."

Nadya *laughed*.

She was dragged out of the room, out of the palace, to a wide courtyard. They made quick work of it, she had to give them that. The pyre was ready to burn the heretic.

"One more question," she said after the guard had shoved her up onto the wooden dais to the cheers of a waiting crowd. "You have the Black Vulture, but you're burning me first?"

"We'll want to break him and show him off before we kill him. You, well, everyone saw what you're capable of. You need to be destroyed immediately."

Nadya's heart hammered in her throat. She couldn't die here. Desperately she rifled through the power she had as she was strapped against the wood, her hands tied behind her. Madgalena brushed her thumb against Nadya's forehead, coating her skin with some kind of oil. It felt like the ground was pulled out from underneath her.

Oh.

They had a way to neutralize her magic; cut off her access to the divine, to herself. She scrambled, reaching, but it was like trying to grasp water. It slipped through her fingers, gone.

She was going to die. Death would not be so kind twice.

Her vision tunneled as panic constricted her. She heard the hiss of a fire being lit. She heard the tinder dropped beneath her feet. Heat against her legs. Fear, finally grabbing her by the rib cage. She had run from so much, survived so much, only to have it end like this.

She would not let them see her cry. She would not let them see her break.

The flames licked at her boots, not quite hot enough to catch, but soon. She closed her eyes.

Something in the air shifted. She heard a rumbling from the crowd, a change in tone, the shift from furious bloodlust to something close to terror. Something shook the pyre, landing hard, and her eyes flew open.

"I've always wanted to rescue someone!" Malachiasz said cheerfully. "What a novel change of pace."

Roiling chaos and absolutely covered in blood. His eyes were murky; he was barely holding on to himself. He grinned at her, sharp-toothed, his expression flickering as the flames licked at his boots. He used one heavy black wing to beat at the fire, irritation crossing his features as a crossbow bolt slammed past both their faces. His claws slashed through the ropes binding her.

"Careful, someone might think you have a shred of decency," Nadya said, shaking. She couldn't feel her power. The hem of her skirt caught fire. Another crossbow bolt flew past, nearly grazing Malachiasz.

"The notion offends me. Shall we go? Be warned, this is going to hurt quite terribly."

He was going to shift them out with magic. *He can still do that?*

"I would rather die than be carried out of here."

"Well, I guess you'll die." He pulled her against him, and the press of his magic slammed down on top of her.

"Let her sleep. The world will wait a few hours more."

Nadya stirred at voices whispering too close. She thought she recognized one, but Malachiasz was dead. A dream, then.

"Will it? You would know, wouldn't you, how much time we truly have."

"It's not like that."

"Malachiasz—"

Wait. No. He was dead. And that was Serefin's voice, the one who had killed him.

"—is she in danger from you?"

A long beat of silence. "Not . . . yet."

"A reassuring pause."

"We'll talk in the morning when she's awake. Right now, we sleep."

She heard the door close. The bed she was on shifted slightly to one side.

"How much did you hear?" Cool fingers brushed the side of her face, tucking hair behind her ear.

She didn't open her eyes, reaching a hand to grasp at the impossibility whispering gently to her.

"I don't talk to ghosts," she mumbled.

He laughed softly. "No, that's probably wise."

She opened her eyes slowly, prepared for disappointment. But the chest her hand rested against was solid, and everything crashed back down on her at once. She was a monster. The Church wanted her head. Her *aunt* was the Matriarch and hated her. They were all going to die, and the world was going to end.

Malachiasz was alive.

She leaned up on her elbow, ignoring the incredible twinge of pain. She reached up to touch his face.

She had broken so much.

They had done so much to each other.

Maybe it *was* better if it all had ended on the mountain.

She let her hand fall.

"Don't push yourself. Your ribs are sprained, not broken, but it still won't be pleasant," he said helpfully. "And fire got your calf, but the burns are minor. Sorry, I was a little late there on the rescue."

He was a mess. His black hair was tangled and wild. He had truly the most impressive smudges of exhaustion under his pale eyes. She could tell he had very little control over the chaos that was his body. The eyes and mouths and horror. He looked like he'd been shattered into a million pieces, and the pieces had been put back together wrong.

He was beautiful.

"Malachiasz," she said breathlessly.

He shivered.

She didn't know what to say. She had a thousand things to tell him, but they all fled her mind at once.

"You look awful."

He swiped at his eyes, laughing, and Nadya reached out and took his wrist. The bones felt fragile under his skin. How was he so strong yet so breakable?

"Why does Serefin think you're going to hurt me?"

"I can't control myself. Chyrnog has everything."

This was all so impossible. That he was here, that she had survived the pyre. The notion that she was an enemy of the Church was crushing. Shakily, she worked her way to sitting—mildly delirious from the pain—patting the spot next to her. Malachiasz hesitated but shifted to sit at the edge of the bed, slowly moving farther in and sitting with his legs crossed.

It was dark outside and the room they were in was sparse. Only a bed with a chest at the foot and a small table to the side. A bundle of sage was nailed to the doorway. She could smell incense and found the censer on the table, burning faintly.

Nadya took his hand between hers. He was trembling. What did she even say?

"When you betrayed me, the first time, had you been planning it the whole while?"

A cluster of eyes opened at his throat. He was wearing a loose shirt, black, the ties at the neck undone and open, showing a fair amount of his pale chest. He had cleaned up a little but ash and blood still streaked his skin in places.

He let out a breathless laugh. "I . . . well, yes and no?"

She toyed with his fingers. His nails were destroyed, the skin around them red and angry.

"I didn't know what to do when we found you. I never—well—I mostly never lied to you. I didn't want to give Meleski the power he was asking for and I ran. When we met you, I knew you could be instrumental in turning it all back in my favor. But you were covered in blood and you were furious and all I could do was give you my name and come to the hopeless realization that you made me feel things I didn't think I could."

"But that wasn't enough to stop you."

"So little is."

She laughed at that.

"You turned it right back on me."

"Did you really not suspect it of me?"

He cocked his head. "I'll answer that, but did *you*?"

"I spent the entire time in Grazyk suspecting it and hoping I was wrong. You've always been too good to be true. Too kind, too gentle, too beautiful. And I've been trying to figure out a world I was in no way prepared for while a boy who's too clever for his own good manipulated me."

"I didn't suspect it of you, no. And I have *never* been good."

"No, you haven't. I don't think you can be. But it came down to impossible choices. I knew what that forest would do to you. I knew when I went down into those mines for you. All we have of each other is our betrayals." She fell quiet, pressing her fingertips against his. "We have a lot to talk about."

He nodded. "More than words can fix." His eyes flickered before focusing on her. "Nadya, can I stay?"

She frowned before she realized what he was asking. *Oh.*

He rushed on, harried. "I don't want to be alone." He paused, considering. "No, I'll go. You need to rest. We're not—we didn't. I don't want to put you in danger and—"

She kept a firm grip on his hand. "Don't go," she whispered. "We can have a good fight about you killing my goddess, later."

"Only if we fight about you obliterating my country."

She shifted over, knowing neither was forgivable. Wincing at the pain in her sides, she let him slide into bed next to her, careful space between them. She wanted to kiss him, to feel the press of his body against hers, but she couldn't make herself reach for him. She didn't know how to cross the chasm that had been ripped between them.

"Where are we?" she asked, deciding benign questions were safe.

He draped an arm over his forehead. She leaned her head on her elbow, reaching her other hand up and twining her fingers through his. It was safe, holding his hand.

"I have no idea. We're a few days outside of Komyazalov, deep in the forests. In an abandoned stronghold of some kind."

"*Days?*"

"You've been out for three days, Nadya."

"How?"

Something sheepish flickered across his face. "Well, the only way to get you out was with chaos magic—it's all I have—and it turns out if you weren't some rather eldritch creation yourself it would have thoroughly obliterated you."

"*Malachiasz.*"

"You're fine! In one piece! Rashid almost tore my head off. Did we know he was a healer?"

"I can't believe you."

"I was helping!"

"Is everyone else all right?"

"Varying levels of what that might mean, but alive, yes."

"Comforting."

"We are firmly establishing I do not know how to be that." He ran his thumb over her knuckles.

Nadya considered. "Is it a Vulture hunter's stronghold, do you think?"

"Oh." He sounded like that hadn't occurred to him. "Yes, you're probably right."

"Be careful."

"She murdered Żywia, she should watch *her* back," he said darkly. "Why does she still have that relic?"

"I couldn't stand to have it near me," she whispered. She didn't know what she saw in his expression, but it made her sad and uncomfortable. "Is there a scar?"

"What?"

She had the hem of his tunic in her hand, tugging it up. Halfway through the motion, she started blushing furiously.

"Blood and bone, stop, let me," he said with a laugh. He pulled the tunic over his head and tossed it to the floor.

The scar was fresh and angry looking, all raised skin and taut flesh over his heart. She brushed her fingers against it, suddenly very aware of the heat of him and how close she was, how easy it would be to tip her face up and kiss him. She ignored the rippling shifts in his body; it had become a benign sort of horror. She glanced up from underneath her eyelashes. His eyes were dark, pupils blasted out, obliterating his pale irises.

"Wait, you have to tell me what the scar on my back looks like," she said, completely shattering the moment. She shifted onto her stomach, letting out a wheezing breath at the pain in her ribs, but ignoring it.

He laughed incredulously and it was a welcome sound. *"What?"*

"I got stabbed in the back by a swamp witch, it was very dramatic, I died for a few hours, you've missed a lot."

There was a long silence. She turned her head to find him watching her with the most agonizingly gentle expression.

"Malachiasz?"

"I felt it. I thought you were gone," he said, voice shaking. "I almost gave up entirely."

She rested her cheek against the pillow. "But you didn't?"

He shook his head slightly. "I don't know. I guess I don't think the whole world should suffer for my mistakes. Serefin's been pretty threatening."

Nadya laughed. *Gods,* it hurt.

He reached out, very carefully sliding his hand under the hem of her tunic. His fingertips were warm against her back as he traced his way up her spine.

"Goodness," he said, flattening his hand out over the spot where she'd been stabbed. Her whole body heated underneath the spread of his fingers. "Did they get you with a rusty saw blade? That's impressive."

"It *did* kill me!"

"Oh, to be so cavalier about such things." There was pain in his voice. He needed to mourn. That they had slipped away from death was a blessing—or a curse, considering Chyrnog's role in it—but it couldn't last. She had tried to save Żywia, but the relics were too powerful.

He lightly traced the scars on her sides from his claws. *"Prszystem, towy dżimyka,"* he whispered.

Those were not words she ever thought she'd hear him say. Apologies were not something a person with no remorse gave.

He leaned down and kissed her shoulder blade, setting every nerve in her on fire. He tugged her tunic down. "Go to sleep, Nadezhda. We won't have the chance to get much in the future."

37

MALACHIASZ CZECHOWICZ

There is a cycle, a turning, gods die and gods are reborn and renewed and remade. The ones who survive, who live eternal, are the ones twisted, mad, wrong. The ones who will destroy anything in their path to get what they wish.

—The Volokhtaznikon

Morning broke too soon. Malachiasz had only just fallen asleep when someone—probably Serefin—pounded on the door. Sometime during the night, Nadya had cleared the space between them, pressing her body to his. After, he'd remained awake for hours. His mind was miraculously quiet, though he couldn't ignore the hunger that sparked from the magic clouded around her. He softly ran his fingers through her hair. It was only a matter of time before Chyrnog made this impossible.

Nadya stirred, blearily sitting up. She dropped her head into her hands, groaning softly.

"My entire body hurts," she whispered.

"We have that in common," he said.

She lifted her head quickly, looking over her shoulder as if she'd forgotten he was there. She firmly placed her hand against his face.

"Not a hallucination," she murmured.

"You did not hallucinate tearing off my shirt, no."

Her face turned bright red, the pale freckles that dusted her skin disappearing underneath the rush of blood. "Oh," she squeaked. Her gaze dropped to his chest. "It *is* an impressive scar," she muttered.

She scooted out of the bed quickly, and Malachiasz held back a sigh. He didn't blame her for the distance. As glad and relieved and thrilled as he was to find her alive, there were a few too many betrayals between them.

"I—" she started and stopped, turning to him. "Before we go out there and have to account for things neither of us have a good explanation for, I'm glad you're here." Her expression twisted. "I— I'm glad you're fighting this."

"Did you think I wouldn't?"

"Frankly, yes. His goals don't seem much different from your own."

It was a blow and she knew it.

"Right," he said flatly, heat burning through his veins. He'd forgotten how infuriating she was. "I'm quite enjoying ravaging villages and consuming those with a bit of godstouched magic. It's been *great fun.*"

She flinched. "All to tear down a divine empire."

"You're telling me you want it standing? After all this?" He got up, angrily jerking his tunic over his head. "Nothing has changed? Just going to continue with your divine delusion?"

Her expression hardened and he hated how it thrilled him. She was delusional, but she was *passionate.*

"It's not that simple," she snapped.

"Seems pretty simple to me. Your goddess was going to murder you. You turned her power against her—"

"I didn't know you were going to kill her!" Nadya cried. She was clutching her necklace of prayer beads and tears welled in her dark eyes. "I was letting you escape. I didn't . . ."

He raked a hand through his hair, lightly distressed at how tangled it was. He carefully gathered the disaster back and tied it.

"You *knew*, Nadezhda," he said as he worked. "I'm not going to let you cling to *all* your fantasies. You had served your purpose."

Tears tracked down Nadya's dirty cheeks. A pang of regret—he didn't want to make her cry. But the tears were very clearly not directed at him.

She wiped at her face with the back of her hand. "I didn't know," she muttered.

"Many things, apparently, but we've established that."

"I didn't know that was going to happen to your magic!"

He found that *very* hard to believe. It was all lies.

"Sure, Nadya." His tone came out more final than he intended. She winced, then shook her head, slamming out of the room. He sighed, falling back onto the bed. It was still warm where she had been lying. He closed his eyes and pinched the bridge of his nose. It was so *difficult* with her.

The door opened a few minutes later and someone perched on the bed. Rosewater and something sharp he'd never been able to put a name to met his nose.

"Parj," he said.

"Fighting already?"

"It's all we know how to do."

He opened his eyes, lowering his hand from his face. The Akolan girl sat cross-legged at the foot of the bed, wearing a muted crimson dress, Kalyazi in style. Her thick black hair was braided down one shoulder. She smiled. There was a mug cradled in her hands, steam pouring off it.

"Serefin says you're feeling a little less than human these days," she continued.

"Understatement," Malachiasz said tersely.

"What happens when he takes control?"

Malachiasz shook his head. It wasn't a feeling he wanted to describe. It was violation, it was torment. She made a soft sound.

"Wrong question, I apologize. I guess I should be asking how long we can expect to have you this lucid?"

It was impossible to say. Especially with Nadya so close. He knew what having her near was supposed to feel like and it was *good*, not this . . . gnawing hunger.

"I don't know, Parj."

"Malachiasz, we don't have anyone here who can restrain you if you turn against us."

He sat up, shooting her a wounded look as he reached for the tea. She placed the mug in his hands.

"Don't give me that. We're fully aware that having you around is like letting a tiger off its leash and hoping for the best."

"Do you have tigers in Akola?" he asked, taking a sip. It was sharp, almost spicy.

"No, they're farther south. I think they're in the far north of Kalyazin? I'm not sure. But still."

But still. He understood her point.

"Nadya could stop me," he mused.

Parijahan lifted an eyebrow. "You assume Nadya understands the breadth of her power."

"Parj, look at you, talking like a mage. Finally embraced it?"

"You weren't supposed to know about it."

"Bold of you to assume I can't feel your rational magic pushing against my chaos."

Her eyebrows raised. "Really?"

He nodded. "Figured it out sometime during the forest. I'm a little hurt you never told me. I'm *more* hurt Rashid never told me about his magic."

"That's a conversation to have with him."

Probably. It explained a lot about the Akolans that he never could quite figure out. The gaps in Parijahan's story.

"That's why they want you back, isn't it? Not because you're the heir, but because you can guarantee they'll get whatever they want?"

"I do love being nothing but a commodity for a power that I cannot even actively control."

"I'd get away, too, if I were you."

"You don't want me to do the right thing anymore?"

"Fuck the right thing."

She laughed. "No, Malachiasz, maybe don't go that far."

He grinned. Her uncanny ability to always put him at ease being explained by magic *did* make him feel better. He liked when things had rational explanations.

"You dodged the question of what we're supposed to do if you snap," she pointed out.

"I sure did," he said brightly, setting the tea on the side table and standing up.

She groaned dramatically, standing to wrap her arms around him. After a beat—he didn't know what to do with all this affection—he returned her embrace.

"I'm glad you're alive," she whispered. "Leaving you on that mountain was the worst thing I've ever done."

"Truly. It was incredibly cold when I woke, the least you could have done was drag my corpse down from the summit."

She pressed her face against his chest and wheezed a laugh. "A nightmare, that's what you are." She let go.

"Where's Rashid?" he asked, taking the tea back up.

"In the kitchens."

He kissed the top of Parijahan's head. He didn't understand why she was friends with him. He didn't understand why any of them were. He didn't deserve them.

He poked his head out of the room, finding a short hallway. "What is this place?" he asked. He'd arrived only the night before with Nadya, the past three days spent getting her here in one piece. The others had gone ahead after he'd gotten her out of the city.

He would be haunted for a very long time by the expression on her face when he'd seen her on that pyre. The cold resignation.

"A monastery? Maybe? Converted into a stronghold and left abandoned. I'm not really sure. There are a lot of rooms. There's a sanctuary and a library up in the tower."

He eyed icons on the walls as he passed. The gold leaf held up remarkably well, though the rest of the icons were faded and almost indecipherable. Parijahan wandered away, saying something about finding Nadya. He made his way into the kitchens. He was starving. He couldn't remember the last time he'd eaten anything, and it made him feel better to know it was a normal human feeling.

The kitchens were small. Rashid glanced up when he entered, his face breaking into an expression of such relief and joy that Malachiasz nearly bolted.

There was a knife in Rashid's hand, and he jammed it down into an apple. "I should put that in you."

"Honestly, that would be easier to take than another hu—"

Rashid slammed into him with an embrace. Malachiasz had to swallow back the surge of hunger at Rashid's proximity. *Oh, no.*

"Do me a favor. Enough with the dying, all right?" Rashid said, letting go.

"I'll do my best." Malachiasz's voice came out strained. He picked up a withered apple and bit into it, sitting down at the table. "Where'd the food come from?"

"Ask Katya."

Never mind, then. Rashid filled a bowl with *kasha* and put it in front of Malachiasz. He let out a grateful breath.

"So," he said around a mouthful. Rashid's sleeves were rolled up to his elbows, his markings visible.

Rashid sighed. "When did Parj tell you?"

Malachiasz blinked. "Wait, what?"

"About my magic?" Rashid cocked his head.

Malachiasz lifted his eyebrows. "I . . . no one told me outside of what I've discovered in the last few days," Malachiasz said. "I rather hoped it was a conversation we could have?"

"Are you going to be insufferable about it?"

"Probably."

Rashid laughed. Malachiasz took another mouthful of *kasha*, listening patiently as Rashid explained, in bits and pieces—while slicing a loaf of black bread and actively not making eye contact— what he could do.

"Rashid, that's incredible," he said.

"Your reaction makes it all the more terrifying. I never wanted to be considered incredible by someone who's entire life was spent pushing the boundaries of magic."

Malachiasz considered the danger he was posing by being there. The danger he was posing to *Rashid* because Rashid's power was sparking something in him that he wasn't sure he could fight against for long.

He didn't want to hurt his friends.

"Thank you for telling me," he said. "I want to help, if you need it."

"Mmm. You'll be condescending."

He grinned. "Fine! Keep having magic lessons with Ostyia! She's *fine*."

Rashid returned his grin and something in Malachiasz's chest shifted. Like a piece of his broken heart had slid back into place. He held out his bowl and Rashid spooned a little more *kasha* for him.

"I'm going to go find my brother."

"Did that feel weird to say out loud?"

"Profoundly."

It took him a bit of wandering before he found Serefin in the great hall. It was a wide room with a long table in the center, benches on either side. A huge fireplace sat at the end of the room, warmth radiating from it. There were more icons, and Malachiasz watched them with interest. Supposedly he should expect them to start weeping from Nadya's proximity, which he thought sounded delightfully macabre.

"What happened to that cultist?" he asked Serefin as he sat down across from him.

Serefin's eye widened. "Oh no."

"You lost the cultist?"

"I lost the cultist!"

Malachiasz rolled his eyes.

"He was with us when the Vultures attacked, but . . ."

"Think he had something to do with the god attack?" Malachiasz asked around the spoon in his mouth.

"Perhaps."

"He is almost definitely in a Komyazalov prison," Kacper said. Malachiasz peered over the table. The other boy was lying on the bench with his head in Serefin's lap.

"Actually, there's a boy who has the ear of the *tsar* that's probably a part of that cult," a new voice said. Malachiasz frowned, recognizing the voice from somewhere. "So, he's fine."

A Kalyazi girl with an armful of food from the kitchens sat down, a safe amount of distance between her and Serefin. She tucked her straight black hair behind her ear.

"Anna!" Malachiasz said. She had never warmed to him, but he was rather fond of her. She'd punched him in the face when she thought he'd put Nadya in danger. It was hard not to respect her.

He was surprised when she smiled at him. "Nadya told me you were dead."

"I was."

Rashid came in with more food and set it on the table before sitting next to Anna. Parijahan trailed after him with the bread, sliding in next to Malachiasz. Serefin thanked them softly.

"May I ask an entirely out of line question, *Vashny Koroshvik*?" Anna asked Serefin.

"Only if you never call me by an honorific in present company," he replied cheerfully.

Anna gave a thoughtful nod. "How did you lose your eye?"

"I tore it out of my face."

Anna paled. "Oh."

"It's mostly fine now. Right?" He looked down at Kacper.

"Don't flip that eye patch up. It may be healing but it's still gross," Kacper said.

Serefin shrugged. It was to that level of brevity that Katya finally staggered into the room. Ostyia joined not long after.

"Oh, I'm absolutely never letting her hear the end of this," Malachiasz heard Kacper say quietly to Serefin.

Malachiasz stiffened when Nadya entered the hall. She had clearly come from the bathhouse. The blood and grime were gone, and her pale hair was damp. She had exchanged her battered clothes for a dark blue dress with intricate purple flowers embroidered at the hem. There was a brown belt tied around her waist. She lifted her eyebrows when she walked in.

"Gods," she muttered. "We're not going to be able to lie low for long with this many of us."

Parijahan shifted over and Nadya slid onto the bench between them, sitting close to him. She glanced over, a steeliness in her gaze that said they were absolutely still fighting. He slid a mug of tea her way.

She frowned for a long moment before she accepted it. When she shivered, immediately after, and he slid out of his military jacket and gently placed it over her shoulders, she accepted that, too.

Katya eyed them all and rubbed her temples. "I don't even know where to start."

Serefin and Malachiasz exchanged a glance.

"Do you want the bad news or the bad news first?" Serefin asked, amiable.

"You are insufferable."

"I'm a delight," he replied. "The Vulture attack seemed to be partially an attempt on my life." Serefin shot an accusatory glance at Żaneta as she walked in. She shrugged, sitting down on the other side of Malachiasz.

He had to talk to her after. He needed to know how many Vultures Żywia had aligned with her. He wasn't optimistic enough to hope it was a significant amount.

Żaneta couldn't seem to decide if she was more afraid of Serefin or Malachiasz's response to what she was about to say, her gaze flicking between them.

"It's down to which one of us are you willing to disappoint first," Serefin said dryly.

She dug both hands into her wild curls, letting out a breath through her teeth. "My father took the throne as regent," she said softly.

Malachiasz watched Serefin. There was a slight fracture in his calm, but he hid it well. He motioned for Żaneta to continue.

"Not . . . unexpected. Reason?" he inquired.

"Competency. There was significant evidence pointing to your mental state being too fragile. There were a lot of excuses made as to why you were not seen in court. That you had lost your mind was the clearest cut."

"And my mother?"

"She stepped aside."

Serefin frowned.

"She was not given a choice," Żaneta continued.

"So, the assassination attempt?"

Żaneta shot a nervous glance Malachiasz's way. Serefin followed it.

"You were with Żywia, you aren't in the wrong here."

"Wait." Katya focused in on Żaneta. "What are you?"

Żaneta's eyes widened. She shifted closer to Malachiasz on the bench.

Interesting. He had expected her to want revenge.

He softly touched her hand where it rested on the table. "She won't harm you."

"You're one of them?" Katya asked.

Żaneta hunched inward. Malachiasz knew they both were thinking about Żywia's broken body. Her blood on Katya's hands.

"You're going to have to live with it, Katya," Serefin said wearily.

"No."

"This is a waste of time," Nadya said.

Żaneta took that as her sign to ignore Katya. "Rozá and Walentyn. They kept trying to crown a new Black Vulture. When it didn't work, they tried to create a new order instead. A lot of the Vultures went with them. Żywia held the Salt Mines. She kept in communion with the oldest Vultures. There was a rift down the middle. Those who questioned you after the business with Izak went with Rozá. Those who were loyal remained loyal."

That wasn't as bad as Malachiasz was expecting, honestly.

"The attack was a joint effort between the Vultures and my father," she continued. "They wanted to lash out at Kalyazin, who they blame for the loss of our magic. And they'd heard you were moving in the direction of the capital."

"And, somehow, they've moved an army through Kalyazin," Katya said, taking a worn and worried-over letter from her pocket.

Under the table, Nadya's hand sought his, finding it where it rested on his knee.

"This war is never going to end," she whispered.

38

SEREFIN
MELESKI

Why are we expected to fix the mistakes of the gods?
Were we the ones who set this horror upon the world, or
was it the negligence of the gods, their arrogance, their
belief that they had sent the old ones to a place from
which they cannot return? We know now that this belief
was false.

—The Books of Innokentiy

It was demoralizing, having all his worst fears confirmed. It was very easy to entertain thoughts of giving up completely.

Kacper took his hand, squeezing gently. "Don't go dark," he whispered in Serefin's ear, kissing his jaw.

He wanted to. He wanted to go back to bed where there had been a few hours of peace, Kacper draped over him—the boy slept like a tornado—and everything wasn't apocalyptic. It had been warm and soft and briefly Serefin had thought everything might work out.

He wasn't so optimistic anymore.

Malachiasz's expression fractured. He dropped his head, pressing his fingers to his temples. Nadya turned his face toward hers with a slight frown. Malachiasz's skin was beaded with sweat.

Serefin tensed.

"I'm fine," Malachiasz whispered.

"Don't lie to me," Nadya replied.

His jaw clenched and he tugged away. "I'm fine," he repeated firmly.

Katya's hand rested against that damn relic. Serefin needed to get that away from her.

"I was going to say my throne was the least of our concerns," Serefin said. "Now I'm not so sure."

Malachiasz rested his head gingerly in his hands. "Chyrnog is the problem."

"Was Chyrnog also behind what happened in Komyazalov?" Katya asked.

Nadya shook her head, tugging at her beaded necklace. "Cvjetko wanted to set free Nyrokosha, the elder god underneath the Komyazalov cathedral."

"I'm throwing myself in a river," Katya muttered. "This is . . ." she trailed off with a helpless laugh. "I don't even know where to begin."

"There need to be four," Malachiasz said softly. He stood suddenly, nearly knocking Nadya off the bench. "Pelageya told . . . us?" He looked at Serefin for confirmation.

Serefin stared at him blankly.

"Oh," Kacper breathed. "The girl, the monster, the prince, and the queen."

It felt like a lifetime ago, hearing the omen in Pelageya's tower. It felt like a lifetime ago, telling Malachiasz about it while waiting to be killed by cultists.

"What," Katya said flatly. "That doesn't even make sense."

Malachiasz wordlessly pointed to himself, to Serefin, and to Nadya. He faltered slightly, glancing between Katya and Parijahan.

"Not a queen," Serefin murmured, and pointed at Parijahan.

"Since when am I involved in your mad witch's ramblings?" Parijahan asked.

"Pelageya is not the most forthcoming. But . . ." Nadya paused. She met Serefin's gaze across the table. He was twelve steps behind the rest of them. "How did you free the fallen gods? Chyrnog?"

Serefin shuddered involuntarily. He didn't like remembering. The earth closing over him, the moss growing on his skin.

"I gave up."

Malachiasz tilted his head at that. He looked *very* pale. There was something wrong even if he denied it. He'd moved a significant distance away from Nadya—*oh*. Serefin picked up a roll and tossed it to Malachiasz, who caught it, a grateful smile ghosting over his features.

"And you broke the connection with Velyos—" Nadya started.

"And Chyrnog—*wait*—" Serefin breathed. He turned to Katya. "It was *you*."

Her eyes widened. "I'm sorry?"

"That *altar*. That was when I first spoke to Chyrnog. That was when he hitched a ride into the forest to be set free. What were you doing?"

She stared at him for a long moment before reaching over and pulling at the ties on his tunic.

"Please don't disrobe him at the table," Kacper said.

Malachiasz glanced at Nadya. She very pointedly did not meet his gaze.

"May I ask what you're doing?" Serefin asked Katya serenely.

She tugged the neckline over to the scar on his chest. "It was . . . nothing, frankly. It was intended to scare you and give me a sense of why your eyes were so weird. It was minor magic. It wasn't supposed to open the channels of communication between you and old gods. What is wrong with all of you?"

The scar on his chest was mostly healed. Katya, satisfied nothing eldritch was going to crawl out of Serefin's skin—yet, anyway—leaned back.

"*Bovilgy*," Malachiasz said.

"That's what Pelageya said," Serefin said.

"I don't—it doesn't make sense."

"You're literally a god, Malachiasz," Nadya said dryly.

He waved a hand, dismissive. "We know by now it has nothing to do with divinity and everything to do with scope of power."

Nadya rolled her eyes.

"And what is all of this but your gods getting antsy because magic has changed? She doesn't use magic the way the Church wants," he said, waving at Katya, who appeared reluctant to acknowledge Malachiasz was right. "You don't, either."

"You think that's what this is about? A petty cling to power?"

"*Sznecz.*"

"Oh, shut up."

"What about your soul?" Serefin asked.

Malachiasz's face grayed. Probably not something Serefin should have shared like that. But if Malachiasz was going to be there, with them, the rest needed to know what they were up against, how far into impossibility they had walked. He knew Malachiasz, how antagonistic he could be, how any moment could be the one where he turned on them, but he also knew Malachiasz wanted to be free of Chyrnog's hold and he would do anything to make it happen.

Parijahan blinked at Malachiasz, while Nadya let out a deeply weary sigh, resting her forehead against splayed fingers.

"Pelageya said I would need help. T-to get it back," Malachiasz said. His voice quieted. "I don't think we can do anything about Chyrnog unless I find the pieces."

"How long do we have, Malachiasz?" Serefin asked.

He glanced at Nadya. "I don't know . . . I took another. I don't know how many he needs, but it's not many more."

Nadya finally lifted her head, meeting his gaze. Her hair had dried to pale white-gold waves around her shoulders. "What does that mean?"

"We're dancing very neatly around the fact that he's eaten

people," Katya said flatly, jamming the relic knife into the table. Malachiasz flinched. "We kill monsters. We don't try to save them."

Serefin put his hand on the hilt of the blade. Katya let him wrench it from the wood. He held it loosely in his palm. "You kill Malachiasz, you set Chyrnog free."

"Every moment he is like this, he and Chyrnog become more indistinguishable," Katya replied.

"So, we move faster."

A muscle in Katya's jaw fluttered.

They were getting nowhere. Serefin sighed. "All right," he said, gently taking control of the situation away from Katya, who looked like she was in turns so bewildered and so furious she was going to sink underneath the table. "Let's lay out what we know and see if it paints a coherent picture."

But when they brought their individual pieces together, there were too many gaps. Malachiasz took out the book he'd gotten from Ruslan and set it on the table.

"Oh, I found so many in Komyazalov," Nadya said, sounding disappointed.

"I brought them," Anna said. "I got your stuff before we escaped."

Nadya brightened considerably. She touched Malachiasz's hand before darting from the room, returning with an armful of books after a short bit.

"Who were the four who bound the old gods the last time?" Nadya asked. "How did they manage that?"

"I have their names," Malachiasz said, flipping through his book. He rattled them off, looking at Nadya hopefully.

"They sound vaguely familiar," she said softly. "Wait, Sofka—abandoned by Marzenya."

Katya lifted her eyebrows. "That would be significant."

"Ruslan mentioned that his cult was in Komyazalov," Malachiasz said. Rashid leaned across the table, taking two of the books, before handing them on to Malachiasz. Their covers had the same stamped symbol.

"So, we have to get his soul back, and the four of us are needed to bind the old gods?" Parijahan asked.

"Simple," Serefin said lightly.

"Should we start with the soul, then?"

Malachiasz appeared lightly distressed but nodded slowly. "Pelageya said she didn't have the pieces anymore. It's only pieces. I have so little left."

"My concern is that the attack on Komyazalov was only the beginning," Serefin said.

"It began months ago," Nadya replied. "We just haven't heard every tragedy. The swamp witches, the dragon in the west, it's happening everywhere. We're out of time."

Serefin returned to the room he had slept in the night before. He was wishing he had something to throw very hard at a wall when the door opened and shut behind him.

"That was not fun," Kacper said, leaning against the wall.

Serefin glanced at him. His tunic was wrinkled, and his hair was a mess, but Serefin wondered if he'd ever been so lovely.

He crossed the room, dropping his forehead to Kacper's collarbone. Serefin's brain wouldn't stop spinning and he needed a distraction. "What if I told you there was a lot of that on your horizon?"

Kacper's hand found his waist, fingers catching underneath the hem of Serefin's tunic. "No," Kacper whined softly.

"State dinners. Meetings with diplomats."

"I'm your spymaster," Kacper protested. "I have to stay in the background!"

"Is that all you want to be?" Serefin asked innocently.

"You're a nightmare."

"This is true."

Kacper tilted his head back with a low groan.

"Did you doubt I'd be public?"

"You're the bloody king. I grew up in Zowecz."

"Hm, well." Serefin dipped his head, kissing Kacper's neck. "Unfortunate for you, I suppose."

Kacper laughed.

"I have no intentions of keeping us secret. I don't—" Serefin paused, frowning. "Stop me if I sound condescending, but I don't care where you grew up."

"A little condescending, keep trying."

"It doesn't matter that you're from Zowecz."

"No, somehow you're getting worse."

"I don't care what the *slavhki* say."

"There we go, less about me, more about your nightmare court."

Serefin laughed. Kacper grinned and kissed him, fast and light. "They'll talk." Serefin's fingers slipped under the hem of Kacper's shirt. "It won't be easy. It would be hard no matter who I chose to be with. I'm choosing you, Kacper."

"Grandiose!"

"You like it."

"Unfortunately, I do. It just encourages you."

"And I only need a little bit of encouragement. I'm a menace."

"You are." Kacper leaned his head against Serefin's shoulder. "I don't know if I'm prepared for your court."

"Well, on the bright side, we don't know that I'll ever take my throne back! We could be stuck here forever!"

"Don't catastrophize."

"I'm not!"

Kacper kissed his throat. He felt a little unsteady. He hadn't even had anything to drink. Well, he'd had *some* wine with breakfast, but not much. He kissed his jaw, his cheek, his temple. "You are," he murmured, lips sliding against Serefin's skin. "It's what you do." He kissed Serefin's mouth gently. "That's all right. I'm here to remind you that things are bad but we're still here and that means there's hope."

A soft sound broke from Serefin's chest, pulling a smile from Kacper's lips.

"If you don't want to be recognized, you don't have to be—I just—I know there's a power imbalance and I—"

"Oh, this too?"

"Y-yeah, yes." Serefin cupped Kacper's face between his hands. "Remember when I said we should talk?"

Serefin huffed.

"Talk to me." Kacper pulled the tie out of Serefin's hair, letting it frame his face, and immediately got distracted. "I can't decide how I feel about this." He ran his fingers through the strands.

It was past Serefin's chin, long enough that he usually kept it tied out of his face. He bit back a smile.

"No?"

Kacper made a thoughtful sound. He ran his hands through Serefin's hair, parting it on the side. "For a coping mechanism, you make it look good."

It stung a little, how frank Kacper was. Serefin pulled back. Thought about all the little things he didn't know about him. Maybe he was right. Maybe they should talk.

"It terrifies me, how good to me you are," Serefin said. "Sometimes it feels like I'm waiting to stumble on your ulterior motive. Like it's a matter of time before this crashes down around me because no one stays. No one cares about me." It came pouring out of him in a rush of words he immediately wanted back.

Kacper was quiet, his brow creased.

"I've fucked up everything with Tranavia. I'm supposed to be the king? Lead a country?" His voice went a little shrill. "I couldn't handle one noble putting pressure on me before I crumbled. I can't do this. But I guess it won't matter because someone's going to kill me or Malachiasz is going to kill me and this is all going to end anyway. You deserve better than constantly propping me up. I'm a self-destructive drunk. I don't deserve that. I don't deserve you."

He spun away, unable to handle Kacper's reaction. After a pause, Kacper's fingers slowly slid into his, tugging him around. He pulled Serefin closer, his movements careful.

"Do you remember when we were ambushed in Rzenski? Not the ambush, but after?"

Serefin had been badly injured.

"How you sat at Izabela's bedside when you were near to bleeding out?"

"I was the one who sent us into that ambush, and she got hurt," Serefin muttered. "It was my fault."

"She barely had a scratch. You almost *died*. But you cared about one soldier in your company of hundreds—sometimes thousands. I watched you care about every single person under your command for three years. You cared about *me* when I was a boy from a farm with nothing to offer. I don't love you because I want something from you; I do what I do because you need help and you'll never ask for it. I don't care about being recognized. You're right, there's a power imbalance between us. You can be insensitive sometimes. Actually, a lot. Actually, you're a bit of an ass."

Serefin blinked, wondering if he should feel stung, but Kacper smiled reassuringly.

"You *acknowledging* the imbalance means you can work on it." He hesitated. "Do you *want* to be king, Serefin?"

The question was a bolt of lightning down Serefin's spine. He had never been more terrified than the day the crown had been placed on his head. But he did want it. He wanted to be a better king than his father. He wanted to save Tranavia.

"Yes," he said softly, his voice hoarse.

Kacper took Serefin's face between his hands and kissed him hard. His eye closed reflexively, his whole body relaxing under Kacper's sure hands. There was something different about the way Kacper kissed him now. They had eased into a relationship that was gentle, almost entirely for Serefin's sake. This was warm and breathless and messy.

"I hate when you're defeatist," Kacper said roughly. "And you're damn right I'm too good for you."

"I hate when you badger me about my perfectly innocent pessimism!" Serefin returned. "And you are, you really, really are."

Kacper laughed, his head tilting back. Serefin took the opportunity to press his mouth to Kacper's throat, knocking him against the door. Kacper's hands were under his shirt, warm as they moved up Serefin's back. Then, in one impressively deft movement, he yanked Serefin's tunic off.

Serefin blinked at him.

Kacper grinned.

"That was something."

"Shut up, Serefin."

"Well, it's only fair if—"

"Serefin." He already had his tunic half off.

Serefin marveled at the taut lines of Kacper's chest. Serefin grabbed his shoulders, kissing the long scar that cut across his collarbone. He remembered when it had happened, a Kalyazi spear grazing Kacper. There had been so much blood that Serefin was convinced he'd died on the field. That had been a very bad day. He never wanted to feel that way again.

Kacper took Serefin's face between his hands. "Two can play at that game," he murmured, pressing by turns careful and sloppy kisses against the many, many scars on Serefin's face.

His fingers very cautiously caught on the loop of Serefin's eye patch, buried in his hair. He gently tugged it off, pausing to see if Serefin would protest. When Serefin remained quiet, he thumbed a scar that cut against the corner of Serefin's chin as he dropped the eye patch.

Serefin closed his eye as Kacper brushed the pad of his thumb over the oldest of Serefin's scars. He gently kissed Serefin's eyelid, keeping up a veritable assault of tenderness to the point that it was near agonizing. Serefin, affection starved for his whole life, wanted more.

"Mm, I missed one," Kacper murmured, pressing his mouth against the scar cutting across Serefin's throat.

Serefin couldn't really keep track of his thoughts after that.

39

NADEZHDA
LAPTEVA

Peloyin presided over the other gods, but that did not mean his power was far-reaching. That did not mean he could not be toppled.

—The Books of Innokentiy

Malachiasz went to leave the hall but Nadya grabbed his wrist. He paused, stilling in a way she found concerning. It wasn't an entirely human kind of quiet.

He twisted his wrist slightly so he could take her hand. She had his spell book. He'd want that back. Something of a peace offering that would last for potentially ninety seconds before they started fighting again.

Serefin had practically run from the room, clearly anxious about the news from Tranavia, Kacper following. Parijahan had wandered off, and Rashid and Ostyia had cleared the table before disappearing.

"Nadya?" Katya shattered any chance Nadya might have had to ask Malachiasz about his soul.

Malachiasz's expression grew irritated. "Your *tsarevna* wishes to speak to you," he said, his voice cold. He tugged out of her grasp.

"We have a fight to finish," she grumbled.

He glanced at her, a smile flickering at the corner of his lips. "I'm not going anywhere," he said.

His words jolted her strangely. She blinked at him, eyes welling with tears. He hesitated but she waved him away. Żaneta followed, mumbling about seeing if he needed any help.

Nadya glared at Katya, who appeared unperturbed.

"Can we talk?"

Not like Katya to phrase it as a question. Nadya glanced at Anna.

"You, too," Katya said to the priestess. "I don't feel great after that. I wish . . ." She trailed off, staring at the doorway Malachiasz had disappeared through.

"You wish we could do this without him," Anna said.

"I wish he was dead," Katya muttered.

Anna turned to Nadya. "How do you reconcile that?"

Nadya picked up the book Malachiasz had left; he'd taken the rest. He'd have them all read by the time she saw him again.

"I can't," she said. "What he's done . . . What he's gone through doesn't make it acceptable, but it does explain him. He's profoundly lonely and broken and I don't think he can be fixed." She shrugged. "He's trying to fix *this,* though."

"You love him, don't you?"

Katya rolled her eyes. Nadya fought the impulse to deny it. She wondered if it was possible for her heart to burst from all the strange, complicated, messy feelings she had for this boy.

She loved him. It was terrifying and awful and going to ruin her life. He was stupid and clever and cruel and gentle and such a mess of contradictions that her heart hurt.

So, all she said was one very soft, "Yes."

"All right, then," Anna said.

Katya shot Anna an incredulous look. "That's *it*?"

Anna shrugged. "That's it."

Nadya nearly burst into tears. Anna smiled gently at her and very carefully took her corrupted hand.

"It's your heart and your decision. After listening to you talk about everything that happened, I can't say I understand it, but I see how much he means to you. I'm not surprised, you became friends so quickly after meeting."

Nadya had wanted to put a knife in his heart from the moment she'd met him until the moment she'd first kissed him. She still wanted to put a knife in his heart after most conversations with him. She said as much.

Katya made a thoroughly disgusted sound. "All those *eyes*," she muttered. "If this is what we're doing, how do we even start? How does someone lose their soul? I was hoping those boys would know more than they did."

Nadya had to agree. She didn't like how Malachiasz had looked for most of the conversation. His skin too pale and beaded with sweat. His pupils too large.

"Have you ever heard the term *bolivgoy* used?" Katya asked.

"The forest, maybe?" Nadya asked.

"It's . . . wildly heretical," Anna said with a contemplative frown.

They were walking through the bare hallway of the complex. Occasional icons hung on the walls and Nadya looked away. She didn't want to see what her presence had wrought.

Katya gestured for Anna to continue as she pushed open the door outside.

"The Church has been calling for the death of such beings. That's all I know," Anna paused. "Is Malachiasz truly a god?"

Nadya took her time answering as they left the walls of the complex—it had definitely been a monastery once. It was cold out—maybe it would never be warm again. Snow had fallen during the night, piling heavy on tree branches and the road before them.

"That brings into question what we think of as gods, doesn't it?" she said. It was all well and good to be told she was made from the same stuff as the old gods, but she didn't understand what that meant. Was her fate to lose the fragile pieces of her humanity and become like those she spoke with? Would that happen to Malachiasz?

"Malachiasz is some kind of chaos god," Nadya continued. "But he's human, still. I do think he was on to something, but there's a missing piece, something he didn't consider that kept him tethered."

Katya made a disgusted noise, kicking a snowbank.

"You, perhaps?" Anna suggested.

Nadya had never considered that. *Could* she be the reason he never made it to true ascendency?

The entropy at his edges. The eyes and changes that shifted across his skin *infected* with darkness. Katya was right. The longer he was like this, the more he and Chyrnog melded together. The thought was terrifying.

"And we want to . . . save Tranavia's Black Vulture," Anna said.

"Gods, it sounds even more ridiculous when you say it out loud," Katya said.

"He has to save himself," Nadya said.

"You're putting a lot of faith in a boy who has proven time and again his willingness to commit atrocities in pursuit of power," Katya pointed out.

"He's the only thing holding back the end of the world," Nadya said.

"How do we know he's not waiting to turn on us? He's done it before."

They came upon a small hut in the snow, chickens pecking idly around it. Katya pounded on the door with an authority she clearly never considered anymore.

The door swung open underneath her hand. Katya frowned. "Lavrentiy?" she called. She stepped inside, cautiously.

Nadya followed. The second she was past the threshold, she sighed. She knew the taste of this power.

"Pelageya," she said, stepping past Katya and into the sitting room.

"Wait," Katya said, stepping back outside and staring at the hut. "Wait, how?"

The witch laughed, clasping her hands together. "You! How un-expected!"

Nadya flopped down into a chair, exhausted. She frowned and worked a small skull out from underneath her, setting it on a nearby table.

"How do you do this?"

"I come when I'm wanted. It's simple."

Katya tentatively entered the room, Anna behind her.

"Was it you?"

"I don't know what you're talking about, child," Pelageya said in a way that only confirmed Nadya's growing suspicions of where Kostya had gotten Velyos' pendant. "Tea? You didn't bring your Tranavian boys? Shame, I've grown quite fond of them. They're so delightfully foolish."

"Why?" Nadya asked, ignoring Pelageya's deflection, but taking the tea. Pelageya made very good tea. "Why did you give Kostya that pendant? Why all the nonsense prophecies and spinning us in circles? Who are you?"

Pelageya lifted her eyebrows. "You know who I am."

"You're a witch," Katya said.

"I'm *the* witch," Pelageya said, tapping the side of her nose. "And what are you, little eldritch beast playacting at something holy?"

Nadya sighed. "Why couldn't I just be a cleric?" she said.

"You are! You talk to the gods; the gods talk to you. You're mortal. You can die."

"Then why does everyone keep telling me I'm not?"

Pelageya tilted her head. "Ah, how did you enjoy Komyazalov?"

Nadya shifted further down in her chair. "I don't know who was worse, Nyrokosha or Magdalena."

Anna snorted softly.

"Magdalena," Pelageya said thoughtfully. "At least with an old god like Nyrokosha we know their intentions are straightforward."

"How are you doing all of this, Pelageya?" Nadya asked.

Pelageya glanced at Katya and Anna and back to her. "It's all magic, child."

"That's not how magic works."

"No, it's not. Not anymore. Magic has changed and its threads race out throughout the world. It infects, blesses, consumes, destroys, and creates. Would this have been possible without you and your Vulture and that king and *prasīt*? I think not. You altered the course of the world. It was always going to change, it was merely a matter of who was going to do it."

"You believe our fates are preordained?" Katya asked.

Pelageya let out a pealing laugh. "Absolutely not. Though," she regarded Katya, "you might be different."

Katya flushed.

"And you! Dear child. Daughter of darkness, daughter of death, you who let yourself be taken apart to discover the truth of yourself. Do you understand, yet, what it means? Godstouched, but not like other clerics, no, because there was already divinity in your veins. You had already been touched by something far darker."

Nadya frowned. She drew her legs up and hugged them. "But my parents . . ."

"Human. You're mortal, dear, or at least, you possess mortality."

Nadya winced. She didn't like how that sounded.

"The pieces in this game have been moving for a very long time. There are so many more old gods than the ones you know. Do they all wish to be free? Hardly. Many are content to dwell in the depths of the universe. But there are as many who wish freedom. Chyrnog. Nyrokosha. Valyashreva. Morokosh. And a few have lost their names, and thus their reason. And what if they knew their time was soon approaching? What if they had been trying, again and again, each time a child was godstouched, to press their hands to that child as well?"

Nadya took in a sharp breath.

"Haven't you ever wondered why the clerics went away, Nadezhda? Why you are the only one left? Why the gods would all speak through one fragile girl when they could be taking clerics of their own? Why vengeful, petty Marzenya would be willing to share?"

"Because they knew what the old gods were doing," Nadya whispered.

Pelageya nodded. "The anointing ceased because there was no way to know if an old god had swept the child up in their clutches."

She had been the child touched by darkness. She hugged herself tighter. "Do you know which one, Pelageya?"

"It doesn't matter," Pelageya replied. "They are all terror and rage. Their hands have shaped you as the gods' have. You are a creature of darkness and chaos and starlight and I have watched you so valiantly try to keep this world from plunging into madness and I do not know if you will succeed or fail. Because it grows harder, doesn't it, child? To ignore their whispers. To not hunger for the magic and power that sustains them."

Nadya thought of stealing Zvezdan's power. "Why not tell me this a year ago?"

Pelageya tilted her head. "Child, a year ago you wouldn't have believed me. You were held in the grip of the Church and the belief that magic should only come from the gods. This is why I don't give prophecies; I merely give you what I see because I don't know in what directions you will move."

"And was my direction expected?" Nadya, who, over a year ago, was barely able to touch Malachiasz's spell book without feeling unclean. Nadya, now, who cut her arms and cast from that same book and kissed a boy so much worse than everything she was taught to hate.

"I never know what to expect!" Pelageya said cheerfully.

Nadya couldn't look at Katya or Anna. This conversation wasn't finished, but she couldn't take any more.

"If I come back, will you be here?"

"Of course, child. Bring your Tranavians! Delightful boys. Absolutely wretched."

Nadya fled.

Nadya didn't wait for Anna and Katya. She wanted to see Malachiasz. To fight, to talk. She was rattled and doomed and they were out of time and she wanted whatever stolen moments together they could get.

She yanked his spell book out of her pack, holding it against her chest as she went in search of him. She was still wearing his jacket and she tugged the overlong sleeves down over her hands.

"Exactly who I was looking for!"

Nadya stopped, turning to Parijahan with lifted eyebrows. "I was going to find Malachiasz, but I guess it can wait?" She wasn't anticipating revisiting their argument. Half of what she'd said to him had only been because he'd looked so infuriatingly self-assured.

"He's in the library."

"Of course he is."

"And he's who I wanted to talk to you about." Parijahan hooked her arm through Nadya's, tugging her in the opposite direction.

"We're a little beyond the 'he's bad for you' speech."

"Have you been getting a lot of those?" Parijahan asked amiably.

"It's been deeply implied in anything said to me now that he isn't dead."

"I'm fairly certain you're allowed to make your own bad decisions."

Nadya snorted.

Parijahan glanced sidelong at her. "To warn you . . . what I'm about to ask will potentially make you want to sink into the floor."

"Ominous! Wait, I'm getting a cup of tea." She disentangled herself as they reached the kitchens, pouring them both tea from the samovar. The coals had recently been stoked underneath it.

"I worry about you! I can't help it! Your education was . . ."

"Specialized?" Nadya offered.

"To put it nicely. And you and Malachiasz are sharing a room and I . . ."

Oh.

Nadya froze halfway to the table. *"Parj,"* she said, her voice strangled.

"Melting into the floor?"

"I'm at least seven feet under."

"It's nothing to be ashamed of."

Nadya was quite certain her face had never felt hotter. She set the mugs of tea down so she could bury her face in her hands. Parijahan laughed softly.

"We haven't," Nadya mumbled.

"No?"

She shook her head quickly. And as if she wasn't living the most mortifying moment of her life already, Kacper came in.

"Sorry, am I interrupting something?" he asked, one eyebrow lifted.

"No," Nadya squeaked, sitting down and hiding her face in the steam from her tea.

"What kind of poisons do you have on you?" Parijahan asked him. This was the worst day of Nadya's life.

Kacper paused in pouring his own tea, glancing over his shoulder. "Are you planning on poisoning someone? I object to Serefin or Ostyia, but anyone else is fair game."

"Is that a yes?"

"Parijahan, darling, I always have a variety of poisons on my person."

"Any thistlerot?"

He frowned slightly, topped off his tea and turned around. "Yes."

"It's a contraceptive in small doses."

"I'm aware," he said. "I can get you some, but blood and bone, don't tell me any more."

"Wait, Kacper," Nadya said. She had an idea now of how to get information without Malachiasz knowing. "Do you . . ." she trailed off, frowning. "Do you have anything to put someone to sleep?"

His mouth twisted slightly. "Well, I have something, but it's slow acting. It'll knock you out, but it takes a few hours to really work."

"That would be perfect. How good are you at drugging someone's tea?"

"I'm offended you have to ask," Kacper said.

"Could you drug Malachiasz's tea tonight?"

A slow smile stretched across his face. "I would love nothing more."

"Worrying but deserved, I suppose."

He grinned. "*And* I'll get you that thistlerot."

"Oh, thank you—wait—" She dropped her face into her hands as Kacper laughed.

"No one here needs to worry about *that* sort of problem," he said.

She groaned softly. "Let's go back to all politely pretending we're not very aware of the states of each other's relationships."

"You are not a particularly private person when it comes to you and that Vulture, sorry to be the bearer of bad news."

"Let me live in ignorance."

He grinned before wandering out of the room. Nadya decided she would die right there with her face in her hands.

Parijahan gently squeezed her shoulder. "Personally, I think you should hold onto whatever happiness you can."

"I don't know if I'll use the tea," Nadya said softly. It was a terrifying step. She knew it was mostly her upbringing coloring everything, and it *was* something she wanted, but she was scared of the actual act of *wanting*. As if she wasn't allowed.

"I will never know! Unless you want to tell me. I was merely worried about you. The two of you are so . . . intense."

Nadya took a long sip of tea. "Worried about me?"

"Nadya, you're my friend."

She blinked, confused. Parijahan tilted her head, eyeing her.

"Are you all right?"

"I'm not used to people caring about *me*. The cleric, sure, yes, absolutely, but not me."

"Maybe you tell yourself that people only care about the cleric when they're caring for *you*."

Nadya made an unconvinced noise. Sure, maybe, but that was undercut by most of them going out of their way to betray her. Malachiasz had wanted her power. Serefin kept her around because she was politically useful. She said as much to Parijahan, who scowled.

"Malachiasz is a lovestruck idiot over you. Serefin ignores people he doesn't care about and he does not ignore you. I admit I struggle with understanding Katya's motivations, but you would be ashes under a pyre if she didn't. Nadya." Parijahan took her hands. "We're your *friends*."

Nadya bit her lower lip to keep from crying.

"Great, then! Now that I've assuaged my fears and utterly embarrassed you, I'll let you be on your way," Parijahan said brightly, standing. She kissed Nadya's head.

"I'm asking Kacper for some mild poison to put in *your* tea," Nadya muttered.

"I would expect nothing less!"

Nadya left the kitchens not long after her, face still burning. Made all the *worse* by Kacper finding her in the hallway and handing her a small pouch with the most insufferable grin on his face.

"If you say anything to Serefin—"

"I can be discreet!" he exclaimed, turning smartly on his heels and disappearing down an adjacent hallway.

"This is a nightmare," Nadya muttered. She needed to not let the previous conversation ruin everything she had to discuss with Malachiasz.

She wondered if she should be concerned that he was off by himself, wandering through the small library at the top of the tower. He didn't acknowledge her as she approached, but his shoulders visibly tensed.

"Can we talk?" she asked, holding out his spell book. She had read every page, looked at every sketch. She knew what this meant to him. His eyes widened, and he made a jerky motion toward her, like he wanted to snatch it away. She gently put it in his hands, taking his dagger and handing him that, too.

He was quiet, fingers tracking over the worn leather, glancing around the icons still pressed into it. It was stained with blood and some of the pages were loose from the number of times he had unbound and rebound it, adding more. He flipped through, a light frown tugging at his tattoos. Could he read the spells he had written? She was afraid to ask.

"Thank you," he said, his voice shaky and thick. He moved suddenly, shifting the book and dagger to one hand and taking her face in the other, leaning down to kiss her.

Oh, she had forgotten what kissing him was like. A warm sunbeam; like drowning. She wanted more, but when he broke away, she didn't reach for him. Their betrayals hung over her like a knife on a fraying thread at her throat.

He hugged the spell book to his chest, grinning, so purely happy that she felt like she'd been punched in the chest. "I never thought I'd see this again, Nadya, *thank you*. Why did you keep it?"

"Because you died." Her fingers tightened in his hair, tugging him down until his forehead pressed to hers. "You died after I had betrayed you so fully and that was it. No more second chances. None of us dying and not staying dead is a second chance. It's the gods toying with us because the best way to control a mortal is to take them when their mortality is slipping away and send them back twisted and broken and wrong."

His breath hitched. He reared back, digging a finger in his ear. "Malachiasz?"

"Sorry, I thought I heard you admit your gods were manipulative? I might be hearing things?"

Nadya groaned. "I never want to admit you're right."

"I'm *right*!"

"I hate you."

He grinned. His spell book was still clutched to him, but his other hand rested lightly against her waist. She hooked her arms around his neck, gently tangling her fingers in his hair.

"You're insufferable. I missed you so much, and it felt like I wasn't allowed to. There are no words for how glad I am you're alive, but . . . this can't last. We all died on that mountain." She fell quiet, listening to the soft sound of his breath, feeling the warmth of his body close to hers.

His hand came up, his fingers a whisper against her jaw. "Are you so ready to give up hope?"

"There's no hope, Malachiasz."

He grunted softly, tilting her head. "What is that?" he murmured. He traced a fingertip down her throat, taking her left hand. He glanced from her hand to her face and gently touched her forehead. Her breath caught as a rush of dread horror surged through her. An eye opened on her palm. He glanced at it, lifting an eyebrow.

"There's one on your forehead, as well," he said. "Well, well, Nadezhda, what *are* you?" The drop in his voice sent a shiver down her spine. "Did I not tell you that your power drew from darker sources?"

She refused to admit he was right. "It's not drawing from them; it's me."

"You're telling me that I have a being of unfathomable power controlling my actions and somehow there is *also* one half my height who is very scary and standing before me?" His gaze roved over her face. "How is that possible?"

"It's . . . complicated."

"I have time."

"Do you?"

He closed his eyes.

"If you're going to snap on me, I would like some warning," Nadya added.

"Oh, you'll know."

"That's true, you are a bit of a horrifying eldritch chaos monster, aren't you?"

He grinned. "Have I not scared you off yet?"

"Are you trying to?"

"Feels like it would come with the territory of being generally unliked and unlovable."

He'd knocked the breath out of her. "Is that what you think of yourself?"

"Nadya, please." He didn't give her the chance to respond, moving to a nearby table. He set his spell book down and beckoned her over, deftly catching her by the hips and setting her at the table's edge.

She was almost level to him, like this. She liked it. He moved between her knees, tilting her head back.

"The light in here is abysmal," he murmured, intently looking at the eye in her forehead. "What are you, my love?" he asked, then blinked, realizing what he'd said.

She blinked owlishly at him. He was *blushing.*

"Nadya," he amended.

She hummed in response.

"Can you see through it?" he asked. He tugged at one of the epaulets on his jacket she still wore, a smile at his lips.

"Do you see through all your truly disgusting eyes?"

He squinted into the middle distance past her shoulder. "Yes."

"Oh." That was unexpected. Gods, it must be constantly nauseating. "Well, no, I can't."

He made a thoughtful sound. "Would you like to try?"

She picked at the hem of his black tunic, running her fingers over the embroidery. "What are you proposing?"

"I'm proposing," he said carefully, "that I help you. We've never really tested the bond you made stealing my power." His pale skin had flushed further.

"I stole a god's power, too," she whispered.

"Did you?" he asked, absent like he was trying to figure out a puzzle but still talk to her.

She plucked at his tunic, not meeting his eyes, and told him everything. Using his spell book. The crying icons. The dark water and the taste of Zvezdan's magic.

He stilled as she spoke, going so quiet it was as if he'd stopped breathing.

"Nadya," he said softly, voice strained in a way she didn't recognize. She realized it was because she never really heard it. Fear. "What you're telling me is impossible."

She flinched. "You don't believe me?" Her voice came out small. Maybe Magdalena was right. Maybe she was mad.

"Why wouldn't I believe you?" He peered at her face. "Of course I believe you."

"Maybe I've never heard the gods," she whispered. She expected a snide remark, another gleeful comment about how he was right all along. Instead, he brushed his fingers across her cheek.

"I've watched you silence the stars, burn a battlefield to ashes, pull a realm apart from ours so much closer, steal my magic and use it as easily as if it were your own. You used my spell book. Something that would kill any blood mage who attempted it. Nadya, I believe you. You've been doing impossible things since the moment we met."

"What did you mean earlier, about your soul?"

His expression shuttered. Her hands fisted in his tunic.

"I didn't know Tranavians believed in that."

"It's *complicated*," he said, a whine in his voice. She took it to mean that it wasn't, it only bordered too close to Kalyazi theology.

"So, it's your conscience—which you've never had—your essence, the pieces inherent in you that make you who you are." She slid her palm up his body until it rested over his heart. He shifted restlessly between her thighs. "The anchor of your name. Your ability to maintain control. Your power, your heart, your clever, sharp mind. Am I right?"

He nodded miserably.

"And you had so little left after the Vultures. You had eroded it down to the smallest slivers. And you gave those slivers to a witch."

His lips parted. A soft sigh escaped.

"And that's how Chyrnog took you."

"Yes," he whispered.

"But he is changing so little. Because you already want what he wants."

Malachiasz's eyes closed. He was trembling hard. "He wants me to put my mouth to your throat and tear it out," he said. "You have so much power. It would taste like wine until it dissolved into ashes." His fingers, tipped with claws, traced lightly down her face. "He wants me to eat your eyes first." He reached her heart. Held his thumbnail over it. Pressed the tip of his claw into her skin. "He wants me to eat your heart next. Fitting, he says, for your last image to be of me, your last heartbeat in my hands. He wants me to destroy every single piece of you."

Fear hammered in her throat. "And what do you want?"

"You," he whispered, and something in his voice made her thighs tighten involuntarily against his hips. A strange sound broke from his chest. He gave a slight smile and kept going. "Alive. Far away from me if that's what it takes."

His claws receded and he slumped against her. He let out a long breath. She kissed his hair.

"You wanted to do magic, do you still?"

He lifted his head. "You want me to?"

"What, exactly, are we doing?"

He hesitated, then carefully cupped her face, his thumbs at her temples. She became very aware of how large his hands were, long fingers twining back into her hair. The prospect of using magic, of discovering, enough to bring him back from the brink. It wouldn't last, and the fear of that moment pounded within her, but there was a heat she couldn't deny, and if he could help her, she wasn't about to stop him.

"I—we," he said, faltering before straightening his shoulders, "are going to test what exactly it is you can see through that deeply unsettling eye of yours."

"Will it hurt?"

Something darkly mischievous flickered over his face. "The way I'm planning to do this will feel very good."

Then he kissed her hard and broke her into pieces.

40

NADEZHDA

LAPTEVA

If I bleed enough, if I sweat enough on the altar stone in the caverns, maybe she will listen. Maybe she will hear me again. Maybe she will tell me what I did wrong. Maybe she will tell me why there are now only spiders.
—Passage from the personal journals
of Sofka Greshneva

All the messy grasping moments of theft, the rushing tides of throwing power at each other in moments of desperation, were nothing like this. Every part of Nadya relaxed underneath Malachiasz's cool fingers as he carefully took her apart, his magic achingly gentle yet toxic and dark.

There was a kinship there. A touch she knew, as recognizable as her own since the night she had slipped a thread of it away from him and kept it for herself.

If that was what she was, a thief, a monster, why did the excited thrum of his magic want to mold to hers so willingly?

She was too hot and too cold by turns, until the heat

overtook her. The heat of his body pressed close. His mouth as he kissed her, slowly, surely. His magic as it enveloped her, breaking her open before him.

No words were needed. She knew what he wanted, what magic she needed to wrap around his as he pressed and prodded, using a power that didn't feel like his blood magic, but bigger, vast and endless and infinitely changing. Chaos refined to singular points of caustic heat as his hands glided across her skin. As she wrapped her legs around his hips and tangled her hands in his hair.

She arched, her head falling back. She could feel him searching. Gentle presses against every closed door within her. Some she opened, others she kept closed and he moved on. She knew what he was looking for but didn't know where he would find it. She welcomed the search. Knew it was only a matter of time before he—*ah*.

A stutter, a pause, as he found the ocean of dark water. She felt his gasp for air, his hand tightening on her waist. His breath hot against her neck as he lowered his head and took a moment to consider.

She whispered his name. Kissed the corner of his jaw and waited for the moment of reckoning. Opened her eyes and watched him from under heavy lids, his pale eyes unseeing, caught in magic's throes. It was an ocean formed by the hands of old gods. She never should have existed. But she did and she was here, now, caught between dark and darker magics and was, at the end of everything, nothing but a girl who had finally realized that the power she had was her own.

She could feel him through whatever this was, his emotions, the sharp sting of them. They were loud and large. No wonder he was the way he was—too much, by measures cruel and kind—if this was how the world filtered to him, in violent bursts and passionate flashes. Here, now, curiosity and heat overwhelmed him.

She didn't know what had changed except his efforts were renewed, he jerked her closer, kissing her harder and the heat of him was so intense she was going to burn up entirely.

He'd found what he was looking for. His magic pulled hers along, frantic, lifting with each breath, each press of his lips against hers, against her skin. It kept going, kept pulling until something . . . *snapped*.

An exquisite rush of torment.

She couldn't help the sharp cry that broke from her, the way her hands tightened and clutched at him. A dread power coursing through her like a flood until—

Until a very different kind of sight.

"Oh," she whispered. Her whole body trembled, aware of the way her skirts had pushed up her thighs, Malachiasz's hand a point of blistering heat far up and underneath them.

Malachiasz let out a long, shaky breath, a smile tugging at his mouth. He pressed an open-mouthed kiss to the inside of her thigh, laughing a little at the hiss of air that broke past her teeth.

She bit her lower lip, closing her eyes, but she could still see. "Wait," she said, tightening her arms around him.

When she was in the realm of the gods, the world looked different. Hues, textures, always slightly off. The dim library they were in was still just a library, but the light was a sickly, diseased green. There was decay on the floor, spreading from where Malachiasz stood.

She'd seen him without his careful mask of magic that kept him human. She had seen him as he was, as the monster, the god. There was no fear of the churning chaos, the limbs and teeth and painful, tangled horror. The spine tearing, the feathers leaving pinhole pricks in his skin. But something nasty dripped between the books, an inky darkness, almost like blood in texture. Poisoned, decaying.

Entropy leeching out into the world with every step Malachiasz took. They were out of time.

"It worked?" he asked, breathless.

"It worked," she murmured.

"It didn't hurt, did it?" He sounded genuinely concerned.

"No, you wonderful boy."

"Oh, that's a new one. I've never been wonderful before!"

She couldn't tell if he was being facetious or earnest. She suspected the former. He buried his face against her neck. She twisted her fingers in his hair.

"How on earth did you learn to do that?" she asked.

He lifted his head enough to cast her a very sly smile. "I know how to do a lot of things."

She was all too aware of the way her face heated. All too aware of that *damn* pouch burning a hole in her pocket.

"Maybe," he continued, his voice rough, "if we survive this, I can show you."

She tried very hard to keep the small plaintive sound from escaping her throat and did not succeed. He grinned.

He smiled a lot. It was one of the first things she had noticed, but his smiles were careful masks to get under people's guards. He never smiled with his teeth unless he was trying to scare someone.

But his wide grins full of teeth, the ones that closed his eyes and made him look his tragically young nineteen years, were desperately real for her.

He kissed her. His mouth moving against her jaw, to her throat. She let out a whimper.

A sharp pain.

The world seemed to slow as she slammed the heel of her hand out against his chest, knocking him away as she shot back, scrambling to the opposite side of the table. He stared at her, eyes wide, her blood trickling down his chin.

"Fuck," he whispered. A pure, stark fear crossed his face that Nadya knew meant only one thing.

His eyes shuttered black.

No no *no no no*. She couldn't watch as what her divine eye saw began to manifest. She rolled off the table, knocking it over and toward him to buy herself some time. She had no weapons. She'd left her *voryens* in her belt on her bed, a wildly foolish thing to do.

Don't panic, she thought, catching a terrifying glimpse of his rows of iron teeth. His claws slid out from his nail beds, giving her an idea.

With a tiny thrill, she let her own claws ease out. A part of her expected disgust from Marzenya and was jarred when nothing came. She was just a girl whose power was her own.

Though she would really like some backup.

"Malachiasz, *sterevyani bolen,* darling, I know you can hear me," she said, taking a careful step back as he moved closer. His movements too smooth, unnervingly inhuman. There was nothing behind those onyx eyes and the monstrous shifts were distorted, infected.

This was Chyrnog.

He lunged and she darted away. She shoved her shoulder into a shelf of books, knocking it over, hoping the noise would bring someone to investigate. It didn't take long for the door to open, the king of Tranavia looking perplexed.

"Nadya, I swear, this is a little too familiar," he said.

A lifetime ago. "You've been traveling with him . . . how do you stop him?"

"Blunt force trauma to the face?" Serefin suggested, watching as Malachiasz's claws got dangerously close to Nadya's throat.

"Why do you not seem concerned?"

"I shut down my sense of fear when I was sixteen and never looked back," Serefin said blankly.

Nadya tipped a chair over in front of Malachiasz, using his moment of pause to kick him squarely in the face, cracking his head to one side.

Serefin stepped into the room, briefly drawing Malachiasz's attention away before it returned to Nadya. He wanted her. First her eyes, then her heart.

"Nadya, if any of us can stop him, it's you," Serefin said.

He was right. What was the point of all this power if she couldn't use it when she needed to? She pulled on the smallest bit of the dark water, not wanting to be overwhelmed. It was a heady, intoxicating rush that she could easily grow too used to.

"Well, at least get in here and continue to be your irritating, distracting self," she said.

"I am here to be your human shield, my lady," Serefin said with a slight bow.

"I'm going to kill you."

"That would be the opposite of helpful if I'm to be your human shield."

"I don't need you alive to take the brunt of his blows."

"You wound me."

Her heart raced too fast, pounding in her throat. She kept using pieces of furniture to barricade herself behind, but they were mostly futile attempts. There would be no reasoning, no bringing him out of this gently. She let magic pool in her hands, heat at her fingertips. She waited for him to lunge, all snarling chaos and sharp teeth and blood, and held up her hand, freezing him in place.

He immediately resisted, slamming his power against hers in a dark spray of sparks that she could barely hold off. Serefin picked up a chair by the leg and swung it into the back of Malachiasz's head.

To absolutely no effect.

"Oh, huh," he said, surprised. "That worked last time."

Malachiasz rammed into Serefin, knocking them both into a bookshelf and toppling it.

Nadya picked up a broken chair leg, hefting it slightly. No harm in trying again, she supposed, and brought it down hard. He flinched away but it gave Serefin time to kick him off as Malachiasz's claws got terrifyingly close.

"My face has seen enough abuse," Serefin muttered, catching some kind of light in his hands and punching it against Malachiasz's chest.

Malachiasz made a panicked screech, clawing at himself. Nadya grasped at her magic and pressed her will down against Malachiasz's—against Chyrnog's—knocking him off his feet.

It was overwhelming, the well of power, and Nadya hardly knew enough to form it into anything that wasn't broad strokes of raw magic, but that was what she needed. She slammed it down against Malachiasz, knocking him unconscious.

Only a broken boy at their feet, bleeding from a head wound.

Serefin let out a long breath. "We're in trouble," he said softly. He sat down with a heavy breath. "What were you doing in here, anyway?"

Nadya felt her face grow hot. Serefin glanced at her and closed his eye.

"Blood and bone," he muttered.

"We were just—"

"I would rather tear out my remaining eye than hear what you do with my brother. Forget I asked."

She was quiet. She started to right overturned furniture.

He held out his hand. "Come here, sit down. We can clean up later."

She didn't want to. Picking up the mess was the only thing keeping her from thinking about how hopeless everything was. She sat anyway, heaving a sigh. Serefin wrapped his arm around her shoulders.

"We can't fight this, Serefin," she whispered, leaning into him. "He's not going to get out alive. I don't think I am, either."

He rubbed his hand against her shoulder, kissing the side of her head. She rested her head against him. He smelled nice, the slightest hint of copper, but mostly like wine.

"There's always a chance," he said quietly. "We always have a chance."

"Since when are you so optimistic?"

"Only when someone is catastrophizing even harder than I am." He paused. "You're shaking."

Serefin pulled her closer. He sat there, with her curled up against him, in silence for a long time. There was nothing to say to make either of them feel better. Eventually a groan broke through the quiet. Malachiasz sat up, cradling his head, and crawled the few steps to them, collapsing over them both.

"I don't like this!" Serefin said.

Malachiasz mumbled something completely incoherent against Nadya. She folded up, pressing her face into his hair. He shifted, flipping over, elbowing Serefin in the stomach hard, almost definitely on purpose.

"He's gotten so much stronger," Malachiasz said, his voice scratchy.

"It's becoming harder to get you back," Serefin noted. "You're going to have some horrifying bruises. Although maybe that would be an improvement?"

Malachiasz glared at him. He reached up and touched Nadya's neck. His fingers came away wet with blood.

"I need to stay away from you," he said.

"I can handle myself," she said.

"As true as that may be," Serefin said, "Malachiasz is an hourglass and the sand is nearly run out."

Nadya sighed and told them about her conversation with Pelageya. Malachiasz frowned slightly.

"I don't think Malachiasz is the only one we need to worry about," she said quietly.

"What do we do with that? Surely the god has weaknesses. Surely you—"

"Wait," Malachiasz said, moving to sit in front of them. "You said the Church was afraid of you; your gods were afraid of you."

"Yes, the whole 'molded by the old gods before Marzenya claimed me' bit is cause for some alarm."

"Why, though?"

The Church was easily explained. Nadya was proof that everything the Church had taught wasn't true. She could shake the Church down to its foundations. The gods, well, wasn't it also her fault Marzenya was dead? After a long pause, she said so.

"I wouldn't have been able to kill Marzenya without you, Nadya," Malachiasz said earnestly.

"The old gods made me; I can't be their weakness."

"Well, not only you," Serefin said, "but it's like Pelageya was saying, wasn't it? It's not only about you. It's about a cleric made by old gods, a Vulture turned chaos god, a blood mage turned . . ."

"What exactly are you, Serefin?" Malachiasz asked amiably.

Serefin held a hand out and a cloud of moths spread out around his fingers. "I'm not sure."

"Godstouched," Nadya said.

Serefin shrugged.

"And a *prasīt* with rational influence magic," Malachiasz said.

"I don't understand *that* at all," Nadya said.

"No, neither do I." But he sounded like he desperately wanted to study what it was Parijahan did without even being aware of it.

"Serefin, it sounds like you're saying we should work together," Nadya said dryly.

"A baffling suggestion after all the backstabbing, I know."

They were all quiet for a long breath. Malachiasz gazed over her shoulder.

"Positively shocked you didn't toss me out that window," he murmured.

Nadya gasped. "I could have defenestrated you so easily. A lost opportunity."

Serefin rolled his eye. "So . . . where does this leave us?" he asked.

Nadya thought of the world she could see. The things she could do. There was surely a place they could go to confront the end of the world.

Even if they were doomed, they had to try.

41

MALACHIASZ

CZECHOWICZ

Morokosh needles his fingers like icicles into the minds
of mortals, driving them into frenzies so deep that one
young girl might slaughter an entire village on her own.
—The Volokhtaznikon

Malachiasz needed to stay away from Nadya.

Nadya clearly had no intention of letting Malachiasz out of her sight.

He was rattled by everything in the library: her nearness, her warmth, the feel of her legs around his hips, the way she posed questions that she knew he wouldn't want to answer while looking at him so intently—*seeing* him—the feel of his teeth cutting into her flesh, the taste of her blood, sweet and bitter and disastrous.

He could still taste it.

He had followed Serefin to the kitchens, desperate to wash away the sweetness. Serefin, delighted in an utterly concerning way when Malachiasz had requested alcohol in a desperate bid to forget all the feelings he couldn't handle, brought out a bottle of vodka with a flourish. Nadya seemed dubious.

"You both have entirely unhealthy coping mechanisms," she muttered. She touched Malachiasz's side and he flinched involuntarily. "*Oh.*" She'd pulled her hand away like he'd burned her. Her dark eyebrows tugged down, expression troubled. "All right," she said, "I should have taken you literally biting my neck as the bad sign it was."

He reached for her. The grief at losing her was still close and he couldn't help it. He gently tugged her hair over one shoulder. The bite wasn't deep but had an ugly look to it.

"Shit," Serefin muttered, frowning at spilt vodka. "I can hit you with a pan if need be," he offered, glancing up.

Malachiasz could feel how close the god had grown, how easy it would be. He was *so hungry.*

"Does it hurt?" he asked Nadya.

She shook her head. "I wouldn't have minded if I didn't know what it meant for you."

Oh. Well, then. That was distracting.

She took his hand from her neck, gently squeezing his fingers.

Serefin swore again. Malachiasz sighed.

"Let me." He took the bottle from Serefin, noting that nothing had ended up in the glass and Serefin was moving his hand from the glass to the spill on the table with a deepening frown.

"It's the eye," Serefin said. "Depth perception. I—no, that's not enough, more than that."

Malachiasz took a sip of vodka while sliding a glass to Serefin. It went down with a satisfying burn. Serefin took the glass—*and the bottle*—leaving the room. Nadya and Malachiasz exchanged a glance. She shrugged before following. Malachiasz hesitated, uncertain.

He should leave before he hurt them all. He had never had anyone in his life before that he cared enough about not to hurt. It was strange and terrifying. He didn't like being *seen.* He liked his masks and lies. They were safe. This wasn't safe.

Nadya poked her head back in. Her hair was still gathered over one shoulder, creating a pale curtain as she leaned in.

"Malachiasz? If you don't come, Serefin is going to drink that whole bottle by himself and he *really* shouldn't."

She still had her left sleeve rolled up, revealing the strange inky stain on her skin that tracked up her neck; her fingernails curled into claws. The eye at her forehead had closed. If she was molded by the old gods—and granted an unfathomable power that had knocked the air out of him—why did Chyrnog want her so badly? Or was that not it? Not a vessel, but a creation in her own right. Something that might shove at the world until it crumbled.

He thought of the girl in the snow, shaking as she offered up her arm, her blood, so they could escape the Vultures. The girl who had nearly tossed his spell book in the river. The girl who stood before him now, her hair no longer in a rigid braid crown but loose at her shoulders, darkness staining her skin and soul.

What if they really were looking in the wrong direction?

Chyrnog stirred. *"I'll have her power, too. She was made to set me and my kin free. Made to unlock our chains. It's only a matter of time."*

Not her.

Her touch startled him as she took his hand. "Come on, *sterevyani bolen,*" she said, tugging him out of the kitchens. "I knew the vodka was a bad idea."

She pulled him through the painfully cold halls and into a sitting room. It was in a sadder state than the other rooms. There were tired furs on the floor and a few threadbare chairs paired with one very battered chaise. The walls held more icons, which Nadya took in with a sigh.

"We can turn them," Serefin said. He'd taken to swigging directly out of the bottle and poking at the oven in the corner, trying to warm the room. Kacper had found him and watched worriedly from a nearby chair. Serefin finally succeeded and immediately flopped onto Kacper.

"I want to see them start crying," Malachiasz said, peering at one.

Nadya rolled her eyes. She opened a trunk, pulling an old blanket out and wrapping it around her shoulders. "Did you read those books I brought?" she asked, settling on the chaise. The books were on a table. She must have brought them with her, along with his forgotten spell book, which she handed to him.

He'd read two of them and had some ideas, but if it all came down to finding his shattered soul, he was at a loss.

"Do you still have that pendant?" he asked Serefin.

Serefin blinked, bewildered, patting at his chest. "I do," he said, tugging the necklace out from underneath his shirt. He tossed it to Malachiasz.

Malachiasz turned it over in his hands, sitting on one of the chairs.

"Can I voice my hesitation at making plans *with* the person the old god currently is possessing?" Kacper said.

"We're not making plans," Nadya said. "We're discussing historical precedence."

Malachiasz smiled slightly. Nadya leaned on the arm of the chaise, taking one of the books into her lap. He flipped open his spell book. He didn't know if having it would help, but he hoped so. If not, there was a pencil in his pocket and the light hit the fall of her hair in a way that made his fingers itch.

"Can you read it?" Serefin asked.

Malachiasz flipped a few pages until he found a spell. It was unsettling. He'd written this spell, knew exactly what it was supposed to say, but there was a terrible disconnect and he couldn't process any of it.

"Can you?" he turned the question on Nadya, who'd sunk down into the chaise.

"I don't understand the mechanics, but yes."

Interesting. He returned to the page before and the first few lines of a haphazard sketch of Nadya. He had missed the safety of this book. The knowledge that all he was could be found carefully tucked within the pages.

"Sofka was abandoned by Marzenya," Nadya said, frowning at the book in her lap. "Lev was chosen by one god, it doesn't say who, and returned from the mountains but couldn't speak and supposedly touched by Peloyin—oh, that's odd."

"What is?" Serefin asked.

Parijahan wandered into the room, moving to sit next to Nadya on the chaise. Żaneta followed, yawning. She handed Malachiasz half a slab of black bread and a cup of tea before sitting next to him with her own cup. He stared at her.

"Serefin mentioned that eating actual food helps with the . . ."

"Cosmic hunger?" Malachiasz offered, but he took it gratefully, sipping at the tea. It would do little to sate the discomfort of being so close to Nadya, but it would numb him, for a time. "Where's Katya?"

"We probably won't be seeing her or Ostyia," Kacper said.

Nadya clapped her hands together. "Where's Rashid, I just won a bet."

"You didn't," Malachiasz said, recalling the many, many bets Parijahan and Rashid made with each other at their expense.

"I absolutely did. Anyway, Peloyin keeps coming up, but he's the one god I've never spoken to. The other gods always avoid talking about him, and information is sparse, for whatever reason." She flipped a page. "The original four were all clerics who either lost the touch of their patron gods or went somewhere and came back changed."

"Like, say, dying then not being dead?" Serefin asked.

"Parijahan hasn't, though," Nadya said. "I still don't quite understand how you're wrapped up in this," she said to the Akolan girl.

"Ah," Parijahan said softly.

Malachiasz perked up. He knew that tone. *Oh.* "It was before you came to Kalyazin."

"We were kids. I was hungry and didn't wait for our tester." She leaned against Nadya's knees. "The poison moved so fast. I was gone before anyone realized what had happened. Rashid was there, but he didn't know I'd died. He thought it was a weak poison. If he hadn't been there . . . that would have been it."

Kacper tucked his chin against Serefin's shoulder. "Is most Akolan magic like this?"

"Akola has a lot of power," Malachiasz said, "and it's true, they hide it, but it also might be true that it doesn't manifest in the ways it does for us or Kalyazin."

Parijahan nodded. "There's a lot we don't know because the mages sequester themselves away in the deserts. And our court mages are more for show."

Malachiasz desperately wanted to figure out how Rashid and Parijahan's magic worked. He wished they weren't here at the end of everything. He chewed at the bread, but it didn't seem to be helping. He was feeling rather ill.

"You can't resist. If you don't take one here, I'll merely force you somewhere else. There is no stopping me."

Malachiasz let out a sharp breath. Nadya's eyes were on him. She got up, downed the last bit of vodka in her glass, and crossed the room, still wrapped in the blanket, taking his hand.

"You need to sleep," she said.

He did. But he didn't want to. His head ached from being whacked and it was easier for Chyrnog to take hold of him when his defenses were down. But Nadya pulled him back to her room. They *needed* to keep their distance. He didn't know how to say no to her, though, because he didn't know how much time they had left.

"I shouldn't be here," he said.

She tapped him resolutely on the chest. "I don't want to be alone, and neither do you."

"I hurt you—"

"You really don't need to act like that bothers you."

He reared back, stung. She glared up at him.

"I—of course it does."

"But you like it, too."

He flushed and looked away. "You know what I am." He paused, adding, "If I'm going to bite you, I would much rather it be something you enjoy."

She laughed. The sound made his heart trip over itself. She sat at the edge of the bed and drew her knees up to her chest.

"We could always . . . not sleep," she said.

He had been halfway through tugging his tunic over his head and he froze. The tunic slid back down, his brain going fuzzy.

"Come again?"

Her head tilted. "We are very likely going to die."

"Yes?"

She flushed. "I . . . I don't want to die not having known what it feels like. Being with you."

"Being with me?" he asked, his voice cracking. He knew what she was talking about. She frowned, hugging herself.

"You're making fun of me. Poor, sheltered, repressed Nadezhda."

"I'm not making fun of you!" he said, quite firmly, before conceding. "You are absolutely repressed."

"Shut *up*," she groaned, falling back on the bed. "I just . . ." she trailed off. She let out a breath.

He closed his eyes because every nerve was on fire and his traitorous body was betraying him, damn it.

"Nadya," he said, strained. "I almost tore your throat out not three hours ago."

She made a thoughtful hum. Blood and bone, she was going to *kill him*.

"I can't believe you're being reasonable," she said.

"I'm being reasonable because I don't want you to *die*."

"I'm not going to die from sleeping with you."

He dragged both hands down his face before allowing a partial defeat and kneeling next to her. She held out a hand, languid in a way that she *had* to know what it was doing to him. He slid his fingers between hers.

"If you're worried about repercussions—"

"What if we *live*," he whispered.

"Kacper has a tea for that."

That gave Malachiasz pause. "Why the hell would *Kacper* have that?"

"It's a poison in greater doses."

"I don't want to know how you know this." He blinked. "Did you *talk* about this with *Kacper*?"

"No!" Her nose scrunched. "I talked about it with Parj," she mumbled. "Who talked about it with Kacper."

"*Nadya.*"

"As if they aren't assuming this is what we're doing in here anyway! Also, it was possibly the worst five minutes of my life. Ranked above your death because it was that mortifying."

He couldn't help laughing.

She tugged on their clasped hands, forcing him to lean over her. "*Malachiasz.*"

"I mean, you *have* been trying to take my clothes off since the Salt Mines," he said, dipping down to brush his lips against her forehead.

She laughed again. It was such a good sound. He wanted to spend the rest of his life hearing it, even if his life didn't last much longer. She so rarely laughed and when she did it was like being doused in sunlight.

"Which, really, Nadya, troubling. All these eyes." But he was grinning.

"It's not that bad," she said.

He lifted his eyebrows.

"Fine, it is. It's truly revolting. Malachiasz, you're a horror." She arched up and kissed him. He closed his eyes, pressing into the kiss.

"Did that hurt your ribs?" he murmured against the side of her mouth.

"Shut up, Malachiasz," she said. Her hands were under his tunic, warm against his skin. "No more 'maybe if we survive.' We're here, alive, now."

She grazed her teeth against his throat, and he shuddered, accepting defeat.

NADEZHDA

LAPTEVA

Nadya woke long before the sun. Malachiasz was asleep, body curled toward her. Her eyes fluttered closed, briefly holding onto the memory of Malachiasz's heat and gentle touch, before she carefully tucked it away. She was allowed to have these things she yearned for, this boy. But it was time to move forward.

The room was bathed in soft moonlight and Nadya risked a glancing touch of her fingertips against Malachiasz's lips. He didn't stir. That had been her worry, ultimately. She knew how badly he slept, and she needed to do this without him knowing.

Before she was really awake enough to be aware of it, she had dressed and was knocking on Serefin's door. After some noise from the other side, the door was flung open.

Serefin's expression wearied when he saw her. "Nadya," he said, his voice scratchy with sleep. "Do you have any idea what cursed time it is?"

He wasn't wearing a shirt, which Nadya noted without much more consideration, and nothing covered his left eye. It was closed, but the eyelid had an odd shape to it, flat without any eye to cover.

"Extremely late. Or early. Put your clothes on, we need to talk to Pelageya, alone."

He looked at her suspiciously. There was rustling in the bed and Kacper sat up.

"Where's Malachiasz?" Serefin asked.

"Asleep. We need to talk to her about him."

Serefin's eye narrowed. "There's no way he didn't wake up when you left."

Kacper mumbled something, slowly sinking back down in the bed.

"What?"

"Drugged his tea."

Serefin turned. "You *what*?"

"I asked him to," Nadya said. "Do you have the relic?"

Serefin's expression shuttered. No longer the boy she had come to consider a friend. Here was the royal, the general, the blood mage.

"Why would you want that? I thought we were working together."

"Yes, I—"

"He deserves a hell of a lot of misery, but I'm not entirely sure he deserves another betrayal from you."

Nadya shook her head. It was so hard to explain. "I'm not . . ." she paused. "We can't let him know this part of the plan. Chyrnog will stop it."

Understanding dawned on Serefin's face. He nodded briskly, turning and haphazardly throwing on clothes. She watched as he leaned over to where Kacper had burrowed back under the blankets, touching his head.

"I heard," Kacper mumbled. "Just let me sleep."

Serefin returned to Nadya, moving to hand her the relic.

"No, keep it. He'll know something is wrong if I have it."

He didn't appear to want to slide it onto his belt, but he did anyway. He waved an imperious hand at her. It was too early to be truly irritated with him.

They made their way outside, into the frigid morning air. When they reached the small hut, Nadya went to knock, but Serefin pushed passed her and opened it.

"How is she always *around*?" he muttered.

Nadya contemplated that. "I think she is more than a witch. Where would we be without her, though?"

He made a grumpy noise that she interpreted as agreement as he stepped inside.

"Well," Pelageya called, "this feels like sneaking around."

Nadya sighed and followed Serefin.

"It's her idea," Serefin muttered, throwing himself into a chair.

Nadya held her hand out to Serefin, who frowned before tugging the relic from his belt and handing it to her.

"Why did you give me this?" she asked Pelageya. "What did you intend for me to do with it, if not kill Malachiasz?"

The witch lifted an eyebrow. "What if that *was* my intent?"

"I was in no state to go through with something like that when we spoke."

"But you were willing to take him to a place you knew would destroy him."

Nadya felt Serefin's gaze fix on her face. She briefly closed her eyes, letting out a breath.

"It was easier to pretend he would survive," Nadya said.

Pelageya snorted. "Well, you're right, I didn't give it to you for him. I didn't know what you would do with it, if you would see how your goddess was stifling you."

Nadya sat down slowly. She had done her best not to think about Marzenya's death. She didn't know how to categorize her complicated feelings, so she'd shoved them aside.

"She was going to kill me," she whispered. "If Malachiasz hadn't killed her."

"You were a divine experiment that failed spectacularly."

Nadya swallowed, turning the relic in her hands, her fingers tightened over the hilt. "Is there any way to free Malachiasz?"

Pelageya sat down. "What is the magic between the two of you?"

"When I set Velyos free, I stole Malachiasz's power—"

"Is his the only power you've stolen?"

Nadya shook her head. "Zvezdan's, too."

Pelageya made a thoughtful noise, motioning for Nadya to continue.

"With Malachiasz, it was like I . . . I sewed his power into mine, but the seams are gone. I couldn't break it if I tried. Death couldn't break it."

"What came from that?"

"I am also deeply curious about this," Serefin said.

Nadya smiled weakly. "It's, well, I can talk to him through it. If I tried, I could read his thoughts. I can feel his emotions if they're strong, and it's Malachiasz, so they're *all* strong. For someone so soft spoken, he is very loud. And if I needed to, I could take more of his power, a rather unnerving prospect."

"*Is* there a way to free him from Chyrnog?" Serefin asked. "Or are we out of luck?"

Pelageya looked between them. An odd smile flickered over her lips. "He is one of the most destructive forces this world has seen in a very long time. And you two want to save him."

Nadya and Serefin exchanged a glance. He nodded firmly.

"Ultimately, it's up to him, but it *is* possible to excise the hold Chyrnog has over him. Weaken it. It will require that blade. And you run the risk of setting Chyrnog free, totally."

Serefin frowned.

"He's currently bound within that boy. You free the boy, you risk freeing Chyrnog. Death must touch him twice."

"I can't do it again," Serefin whispered. "I'm sorry."

She held the hilt of the blade close to her chest. "There's no other way?"

Pelageya shrugged. "There are other ways, but not with what you have on hand, and not with the time left."

"He and Chyrnog are . . . melding," Nadya said softly.

"Chyrnog doesn't merely want a hand on the world. He wants to *be present*. If he can weld himself into the Vulture's bones until he no longer realizes his thoughts aren't his own . . . well . . ."

Nadya cast a despairing look Serefin's way.

"We'll do what we can, Nadya," Serefin said.

She squeezed her eyes shut as they welled with tears, nodding. A hand on hers forced her gaze up. The witch stood before her.

"It must be you; it cannot be the king. You have stolen his magic and know the shape of it. You must cut only the pieces that are not the Vulture. It will be dangerous. His second death might be permanent. But if you wish to save him, you must try."

MALACHIASZ

CZECHOWICZ

It had been so fast, the fall. He had been so focused on his magic, on *Nadya,* that he hadn't noticed the hunger as it clawed through him, as Chyrnog used it to remind him, so vividly, that taking Nadya's power would be enough to finish everything. It would set Chyrnog free. It would stop all of this.

"I would leave you, you know. You could go on with your violent ways. It would be so easy. One life given for the rest of eternity. I have shown you true power and still you resist. Still you fight. Is it worth it?"

Chyrnog stripped Malachiasz's will away, taking it apart, laying out the bones of his spine and selecting the ones he found most agreeable. There was no escaping him in this place. Malachiasz knew not to fight.

"You are ready to align with me."

I won't kill her. I have few limits, but that is one.

"She won't truly die," Chyrnog said. *"She's beyond that. She's practically immortal."*

Maybe the god was telling the truth. He didn't know. But he was tired of fighting and it was very easy to consider doing what he knew best—turning on everyone. Maybe he could only be as he had always been.

"Exactly. You want to be noble? I am giving you noble cause. That girl will destroy the world. The others of my kind, they call to her, and their songs are so very sweet. She has spent her whole life listening to the voices of gods. She's known nothing else and will comply with what they

wish. I want one thing. To cloud the world in darkness, nothing more. Is that so much to ask?"

Malachiasz couldn't even go out in the sunlight anymore. He hated how compelled he was by Chyrnog's words. Of course Nadya would fall. She had fallen before. What if he had to stop her?

"There is always another choice. Let me have her power and she will be the thing that survives."

Malachiasz could do nothing without his fragmented soul. Nadya acted like it could be *found.* Serefin, though dubious, seemed to agree. She dragged Malachiasz, Serefin, and Parijahan out of the safe house the next day and to a nearby hut in the woods. Malachiasz caught sight of the benign building and planted his heels.

"No."

"Malachiasz—"

"I'm not going through this *again.*"

"She's asked for us. We should hear her out."

"I can't shake the feeling that this is *all her fault,*" Malachiasz replied acidly.

"Probably," Parijahan muttered, going inside anyway.

Serefin glanced at Malachiasz and shrugged, following the Akolan girl. Nadya looked plaintively at him in a way that made it very hard to argue with her.

"Did you sleep all right?" she asked.

"I slept," he replied. Seeing her dissatisfaction, he sighed. "Not particularly, but I never do. That I slept at all is nothing short of a miracle."

He tried to remember what had happened with Chyrnog, but it was fuzzy in the daylight. It had been hard to convince him to even go out, but Nadya had thrown a cloak at his face. He was uncomfortable, but his skin wasn't burning off, so that was good at least.

"Nadya, I—"

She shot him a look, taking his hand. He ignored the churning hunger that came every time her skin touched his. The desire to take that ocean of power. She had so much, and he couldn't help imagining what he could do with it.

He followed her into the hut.

This one was cleaner than the last. Odd, because he was fairly certain they were all the same. Parijahan was sitting in an armchair with a cup of tea, looking delightfully pleased.

"You have Akolan tea," he said flatly.

"She has Akolan tea!" Parijahan chirped brightly.

"Bribes are beneath you, Pelageya," he said, perching on the arm of the chair Nadya chose.

The witch shrugged. "Have you admitted you were wrong yet?"

"You cannot tell me that the balance of the world hangs on me saying that I made a few mistakes."

She bared her teeth at him. He hated her so much. She looked young, her hair jet-black but for a shock of white, out of place with her smooth features.

"Mistakes seem a light word for what he's done," Parijahan said.

"Catastrophic screw ups," Serefin offered.

"Atrocities," Nadya said simply.

"Succinct, thank you," Malachiasz said, kissing the side of her head.

"Tell me where to find the pieces of his soul," Nadya said to Pelageya, the switch in her focus scarily intent. "That's what we need, right? That's what leads us to Chyrnog. They're in the same place."

"You're not thinking abstractly enough. It's in a stone, in an egg, in a duck, in a hare, in a tree, on an island, in a forest, on a mountain."

Nadya flushed. "Children's stories aren't going to get us anywhere."

"Child, do you think I treat in children's stories?" Pelageya asked dryly. She lifted a teacup and an eyebrow at Serefin.

He was nodding when Pelageya snapped her fingers. "Wait, you need this." She tossed him a bottle.

"This is still bribery," Malachiasz said.

"Malachiasz, please, this is a bribe I will accept," Serefin said.

"I am strangely not comforted with the knowledge that foreign powers can bribe you with a bit of hard liquor."

"Hold on," Serefin said, sliding a signet ring off his finger and tucking it away. "Just Serefin now."

"You're an idiot."

Serefin winked at him, an effect somewhat diminished by his single eye. "I've lost my throne to Żaneta's father, a warmonger. You've lost your Vultures to, well, more warmongers, actually. Tranavia is terrible, I miss it so much. Please, let me have this."

"Is that a problem you wish to fix now?" Pelageya asked.

"We're in the middle of Kalyazin," Serefin replied.

Pelageya rolled her eyes. "Open the door."

Serefin groaned but did as she asked. The door opened to a balcony Malachiasz recognized immediately.

What?

He got up and followed Serefin out. The balcony led to a staircase that spiraled down to the floor level of the palace in Grazyk.

Malachiasz and Serefin exchanged a glance.

"Are you entertaining the idea of shutting the door and forgetting all this divine nonsense?" Serefin asked softly.

"Exactly that," Malachiasz replied. But he also deeply wanted to know how Pelageya was able to do this.

"All right," Serefin said, taking a step back. "It's becoming more enticing the longer I stand here." He fled into the hut.

Malachiasz hesitated. But Chyrnog would still have him, even in Tranavia. He sighed and followed Serefin inside. The door shut behind him. When he opened it again, he found Kalyazi snow and forest.

"How do you do that?" Malachiasz asked.

"Magic," Pelageya said, helpfully.

"Could I do that?"

"Only people who admit to their mistakes can do big magic like that."

"Pelageya, I detest you."

She grinned at him, handed Nadya a cup of tea, and stood. Nadya offered it to Malachiasz.

"She won't make you one," she said softly.

He *almost* laughed.

"Children! You're all children! And yet here you are at the end of the world. An end you have managed to bring about *faster* yet also kept from consuming us."

"We're wildly talented," Malachiasz said dryly, returning to his perch by Nadya.

"You did ask for help," Pelageya said, equally dry. "I'll give you that. There might be hope for you yet."

"Is there somewhere we need to go?" Nadya asked.

"Why? The battle is all around you. You can see it now, can't you? The flow of your power has changed."

Nadya's face went bright red.

"You don't have much time, though," Pelageya said. "There's someone else vying for those pieces and while I hid them well, perhaps I did not hide them well enough."

"What?" Parijahan asked. "Did you tell someone?"

"Me? No. But Chyrnog isn't only speaking to *him,* he has others trained to survive the sound of his voice."

Malachiasz felt the blood drain from his face. "Ruslan."

Nadya frowned. "How did I never know of Chyrnog?"

"The average Kalyazi wouldn't," Pelageya said with a shrug. "But a Kalyazi disgruntled with the church? Who thinks the gods have abandoned us because there are no clerics and an unceasing, ruinous war? Well, they might go searching. They might learn about old gods who ruled with a very different kind of iron fist."

"This is the whole problem with a religion that blankets the entire country," Malachiasz muttered.

"Shut up, Malachiasz," Nadya and Parijahan said. They smiled at one another and he frowned, lightly offended.

"You'll have to run to make it there first. They built Komyazalov so close to the place where dead gods are buried, to the end of eternity. Could be worse, eh? You could be halfway across the continent with a kingdom falling around your ears."

Serefin grimaced. He glanced at the door. "Pelageya . . ." he trailed off.

The witch seemed to know what he could not ask. "I won't lie to you. You who have come to me for so much. You are your mother's son, more than that one." She waved dismissively at Malachiasz. "The situation is dire. The old gods are waking up, and the old gods in Tranavia may yet rise if you do not stop this."

Nadya let out a long breath. "Oh," she whispered. "That makes sense."

"They were everywhere once," Pelageya continued. "Everywhere and nowhere and they lived and they died and they salted the earth and made it fertile. This world has turned for so very long. You fight powers that have seen eternity, and you cannot possibly succeed. But you must, or everything falls. This one will take the sun and crush it."

"Honestly, I'll probably eat it considering how things have been going," Malachiasz mused.

Pelageya barked out a startled laugh. Malachiasz was a little alarmed.

"How many has he forced you to consume? How have you enjoyed it?"

Malachiasz shifted. Nadya reached up, touching his hand where it rested behind her.

"That doesn't matter."

"It does, *sterevyani bolen*. In you, he has found his match. The one mortal who is a little less and a little more, who hungers, has always hungered, reached for more, farther, higher, and with a little prodding, will fall. You must not, for we will all perish."

"I *know that*," Malachiasz snapped.

"I have a question," Parijahan said delicately. "You may not be able to answer, but . . ."

"Why you? Why a girl from the southern lands who has never dabbled in magic, never dabbled in the divine?" Pelageya asked.

"I wouldn't say *never*." Parijahan shrugged. "I knew what I was doing when I chose the clever boy from Yanzin Zadar to be my guard, when I took him out of the palace on days when the mages wanted to test him. I knew what I was doing when we fled."

"But you didn't, truly, because you never knew what the boy could do. What *you* could do."

"I keep him in check." Parijahan said, sounding unsure, looking at Malachiasz.

He could feel it, his own frantic power quieted by Parijahan's sheer presence.

"And you didn't even realize it. You could, though. You will never see outward manifestation like these mages do, but you could hone the numbers and the formulas into chance and providence."

"We don't have time for that," Parijahan said, a touch mournfully.

If they survived this, he so desperately wanted to help Parijahan harness her magic. Nadya's hand went to his wrist.

"That is not the puzzle to solve right now," she said.

"It may never be," Parijahan said resolutely, but her gaze met Malachiasz's. She wanted to. If they survived—such a weighty *if*—they had to try. "What about Rashid?"

"He should be here for that conversation, no?" Malachiasz asked.

"Why isn't he here?" Pelageya asked. "And I've never seen you without your little entourage," she said to Serefin.

"I can survive without them for an hour," Serefin replied defensively.

"You can't."

He hunched down in his chair and took a sulky sip of vodka.

"The Akolan boy's role is different," Pelageya mused, a finger winding one curl around another. "Nevertheless, you are correct. Your country knows what it has lost in you and the boy."

Parijahan looked ill. "I can't go back," she whispered.

"You may not have to. We're probably going to die," Serefin said cheerfully. Parijahan glared at him.

"If you continue to make silly jokes, almost certainly," Pelageya said, narrowing her eyes.

Serefin's fingers tightened on the neck of the vodka bottle. Malachiasz hated feeling powerless. All he had done for Tranavia, and there was nothing he could do to save it.

Nadya's thumb gently worked a circle at the base of his wrist. He felt a pang of hunger.

Pelageya's eyes went to him. "Careful."

"I'm fine," he replied, voice strained.

Parijahan stood, a light frown creasing between her dark eyebrows. She crossed the room and took Malachiasz's face between her hands.

"You're like a storm and you are driving me insane," she said, her eyes closing. "Let me try this."

Her fingers light against his temples, the metal rings on her fingers cold against his cheek. Even when blood magic was all he had, there had always been an element of chaos to it, his power too great. Everything was always too loud and too complicated and too much.

This was a careful string, fragile but without breaks, without tangles, strung from her to him. Was she . . . counting?

But the hunger slowly eased. Chyrnog snappish but abating.

"What did you just do?" he whispered.

"I have no idea!" She smiled, the cool gray of her eyes meeting his.

"Take this moment of peace and run," Pelageya said. "Go to the graveyard of gods."

42

SEREFIN

MELESKI

The longer Peloyin is silent, the more I worry that something has happened. But that's impossible. The gods cannot be killed. They're gods.
    —Passage from the personal journals
        of Lev Milekhin

They were going to lose any advantage they had by arguing about who was going.

"There's too many of us to travel as quickly as we need to," Malachiasz pointed out.

But Kacper and Ostyia refused to let Serefin go without them, and Rashid felt the same about Parijahan. Katya outright scoffed at the idea of staying. Żaneta was the only one who was willing, but Malachiasz refused to leave her at the mercy of the Vulture hunters.

"We all go," Nadya said, ending the discussion. "We'll need a veritable army for what we're about to face."

Things were admittedly awkward with Żaneta around. She had noticed Kacper's closeness to Serefin immediately, and her pointed looks had been bitter until cornering Serefin to ask if he was happy.

"Żaneta, I struggle to believe that my happiness is something you care about."

"I do, Serefin." She sounded sad.

"Why did you do it?"

She had been quiet, but it didn't seem like something she had not thought about. "I felt threatened. By Nadya, of all people. I saw through her game early on, and that you didn't seem to see through it at all, well, I thought you were . . ."

"You thought me an idiot drunk who was going to hand the country over to our enemies because I found one mildly interesting," Serefin said flatly.

"Well, yes," Żaneta admitted. "You make it hard to remember how clever you are when you're in Grazyk. You become an entirely different person."

"When did you see me away from Grazyk—ah, wait. I remember." She had been at the front for a handful of months, a necessary formality for a child of the court, before she was swept back to safety.

"You were brilliant there, and when you returned, you were . . ."

"A drunk," Serefin offered. "I'm the king, Żaneta," he continued gently. "I am sorry about what we might have had, but you sold me out to my father."

"Does he make you happy? The soldier?" She looked at him intently.

Serefin thought of Kacper's surety, his calm demeanor that could quickly fracture into anxiety. His wry, crooked grin and the scar that cut through his left eyebrow. His absolutely abysmal sense of humor.

"Ah, you don't have to answer," Żaneta said with a small smile. "I'm glad, Serefin. Truly."

"Have you spoken to your father?" Serefin asked.

Żaneta's face shuttered. "No," she said softly. "He wouldn't want to see me like this."

Serefin had no idea if that was true, if Ruminski's quest to get his daughter back was because he cared or political in origin. He hated—for her sake—that he couldn't tell.

"Like what? You are radiant as ever," Serefin said cheerfully.

"And you're a flirt."

"Kacper doesn't mind."

"Don't be so certain," Żaneta said wryly, squeezing his hand gently.

"If we make it back . . . you know what I have to do, right?"

Agony cut her expression. "Yes."

"Żaneta, I should have done it when I took the throne."

"I know," she whispered.

"I can't make the same mistake a second time."

She nodded. "I understand, Serefin, I do. I'm trying to keep my own head on my shoulders. My father's mistakes are his."

"Well, I don't have the authority to execute you, anyway, that's Malachiasz."

"Comforting, Serefin!"

They were to the north of Komyazalov and needed to go south. If they took the roads, they would skirt dangerously close to the city, and Serefin doubted the Matriarch had stopped her search for Nadya.

Nadya regarded the map impassively. She had been different since Serefin found her in the library with a feral Malachiasz. He couldn't place how, but something about her seemed old and tired and sad.

Malachiasz perched on the table. "I would rather not take a horse," he said. "They don't like me. Won't like Żaneta, either."

Serefin had forgotten that Malachiasz had wings hidden somewhere underneath all that magic keeping him in human form. Did Żaneta have wings? He glanced at her. She nodded with a wry twist of her lips.

"Still a lot of horses," Katya said, regarding the map with a sigh.

"If I go with Malachiasz, what do I do if I lose him?" Żaneta asked Nadya.

"Hit him as hard as you possibly can," Nadya replied.

Malachiasz gingerly touched the bruise on his face. It was yellowing as if it had been there for weeks, not twenty-four hours.

"Hit him so fucking hard," Nadya continued.

"Nadezhda."

"Blunt force trauma to the face," Serefin added helpfully.

"Got it!" Żaneta said gleefully.

Nadya smiled at Malachiasz. Her expression flickered, driving a spike of panic through Serefin. Malachiasz's posture had subtly shifted. His pupils were blasted out, black leaking into the whites of his eyes.

"Katya, how close are we to civilization?" Nadya asked nervously.

Katya turned, her face paling. Her hand went to her waist and she growled when she realized she didn't have the relic. It was tucked safely in Serefin's belt.

"Stop him," she snapped, which Serefin took to mean they were rather close.

Malachiasz was watching Nadya carefully, hungrily, every muscle tensed. She approached him, holding out a hand, stained and monstrous. He slid backward, his eyes going pale, blood dripping from his nose.

"Nadya, I can't," Malachiasz whispered, his claws digging into the table, splintering the wood. Something washed over him and he stilled to an eerie silence. Serefin sensed it before he struck, yanking Nadya away. A snarl of iron teeth; blood spattering on the floor.

And he was gone.

"Absolutely not," Nadya muttered, and she took off after him.

There was a beat of silence.

Katya started, "Well I guess that solves—"

Serefin rushed after them, Katya letting out a frustrated groan. When he reached the outside of the compound, Malachiasz was nowhere to be found. Nadya spun in a slow circle, her eyes closed, murmuring what Serefin thought was a spell until he realized it was an impressive stream of profanity in Kalyazi *and* Tranavian. Parijahan came up behind him.

Nadya went still, the eye at her forehead opening disconcertingly. "That way," she said, heading into the woods.

"Oh, I don't like that," Parijahan whispered.

Serefin didn't either, but he followed her and hoped, for Nadya's sake, they were too late to witness what was about to happen.

NADEZHDA

LAPTEVA

Malachiasz was still the profoundly broken boy she knew, who knew her, the darkness in him steadily amplifying as Chyrnog crept closer. She didn't think she would know when the final moment happened. When he was gone for good. That frightened her most.

She stumbled past a broken fence and onto a forest road. The crumpled remains of a person were slumped beside it. Bile rose in her throat and she swallowed it back.

He did this. The gentle anxious boy she loved.

He was capable of this even without Chyrnog. It was the truth. It hurt.

She followed the road until she came upon the first of a few small houses, barely even a village. They were worn down, the painted flowers and blocky patterns adorning them faded.

The door to the first house hung open on its hinges. It was deadly quiet. She pushed the door open farther, her world jarring painfully as she took in the blood splashed across the floor. The scattered remains on the packed dirt. She forced herself to look.

She heard another door slam. A scream, fast cut off. Nadya ran toward the house that didn't seem to be touched. She could warn them, stop this. She shoved open the door with her shoulder, feeling that weird unreality like when she saw some other realm.

She was only in time to witness what she would never be able to forget. His claws going through a man. His teeth parting flesh. Blood and blood and bone.

Wide-eyed with horror, she had once watched his body roil from boy to monster, her fear never truly leaving when chaos added teeth and mouths and eyes and eyes and eyes, but quieting, some. She had learned to see past the horror, some. She had forgotten what he was, some.

Monsters were made for destruction.

She closed her eyes; she would not watch this. She didn't know when it ended. She flinched when she felt a hand over her mouth, against her waist, pulling her into the house, her feet sliding across so much blood.

This was not Malachiasz. Or, Malachiasz, but ravaged and beaten. Halfway consumed, halfway divine, monstrous and eldritch. She could see his jawbone under decayed and corroded flesh. His eyes were strange—not onyx black, but pale and ghostly, the pupils clouded.

"Oh, don't look at me like that. He doesn't have me totally," he snapped, confirming her fears.

She blinked.

"Enough—we're the same, he and I, of course we are, but I'm still here."

"Malachiasz—"

He shuddered, wrenching back from her, a low whine breaking from his chest.

Still Malachiasz, at least a little. Nadya didn't know what to do. She glanced over her shoulder—where were the others?

"They'll be dealt with," Malachiasz said, as if reading her thoughts. She wondered if he could. "We have to go; we have to find it first. *Towy dżimyka,* please, you have to help me. I need your help."

This was wrong, something was wrong.

406 ÷ EMILY A. DUNCAN

"Remember when you killed that creature pretending to be me? Nadya, I'm me."

"You have an old god controlling you. I can't—"

"You can hear their songs and *survive*. Nadya, we're the same." There was desperation in his voice, and he sounded like Malachiasz. She realized she didn't know how Chyrnog sounded. He took her corrupted hand, clinging to it. "You're as monstrous as I am."

Tears pricked her eyes.

"They thought if they sheltered you, you would never know what you are." Nyrokosha's voice was sly and smooth in the back of Nadya's head. *"But all truths must come to light eventually. We have waited so long, and here you are to set us free."*

"Please, Nadya. He wants to destroy you, to steal your power, but why? We can work together. Finish this together. You terrify him, the others, all of them—you don't realize what you can do."

What could she do? "Serefin and Parj, they—"

"They aren't like us, Nadya. They won't understand." There was a strange, manic light in his ghostly eyes.

Even amidst all the divine nonsense, Malachiasz's skepticism of the gods had always held firm. It was jarring to hear him talk this way, like Chyrnog might be right.

"No, Malachiasz, no, this isn't the way."

He whirled on her. She froze, holding her ground. "How do you not understand? Setting these beings free will stop the chaos. We'll finally have the power to stop what's happening. You can take down the Church that tried to execute you. I can save Tranavia. Nadya, it's the only way. Please," he begged, his voice thick. "I can't do this alone. I need you."

Maybe this was Malachiasz, after all. Maybe they were doomed to play out this terrible cycle, again and again. Except she had no blades poised over his back. She only had the earnest hope that he would claw out of the hole he was being buried in, not dig further, deeper, and let himself be consumed.

"Were you planning this the whole time?" Nadya asked, her voice dead. "Another betrayal?"

"What?"

"Everyone will die if I do as you ask, including Serefin. Do you realize how much Serefin cares about you?"

"Serefin can't stand me."

"You're his brother."

"I have no one!" Malachiasz cried, yanking his hand from Nadya's. "I am nothing. I was created in darkness and darkness is all I have. There is no saving me, Nadya. There is no happy ending. Help me, or you die with the rest."

She closed her eyes. "This isn't you."

"This has always been me. You don't know the depths of what I have done. This? This is nothing. This is a drop of water in the ocean of my sins. I would let you all die if it meant turning back what has happened—what you did—and finally achieving peace."

That wasn't true, it couldn't be true. She knew how much he cared.

"You're lying," she said.

He shook his head in disgust, turning away.

"You can't act like none of us care about you. Serefin's been carting you across the country trying his damnedest to keep you alive."

"Don't you dare—"

"Parijahan and Rashid remained in Grazyk after you abandoned them, hoping you would return. They could have gone home! Survived this whole mess! Instead they went to the Salt Mines. *We* went. For you. You can justify this however you want, but don't you dare say it's because none of us love you."

He stilled. She took a step closer, cupping his face in her hands.

"Malachiasz, come back to me," she whispered. "You don't want us all to die for the sake of reversing something that cannot be reversed. If we stop Chyrnog, we can find a way to fix my mistake, together."

Everything was quiet. Terrifying and unnatural, broken only by the sound of Malachiasz's strained breath. His eyes were closed, long eyelashes dusting the tops of his pale cheeks. She couldn't tell how much of him was left. Much less than he was telling her, she gathered. Because for all of Malachiasz's thousands of faults, she knew he cared.

His hand reached up, fingers twining between hers. He gently kissed her corrupted palm.

"Your hands are warm," he murmured against her skin. He pressed her palm to his cheek.

"Your face is freezing."

He smiled slightly. Something loosened in her chest. *This* felt like him. She could bring him down again, keep him close a few hours more. She rubbed her thumb against his cheek. Gently, she took his hand, starting for the door, and was jerked back.

He pulled her farther into the darkness of the house, dropping her hand. "Death, then, I guess," he said, his voice cold. He moved away from her and turned, leaving the house.

That was it? After everything, it ended here?

It should have ended on the mountain. It *did* end on the mountain.

She closed her eyes, straining to hear anyone nearby, but there was only the uncomfortable silence.

"Fine," she muttered, trudging out. "Fine." She would find his damn soul herself. And if he didn't want it, she would at least keep it away from Chyrnog. "Could have stayed in Kalyazin and met someone nice, someone who goes to Liturgy and doesn't try to kill you every other day but nooo, Nadya, no, it had to be Malachiasz Czechowicz, Tranavia's greatest idiot. Gods, I hate him." She kicked at a rock, sending it flying and hitting a tree near Serefin's head.

"Tranavia's greatest idiot has been my title for twenty years, actually, and I won't be ceding it to Malachiasz," he said. "I take it you found him."

"Don't talk to me."

"So it went badly."

"Serefin." Nadya wavered on her feet, and in a mortifying rush, burst into tears.

"Ah, damn," Serefin said. He crossed the space between them, leaning down so he was level with her, and took her face in his hands. "He's possessed, Nadya. Whatever he said—"

"He's going to let us die because he thinks he can use whatever Chyrnog gives him to fix everything," she said, sobbing. The dam had broken, and everything she had been shoving aside was going to swallow her. "He wants me to help him and I'm terrified, Serefin, because I *want* to. I've ruined so much, and *I'm going to make everything worse.*"

He pulled her against him, which was wildly unexpected but so very needed.

"Are we friends like this?" she mumbled against his chest.

"Yes, Nadya, we are, and I'm going to say this as gently as I can . . . we really do not have time for you to have a meltdown."

A loud scuffle could be heard in the trees, and Serefin quickly kissed the top of her head and let go, taking off. Nadya shuddered, wiping at her eyes before she followed.

Parijahan leaned against an impressively long stick, Malachiasz unconscious at her feet.

"Please, tell me you hit him," Serefin said, delighted. "Please tell me you just stopped an elder god by hitting him with a stick."

Parijahan looked up. She lifted a hand, spreading her fingers. "Well, the stick helped."

43

SEREFIN
MELESKI

There's no way to stop this. The gods never cared for us, not truly, and I feel as if all I can do is watch as Innokentiy and Sofka descend further into madness looking for a solution that doesn't exist. We've been left to our fate. Our gods are not stronger than the ones who have awoken.

—Passage from the personal journals
of Milyena Shishova

They chained Malachiasz up. Serefin wasn't sure that would hold him, but it was what they had. Nadya returned with Serefin to the village where they dealt with what little was left in silence. Serefin pretended not to notice the tears tracking down Nadya's cheeks.

They returned to the stronghold to find Malachiasz awake and struggling. Katya eyed him dispassionately. She held out a hand when Parijahan tried to go calm him down.

"You cannot stop the inevitable," Malachiasz said, a dark void in his voice. "It's already begun. I'm going to kill every last one of you."

Nadya took in a sharp breath. He noticed her, and his demeanor changed completely. Eyes, still murky but sharper, widening, his shoulders dropping. He struggled against the chains, but it was less about escaping and more about getting close to Nadya.

"Nadya? Nadezhda, *towy dżimyka,* my love, please, this isn't the way to stop him."

Serefin put a hand on her arm. She glanced at him before her gaze returned to Malachiasz.

"Cover his mouth," she said.

For a split second, Serefin worried that this was another twisting of another knife. He eyed Nadya, trying to gauge what was happening, who he was supposed to be helping.

"Nadya?" Malachiasz's voice was small and bleak.

Her eyes flickered closed. She waved a hand to Katya.

"N-Nadya, please, I'm not—this isn't—Nadya, this is *me.*"

"Then you know why I'm doing this, Malachiasz," she replied. Her eyes narrowed slightly, and she reared back, staring. "Gag him."

"Nadya!"

Katya did so, with a little *too* much enthusiasm.

"We need to leave," Nadya said.

They got Malachiasz on a horse, which did *not* appreciate having the Vulture dumped on his back. Malachiasz had simmered down from wide-eyed panic to a kind of cold fury that, frankly, Serefin found terrifying. Nadya seemed unconcerned.

"I need to know how you're so confident about this," Serefin said to her.

They left in a hurry. Malachiasz snapping was the sign that they were out of time. This had to end, and fast.

"When Malachiasz is himself, hearing his own name makes him twitch," she said.

Serefin frowned. "What?"

"You've never noticed?"

He couldn't say he had. "You might be a bit more observant of my brother's finer quirks than I."

"He heard his name without so much as blinking."

Serefin couldn't help but sigh. "I don't understand."

"He and Chyrnog are the same," Nadya said softly, her words chilling Serefin to his core.

He glanced over his shoulder to where Malachiasz was along for the ride, Parijahan nearby and anxiously trying to calm his chaos.

Malachiasz stared at the back of Nadya's head with murderous intent. For a bizarrely chivalrous heartbeat, Serefin wanted to protect Nadya, but quickly realized that if—or, perhaps, when—those two went after each other, he would want to be far away.

"How do we move forward?"

"Go to this graveyard. Find his soul. Hope it's enough to get him back so we can bind Chyrnog."

He cast her a sidelong glance. "You don't think it will be."

She was quiet for a long time, clearly struggling. "I think that's up to him."

Serefin winced. They both knew what that meant. "If we survive this . . . he's never going to be better, is he?"

"That's up to him as well. I doubt it. But if we survive—gods, Serefin, what a horrifyingly big *if*—and he has us still . . . Maybe. I don't know. I mean, he'll always be an ass."

Serefin laughed softly.

"But," she continued, "I think it would be naive of us to act like he's helping for any other reason than self-preservation."

The handful of days spent in the safe house had been protecting them from more than Serefin had realized. The air outside felt . . . bad. He didn't know how else to describe it. The horses they rode were consistently on edge, which made for a deeply unpleasant journey.

Nadya existed in a state of constantly looking like she was

about to throw up. If anyone asked her if she was all right, she would wave them off. She had taken a headscarf from Anna and tied it around her hair, a band covering her forehead, temple rings swinging at the sides of her face.

The first day was rough. Snow fell the entire time and the roads were almost impossible to cross. At one point their only option was crossing a frozen river or tracking west to a bridge that would take them dangerously near Komyazalov. Nadya had simply dismounted, taken her horse's reins, and begun the tense trek across the ice.

"I hate that girl, sometimes," Kacper muttered, dismounting. "I hate Kalyazin. I hate all this snow."

Serefin laughed. He dismounted, grabbed Kacper, and kissed him.

"What was that for?"

"We're going to a divine graveyard where we will probably die and you're complaining about the snow."

"Yes, well, that all sounds impossible. I can't complain about the impossible."

"Think of the stories you can tell your siblings back home."

Something flickered over Kacper's face. "I don't know if they would want to listen."

Serefin frowned but Kacper grinned.

"If we die here, at least I'll never need to have the wildly uncomfortable conversation that would be telling my family I got involved with the king!" he continued cheerfully.

Ah.

Sometimes it was easier to think of the small, inconsequential battles they could be fighting, instead of the ones they were about to face.

"I'll take off my signet ring when I meet them, then I'm just Serefin," he said.

Kacper laughed and shot him a sad smile. "I wish that was all that was needed."

It was only a few more days of travel but moving through the snow was a struggle until the path cleared from the east. It was bewildering to see the tamped down snow, until Serefin realized what it meant.

"The army. We found our Tranavians," he said, feeling profoundly miserable.

"What are they doing, Serefin?" Katya asked, her voice level and low.

"It's Ruminski," Serefin replied. "He's not a strategist. This is . . . suicide." He scanned the fields. They were moving toward Komyazalov. Blood and bone. Judging from the size of the cleared area, this wasn't an army large enough to engage in a successful attack on Komyazalov.

Ruminski was desperate. Ruminski was a fool.

Ruminski, Serefin considered, had no blood magic. So, what else was he supposed to do?

Anything but this.

"What do we do?" Anna asked.

Serefin didn't think they *could* do anything. They had a more important battle to win. "We keep going."

44

MALACHIASZ
CZECHOWICZ

We cannot kill him. We cannot send him back from whence he came. The gods have abandoned us to this horror that they unleashed.

—Fragment from the personal journals
of Lev Milekhin

There was an awakened one nearby. It was a song he couldn't resist. The taste of copper flooded his mouth as he worked at his chains, pulling on Chyrnog's power. His hand burned, the chains falling away. He rolled his shoulders, glancing down. He was missing the tip of the little finger on his left hand. He stared, some far away, distressed piece of him going silent.

He had to go. He was hungry.

No one in the camp seemed to notice. Ostyia was on watch but facing the other direction. Something made him pause, hesitate, claws sliding out, teeth sharpening in his mouth.

No. He wasn't going to hurt them, not if he didn't have to.

He slipped into the night, veering east. He didn't know

how far he'd gone when he was ripped from the sky and went crashing to the ground. He was on his feet in an instant, whirling and pulling the threads that made his order listen because how *dare she*—

Something hit him hard in the head and he went down.

"Oh, that does work," Żaneta said. "Where are you going, Malachiasz?"

Shit. He lay in the snow, feeling it bleed into his skin, the cold, the ice, as all those distant emotions slammed him at once.

His hand hurt *a lot*.

He hadn't even realized Chyrnog was controlling him. The god had grown insidiously quiet, his threads wrapped so tight around Malachiasz that soon they'd choke him completely. There would be nothing left of him to fight.

He swore softly, choking back tears, sitting up and holding his head in his hands. He lifted one hand when Żaneta hefted the branch. "Don't, please, blood and bone, you have an arm on you."

Żaneta lifted an eyebrow. "Surprised because I'm only a *slavhka*? A mistake?"

Malachiasz winced. "You know what, have another go, I deserve it."

Żaneta snorted softly. "You sure do." She sat down in front of him.

They were in an empty field. Where had she even gotten that branch? There was nothing around except blinding white snow.

"Where were you going?" she asked again.

"I'm so hungry," he whispered.

He sat there, letting it abide, just a little, when it returned full force, threatening to swallow him whole. He hunched over, covering his head as the pain tried to flay him to pieces.

"*Stop fighting,*" Chyrnog hissed. "*Do what you're meant to. You're not strong enough to fight me, haven't you learned? How many times do I have to teach you this lesson?*" Something shifted, a reconsidering, and suddenly Żaneta looked very different to him in the dim light.

Alarm crossed her face. "Malachiasz?"

Malachiasz.

Taszni nem Malachiasz Czechowicz.

He let out a long, shuddering breath. No one with magic was safe around him. He was too far gone. Chyrnog was too close. His stomach churned, chaos starting to tear through his body.

Żaneta reared back. "Oh," she whispered.

He knew what she was seeing. The shifts, the changes. Eyes and teeth and limbs and horror.

Malachiasz thought of Parijahan's magic. The numbers.

It wasn't enough, but it was something. He grasped the spell and molded it into a mantra. He struggled to his feet. He didn't speak, afraid he would break the spell. Chyrnog battered against him, turmoil and rage and *darkness darkness darkness* and it was so much and his heart raced with fear.

Chyrnog had never been denied before.

Chyrnog was going to destroy him for his disobedience.

There was so little of Malachiasz left.

They walked. If Malachiasz did anything more, he was going to shatter. The awakened one passed into the distance, a faint memory. A poor soul who would be hunted by Kalyazin's Church for something they had not asked for and likely had not wanted.

How much of the world would change because of the way magic had fractured?

A part of him was thrilled there would be so much to learn. So many avenues of magic that he had never known before, ready to be discovered. How did Nadya's power work? That vast ocean of dark water was as terrifying as it was thrilling. The taste she had given him was not enough.

And Parijahan? The numbers were *new*. He'd used calculations in spells before but unrelated to the actual application of his magic. For her that was all it was, and it resided entirely in her head. No outward manifestation. It was fascinating.

Chyrnog raged within him. He kept his mind trained solely on contemplations of magic, a distraction. He didn't know how long he had before—

It came as a sudden grip. He choked, blood filling his mouth. It felt like his rib cage was being wrenched open, something clawing up his throat. He tripped, landing hard and jarring his bones, immediately throwing up blood. Żaneta's hand touched his shoulder. He tried to shy away but his body was no longer listening.

No no no. He had to keep it together. He was so close and had fought for so long.

"You're much too weak for that," Chyrnog said. *"With each day that passes you become more like me. There's no getting free. I have you completely and there will be no more fighting. All will be quiet. Don't you want peace?"*

Malachiasz spat out another stream of blood. Żaneta made a soft, disgusted sound, which was rather silly, Malachiasz considered, because she was a damn Vulture, because of him, because all he did was corrupt and destroy and make good things terrible. Chyrnog was right, there wasn't much left of Malachiasz that wasn't entropy and destruction and darkness, but there had never been much of him that wasn't that to begin with. He had been created for chaos. He had been made of pain, for pain, by pain. He couldn't fight it because there was nothing to fight. It was his true nature and always had been. All that was left was to allow the inevitable.

Malachiasz collapsed, and everything shuttered dark around him.

45

NADEZHDA

LAPTEVA

The god of war is known to deal with his clerics with a soft hand. A hand that turns hard against Kalyazin's enemies.

—Codex of the Divine 38:76

Malachiasz was gone in the morning. Żaneta, too.

It was difficult not to despair.

Serefin looked to Katya for what they should do. Katya looked to Nadya.

"We get there first," Nadya finally said. If Chyrnog was taking Malachiasz to the same place, they had to get there before Chyrnog could consume the vestiges of Malachiasz's soul.

Katya estimated they had two more days of travel. It went faster while they followed the army's path, but soon they veered farther south and were back to tramping through piles of snow.

They set up camp and it felt like they were all waiting for

the end. Nadya sat next to Rashid by the fire they should not have lit, but had to for survival, and leaned against him.

"I hope he's all right," she whispered, knowing he wasn't.

"What happens if he gets there first?" Rashid asked.

Nadya shook her head but looked up at Serefin where he stood before them. He shrugged helplessly.

"We have to hope," she said. "That's all we have."

Rashid scratched at his arms, as if his markings were perpetually itchy. He'd discovered that if he thought really hard, he could make the snow melt away, green growth shooting up, but the cold quickly choked it down. He toyed with it as they sat.

Parijahan came over, sitting on Nadya's other side. She knew Parijahan wanted to know if she had a plan. They all hoped she had a plan. She did not.

She had the few things she was confident about. She knew there was no reasoning with the old gods—they were more power than anything else—and that her knowledge about power structures and hierarchies would do her well because that was what it came down to, ultimately. Her gods weren't on the same rung of the ladder.

But if she was molded from the old gods, did that make her one, too?

"It's not that simple."

She flinched at the unexpected voice. Rashid cast her a glance before getting up to help Ostyia with dinner. Ostyia was not great with food.

But the voice had been so unexpected and so dearly wanted. *Veceslav.*

In the pantheon there had only been a few gods who spoke to her as regularly as Marzenya, and the one she was most fond of was Veceslav. Of war and peace and iron. He was kind—as much as a god could be, she realized now. His silence had wounded her the most; that his silence had continued after the gods had started to speak again had been equally hard.

"Hello, child." The god's voice sounded warm and Nadya knew to be wary. Marzenya had taught her caution.

I could ask you a thousand questions. I could ask why you left me. She got up, gently touching Parijahan's shoulder.

"I'm going to take a walk," she whispered, holding up her prayer beads by way of explanation.

Parijahan nodded. "Stay close."

I want to understand, Veceslav. I feel as if I have pieces but still so much is being hidden from me.

"*There was fear, when Marzenya claimed you. We had stopped claiming mortals because of one who had fallen to Chyrnog before you.*"

Nadya frowned. *Who?*

"*Oh, you've heard of Celestyna Privalova. They were never stricken from record.*"

Fragmented passages in old books didn't paint a clear picture.

Nadya crunched through the snow. They were in a forest, less dense than the ones they had trekked through to Bolagvoy, but darkness still held the air around her. The trees were oppressive even if they weren't tucked so close together.

Celestyna was said to be the reason Kalyazin was losing the war. It had been evenly matched—neither side gaining a true advantage—until the day Celestyna had betrayed General Khartashov to a Tranavian blood mage, *for* a Tranavian blood mage. The army had suffered devastating defeats. The clerics had died. Then there was only Nadya.

But she was a cleric?

"*She was mine.*"

"Oh," Nadya breathed. She had known Veceslav had a cleric that he never spoke of. But that couldn't have been that long ago. "Was Chyrnog awake?"

"*He has always been able to whisper from a place past oblivion. Able to twist and tug those who are weak to him into doing as he desires.*"

You think you're seeing it happen again.

"*Marzenya was convinced you could be controlled. She thought that if she held her grip tight enough, you would never know. If she covered your ears, you would never hear their songs. If she shielded your eyes,*" *you would never see how this world turns. You would never feel your own magic and realize that you could act apart from her."*

Nadya frowned. *That's why you stopped talking to me.*

"I feared another tragedy," he said.

It was . . . strange. To be talking like this to a god once more. To feel like one knew her, even cared, though she knew not to go that far. Not to ascribe human emotions to these beings who were not human.

But who might have been, once.

Veceslav, why are you talking to me?

"I would like to make things clear."

Sounds like a job for Vaclav.

"If you'd like. He is willing as well."

Nadya blinked. *What?*

"This is . . . not a universally held opinion. Most of us are willing to extend our voices to you once more to try to prolong the inevitable. We are all in danger."

You think I'll fall to the old gods.

"You already have. It's simply a matter of how it will manifest."

Nadya winced. Nice to know they believed in her.

And so it's self-preservation that brings you back.

"Do you wish to hear our voices, truly?"

She closed her eyes. Yes and yes and no.

And this wasn't about them anymore. She was making her own decisions to save the world, to save everything, to save a Tranavian king who drank too much and had fallen hard for his lieutenant, to save an Akolan girl who was calculating and far more manipulative than she ever let on but was so very kind, to save an Akolan boy who was gentle and good and so ready and willing to die saving his friends. She wanted to save the dry Tranavian girl who was terrifyingly loyal.

She wanted to save a monster. A monster with sharp claws and teeth and cold eyes. She wanted to save a boy with careful hands and a soft voice and gentle smile.

There was no saving him.

"You were taken by the dark. We wait to see if you will be strong enough to fight it. But I am here to tell you that I want to help."

She tugged on her prayer beads, her fingers finding Marzenya's. A crack had run through it, right over the symbol of the open-mouthed skull. She pressed the pad of her thumb against the splinter, thinking. Considering how everything she had known about the world had shifted. Wondering how a boy who hated the gods so much yet was possessed by one could be saved. Thinking about how, even if the gods spoke to her now, nothing would ever be as it once was.

What will this ask of me?

"Everything."

There was no marking on the map. Pelageya had called it *Stravhkinzi'k Volushni*. It was an archaic name, old and foreign to the tongue. There would be no trite Tranavian translations to paint a better picture of what they might see.

What would a graveyard of gods be?

Nadya thought of the clearing. The circle of statues. That feeling, impossible to shake. The bad luck that had followed her and Malachiasz ever since.

This was worse.

Without warning, Serefin fell from his horse, choking. He waved Kacper off and hunched over his knees. When he straightened, his eye had collected more stars. A burst of moths clouded around his head. He rested a hand on Kacper's chest for balance, not looking at him. Whatever Serefin was, he was sensitive to the divine. He swayed on his feet before leaning over and spitting out blood.

"Not alarming in the least," Katya said, voice dull.

Nadya dismounted, tossing her horse's reins to the *tsarevna*. "We go on foot from here." Nadya walked over to Serefin and, with a glance at Kacper, wrapped an arm around his waist.

"How have you not been bowled over yet?" Serefin asked blearily.

"I was made for this. You had it forced upon you."

One foot in front of the other. Ahead, Nadya could see the steep drop off of a ravine. Making their way across the distance seemed to take the entire day. When they reached the edge, a boneyard met their gaze.

It scattered for miles in every direction. Bleached white from a millennia of sunlight. Vast and huge, bigger than any city she had ever seen. A rib cage that stretched for miles. A skull that appeared capable of blocking out the sun.

Kacper frowned. "It's just another forest."

Serefin blinked at him.

Nadya ducked out from underneath Serefin's arm. He wavered slightly. "Do you want to see it?" she asked Kacper.

He hesitated.

Already something was beginning to pick at Nadya's edges. She could hear singing, a low, haunting, infuriating melody. Mad and hollow and *repetitive*.

She waved at her head as if batting away a fly.

"I want to know," Kacper said.

"Tell me when it becomes too much," she said. She didn't want to break him. Bodies were strewn among the bones, and she couldn't tell if she was seeing reality, the past, or another realm entirely.

She pressed her fingertips to Kacper's forehead, sharing her sight. The boy stiffened, hand clutching at her elbow. He shivered, jarred and unsteady. He had seen enough. She lowered her hands.

His expression was one of sheer horror, his dark skin tinged a sickly gray. "Oh," he whispered, casting a desperate glance Serefin's way. "He sees that?"

"I think he always sees divine influence now. That eye is . . . something else."

"Do you see someone on the other side of the ravine?" Serefin spoke up suddenly, making them jump. Ostyia came up beside them but did not ask to share in what Kacper had seen.

The other side of the ravine was too far away. She cast Serefin an uncertain glance. He kept rapidly blinking his one eye and messing with his eye patch.

"No," Ostyia murmured, taking his hand. "It's gone, Serefin."

"There's—Oh," Serefin whispered. He closed his eye. "It's *that* eye. He's over there. There's an army on the other side of the ravine. Two, I think."

No.

"I can't tell what he's doing. I . . ." he trailed off.

Nadya didn't understand.

"It's my eye." Serefin answered the question she had not asked. "He ended up with it. I don't really know how. We left him on that divine mountain, and it twisted him up. There was so much blood, and it doesn't matter what you did, Nadya, blood is power. Blood has always been power."

Kacper swore softly and grabbed Serefin's hand. "Hey, come here." He tugged Serefin closer, sliding his hand up the back of Serefin's neck, pulling him down so his face buried against his shoulder. "Serefin, stay with me."

Nadya's stomach tightened. She'd never be able to touch Malachiasz like that again.

Serefin twitched. "He's not Malachiasz, Nadya. Hitting him real hard isn't going to fix this."

46

SEREFIN
MELESKI

They struck down Milyena and cast out Sofka. Inno-
kentiy lost the voice of his god and Lev lost his voice.
Who else would fall from the graces of the gods? Who
else would be cast aside for a single misstep?
—The Letters of Włodzimierz

Serefin's stomach roiled. The air here was heavy and suffocating. He felt bad Kacper had been forced to see the boneyard. He felt worse that they needed to enter the boneyard.

"Why?" Nadya asked, horrified.

"No questions." Malachiasz—Chyrnog—was going to
strike and they couldn't fight an army. Serefin knew how
to look at a battlefield and immediately understand what
strategy would get the highest number of his soldiers out
alive. Sacrifices would be made, but sacrifices were necessary in war.

Was this war? He supposed it was.

The climb down was arduous, but they managed it. Nadya

kept close to Serefin's side, aware he saw things she could not. But her time would come. The graveyard was shifting for her, rumbling at her presence. A new age was dawning, one that had been waiting for Nadya, the girl with darkness in her veins.

"Is he gone?" she asked softly.

They stood sheltered from the snow by what Serefin thought was a rib bone. It was so large to have lost its articulation completely. He eyed it before looking down at her.

"Yes."

Agony cracked across her expression.

"Maybe he's in there, buried deep, but . . ." Serefin shook his head. It was disturbing how Malachiasz still looked like Malachiasz. Maybe Chyrnog and he were too alike for it to have changed him.

"But not likely," Nadya said. "The inevitable come to pass."

Perhaps. Perhaps they were doomed to die in this place. Perhaps Pelageya had been coordinating their downfall since the beginning. Serefin didn't believe that, not truly, but it was impossible to know.

"We have to find his soul," she said.

"How are we supposed to do that without him? How do we know he doesn't already have it? Or the god destroyed it?"

Nadya's fist clenched. "Because that would mean we've failed."

Żaneta stumbled into their group. That wasn't ideal—if she could find them, so could the rest.

"I'm sorry," she said, trembling. "I don't know what happened. He was fine and then he was . . . not. And now the Tranavians are here and the Kalyazi army has mobilized and it's going to be a massacre."

She was bleeding from a messy head wound, and Serefin couldn't tell if it was benign or serious. He almost joked that she must not have hit Malachiasz hard enough, instead motioning for someone to help her. Rashid rushed over.

"Why are they here?" Ostyia asked. But she knew, same as him.

The war had to end sometime. He just hadn't expected the last stand to come like this.

Serefin exchanged a glance with Nadya. He was rather hoping she would know what to do next. Bile churned in his stomach and the whispers settling in the back of his mind reminded him terrifyingly of his time in Tzanelivki.

You wanted this, he said, accusatorily, to Velyos.

"*I wanted my freedom. Chyrnog came with you wanting that Vulture dead.*"

Well, that failed, didn't it?

"*Things don't always work out as planned.*"

But you'll suffer, too, if he truly breaks free from Malachiasz, won't you?

A long pause.

"*You play in the realm of the gods, now. Go find your brother's soul.*"

Something landed at Serefin's feet. An arrow. He stepped back behind the rib bone.

"Don't you dare say we need to—" Kacper started.

"We need to split up," Serefin said.

Kacper sighed.

Nadya looked nervous. The longer they stood there, the more she changed. That strange, shivery halo flickered around her, fractured and tainted. It had been mostly whole, a few fine cracks, when Serefin first saw it, but jagged knives had since punched through. Her left hand had sharpened claws curling outward. Her white-blond hair was in a single thick braid over her shoulder and when she spoke her teeth were strange and wrong. Serefin couldn't shake the feeling that she would alter more the longer they were here. That he might, too.

"We're not splitting up," Katya said. "It'd be the forest all over again."

"In case you haven't noticed, dear, we're right back in the thick of the divine nonsense that happened in the forest," Serefin snapped.

A volley of arrows landed at their feet. They couldn't stand here anymore. It was clear no one was actively trying to kill them, but a stray arrow could do the job just the same.

"Each minute we stand here arguing, Chyrnog gets closer

to Malachiasz's soul," Nadya said softly. Her voice was weirdly tonal, like more than one person was speaking. When she looked up at Serefin, her dark eyes were shot with gold. He flinched. "He's your brother, and you're the one who can see this place as it is. When I try, I . . ." She faltered, falling quiet. "It's better if you lead on."

Serefin wanted to run. It was the comfortable choice. He loved Malachiasz, even after everything. He could admit finally that he loved his brother, but they were also racing headlong into disaster. This was doomed.

But he was no longer the boy who ran. He had one godstouched eye, a cloud of moths that followed his every step, and the voice of a god he didn't particularly want rattling in his head. He wasn't the same person who had staggered home from the front. Serefin was a king. Beaten and battered by magic, but a king, nonetheless.

He had helped start this nightmare; he had to help stop it, somehow.

And it would be better if they split up.

"If this place wanted us separated, it would do that itself," Anna pointed out. The priestess had been quiet, and her voice came out sharp and unexpected.

She was right. It wasn't the same here as the forest. If he turned away, everyone else wouldn't disappear.

But this was a graveyard of the gods. Much worse could be lurking here, hiding among the pale white shards. The bones were too large to consider, so vast that sometimes they didn't even register as bones, but as strange pale trees with no branches, smooth and eerie.

Nadya slipped her hand into his, jarring him. Her hands were freezing.

"We need to stay together," she said quietly. "At the very least, us and Parj."

Parijahan glanced over at her name. Right. The four. Pelageya's strange omen. They couldn't do much without Malachiasz.

One step at a time, he thought.

Where would Pelageya hide a soul? He took out the disc of metal tied to Malachiasz. The Kalyazi spellwork scrolled around the edges was structured in a way that was familiar, like blood magic. A lifetime ago he had found those spell books scrawled with Kalyazi prayers and wondered if the Kalyazi weren't as devout as he had believed, and now he had more evidence of that very fact.

He supposed he was getting his answer.

"Blood has always been power," Serefin murmured.

He gently pulled his hand away from Nadya's, taking the blade from his belt, and with a nod, Kacper's *szitelki* from the sheath at his hip, rolling up one sleeve, then the next.

He crouched, motioning for Nadya and Parijahan to do the same.

"Let's start with those of us we know are wrapped up in this," he said, his voice soft. "If we need more, we can get more."

Nadya frowned. "Serefin, what—"

He flipped the blades, and in one swift motion sliced both his forearms at once. The initial rush of power that always came when he cast magic did not come. He missed it. This was slower, sluggish, building in intensity until something pulled steadily at his heart.

He flipped the blades again, wiping them deftly on his trousers, and started to hand them to Nadya, but she was already dragging her *voryens* across her forearms. Parijahan swiftly followed suit. The ground grew wet beneath them.

He let his blood seep into the earth, closing his eye, hoping the blood of the godstouched did something, anything, in this place of divine memory and death. He heard Nadya's low intake of breath. When he opened his eye, a trail of flowers was sprouting, leading off into the bones.

"Do we follow it?" she asked.

He gave a nod and straightened. Nadya touched the bone nearest to them as she rose, staining it black. His gaze lingered on the imprint of her fingertips.

Serefin took the first step. Tiny bones snapped and crunched beneath their feet, not those of the gods, but of simple creatures who had stumbled into this terrible place and been found wanting. Bones of gods caged them in as they walked. A jawbone. A rib cage. A skull that took a significant amount of time to walk past.

Eventually, they arrived at the skeletal remains of a god, somehow intact, and in the center, where the god's heart would have been, was a vast lake that Serefin was certain was made of blood. Little creeks like veins spread out from the lake. He stepped over one.

"Didn't Pelageya say it was on an island?" he asked.

Nadya's eyes closed. "In a tree in a rabbit in an egg or some nonsense. It's from a children's tale."

"Well, we're children."

She laughed at that, which was good. Serefin didn't think he could handle another Nadya meltdown. Seeing her crack scared him in a way that was hard to define because she had always been so unflappable.

"You're twenty years old," she said.

"Details."

They reached the shore of the lake. There wasn't sand, or if there was, it was the wrong color. Black and glittering. It would almost be pretty if it weren't so macabre.

"For a country horrified when you get a paper cut, there sure are a lot of bloody pools here," Kacper commented.

Katya crouched at the edge. "Truly, we've been in this long enough to realize Kalyazin has been overcompensating for something."

Nadya snorted. Parijahan held her hand out over the water—well, it wasn't water, but Serefin didn't really want to think of it as anything else.

"We have to cross it," Nadya said.

"You think this is the place?" Rashid asked.

"Do you have a boat?" Kacper asked.

She shot them both withering looks and moved closer, digging a heel into the sand. She narrowed her eyes at the water, plunging her hand in. Katya hastily shuffled back and Parijahan reached out as if to stop her. Kacper took a step forward, but Serefin put his hand across his chest.

"Let her," he murmured. "We have to work on instinct here and it will lead us to strange places."

Nadya's eyes began to glow, cracks of golden light forming under her skin. Her strange halo shivered and grew brighter.

The ground shook. Serefin turned slightly, studying the path behind them. He couldn't shake the feeling that they were being watched.

"Of course you're being watched. The gods, the freed, the never caged, the old ones, we all watch. We wait to see how you will shift the world on its axis. If you will balance it or plunge it further into chaos."

Did Pelageya start all of this?

Velyos laughed. *"The witch? Pelageya has power enough to become a god if she wishes, but every day she turns away from that path. Pelageya is many things, but where you are is no more her fault than it is yours, or that cleric's, or that Vulture's. The world turns. Choices are made. Yes, I had hoped someone would set me free. Yes, I called to Pelageya to take the pendant and place it somewhere it might be used. Yes, she complied."*

So, it's your fault, then.

"I have always been one for mischief," Velyos replied.

This is a little more than mischief. You got what you wanted. You got your freedom and your revenge; what about this four songs nonsense? That was you, wasn't it?

"Chyrnog has worked for far longer than I. He has been nudging the pieces of this game for a millennium and you have all complied exactly as he wished. Mortals are predictable. This isn't revenge, this is simply his nature. His nature is to devour, to consume, this is simply what he knows. And he found in your brother a mortal made for the same."

Pillars of dark stone began to lift up from the bloody water, forming a bridge that disappeared into the distance.

Nadya stood, the gold slowly siphoning away.

"The four songs? Yes, that was me. Chyrnog was always going to break free. Chyrnog was always going to need to be contained. That's the way it has always been, but it has been so long since he last escaped that the world forgot him. You mortals thought if you no longer spoke of the terrors of the deep, they would be condemned to myth and no longer ravage the world. Alas, it's not so easy. This was all inevitable."

Inevitability is too Kalyazi a notion for me, Serefin replied.

"I didn't choose Tranavians intentionally, but you have made this game so much more interesting, so I have to thank you for that."

Serefin rolled his eye.

What about her?

Nadya wavered on her feet, turning to him. He took a step toward her as she hesitated.

"I've never seen anything like her. She makes things so much more unpredictable. Delightful, really."

Serefin didn't like the sound of that.

"She has their power in her bones, but it wasn't enough to make her like them. Or, maybe it was."

"What do you think we're going to find?" Serefin asked aloud.

Nadya glanced over. "Whatever it is, it's not going to be pretty," she said simply, then set off across the bridge. Serefin let out a breathless, incredulous laugh, before jogging to catch up with her.

"How did you do this?" he asked.

"Magic. What else?"

Like no magic I've ever seen, he thought. He didn't really understand what Nadya was, but apparently neither did the gods.

"Don't mistake my not telling you things you did not ask for ignorance," Velyos snipped. *"She is what happens when the darkest divinity is harbored in a mortal. A girl, divine in one breath, monstrous in another. That she has survived this long is remarkable. And truly, the old gods must have something very specific in mind for her. Their voices should have driven her mad long ago."*

But she can hear the voices of the gods, that's her whole thing.

"Yes, and no mortal should be able to stand as many voices as she does. Perhaps she isn't as sane as assumed."

Serefin frowned. He cast Nadya a glance, but her gaze was locked on the island they drew near.

"What if we didn't make it here first?" Serefin whispered, as Nadya stepped off the bridge and onto the glassy black sands.

"Catastrophizing again?" Kacper asked, coming up behind him.

Serefin should have asked everyone else to wait on the other side of this strange water, but he was grateful for Kacper's presence. Here, the beach broke into forests, dark in a way that terrified Serefin.

"Hypothetically speaking," he said to Nadya, "the only place where the gods could walk in our realm was on that mountain, right?"

"Hypothetically, yes," she replied, eyeing the forest with trepidation. "But this place doesn't play by the rules either, so we shouldn't count on being safe from that."

Great.

"I'll wait here," Katya announced. "Hold the bridge if needed." It was very clear that she simply did not want to go into the woods.

Serefin took the bone relic from his belt, holding it in his palm.

Nadya's face paled. "I need that," she whispered, taking it with trembling fingers.

Anna glanced at Nadya, who nodded slightly. The priestess sat down next to Katya.

Kacper grabbed Serefin's hand. "No, you—"

Serefin cut Kacper off with a kiss.

"I'll come back," he murmured against Kacper's lips. "I promise. I love you."

Kacper's expression cracked. He grabbed Serefin's face and kissed him harder. "Don't you dare make this sound like a goodbye. I love you, and you're coming back to me."

Ostyia took Kacper's hand and tugged him away, directing a look at Serefin that said that if he didn't come back, she would resurrect him to kill him herself. He'd missed having her around.

"Come along," Parijahan said, stepping past Nadya and Serefin.

His breath caught. He had known Parijahan was as trapped in this as the rest of them, but he'd thought the visual cracks in their mortality wouldn't extend to her. Nothing ever seemed to really touch her.

Her black hair was tied in a loose braid, but small triangular horns pressed out from her forehead. She glanced over her shoulder at them. Her gray eyes were gold, the pupils the wrong direction, slitted like a snake's. She grinned.

"I want to save my friend," she said brightly, setting off into the forest.

"She's going to be the only one to make it out alive, I swear," Nadya muttered, then ran after her.

It was too late to turn back, too late to run. And as much as he wanted to, as much as he couldn't shake the feeling that they were walking directly into a naked blade, Serefin followed them anyway.

interlude vi

TSAREVNA

YEKATERINA

VODYANOVA

The cleric, the king, and the *prasīt* all disappeared into the tree line. After a few tense moments of silence, Rashid let out an irritated huff of air.

"No," he muttered. "She's not doing this alone." Then he ran into the forest.

Anna called after him, but Katya held out a hand to keep her back. It was his choice.

"How can we let them go off by themselves?" Anna asked.

"You saw them. This place is changing them. I don't think we could survive anything in there. I don't think we'll survive being out here, quite frankly."

Katya eyed the sky dubiously. She had spent her whole life studying the strange and the occult, but she had always rather thought it was an exaggeration. The sun had dimmed, like something rested beside it, casting a long shadow. How much longer until the whole world was plunged into darkness?

She gritted her teeth. She wasn't going to die here. She wouldn't allow it. Besides, her time wasn't up yet.

"Do we . . . wait?" Ostyia asked, sitting close enough that their thighs touched. After a moment of consideration, she took Katya's hand, kissing it gently.

Katya let that warm her chilled heart. It was so cold here.

Ostyia rubbed her thumb over the back of Katya's hand. "I'm worried about Serefin," she said softly.

Kacper glanced over at them. "He's not as bad as he was before, when Velyos had him."

"No, he's not, but . . ." She shook her head slowly. "He's not exactly himself, either."

"Neither is Nadya," Anna said.

"I don't think we're going to see them again," Kacper whispered, tears in his dark eyes.

Ostyia squeezed Katya's hand, kissed her temple, then got up and wrapped her arms around Kacper. Katya wondered how long they had known each other, how long they had circled in the king's orbit. Serefin was charismatic, as much as he tried not to be. How many people hadn't made it close to him like these two?

"Stay here," Ostyia said fiercely. "I can't lose you both, I can't."

"We can't lose *Serefin*!" Kacper cried.

Ostyia's face was bleak. "No, we can't. But if he doesn't do this, we lose him anyway." Kacper folded down, burying his head against Ostyia's shoulder.

The air around them changed sharply. Katya stood, frowning, reaching for her sword. The Vulture—gods she'd been ignoring the girl—looked up at her, tensing.

"What is it?" Her Kalyazi was surprisingly sharp. There wasn't a hint of a Tranavian accent in it.

Anna lifted her head. "I feel it, too."

Something heavy, falling down on top of them, smothering

them. A trembling in the earth, as if something very deep was clawing its way up.

"What did they say would happen if Malachiasz got there first?" Żaneta asked.

Katya shook her head wordlessly. "Chyrnog is entropy. He's the end of the world."

The sky darkened at a terrifyingly rapid pace. The sun dimming with each passing breath. Katya's grip tightened on the hilt of her sword, her palms starting to sweat.

"Ostyia?"

Ostyia made a soft sound of acknowledgment. She still held Kacper's hands but was staring up at the sky.

"Remember when all those corpses attacked Voczi Dovorik?"

"I'd rather not."

There was a shift as something rose on the horizon. Muscle and sinew and flesh lifting onto a pile of bones, forming a body. There were too many limbs, a roiling chaos in vaguely human shape. It was far away but Katya knew with dread certainty that it would be very close, very soon.

"I never thought I'd say this, but I wish you had blood magic right now," Katya said.

Ostyia scrambled back from Kacper and to her feet. Her spell book was at her hip, Kacper's at his. Useless.

"Me too," she said.

Another figure lifted in the distance. Vast and incomprehensible, a twisting facsimile of vague life and pure horror. Gnashing teeth and blood dripping down bones as it became something more. One at a time, then all at once, others followed, horrific and indescribable. This was no longer a graveyard.

"How religious are you feeling, Katya?" Anna asked, her voice good-natured for someone who appeared terrified out of her mind.

"I'm thinking of committing some high blasphemy," Katya replied.

"Yes," Anna agreed. "Me too."

47

MALACHIASZ
CZECHOWICZ

Rohzlav watches Chyrnog from the shadows, as the
one hungers, the other delights in the act of starvation.
—The Volokhtaznikon

"*You said she would be easily swayed,*" he hissed at . . . himself?
Wait, no, Chyrnog hissed at him. Malachiasz was separate,
there were broken parts of him left. Small pieces.

"*She can hear my songs. The songs of my kin. She is darkness*
and divinity and she can raze this world to the ground! Stubborn
girl. Why doesn't she listen?"

Chyrnog, ever confident, ever arrogant in his power, had
been the one to speak to her. Appealing to her emotions,
appealing to Malachiasz's vulnerability. He had failed.

Her darkness, thrilling as it was, had never turned to destruction. If it had, Tranavia would have been ashes a year
ago. Serefin would be dead, Malachiasz, too. The sanctuary
where she had been betrayed would be dust. She wouldn't
be convinced.

Chyrnog didn't care.

Malachiasz retreated. He had finally found a battle that was too much for him. There was only one path for him to take. More chaos. More pain. It was all he knew.

He pressed out. There was a pulling at his chest and he recognized the pieces of his soul that he had thrown away. He needed them back. But then Chyrnog would have them, and what would he have left? Nothing and nothing and nothing.

"No," Chyrnog snapped. "They're here."

On an island in a forest in a tree and Malachiasz couldn't remember how the rest went but before them was a small temple. Cut from bone. The bones of a god carved into doors and windows and towers. He saw Nadya turn, her face going pale. She touched Serefin's arm and he followed her gaze.

The end was destruction no matter how it went.

SEREFIN

MELESKI

"Go inside," Nadya said. "Take whatever you find."

He shot her a dubious look, blanching when he saw the relic in her hands. He turned to Parijahan.

"She stays," Nadya said. "I need whatever it is she does that keeps his chaos at bay."

Parijahan took a deep, shaky breath. Sighing, Serefin steeled himself and walked into the temple.

And right into a nightmare.

He should have expected it, honestly. Where else would his brother's soul be comfortably hiding? The floor was strangely squishy under his boots, like he was standing in the mouth of a great beast. Glowing candles, held up by grotesque hands on the walls, cast a sickly light on blood trickling down from the ceiling.

He pressed past it. Past the screams, full-throated and mad, past the eyes that opened on the stone walls, watching him silently as he walked. He stepped over a body and did not investigate it further. Who would come to this place of dread horror?

Well, him, he supposed.

The dim hallway broke into a wide sanctuary, primal and jagged, and Serefin had the feeling of having been here before. A blade poised over his heart, carving out his chest. His blood splashed across the stone altar.

It was all the same. A space folded over and over again in time.

The small stone church, the clearing of horrifying statues, and a thousand other spaces where people had been sacrificed to the old gods. Where blood had spilt for the sake of divinity. No different from how it was spilt for magic. It was the same. *They* were the same.

There was a tree carved on the stone altar, blood spattered against it. A box rested in the pool of blood, and when Serefin opened it, the ground shook. The gods turned their eyes on him all at once and a shiver cracked down his spine.

He found a single black feather, blood staining the tip, and laughed.

NADEZHDA

LAPTEVA

Nadya didn't understand Parijahan's magic, but every blow he tried to land, every claw grasping for her flesh, missed. She didn't want to take the next step, better to fight him forever.

Distantly, she knew Serefin had returned, a box in his hands, and it was time. There was only one way to do this. Pelageya had told her that it would hurt him, and he must be separate from Chyrnog for it to cling to him. And he had to want it.

She caught Malachiasz's hand, letting his claws dig into her palm. She pulled him closer. She had expected that when Chyrnog finally won, he would take the chaos god, the monster. But instead, he had taken the boy. Fitting, she supposed, as all Malachiasz's atrocities were done when he looked his most harmless.

"*Dozleyena*, Chyrnog," she said, her voice soft. "It's time we talked, you and I."

A slow smile stretched over Malachiasz's face, but it wasn't his. It never reached those haunted, murky eyes.

"Are you ready, then, for oblivion?"

Nadya had known oblivion. She had walked amongst the gods. She had died and been reborn. There was nothing this being could do to her that had not already been done. There was nothing she had not already lost.

"Your power grows with each passing moment, but it's not enough, is it? There are so many gods who would fight you. Willful, cruel beings who still recognize when one means true harm. You want me because I am all you are not. You are nothing but a sad glimmer of darkness in eternity."

"I am everything," Chyrnog snapped.

"Are you? You were locked away once, you can be locked away again." Nadya grinned.

She jerked him closer, slamming her hand against Malachiasz's forehead and diving deep. If only she had known, when she had carved into his palm, what she would be creating. A way to know what was him, what wasn't, a way to yank hard at the void Chyrnog clung to and separate it from Malachiasz.

She took the relic and stabbed it into Malachiasz's chest.

"I'm sorry, my love," she whispered in his ear at his little gasp of surprise. "I had to." She twisted the blade a little farther, severing Chyrnog's hold as much as she could.

Malachiasz fell to his knees. Nadya knelt with him, tears streaming down her cheeks.

"Serefin?" she called, beseeching.

She felt his hand on her shoulder. He fumbled with the box,

opening it, revealing a single black feather. She let out a helpless laugh.

"Always a Vulture at heart," she whispered. She took the feather and pressed it past his lips, and pulled the blade from his chest, holding her palm over the wound as it bled.

Another hand landed over hers. Brown skin and careful, long fingers. He shouldn't be here. Rashid furrowed his brow, flowers blooming from his fingertips.

"No, he has to die," she said. "He has to die for it to work."

"Nadya?" Malachiasz's voice, soft and weak.

"Malachiasz." She took his face between her hands. "Twice death-touched boy, this will work. Please trust me."

Serefin made a strange sound from behind them. Nadya glanced over her shoulder. There was an odd red light emanating from within the temple. Her vision split jarringly. The temple was a clearing—that horrible clearing—the altar in the center soaked with blood. Malachiasz let out a long, pained breath through his teeth and struggled to rise.

"No, no, no," she said, trying to keep him in place. Not the clearing. Not the place that had stripped him of his humanity and showed him as he truly was. Keep him here, keep him safe, set him free. "You'll die for good."

He pushed past her hand on his chest, kissing her. His lips were soft against hers, leaving an ache that nestled beneath her ribs.

"Maybe it's time for that," he whispered.

"What? *No*." She tried to cling to him, but trembling and bleeding, he stood and moved away from her. He gently pressed his lips against Rashid's temple. He rested his forehead against Serefin's and gave a sad smile.

He's saying goodbye, Nadya thought, horrified.

He cupped Parijahan's cheek in his hand. She knocked it off, shaking her head, saying something, but Nadya couldn't hear past the rushing in her ears. Malachiasz stepped into the temple.

"No," Nadya breathed, getting to her feet. "This is not the time to be a hero."

Serefin closed his eye. "I can't believe I'm about to do this." And with a muttered curse, he followed.

It was the clearing. It was that clearing and those statues and every dead and living god and they would all be unraveled. This would kill them.

Parijahan glanced over her shoulder at Nadya and Rashid, and without another word, she went, too.

Nadya didn't let herself think about how she would be destroyed by this. She ran into the temple and let herself be devoured.

48

MALACHIASZ

CZECHOWICZ

Spiders poured from underneath Sofka's door.
—Fragment from the personal journals
of Lev Milekhin

"He's torn free from you."

Malachiasz opened his eyes slowly, the light blinding. He winced, expecting his flesh to burn, but there was nothing. He sat up slowly.

He was still in the temple. Snow covered the floor, but it was less a home for nightmares, and more like a place where there had been worship, once. Cool stone walls, an altar of polished marble, no blood anywhere.

"Does that mean I'm dead?" he asked. He didn't recognize this voice. It was warmer, less painful than Chyrnog. No damned singing.

"More or less."

"It's final, this time?" he asked, uncertain. He tilted his

gaze upward to find a dark sky scattered with millions of stars. His breath caught in his throat.

"Oh."

"Not my domain, those, and I doubt you really want to talk to the one who controls them."

Malachiasz glanced over, instantly recoiling.

The figure had been impaled on countless spears and swords. He hunched over the weight of them, clearly once tall and proud, but no more. His face was impossible for Malachiasz to make out.

"That you can see me at all means you've not much humanity left."

Malachiasz felt different. Anxious and thrilled and impossibly sad. There had always been a hole where his heart had been, but the void was a little less all-consuming now.

He'd gotten his soul back, whatever that meant.

"What's your name?" Malachiasz asked.

"Veceslav."

He recognized that name. But why? His bewilderment must have shown.

"I am fond of the cleric. I have agreed to do one thing for her, though I don't particularly wish to. But Chyrnog is free, and after he razes your world to ashes, he will turn to ours. Call it self-preservation. I give you a choice."

Nadya's voice had always been fonder when she spoke of this god than Marzenya.

"I don't understand," he said with a frown.

"I was warned that working with a Tranavian would be particularly tedious . . ."

"You've killed so many of my people," Malachiasz said, crossing his legs underneath him.

"Vulture, how many have you destroyed in your quest for knowledge?"

Malachiasz didn't have a number, but he knew the toll was high.

"You're the god of war," he said.

"I am. And you can claim that divinity you want so badly. Be like me. Godling that you are, it's but a short step higher."

Malachiasz got to his feet. "What are you saying?"

"Your mortal logic was flawed, but your path was right. It's simply a matter of seeing it to its end."

He could do it? He could have the power to finally stop this? He had worked so hard and sacrificed so much and to know that it was only inches away, that he could finally have what he'd been looking for—

But . . . was that what he was looking for? He had plotted the king's death and that ritual because the king had wanted the power of a god and Malachiasz knew it would be better served in his hands. But the power of a god untempered by mortality? That was a very different thing.

But he could put an end to Chyrnog. He could fix everything. He could bring peace.

"Ah, an easy choice, then."

Malachiasz almost agreed, greedy for an end point to his years of research. Greedy for an end to all of this.

He hesitated. "What is the other choice?"

"Mortality," Veceslav said with a shrug. "But mortality with my implicit touch."

Malachiasz recoiled. He couldn't live like this forever, with his will constantly smothered.

"I have no interest in consuming you," Veceslav said. "I have little interest in you at all. I claimed a mortal once, and it ended badly, and I can't imagine it won't end badly here. But Nadezhda has asked that I offer, and so I am. Godstouched once is godstouched forever and if you succeed against Chyrnog you will leave yourself open to other horrors."

Malachiasz shook his head. "I tried to destroy all of you."

"You weren't the first, you won't be the last."

He pressed a hand against his chest. "What will happen to me?"

Veceslav was unmoved. If he'd had a face, he might have lifted an eyebrow.

Malachiasz said, his voice very small, "I don't want to lose myself anymore."

"Anything you have done to yourself is your burden to bear. The chaos, the loss of control. If you were to take the next steps, I can't tell you what might happen."

"But if I choose mortality, that's it?"

"You won't have those vast swells of power you desire. You will keep what you stole, to take that away would be to rend time. The world is already crumbling from the rending that Marzenya had Nadezhda do. It will not survive another. Will you sacrifice those golden ideals of yours, to live? Or will you shed the final bonds holding you back?"

Malachiasz didn't know. "What if I don't choose either path?"

"Death."

Malachiasz didn't want to die. He wanted to live. He wanted to take Nadya to Tranavia when there was finally peace and show her how beautiful his country could be. It wasn't all monsters and swamps and blood, though that made up its beating heart and he loved that, too.

But Malachiasz had worked so hard. He had bled and struggled to keep Tranavia out of the sway of the gods. Would he toss that aside? For what?

Was life truly worth it?

49

SEREFIN

MELESKI

Valyashreva waits to rake her plague back over the land. One misstep and she will consume us all. There is no record of her death or containment.
—The Volokhtaznikon

Oh, I've been here before. Snow and ash and bloody footprints and songs and music and moths and stars. Serefin knew this place. He had never wanted to return.

"Dead again?"

"Dead again!" Velyos said. "It's becoming almost comical!"

"Huh." Serefin had known following Malachiasz into that temple was a bad idea, but he hadn't expected it to be *that* bad. "Well, that's less than ideal."

"Walk with me," Velyos said amiably, and Serefin, who had resisted this god—not a god—for so long, fell in step beside him. The tall cloaked figure with his deer skull head.

"You chose to cross over by going into that temple," Velyos said.

"Ah."

"Thought you might like that cleared up."

"So, Malachiasz is dead as well?"

"Oh, most likely. He'll have a choice just as you'll have a choice. Let's make it a lofty one. One of big ideals and kingly necessity. Barely a king, you are, but it's never too early or too late to start making the messy decisions."

Serefin didn't like the sound of that at all.

"There were four songs and I wanted all four songs; it would have been so easy with four songs. A quick break, for me, for those locked away, but perhaps not for Chyrnog, but who can say, I can't see the future! I can only guess and predict how you predictable mortals will act. And you do always seem to act as I suspect."

"There need to be four of us to bind Chyrnog back into the earth," Serefin said.

"That will be more difficult now that he's broken free of the boy."

That hit Serefin like a punch to the stomach. Somehow it had felt survivable when the old god was locked inside his brother's head. Even when he thought about giving up, Malachiasz was still fighting. Serefin hadn't had, well, *hope* exactly, but he'd thought maybe they would have a chance.

"What will happen?" Serefin asked softly.

"Why ask when you already know? Those friends of yours will be the first to go."

Kacper. Serefin's heart clenched. No, he told Kacper he was going to return. He wasn't going to die.

He was . . . already dead.

"Then, the rest of the world! And the next one! The gods will fall, Alena will be eaten, and the sun will go dark! Chyrnog will finally have the total destruction that has been his due since the beginning of time."

Serefin closed his eye. "What is my choice?"

"Do you want the power to stop the old god? Stop all of this in its tracks?"

Serefin froze.

Velyos walked a few paces more before he looked back. "Seemed a simple enough statement. Are you denser than I thought?" The skull tilted.

Finish . . . everything? Have the power to save his kingdom? It was too much, too good, it was . . .

"What would that entail?"

"Ah, ah." Velyos tapped a spindly finger against the side of his skull. "That's not the way this works. You have two paths and must choose the one to walk."

Serefin didn't trust the gods. That he would be *given* the means to stop Chyrnog didn't seem possible. As sweet as it sounded, as good as it seemed.

He wanted to know with utter certainty that Kacper was safe. That Ostyia and Żaneta were safe. That he might go to Katya's father and entreat him to begin the arduous process of coming together with Serefin to prepare a peace treaty. He wanted to know that his kingdom would have peace in his lifetime.

He had seen so much death.

He had killed so many.

It wasn't something that he ever truly allowed himself to dwell on, because he knew if he did, he would drown in it.

Could Tranavia have a king like him? One so stained with blood? One who was battered with the echoes of the front every single day? One who woke each night from the death of a friend being played out in his nightmares? This would be how he lived for the rest of his life. Serefin Meleski of the scars and trauma and decorated military jacket.

Was it an impossible choice, truly? How much he would love to wipe away everything he had done and everything he still had to account for; how easy it would be to turn the world away from the wartime sins of his people.

How thrilling to be the one to finally stop this damn war on sheer power alone.

But he didn't like the catch that he didn't know. The gods would ask for something in return that he would not want to give.

Serefin shook his head. "No," he said softly. "I want to stay me."

"You, godstouched, with your moths and stars and broken mind?" Velyos asked skeptically. "That could be fixed, easily. Your eye, too. You've kept such good track of it. We know exactly where to fetch it from."

Oh, it was tempting. But he didn't know who he was without the scarred mess. Without the war trauma and the nightmares. They had been with him for so long, they were part of him. And that was trite, it was cavalier, but he couldn't imagine a reality for himself like the one Velyos was describing.

"If you choose the mortal path, it is very likely that everyone you love will die," Velyos warned.

"Likely," Serefin repeated. "But not a guarantee?"

"Nothing in your world or mine is truly a guarantee," Velyos replied.

Serefin nodded slowly. "Then we fight back. Mortal and broken, as we are."

"Very well," he said. "What a choice you have made." And Serefin could have sworn that, somehow, Velyos was smiling.

interlude vii

PARIJAHAN

SIROOSI

"I'm not playing this game with you," Parijahan said.

She was quite tired of being toyed with by these Kalyazi gods. She had followed Malachiasz into this damn temple because she had a role to play in this madness, but she didn't have to like it.

"No?"

She sat cross-legged, her hands folded in her lap. Eyes closed.

"Do you think you have that kind of power? That you can deny my games?"

"Who am I talking to?" Parijahan asked, begrudgingly opening her eyes. She closed them again with a shiver.

The being was amorphous and fluid, a pale featureless mask over its face, talon-tipped wings that looked treacherously sharp instead of arms.

Parijahan thought it better if she just didn't see that.

"My name is Bozidarka."

Parijahan inclined her head slightly. "And why is it you're talking to me? I'm not one of your northerners."

"Do you think we only care for those of our territories?"

"Well, yes." Parijahan opened her eyes, she couldn't help it. She winced at the visual assault of the goddess's appearance. "That's been the general consensus."

"And yet, here you are."

Parijahan frowned. She lightly pressed her fingers against her chest, finding no heartbeat. "Am I dead?"

"What did you think was going to happen?"

Fair enough. What *had* she expected? She only knew that she had wanted to help and didn't know how. She didn't know how to make this power she supposedly had work; she didn't know how far Rashid's magic could go, truly.

Rashid. He would know not to have followed them, wouldn't he?

She couldn't fool herself. Rashid had followed, for her. She sighed.

"I don't see what you want with me."

"The same thing that we want with the rest of you mortals."

"Why should I comply with any of your wishes? You can say this is our silly mortal fault, but it's not like you haven't been manipulating Nadya from the very beginning."

"Fair enough," Bozidarka replied.

Parijahan frowned, not expecting that response.

"But this isn't about Nadezhda. This is about *you*. This is about offering you the power you have run from for so long."

"Offering me *what*?" Parijahan stood. "No, no, no, thank you, very much, I don't want anything to do with this. I've been running from power my whole life, I'm not about to change my mind now."

"If that's what you truly want . . . but you could save that boy you're so worried about."

Parijahan hesitated.

50

NADEZHDA

LAPTEVA

If there's one thing Horz would never do, it's hide away the stars he's so very proud of.
—Fragment from the personal journals
of Leonid Barentsev

When she died, Nadya had always thought Marzenya would be waiting for her. But Marzenya was dead and Veceslav was . . . occupied. Still, she figured one from her pantheon would greet her.

Honestly, she should have known better.

Nadya kicked her legs out over the wide cavernous expanse. A few small spiders ran up and past where her hands were resting. She did her best not to flinch.

"You've done all you were meant to, daughter of darkness. Chyrnog's daughter, Marzenya's daughter, mortal, but so much more, so much stronger. Are you ready to shed all that is holding you down?"

Nadya tilted her head back, closing her eyes. She felt a ripple in herself, a stone dropped in the ocean of dark water.

"I set Chyrnog free," she murmured.

"Clever little thing."

"I did it so Malachiasz would live, but that didn't happen, did it?"

Of course not. The four had fallen and Chyrnog would never be chained again.

"Now, you only have to set me free," Nyrokosha said, a gentle prod. "It would be easy; my chains are not bound nearly so tight."

Nadya made a soft sound of assent.

She had known what cutting Chyrnog's threads from Malachiasz would do. She wondered, though, if anyone would realize. What had Malachiasz said once? Betrayal serves itself. But she hadn't been serving herself, she'd been thinking of Malachiasz. Of the boy from Tranavia with blood on his hands, who loved art and magic, who was so much more than anyone knew.

She had been selfish.

It was strange, at the end of everything, at the threshold of death and oblivion, to feel so calm. Nadezhda Lapteva, the savior of Kalyazin, had set its destruction upon it. It was strange to feel no regret.

The pieces were finally lining up, the nonsensical riddles, the countless nonanswers. She was a girl whose magic had come from the dark and been threaded with light. It was everything and nothing.

That crystal jar strung with teeth, found in that place beyond the well of blood, had been her own essence. She who had taken the stars out of the sky—maybe that had been Horz, maybe Nadya had done it herself all along. She held out her hands before her, finally opening her eyes, ignoring Nyrokosha's cruel whispers.

One hand pale, her fingernails worn down, her palm worn with callouses. The other stained with long, ugly claws digging from her nail beds. One pale, thin wrist and arm, the other changed. Magic lit in her palms, a simple thing. A drop of water in an ocean. It had been withheld from her because of fear, because those in power—mortal and divine—had feared. What she might do if she realized that the world didn't turn in the way that they wished it to. What might happen if she learned magic was a road that went in a thousand directions.

What might happen if she listened to a Tranavian explain why his way of life was so deeply important to him, even if it was very different from her own.

They had feared.

It was time for the world to change. She had spurred it on in terrible ways, she knew. Sometimes it took a terrible thing for those in power to realize something was very wrong. The death of a god. The birth of an eldritch power.

"I could let all this go," she said.

"Yes," Nyrokosha whispered from the depths.

"I could crack this world into pieces and shape it anew. No more war. No more suffering."

Malachiasz, bloodstained in a ravaged village, beseeching her to help him finish this. His hair tangled and his form monstrous, but still the boy she had fallen in love with, the one she so desperately wanted to help. But he had died, hadn't he? And Serefin with him. And gentle, cunning Parijahan who didn't deserve to be dragged into their chaos.

Maybe their lives were worthy sacrifices.

Maybe that was how it was to be. They were to die here, these four, and change would finally come.

It was poetic. It was the stuff that her books of martyrs were made of. Necessary sacrifice. A dawning of a new age. One less cruel, less cold, a little less bloody. No blood magic, no more clerics, nothing but vast new avenues of power that still had to be forged and discovered.

Nadya could take this mantle of godhood and fix so much more that way.

She didn't realize that she was making the decision in her heart.

She didn't realize—until the legs of a massive spider started to slam out from the depths. Nadya scrambled away from the ledge, something snapping within her.

What am I doing?

She didn't want this.

She wanted to dig into the dirt and the blood and the chaos and bring something good and beautiful back into the nightmare she had helped create.

She wanted Malachiasz's hand cradling the back of her head. Wanted him to lean over her shoulder to scoff at her Codex. To see the intense look on his face when he was curled over his spell book, the look that she now knew meant he was sketching.

She wanted to spend another afternoon in a library with Serefin, him spending the first hour complaining that every book he picked up was too dry before one finally caught his attention, and his wine, for once, went unattended to.

She wanted another evening with Parijahan, drinking tea while she braided Nadya's hair, cajoling Rashid to tell them stories if he insisted on hanging around.

Quiet moments of humanity with those she loved so dearly. Power wasn't worth losing that.

There were bones rattling off the spider's legs as she hauled herself up the crevice. Nadya backed away. She hadn't meant to do this. She hadn't taken the divinity.

She turned and ran, making her final choice.

interlude viii

RASHID

KHAJOUTI

Rashid stood at the entrance to the temple. He waited for the light to fade. He waited longer, still, for someone to come out from the darkness. Anyone, but Parijahan most of all. He didn't think the others would be offended if they knew.

But there was nothing but an ungodly silence. A godly silence?

Then came a trembling in the earth and through the trees of bone he saw great figures rising in the distance. They were out of time.

He knew this might kill him. But he had followed Parijahan this far, he wasn't going to let her face this alone, either.

Inside, the temperature plummeted. Flowers grew up around his feet, filling his footprints as he walked down a darkened hall. The torches had all gone out. It didn't take long to reach the temple proper. To take in the four altars that held the bodies of his friends.

His breath caught in his throat. He tried his hardest not to panic but his heart thudded heavily in his chest.

Parijahan was lying on her side, her hands cradled close to her chest. She wasn't breathing.

Tears were immediate. Before he fully registered what he was seeing. Before he felt how cold Parijahan's skin was underneath his fingertips.

"I don't know how to live in a world without you in it," he whispered.

It was excruciating, walking away from her, but he had to check the others. They looked like they were sleeping. Malachiasz curled up protectively, his dark hair splayed out. Serefin on his back, one hand resting on his chest, the signet ring on his little finger a strange kind of irony. Nadya was the most disturbing—it was as if every muscle in her body was tensed.

All of them cold. Not breathing.

He had to tell the *tsarevna*. Tell Kacper and Ostyia. But he was drowning under his own grief, and he couldn't stand to watch the Tranavians grieve their king.

He returned to Parijahan. A lifetime ago he had been dragged from his home to work in the household of a Travash, to accept his fate. He hadn't expected to find the young *prasīt*. A girl his age, mostly relegated to her rooms to stay out from underfoot—because she most certainly got underfoot. A girl, black hair wild, robes disheveled, who had locked eyes with him, something discerning in her cool gaze, before grinning and running off. Later he'd found out she had run to the keeper of the house to say that she wanted her own personal guard and wouldn't that nice boy from Yanzin Zadar do well?

He hadn't left her side since. For nine years. *Nine years* making sure no harm befell the *prasīt* of Travash Siroosi. It hadn't been about duty, not strictly. But because he loved her. It was an impossible love to describe. He didn't want her. He didn't want like that. He only wanted to keep her safe, always. Even when she dragged him into the heart of a country at war and told him she was going to burn down Tranavia in revenge. Very well, he'd said. Even when she'd dragged a haggard Tranavian with blood on his hands into their camp. Even when she'd taken a Kalyazi cleric and shown her the path to a country's downfall. Very well, he'd said, to it all.

He didn't notice the flowers blooming where his tears fell. Or the flowers under his fingertips, at her skin. He only noticed her grow warm beneath his hands. She took a gasping breath.

"Parj?"

Parijahan's eyes opened. Still strange and snakelike. Horns had sprouted from her forehead like a sharp crown. But she let out a pained laugh.

"Help me up," she said, eyes rimmed with tears. He pulled her up, and she wrapped her arms around his neck, burying her head against his. Her shoulders shook with sobs. He'd never seen her cry like this.

"Parj, I thought you were dead."

"I was," she whispered. "I'm so glad you're alive."

"Me too." He gently pulled away, noticing the flowers. "Hold on, I need to wake the others."

"What?" She scanned the room, her face ashen.

Rashid took the king of Tranavia's hand first, frowning. He didn't really know what he had done. He couldn't—this wasn't raising the dead, was it? That was too much to consider. Flowers, crimson and pale blue, began to unfurl, before bursting around his hands.

Serefin immediately coughed, leaning over and retching. Rashid jumped back. Serefin rolled off the altar, landing in a heap on the ground, his cloud of moths frenzied around his head.

"Blood and *bone*," he said. "I'm sick of this dying business. Never again."

"I don't think you're immortal, alas," Rashid said.

Serefin let out a shaky laugh. "That prospect sounds even worse." He leaned back against the altar, clutching his chest. Parijahan sat next to Serefin, taking his hand and whispering something Rashid couldn't hear.

Rashid moved on. He had barely brushed his fingertips across Nadya's cheek when she awoke, gasping, her hand snapping out and clutching his wrist so hard he thought his bones would crack.

Her eyes were strangely cloudy, gold and crimson and terrifying. She took in a hitching breath, and fell back, her body relaxing.

"Nadya?" he whispered.

Straightaway she made to get off her altar, and Rashid rushed to help her. She crawled over to Serefin and Parijahan, curling between them, pressing her face to Serefin's shoulder. Rashid could hear her sobs.

He had saved Malachiasz for last. There was so much blood dried on the front of his tunic and his lips, and it was too much to hope that he would survive whatever this was. Rashid took Malachiasz's hands in his.

He cared so much for this terrible boy. It was hard not to be charmed by his wide grins and quiet, careful kindness, even when it was so frequently couched in darkness.

Flowers, black and white and the deepest purple, bloomed at his fingers as he touched Malachiasz's pale, cold skin. It took longer—there was a terrifying moment where Rashid thought Malachiasz was truly gone.

He took in a rasping gulp of air, instantly shielding his head with his arms.

"Malachiasz, it's all right," Rashid said, taking his wrists and tugging his hands down.

He looked horrible. There was too much monstrosity caught inside him now. He moved to stand but his legs were too weak, and he stumbled into Rashid's arms.

"You're alive," Rashid said. "Are you . . . ?"

Malachiasz nodded against Rashid's shoulder. Rashid clutched at him a little tighter.

"N-Nadya—"

"She's alive." He felt Malachiasz relax against him.

It took a few more seconds before Malachiasz was steady. He took a step back, something hard to decipher in his eyes. He scanned the room, a slight frown on his face, before his gaze landed on Serefin, Nadya, and Parijahan. A strangled sound caught in his throat. He lurched over to them.

Nadya lifted her head from Serefin's shoulder. "Malachiasz," she whispered, her voice thick with tears. She scrambled up and threw herself against him.

Rashid flopped down onto the ground next to Parijahan. She leaned her head against his shoulder, taking his hand.

They would all be dead if I wasn't here.

"You're impossible, my dear," Parijahan whispered.

It was an uncomfortable thought.

51

NADEZHDA

LAPTEVA

There are ties, connections, Alena and Chyrnog and Marzenya and Milyena and Nyrokosha. I cannot tell what they mean. I cannot decipher why clerics of Marzenya are accounted as speaking to Nyrokosha. Clerics of Milyena speaking to Chyrnog. As if there were a time when clerics could speak to other gods than their patrons. The idea is baffling.
— Passage from the personal journals
of Innokentiy Tamarkin

Nadya wanted to press her face to Malachiasz's chest and disappear. She wanted to pretend, only for a moment, that everything was all right. He was warm and *himself.*

But Chyrnog had been set free.

And Nyrokosha as well.

Nadya leaned back, Malachiasz reluctantly letting her go. Gods, he looked horrifying. All eyes and teeth and mouths.

This was how it was for him, forever. The chaos, the horror. She leaned up and pressed a fast kiss against his lips.

Malachiasz stepped away and hauled Serefin to his feet. They eyed each other for a long, tense moment. They were so similar in profile. Serefin's hair had fallen out of its tie and was long and loose at his shoulders, hanging in his face.

Parijahan wrapped her arms around Nadya's waist, and she nearly sobbed.

"What do we do?" she asked, nestling her chin against Nadya's shoulder.

"I . . . uh . . ." She closed her eyes, but not before she saw Serefin give Malachiasz a hug, quick, like it would burn him if he did it, but he needed to anyway.

Brothers.

"I set Chyrnog free," she said, rapid and rushed. "I had to or Malachiasz would have died." She kept her eyes closed. "And I—I didn't mean to, *I swear,* but I set another free as well. Nyrokosha. She wanted me to become a god and I thought—I almost—"

"Nadya, shh." Malachiasz's hands went to her shoulders. "Did you choose it? This divinity you're owed? Eldritch beast that you are?"

She tipped her face up, laughing. It wasn't funny. At all. It was horrifying, wasn't it? Maybe not. Eldritch beast that she was. "I didn't. I almost did. Think of all I could do no longer tethered to the ground."

Malachiasz kissed her, gentle and quick, a promise, of what she wasn't entirely sure.

Serefin blinked rapidly at them, and whispered. *"Kacper."* And bolted from the temple, Rashid and Parijahan following swiftly behind.

Malachiasz waited for Nadya. He glanced up as the ground trembled, dust raining down as the world shifted.

"Lie to me," she whispered. "Do what you do best."

His expression was difficult to read. "We're going to live," he said finally, his voice hoarse. "We're going to live and put a stop to this and convince our damned countries to end this war. I'm going to leave the Vultures and take you somewhere far away and you can be just Nadezhda, the nightmare girl who stole my heart. We're going to be happy, finally."

Tears slipped down her cheeks. Beautiful, wonderful lies.

He gathered her in his arms, she could feel the tension in him— they were wasting time they did not have. He kissed the top of her head.

"I love you," he murmured, kissing her forehead. "Not a lie. You are the only good thing that has ever happened to me." He kissed the bridge of her nose. "Not a lie then, not a lie now."

"I love you, too," she said. An iron weight on her chest lifted at finally saying it. "And you are *absolutely* lying to me about leaving the Vultures."

He laughed and took her hand, gaze roving over her body in a way that made her feel far too seen.

"A monster born, not made," he murmured.

She shivered.

"Can I see you? As you really are?"

She flinched. "I don't—"

"Not if you don't want to. I suppose we don't have time for that."

But she did want to. She didn't know what it would be like, feel like, but if anyone was to see her that way, she wanted it to be him first.

She thought back to that ripple while talking to Nyrokosha and let herself sink into it. Her vision shifted strangely, her peripheral vision becoming significantly more pronounced. Malachiasz's breath left him in a soft rush.

"Ah," he murmured.

He took her hand, pressing her fingers to her temple, dragging them up something that was smooth and hard and thin, like bone, like horn.

"It's like a halo," he said. "Fitting. Do you want to know about the eye situation?"

"I'd rather not!"

He laughed. "You're perfect," he said softly, leaning toward her.

There was another trembling in the earth and stones came crashing down. His hand grabbed for hers and they fled. Right into a churning nightmare. The sky was dark and acrid and figures, large and monstrous and so difficult to comprehend, filled the expanse.

Are these gods?

"*Not gods,*" Veceslav said. "*Echoes of the fallen. Echoes of those who have died. They could return, be brought back by elder powers, but for now they are only angry memories.*"

"Oh," Nadya whispered. "Don't do anything stupid," she said to Malachiasz.

He grinned. "I only know how to do stupid things." He darted off in the direction of the beach.

True enough, Nadya thought, running after him. He seemed lighter without Chyrnog's presence, but she was scared to consider that she might have been too late. Chyrnog might have melded deeper than she was able to remove, poisoning Malachiasz to his bones.

And she might have doomed them all.

"Who's responsible for the giant spider?" Katya yelled when they made it to the beach.

The bridge was gone, and the sun was dark. It was almost impossible to see. Nadya chewed on her lower lip, darkness crowding in at the edges of her vision. A hand slipped into hers. Anna squeezed it, smiling.

"You look terrifying," Katya said.

Anna rolled her eyes, then added. "I mean, you kind of do."

Nadya grinned. "We need to mobilize those armies."

Serefin jogged over to them. If she and Malachiasz and Parijahan had become monstrous, Serefin had become resplendent. Stars rotated around him in loose constellations and tight circles of unearthly light. Moths fluttered around each movement. There was a bright glow at his edges, some power Nadya couldn't name, so different than whatever Nadya and Malachiasz were toying with. The scars on his face were like burnished gold.

"Who did you talk to?" she asked him.

"Velyos," he said.

"Huh."

"We need to get back to high ground. Bring the bridge back."

"Do you think the armies have already met?" Żaneta asked.

"If they have, this will have given them pause." He looked to Katya. "Shall we?"

"Show me why they gave you command of the army so young," Katya said, a well-meaning challenge.

Serefin winked. "I am *incredibly* charismatic, haven't you heard?"

Nadya gazed around her. The figures were everywhere. One that stood as a vast skeleton, one with hundreds of wings covered with eyes, one with dozens of arms all holding masks but with no face to place them on. There were so many, all so unfathomable, that Nadya couldn't quite comprehend killing one. But they had to. They had to stop Nyrokosha. They had to stop Chyrnog. And she was on her own. There would be no help from her gods.

"What did you think that was at the temple?" Veceslav asked. *"Did you think that was not help?"*

I have no idea, frankly.

"When the last four bound Chyrnog, there had to be sacrifice. They chose differently. They chose death. What have you four given? An eye, a soul, safety—"

Blood.

"But was it enough?"

Nadya glanced to where Parijahan stood with Malachiasz, her fingers pressed against his forehead. His eyes were closed. Chaos and reason.

"Nadya?" Serefin prodded. "We have about thirty seconds before the one east of us slams that fist down and I'd rather not be on this island when it does."

Ignoring his commentary, she plunged into her ocean of dark water and drew up a sea of power. Stone after stone, lifted from the pool of blood.

"You."

Chyrnog's voice was a blade driven into her ears, nails dragged down slate, screeching, clawing, cloying.

"How much more will you resist, child? Let me in. Let me help. I know the desires of your heart. This world of peace that you dream of. It would be so easy."

Bile flooded her throat. She drew up the bridge and retched, wavering on her feet as Serefin and Katya raced off, Kacper and Ostyia at their heels. Anna hesitated, glancing at Nadya, who couldn't speak. If she did, she would break. Anna nodded once and took off after the others.

A soft touch at the small of her back.

"How loud he is," Malachiasz murmured.

"I'm going to break," Nadya said, her voice trembling. She wasn't strong enough to fight this. Gods, how had Malachiasz withstood it for so long?

"You aren't. You're more powerful than he knows. Now, what are we to do while Katya and Serefin rally the armies?"

"That's trusting they *can* rally the armies," Rashid said, sounding skeptical.

"We have to kill Nyrokosha."

"The big spider?" Żaneta asked.

"An old god."

Żaneta nodded. "You worry about Chyrnog. I'll take care of Nyrokosha."

"Wait." Malachiasz grabbed her wrist. "Żaneta, be careful. I won't lose another of my order."

She blinked at his hand on her wrist. She tilted her head at Rashid. "Do you think my odds are better if he comes along?"

"It might even them out."

Malachiasz let her go and she and Rashid took off to where a monstrous spider crushed down on the bones of gods.

That left Nadya, Malachiasz, and Parijahan.

Three, not four. They needed Serefin.

52

SEREFIN
MELESKI

Her words are like needles in my ears and they're constant they're constant and I can't hear Veceslav and I've lost Odeta and it's over it's over it's over.
—Fragment from the personal journals
of Celestyna Privalova

The climb out of the ravine was treacherous. The gods around them were fighting each other and everything shook, a blessing in disguise until they inevitably turned on the fragile, breakable mortals.

"What are these, anyway?" Katya asked.

"Why on *earth* are you asking me?"

"Right. Tranavian."

He laughed. They scrambled up onto a battlefield.

And Serefin Meleski was rendered completely useless.

He would never escape. There would only be war, the screams of battle and sounds and smells of death, forever. That was his fate. War, eternal.

Someone's hands were against his face, directing his attention away from the battlefield.

"Give him a moment." Kacper, that was Kacper's voice. "He'll be all right."

"We don't—" Katya started and stopped. He heard her sigh.

She was right. They didn't have time for Serefin to be acting like this, but it was so much and so loud and this was all going to be in vain. They were going to die, and this time it would be final.

He squeezed his eye shut. "I'm fine," he said. He took a long, shuddering breath. He had to be fine. He reared back, Kacper squeezing his hand before letting him go. *He had to be.*

The battle had stalled in the wake of the horror around them, for now. Serefin could feel the tensions he knew too well, the crackle before it started up anew. Someone's crossbow would set off a bolt and everything would fall apart. He had seen it again and again and again.

Malachiasz landed gracefully next to him, carefully folding his heavy black wings up against his back.

"Even if they refuse you, my Vultures can't refuse me," he said to Serefin. "Katya, go to the Kalyazi."

"Don't tell me what to do," Katya said, but she was already moving.

Serefin jogged to catch up with Malachiasz, who was already striding off. He didn't want to think about the army before him.

He paused in the field. It took Malachiasz a few seconds to notice and turn back around. Kacper and Ostyia had caught up to him by then.

"I can't go back to this," Serefin said, voice soft. Not another battlefield. Not another warfront.

"You're not," Kacper said, taking his hand. He shifted the signet ring so it was facing out. "You're the king. You're going to be the king."

"Also, I'm not good at rousing speeches," Malachiasz said. "So, I'm gonna need you to make a rousing speech."

Serefin shot him a dry look. Malachiasz shrugged.

"I'm the one with the occult throne."

Something slammed into the ground nearby, making all of them jump. One giant misshapen skull. Serefin took that as the sign they needed to go.

When he got closer, he recognized the standing commanders and immediately relaxed. Ruminski had done his time at the front, but he had never led the army. The other generals didn't know him the same way they knew Serefin. The military would be on Serefin's side.

Oliwia Jaska jolted when she saw him. A tall woman with dark skin and hair shaved down close to her scalp, she looked far more worn and frayed than the last time Serefin had seen her, more than a year ago.

"Meleski?" she yelped, in a way that did not sound altogether horrified. Rather it sounded like she never thought she'd see him again. She stared. "Apologies, *Kowesz Tawość*."

"My feelings about honorifics haven't changed, Jaska," Serefin said, his spine straightening just by being back in this environment.

She bowed. His heart hammered in his chest.

"We were told you . . ." She trailed off.

"You were told I lost my mind, yes, like my father. I made it rather easy for Ruminski, I'll admit. So, you're here on a suicide mission against the Kalyazi?"

She lifted her chin. "We are here to end this once and for all." Her gaze went over his shoulder to where gods clashed. "That was unexpected."

"If I were to give you orders, would you listen to me?"

"You're the king," she said, sounding puzzled. "You also outrank me."

Serefin grinned. "I do! I outrank everyone!"

Kacper closed his eyes briefly. "I thought you had considered that walking here."

"I *hadn't*!"

"We don't have time for this," Malachiasz muttered.

Oliwia's gaze went to Malachiasz and her expression twisted.

"Are you with me, Jaska?" Serefin asked.

There was a beat of hesitation that Serefin did not like—until he realized it was simply because of, well, everything. The Kalyazi army. The gods clashing around them. They were so small and this was so big and it was very hard to see anyone coming out alive.

Finally, she gave a sharp nod.

"I must ask what you will not want to hear." Serefin pitched his voice, catching the attention of those around him. He hopped onto a cart, climbing to the tallest part and balancing precariously. "I don't need to tell you what's happening around us, we all see it. Also, hello, it's been a while. I never abandoned my people, though I suppose it did look that way." He gazed out at the soldiers, vaguely recognizing many. His stomach did a nervous swoop. "And it is long past time to settle our grievances with the Kalyazi—I agree— but not here. Not today. Not like this. Today, we have something bigger to fight. Literally."

Someone groaned. It might have been Kacper. He deserved that.

"Things have spiraled greater than this bloody war. What happened to our magic is terrifying. We're desperate. But if this is our final stand, let it be against the beings that would seek our destruction, not the people who would also be destroyed."

There was little reaction as Serefin clambered off the cart, hopping down. But then Jaska clasped him on the shoulder with a grin, and someone else ruffled his hair—which was not something he thought one did to their king—and suddenly there were a lot of voices talking to him at once and he had to be yanked out of the crowd by Malachiasz. Jaska regained control.

"Does the job," Malachiasz noted.

High praise, coming from him. Katya drew a horse up in front of them, shoving a bundle off her saddle. It landed with a hard thud and groaned. The cultist.

"Look who I found," she hissed. "Whispering his lies to my armies. No matter. My people will help."

Ruslan glanced from Malachiasz to Serefin suspiciously, his

eyes darting to where a god rumbled near, focused on a strange, birdlike creature across the ravine.

"This is Chyrnog's will," the boy muttered.

"Is it?" Malachiasz said. He pulled a ring from his pocket, flipping it between his fingers. Was he missing part of a finger? "How many more pieces of yourself are you willing to let him consume?"

Serefin glanced up at the blackened sun. *That* was Chyrnog's will, he rather thought, all the rest was incidental.

Ruslan sneered. "As much as possible."

"Now really isn't the time to hold onto your ideals," Serefin said. "This is the end of the world. If you'd like to die here, fine. I'll throw you over that ravine and you can die knowing you've wasted your life on a being who doesn't give a shit about whether you live or die. *Chyrnog doesn't give a shit about you.* Do you want to live, boy? Or do you want to die with your life wasted in the mud?"

Ruslan's mouth fell open slightly. Something flickered over his face. Malachiasz gave Serefin a slight nod, and then paled, his entire body tensing.

Giant limbs had begun crawling out of the ravine, dissonant screeches puncturing the air. Someone slammed into the spider's body only to be flung right off.

"What is that?" Ruslan asked, horrified.

"An old god. Not quite what you imagined? Well, why don't you have a go at killing it anyway." Serefin said.

While we try to destroy the truly unkillable one, he thought wearily.

Ruslan looked to Katya, exhausted and beaten down. Her face was dirty. Her hair had fallen out of its braid.

"I'm not forgetting what side you were truly on," she warned.

He smiled, smug. "I wouldn't want you to."

That was all they could do about Nyrokosha. Serefin had to hope it would be enough.

The ground had started moving, corroding, like something was tearing through it, *eating* through it. The graveyard looked strange, like the edges of it were being ripped, shredded imperfectly, caught by the wind, except the air had gone perfectly still.

"What is that?" Katya asked.

"That," Malachiasz said, his expression darkening, "is Chyrnog."

Serefin had expected Ruslan to be delighted. That was his god, after all. But there was only fear on the boy's face. Reality striking.

"You know," Ostyia said. "I expected it to be more . . . tangible."

"You can't fight that," Katya added. "There's nothing *to fight*."

Malachiasz glanced at Katya. "Take the armies and deal with Nyrokosha. We'll . . ." he faltered, his expression fracturing. "We'll deal with Chyrnog."

The giant spider was horrifying, to be sure, but it was *something*.

Serefin turned to Kacper. "Stay with Katya."

"But—"

He grabbed Kacper's face and kissed him hard. "Please," he murmured against his lips. "I love you."

This time it was potentially a goodbye.

Kacper's dark eyes filled with tears. *"Serefin."*

"It'll be heroic, yeah? One for the history books."

"There's no glory in being another dead king."

He didn't know what to say to that, so he kissed Kacper's cheek softly, and turned away, toward Malachiasz.

"Kill a god with a god," Malachiasz said.

"That's all well and good, but we decided it would be better not to go down that road," Serefin said, following after the roiling chaos of his younger brother as he headed to where the field had started to look like shredded linen. "Surely he has a weakness?"

Malachiasz wordlessly gestured to Nadya.

She stood thirty paces away, her head lifted to the sky. Dark clouds swirled, lightning striking from one to the next. A huge chunk of the graveyard was suddenly gone, swallowed up into an unfathomably large ravine. Something slammed onto the ground much too close to where Serefin and Malachiasz stood. It took a moment to register another giant skull of a risen god.

"We won't survive them killing each other. We won't survive Chyrnog, what's the point?" he mumbled.

Malachiasz glanced at him. He was quiet for a long time. "One good thing," he finally said.

"What?"

"I have to do one good thing. I have done so much wrong, Serefin. I have to try."

"Who are you and what have you done with my brother?"

Malachiasz laughed. "There's no changing me. But I have to fix this, somehow. She's going to blame herself, and it never would've happened if she hadn't met me. If I hadn't decided that the only way for us to live was to eradicate the Kalyazi gods."

"You don't believe that anymore?"

Malachiasz gestured to the madness surrounding them. "Oh, no, I believe that. But I don't think it would change anything. New gods would simply rise to take their place. It will go on forever."

"At least we won't have to worry about that after we're all devoured by this deity of entropy."

"Serefin, so good of you to be optimistic," Nadya said. Her voice was a chorus. It was wildly unsettling. Nadya turned, her eyes like a spider's, too many wrapping around her temples. "Do you have that pendant? Velyos' pendant?"

"I would never lose a beloved momento of such a horrible time."

"We're going to trap him in there."

"How?"

She glanced at Parijahan, then Malachiasz, and smiled.

"Absolutely not, Nadya," Malachiasz snapped.

"You're not going to stop me."

"This is not your sacrifice to make."

A great groaning crashed around them, a hole opening in the sky. Darkness where there had once been a horizon. Serefin swallowed hard. "What's your plan?"

"*Nadya,*" Malachiasz interjected.

Parijahan put a hand on his arm. He relaxed ever so slightly, but still looked ready to argue.

"I need you to cast all that wild, chaotic power you have," she said, cupping his cheek with her hand. "I need you to be *alive.* It won't work if you're the one he takes. He's already had you. You and he are the same."

Malachiasz flinched.

"Serefin, the stars?"

He frowned, plucked one out of the air around him, and held it out to her.

"Magic, condensed," she said softly. "Folded again and again. Weave it into a prison, Serefin."

He nodded, curling his fingers around the light.

Nadya took Parijahan's hand. "I do not want to ask this of you," she said, her voice—voices?—trembling.

Parijahan smiled. "You didn't think I would let you face this alone, did you?"

53

MALACHIASZ
CZECHOWICZ

*There were four, there were always four. There always
needed to be four to bind the horrors into the earth and
contain them for another cycle. The songs, each playing their careful part. Tamarkin and Shishova and
Milekhin and Greshneva. They died, but they died
martyrs, and they died to reset the cycle.*

—Fragments from a personal journal,
author unknown

Nadya went to Malachiasz, yanking him down to kiss him
hard.

There was a storm churning before them, ripping pieces
of the world away. Every second it grew a little stronger.
Chyrnog grew a little stronger.

"One last fight, my love. Together, this time," she whispered.

He pressed his forehead against hers. "I have made so
many mistakes, and I am sorry for it."

She pulled back, laughing. "Are you only saying that because Pelageya said you have to apologize before you can do big magic?"

He lifted his eyebrows. He wanted to know that doorway spell *so badly.*

"No remorse! Terrible to the end! The apology has to count and you're not sorry." She grinned up at him. This would be the last time he ever got to see her smile. See the freckles that dusted her skin and the way she scrunched her nose up.

He kissed the bridge of her nose. "You're certain of this?" He wanted there to be another way. Some way that didn't mean her stepping into Chyrnog's jaws.

"I have the two most powerful mages in Tranavia looking out for me," Nadya replied. "I'm not certain of anything, but I have to. It has to be me." She tugged out of his arms. She hesitated, then darted over to Serefin, kissing his cheek.

"You're insufferable," she said.

"Deluded menace," he replied.

Malachiasz turned to Parijahan, who tilted her head.

"I don't want you to do this, either, for the record," he said.

She smiled sadly at him, taking his hands. "I'm glad you crashed into Rashid in that alleyway, Malachiasz Czechowicz. I'm glad to know you."

"Few people would say that!" He kissed her forehead.

Nadya returned, taking Parijahan's hand, and they walked into the storm together.

Serefin let out a long breath. Malachiasz immediately got to work. He took his spell book from his waist, tossing it to the ground. It wouldn't do him any good, but blood would. Blood had power. It always came back to blood magic, even with blood magic as they knew it gone.

"I can see you forming a spell and you need to tell me what you're planning. I can't read your mind and you need my help," Serefin said.

There needed to be four. Four directions, four corners of the earth, four corners of a cell. It made sense, but he didn't think the pendant would work.

"The pendant has Velyos' symbol on it, it's useless."

"Velyos says that's rude," Serefin told him primly.

Malachiasz stared at Serefin for a long moment before shaking his head. He didn't watch as Nadya walked into entropy. He couldn't.

He yanked his blade from his belt and began to cut lines in the ground at each corner of his spell book.

"You are an enigma," Serefin said.

"How's that giant spider doing?"

Serefin glanced over his shoulder. "Still standing but she doesn't look good. Hey, what was with Nadya's spider eyes? Those were horrifying."

"We should have had the girls bleed on these," Malachiasz murmured. He frowned, thinking. No, it would be fine. He could work around that. Hopefully Parijahan would keep the entropy from devouring her and Nadya completely.

He tensed, pain stabbing through him. A raw hunger scraping at his insides. He doubled over.

"Malachiasz?" Serefin said, alarmed.

He'd thought he was free, that Nadya had severed the ties, but Chyrnog had dug too deep. He had molded himself too fully to Malachiasz. He would never escape. They could bind him to the earth, and Chyrnog would still have his hooks deep within him.

He held out a hand. "Don't come closer," he said through clenched teeth.

He had to get through this first. *This first.* Then he could throw himself off the ravine and into the boneyard and spare everyone a fate worse than death.

Well, they would all probably be dead anyway.

He straightened, fighting through the pain, the hunger. No voice from Chyrnog, but the *need* remained. To consume, to devour, to destroy.

He cut his forearm, bleeding into the tracks he'd dug. The north and the south. He gestured for Serefin to do east and west.

His brother frowned but rolled up his sleeve—there were cuts on his forearms already. What had he been doing?

Serefin scowled. "Are you not going to tell me?" He sounded wounded and there was *no time for that*.

"We can't trap him in a vessel that's been used. We're going to use my spell book."

Serefin blinked. "That will destroy it."

Malachiasz closed his eyes. Years of spell work. Of sketches. He had sketches of Żywia in there and she was gone forever. He'd had that damn book since he was sixteen years old. It was a compendium of the past three years of his life. The first sketches he had ever drawn of *Nadya* were in there. It was all of his research, all of his collected knowledge. Everything that was *him* was in that book and it would be gone.

"It's useless to me anyway," Malachiasz said, his voice thick.

Serefin hesitated, then swiftly cut his forearm, bleeding on the other two points.

"Weave a prison," he murmured, then stars and moths burst out in a cloud around him.

Malachiasz looked up at the storm before them. He watched as it sucked in a massive god that drew too near it. The god corroded into dust before them. The darkness edged toward the armies and Malachiasz dropped his eyes as soldiers were torn into pieces.

Malachiasz sat down before the book. After a moment, he felt Serefin sit down next to him.

"Blood and bone, we're going to die in a field outside *Komyazalov*," Serefin muttered.

Malachiasz couldn't help but laugh. "You're going to have to haunt a field outside Komyazalov."

"I wanted to haunt an alehouse. What is *wrong* with these people?"

"About as much as is wrong with us."

Serefin laughed softly. "Can I be bleedingly sentimental for a second?"

"I'd rather you didn't."

Serefin glanced at him before his gaze went back to the storm, dark and heavy and churning. The lightning that cracked within it was strangely distant, barely putting off light. Parijahan and Nadya could no longer be seen.

"I'm . . . I'm glad we had a chance to figure out this whole thing. I could've done better in the little brother area, but I suppose you'll do."

"Serefin, I hate you."

"You don't."

He supposed he didn't.

Malachiasz reached for the thread of magic binding him to Nadya. It was so much weaker, shorn and remade, but she was on the other side. She was and she wasn't, and she was so brilliant, the sheer raw power within her more than Malachiasz could have fathomed. The girl in the snow had power, but that girl and this one were so very different. The darkness Nadya harbored that she no longer shied away from made her more terrifying than any mage he had ever known.

He waited. He waited for her signal. He waited for her to be consumed, and for Chyrnog to realize his mistake.

54

NADEZHDA LAPTEVA

It's all spiders. It's all spiders. It's all spiders. There is darkness there are spiders there is her.
—Fragment from the personal journals
of Sofka Greshneva

Nadya walked straight into the jaws of entropy.

She clung to Parijahan's hand, the storm swirling around them. If she lost the cool rationale of Parijahan's magic, it was all over. She would be swallowed whole. All the power she and those Tranavian boys had, but nothing would matter without Parijahan.

"Tell me what you need," Parijahan had said before they'd walked into the storm.

"Chyrnog has merged with Malachiasz and Malachiasz's chaos has influenced Chyrnog just as Chyrnog's hunger has bored deep into Malachiasz's bones," Nadya said. "I need that chaos soothed."

And Parijahan had given that to her. It was fragile armor, but it was armor all the same.

Nadya, with all her layers stripped away. Whatever creature she was, laid bare. All that she had been running from, all that had been hidden from her, all that had never truly made sense, in one girl, more than a little bit monstrous, more than a little bit divine, but in the end utterly mortal.

They were all wrapped up in the exact same thing. Different shades of the same parts.

"What do you think you can accomplish here? You who have already helped me, already freed me, do you think you can turn on me so quickly? Are you so quick to betray?"

Nadya almost laughed. The storm raged around her, all darkness and flashes of light and glimpses of monstrosity. A hunger that Nadya could feel as she stood within it. An ache. A burning need to consume all that stood in Chyrnog's path. There was no reason here. There was no killing this. She didn't expect to walk away from this. She could only hope to manage the impossible.

Have you not been paying attention? Betrayal serves itself and I am so very human, and I want to live so very much. Of course I will betray you. I'll betray all of them. I would betray every god who has ever shown me kindness if it meant living.

"What a fool you are."

She wasn't here to exchange platitudes with unknowable darkness. Who knew how far Chyrnog had stretched?

"I have already consumed so many cities, so many forests. All will fall underneath me."

Yes. That was what they had to stop. Entropy was everywhere. With each second that passed, thousands more would die.

Malachiasz would die.

Serefin would die.

Nadya remembered the girl she once was. In the snow, *voryens* clutched in her hand, running from one boy she now called her friend and into the one who had captured her heart. The girl who believed so fully in the will of her gods. Who believed the Church was right and unerring and she had divine providence on her side and mistakes were not things a cleric could make.

Utterly mortal and utterly naive.

Ljubica had said hold tight to her mortality, and she had. It would have been so easy to give into the songs. To show her country that she was more than the sum of her mistakes. That there was a reason she had grown to love the Tranavians. That they were as good and as terrible as any Kalyazi and this war between their countries had raged for too long.

But Chyrnog didn't care about any of it. Chyrnog only cared about consumption. About razing the world. About tearing through to the realm of the divine and destroying it as well. Eating the sun. Killing Alena. Ending everything. That was his purpose. That had always been his purpose.

The gods were not as mortals, even if they had been, once. They could not be turned away from the paths they had set upon. The gods could not be *changed*.

So, it was up to Nadya to change. For her to see her enemies as friends, as family. To recognize that her beliefs needed to adapt to the world as it truly was. To allow them to live alongside the beliefs of a boy who thought differently, instead of smothering down what he cared about.

It was idealistic.

But Nadya was idealistic. She was idealistic and too empathetic and too hopeful that things might change, one day. That maybe she would never end the war, but she had tried. She had tried by extending a hand to the prince who had burned her home and destroyed her family. She had tried by falling in love with the boy who had done so much harm, so much evil, but wanted to be better.

She didn't know if he could. But she hoped.

It was that hope that kept her standing as Chyrnog began to take her apart. As he started to rip her into more palatable pieces. As he decided that her bitterness on his tongue wouldn't be quite so bad after all.

Just a girl at the end of everything, power all her own because it didn't matter who had given it to her. It was hers and she wanted it and she would use it.

She held Parijahan's hand tight and prayed to every single god she knew that this would work.

She let herself be devoured.

55

MALACHIASZ CZECHOWICZ

It's death. It's always been death. The final piece, the final key, the thing that has been driving us all. There's no escape. There never was.

—Fragment from the personal journals
of Innokentiy Tamarkin

It was when the tether that tied Nadya to Malachiasz snapped that he struck. It was through an overwhelming tide of grief that he channeled all the chaos of his power into throwing the storm before him into the trap he had built within his spell book.

It was too much.

Even with Serefin's power alongside his own. Even with what he knew was Parijahan's calm in the storm. Even with the last dregs of Nadya's dying eldritch magic. It was too much.

Malachiasz knew when he was overwhelmed. Chyrnog's smug satisfaction. They hadn't been strong enough. If they hadn't all chosen mortality, would they have been able to

trap him? If one of them had sacrificed more, would it have been enough?

He didn't know. He didn't know. He didn't know.

He pressed his hand against the worn cover of his spell book, blood dripping down his arms, from his eyes, from his nose. He worked to form the magic swirling around them.

He . . . failed.

So, he pulled on Chyrnog's power. He formed the entropy into himself. It would take him. It would eat him. But maybe it would be enough.

He dimly heard someone swearing. Felt someone's hand over his. Too late. It was too late. They weren't strong enough. They wouldn't ever be strong enough. They chose to be human; they chose to live.

And so, they chose to die.

56

SEREFIN MELESKI

I'll defect. They cannot keep me here, I have always been their toy, their pawn, their weapon. Veceslav cannot hold me where I do not wish to remain. The gods are not nearly as powerful as they claim to be. The Tranavians, not so wrong, after all.

—Fragment from the personal journals of Celestyna Privalova

Warmth played across Serefin's skin. He frowned, dimly aware he was waking, but not enough to open his eye.

"He's breathing, at least."

He knew that voice.

"And the others?"

A sigh. "Breathing, but comatose. I don't know. It's been weeks. They might be gone. I don't know what they did."

"Let me know if anything changes, please."

"Of course."

The sound of a door closing. The feeling of someone taking his hand.

"Your eye is twitching, which is more than I've been getting from you." *Kacper.* "Maybe you're still in there. I hope so. I miss you. Also, I cannot keep these moths from chewing through the bedding and Katya's servants are going to *murder me.*"

It was the urge to laugh that knocked him through the wall holding him back. He stirred. He heard Kacper's sharp intake of breath.

"Serefin?"

It took monumental effort to open his eye, but he did.

Kacper's breath left him in a rush. "Serefin."

Then he was being kissed and it was all very overwhelming, and he didn't think he was really in a state to be kissing, but that didn't deter Kacper who moved right on to kissing the scars on Serefin's face.

"I shouldn't've done that." Kacper leaned back. "You need space, sorry. I'm sorry. Serefin, I'm so glad you're all right."

Serefin didn't know if he was. The last thing he remembered was losing Malachiasz, feeling Chyrnog consume him totally.

He closed his eye.

"Give me a moment," he said, his voice scratchy from disuse.

Kacper took his hand. He was freezing, suddenly. Had he died again?

"Who were you talking to?" he asked without opening his eye.

"Katya. I should tell her you're awake."

"Don't leave!" Panic clutched at Serefin's chest. There was nothing and nothing and nothing. He had lost something to Chyrnog—what? He was scared that he didn't know.

"All right," Kacper said softly. "You're the first to wake up, but . . . I think you were the one outside of Chyrnog's path, at the end."

Tears welled in his eye. The feeling of everything being torn away from him as Chyrnog ate and ate and ate was much too close.

"What happened?"

"You four . . . did it. At least, I think. I don't know. There's a rift in that place now. It's terrifying. I don't think we've seen the last of whatever will come out of that."

Serefin made a soft sound of assent. Kacper brushed his hair away from his face.

"Żaneta and Katya killed Nyrokosha. She's warmed up to the Vulture."

"Where are we?"

"Somewhere on the outskirts of Komyazalov. Katya has been trying to talk to her father, but it hasn't been going particularly well. It sounds like the tsar refuses to talk while your status is up in the air like it is, but . . . if we can get Żaneta home and Ruminski off the throne, there's a chance, I think."

Serefin couldn't be hearing this. "What?" He turned his head, looking Kacper more fully in the face. *"What?"*

Kacper only nodded. "It might be over soon? I can't hope. I know what those talks will be like and we have to deal with Tranavia first, but we might be nearly there."

"Come here, please."

Kacper climbed into the bed next to him. With some effort, Serefin turned, pressing his forehead against Kacper's.

"You're saying ridiculous things," he murmured.

"I know."

"I think I died in a field outside Komyazalov."

"No one really knows what happened. You and the others have been unconscious for weeks."

Serefin's hand found Kacper's. He felt strangely empty inside and it was terrifying. What had changed?

Where was Velyos?

If he called, there was no reedy voice to answer. What . . . what had they done?

Kacper leaned closer, kissing him gently. "Let's go home, Serefin."

The manor they were staying in was, Katya assured them, just out of the way enough that no one was going to come looking for them. Serefin was trying to plot his return to Grazyk and trying his very hardest not to panic.

Ostyia sat down next to him at a table in a dusty, underused study. She leaned her head against his shoulder.

"I've been meaning to talk to you," he said. It wasn't a conversation he wanted to have.

"I know."

They both knew what needed to be addressed. They knew each other too well to continue dancing around it.

"You can stay here, with her, if that's what you want."

She took in a sharp breath. It wasn't what she was expecting.

He glanced at her and she was staring at the mess of papers and maps in front of him, her blue eye glassy. "You've been by my side for so long. I can't hold you there forever."

"The thought of a country between me and you and Kacper is unbearable," she said softly. "But, blood and bone, I like her so much."

"Have you talked to her? About staying?"

Ostyia sighed. "She's *Katya,* which means she told me to stay and to go in the same breath."

Serefin nodded thoughtfully. "What if you stay? It doesn't have to be forever."

"You need help. You're going to go depose Ruminski quite dramatically and I cannot miss the look on his face when it happens."

Serefin laughed. Ostyia groaned, rubbing her hands over her face.

"This is the worst. What are Nadya and Malachiasz going to do?"

"Well, assuming they ever wake up, that's a conversation they're going to have, too. I don't really know what they'll decide."

Ostyia frowned.

"I don't want to push you to return with me, but what if you do until we get this peace treaty into something that's real, and then you can come and go as you please?"

She considered that. "It doesn't feel like we could possibly ever get to that point."

"Well, I'm going to try."

"He's being stubborn."

Katya poured them both overfull cups of wine and slid one to Serefin.

"My father is inclined to believe the claims Ruminski is making about your competency."

"We kept his entire country from falling down around his ears."

"Tranavia also brought an army here," Katya pointed out. "And we haven't even discovered how much damage Chyrnog did to the countryside yet. It's not good, Serefin."

He couldn't really deny it. He sighed, pressing at his forehead. His head hurt.

"It's not hopeless," Katya said softly. "It's just going to take time."

"Time that will waste more lives at the front," Serefin replied.

He appreciated that she was trying, he did. But he wanted to do something. He wanted to go home, frankly. Maybe that was the next step.

"I need some kind of assurance that if I go home and deal with Ruminski, your father won't immediately forget that he ever entertained the idea of a peace treaty," Serefin said.

"The entire country almost fell and we're risking invasion from the north any day," Katya said. "I've been trying to pull troops back from the front to head north for months and no one listens to me."

Serefin frowned.

"The Aecii Empire hasn't had a century of war to hold it back," Katya said. "They've been eyeing us for years." She went quiet for a long moment. "My father isn't well, Serefin. He hasn't been for a long time. I don't know how much longer he has left. If we can come to an agreement soon, then I want that dearly, but if we need to wait until public opinion settles and I have the throne . . ."

"I cannot let the front continue as it is," Serefin said.

She nodded. "Understood. So, we press on. There's also the matter of your brother."

"Leave him."

"Serefin."

"Katya, we would all be dead if not for him."

"Thousands are dead because of him."

"A moral quandary we're going to have to accept. Tranavia is unstable. I need the security of knowing the Vultures are under control and I will not have that if he doesn't return with me."

"You and I, we get along, but if he ever makes another move like he has in the past year, I will send all the finest assassins in Kalyazin to take him down."

"And ruin the blossoming friendship between our countries?" Serefin very much doubted Kalyazi assassins would so much as faze Malachiasz.

"Don't fool yourself, Serefin. We're in for long hard years of being hated for compromising."

That they were.

"I'm willing to risk the tension to rid the world of someone like him if necessary," Katya continued.

"I need some kind of assurance from you that your gods aren't going to burn down Tranavia."

"You don't have blood magic anymore."

Serefin didn't respond to that. Malachiasz would put his mind to it the moment they were home. Maybe it would never come back, but Malachiasz would certainly try.

"That wasn't an assurance."

"Talk to Nadezhda about that. We're about to deal with an upheaval in the Church, so I believe we'll be too busy for our heretical neighbors."

That would have to do. He didn't know how much further this conversation could go, what with his authority not being recognized by Kalyazin and Katya having no true authority. They were in the same spot they had been in when they met in that Kalyazi village.

But there was hope. Sure, it would be a mess wrenching his throne back from Ruminski. Żaneta had agreed to go against her father in whatever capacity was necessary, and the man would not go down without a fight.

He would go down, though. Serefin was done running. Serefin had a country to rule.

57

NADEZHDA

LAPTEVA

There will be peace, one day, I have to believe that, because I have nothing else left.
—Fragment from the personal journals
of Milyena Shishova

The silence was profound.

Nadya wasn't sure what it was they had done. Bound Chyrnog, perhaps, but the rest of the gods had gone silent with him. Nadya had woken up and promptly burst into tears. Anna had been at her bedside and crawled in next to her, tucking her head against Nadya's shoulder.

"What did we do?" Nadya whispered.

Anna was quiet for a long time. "It was hard to watch. You all were shifting and changing and being . . . unraveled. The sun was gone, and then a horrible quiet, perfect stillness."

"How am I alive, then?"

Anna took Nadya's hand, lifting it up. Nadya jerked, not quite able to comprehend what she was seeing. The tips of two fingers on her left hand were gone, the littlest and the ring finger.

"Oh," she whispered, not quite able to wrap her head around the missing pieces. Maybe the gods had helped after all.

Something in her chest shifted.

"Where's Malachiasz?" she asked.

Anna didn't immediately respond and panic gripped Nadya. He must have made it. If *she* did—and she was in the heart of the storm—he had to be all right.

"Come with me," Anna finally said softly.

Dread filled Nadya. She got up slowly, her entire body aching, the silence in her head enough to give her a headache.

Nadya frowned. "I can't, uh, look—"

"No. Only the hand. The rest was quite a lot, though."

Nadya smiled. "Think of what Father Alexei would say." She began rummaging in the trunk at the foot of the bed for something to wear.

Anna's expression faltered and then she said, "I think he'd be proud of you."

Nadya froze. She stared into the piles of fabric and had to swallow back her tears. She tugged a black dress, red embroidery at the cuffs, out of the trunk and pulled it on. She debated whether to braid her hair but left it down. She was no longer that girl.

Anna took her through a hallway. They appeared to be in a large house. Simple in style, though. Anna squeezed Nadya's hand before knocking lightly on a door and shouldering it open.

Nadya didn't know what she was expecting, but it was the worst. Malachiasz dead or someplace where she could not reach him. Gone from her forever. A monster. Eldritch chaos god that he was, all he was.

She didn't expect Malachiasz alive and awake, arguing with Serefin while Parijahan listened wearily in the corner. He was leaning on crutches—why was he—?

Oh.

His left leg was gone just under the knee. Chyrnog taking

his final dues. He glanced over Serefin's shoulder, catching sight of her, his face breaking into the most exhausted but happy smile she had ever seen from him. It took everything in her not to slam into him.

His hair was clean and loose around his shoulders, parted on the side and threaded with beads, and there was a new ease to him. With a shiver, a cluster of eyes opened at his jaw. She crossed the room and maybe she did throw her arms around him a little too hard because he let out a soft *oof* and wobbled.

She clutched at him, burying her face in his chest. She was going to cry, and she didn't want to keep crying but he was *alive* and he was *whole* and he was *here*.

"Nadezhda," he murmured, his face in her hair. There was some awkwardness as they navigated the crutches, but she didn't care.

She pulled back to take his face between her hands, trace the corners of his smile. "You survived," she whispered.

"Mostly."

"Me too!" She held up her hand.

He took it, rearranging the crutches underneath his arms, skimming his fingers over the aborted knuckles.

"We almost match," she said, pressing her fingertips to his and lining up where his little finger cut off suddenly.

He let out a breathless, incredulous laugh.

"What happened?" Nadya asked.

"He thought consuming you would strengthen him; the opposite was true. Serefin made the prison—"

"I helped!" Serefin said cheerfully.

Malachiasz rolled his eyes, fondly. The rift between the brothers would take time to heal, but perhaps the healing had started.

"It nearly failed. But . . ." he trailed off, pain flickering on his face. "He molded himself to me, thus his power was mine to use."

She tugged Malachiasz down and kissed him. Awkward and gentle and messy because he couldn't stop smiling through the kiss and she couldn't, either.

She stepped back and Malachiasz readjusted his crutches.

"Comfortable?" Serefin asked.

He nodded, taking a tentative step. It was ungainly, nothing like his usual grace, but he didn't appear particularly bothered. She sensed that was a dam that would break eventually.

"We'll figure out a more permanent false limb when we get back to Tranavia," Serefin said.

Malachiasz shot him a grateful smile.

After rallying the armies, and with the Kalyazi king ill, Katya and a general in the Tranavian army had carefully arranged an armistice. It wasn't peace, but it was something.

It was harder than she expected, living, after everything. It all felt strangely empty, and she wondered if it was her or if it was this strange silence.

She only told Malachiasz, much later. He took the news with a carefully neutral expression. "Is it like what happened before?" he asked. "When they stopped talking to you?"

They were in the manor's small library. Malachiasz idly flipping through a book at a table, Nadya sitting on top of it next to him. Parijahan and Serefin had been talking about how they would get back to Tranavia—if they could find and convince Pelageya to let them use her strange magic to return—and Nadya, realizing she was about to lose them all, had panicked.

She hadn't considered that Parijahan and Rashid would go back with the Tranavians. That was silly, of course they would. The moment Malachiasz was awake he had set to figuring out how it was the Akolans' magic worked. Rashid was willing but wary; Parijahan couldn't make up her mind.

"I don't know. Maybe I'm not a cleric anymore."

He cast her a sidelong glance. "You're more than that."

She knew, but the title had meant something to her. What was she without it? And did it mean there would never be more clerics? No clerics, no blood magic? She didn't know. There was no one to go to anymore. She had to live with the not knowing.

He squeezed her hand. There was quiet between them, and she liked the quiet, but she couldn't shake the fact that things were starting to move, and she didn't know where that left her.

"What are you going to do?" she asked.

He looked up, closing the book. "Well, if I don't leave Kalyazin soon, Katya is going to push to have me hanged."

"For your crimes."

"For my crimes, yes."

"And you'll go back to Tranavia and retake your throne, execute the ones who wronged you, and spend the rest of your life on the cusp of godhood and trying to crack open the mysteries of the universe?"

"Dramatic. I would like to take a nap as well." He peered closely at her. "You're doing that thing where you don't tell me what you're actually trying to say. I can't read your mind."

"You can, actually."

"It might be a bit rude of me to make it a habit."

She smiled. He relaxed enough to make her aware of how tense he was.

"I guess I'm wondering what I should do now."

"What do you want, Nadezhda?"

Had anyone ever asked her that before and meant it? Had she ever been allowed to want anything in her life? She was the cleric, she was a girl from a monastery, she was made to do the Church's will, she was made to enact the will of the gods.

What did she want?

"I want to go home," she whispered. She didn't know what that meant. Her home was nothing but ashes.

He made a soft sound. "Kalyazin, then?" Two words and a ravine of a question.

Nadya reached out, sliding her fingers across Malachiasz's cheek until she gently cupped his face, tilting it toward hers. "It's you," she said. She kissed the tattoos on his forehead. "You're my home."

In truth, it was him and Parijahan and Rashid and, gods, even

Serefin and Kacper and Ostyia. It was Katya, though Katya would remain here.

Katya had pulled her aside and explained very seriously that as much as she wanted Nadya at court—as much as Kalyazin *needed* Nadya at court—she could not promise that the Matriarch wouldn't try for another pyre.

"I could desperately use you near," Katya had said with a rueful shrug. "But I can't put you in danger while Madgalena is still in charge. But I sense she won't be for long. Time to root out the poison."

And now, sitting in the library with Malachiasz, Nadya realized that was all right.

Malachiasz flushed at her words. He dropped his gaze down at the closed book. One of his hands nervously rubbed at the stump of his leg—while he'd told her it didn't hurt too badly, it still felt like his leg was *there* sometimes, and it was jarring to suddenly realize it was gone. The echoes of what the god had done to him scarred deeper than could be seen. It would take a long time for him to heal—if he ever did.

"I want," Nadya continued into his silence, "to figure out what my magic means—if it's really so different or if there are similar accounts that we haven't found yet."

He perked up. She smiled slightly.

"I want to help Serefin draft a peace treaty, even if it takes years. I want . . . a lot, but I mostly want everything to be quiet, for a while. I want you."

There was something vulnerable in his expression that she didn't expect. "Would you go back to Tranavia with me?"

She tucked a lock of hair behind his ear. "I think so."

"I'm still the Black Vulture."

"I know."

"I was lying about leaving the Vultures."

She laughed. "I *know*. Would you? If I asked it of you?"

He only hesitated for a heartbeat. "If you asked, yes."

Warmth flooded through her chest and it took everything in her not to yank his face closer so she could kiss him. She let her thumb brush over his cheek, skirting past an eye that blinked—there and gone—on his skin. "A shame, then, that I love each and every wretched part of you: Black Vulture, chaos god, and all. I won't ask it of you."

"All my parts are terrible, that's true. It would also be impossible, so I'm glad you're not asking it of me."

She did kiss him, then. Softly, because they had time now. Because she could kiss him whenever she wanted, and it was a thrilling feeling. To be able to tangle her hands in his hair and not have to prepare for him to be ripped away.

He sighed. "I never imagined you would leave Kalyazin."

The thought hurt, she couldn't deny that. But the thought of letting him go, even for a little while, hurt so much worse. And she was tired of hurting.

"There aren't really churches in Tranavia anymore. Would you—is that a thing you would want?"

"I don't know! I gave everything I was to this damn church. All for nothing."

He took her hand, kissing her fingers. "Not for nothing. You stopped an old god."

"We *contained* an old god," she corrected.

"We killed Nyrokosha."

"Oh, are you taking credit for that, too?"

"It was one of my Vultures," he said, a little smugly.

She sighed. Nothing was going to be easy. She had to learn to live with what she was and what that meant. She had to live with all she had done.

"Come home with me," he said, cradling her hands in his. "I will harass Pelageya mercilessly until she teaches me how to do that strange transportation magic. This won't be the last time you'll see Kalyazin."

"She will never teach you that."

"I will be so persuasive and charming and nice; she will not know how to refuse. Nadya, there's so much magic we never knew about! I want to figure it out with you."

A different place, a different Malachiasz, the same beseeching question. How long until the study of magic wasn't enough for him?

"Someone needs to put a chain around your ankle to keep you on the ground," Nadya said with a soft laugh. "You're going to burn up again and start another apocalypse."

A flicker in his expression. He thought she was refusing.

"You fought him off, in the end. I suppose I'm still surprised."

"Veceslav took his place," Malachiasz said in a rush.

What? She had asked Veceslav to help, but she hadn't expected that.

"I accepted."

"You?"

He laughed softly. "I think I've been wrong about some things, too. And there really wasn't any other option."

"Who are you and what did you do with Malachiasz Czechowicz?"

A shiver at the sound of his name. That would never stop. Eyes still flickered open on his skin; his hands still trembled. He might have broken free from Chyrnog, but he would never be free of the damage he had wrought upon himself.

"I don't know how to be better. I don't think I ever will, really, but . . . I'm tired of death."

"You have to go home and literally execute people."

"How do you always ruin it when I'm trying to be earnest?"

"It's a very special talent of mine."

But that they could be here, arguing like this, was a blessing Nadya hadn't let herself dream of. He gave her a kiss on the cheek, mumbling something about tea, and left the room.

Maybe she would go to Tranavia with him. Parijahan was going. And with Parijahan would go Rashid. Nadya couldn't watch as everyone in her life went a world away and left her alone.

But she wouldn't be alone. No matter what, she would have

Anna. When she'd brought up the possibility of leaving, the priestess had lifted an eyebrow and said, "Of course I'm coming with you."

The last ones left from the monastery making their homes in the heart of Tranavia.

Ostyia was the most torn. Nadya never did find out what Katya said to convince her to go home with Serefin.

And Serefin, the boy who she had watched from across a courtyard as he burned her home. She watched him now across the room as he read a report by firelight, Kacper asleep beside him with his head on Serefin's shoulder.

He glanced up from the report, meeting her eyes. He smiled slightly. May nothing ever put them across a battlefield from each other again.

The battle was hardly over. She had sat in on some of the meetings between Serefin and Katya—before they devolved into drinking games while Kacper exhaustedly discussed actual matters with Milomir—and they were a long way from peace. They were a long way from understanding.

She might never have it with her Church. Or understand why the Matriarch hated her so profoundly. If it was more than Nadya's strange birth and her magic that was so difficult to explain. If she was just a scapegoat for all that was changing in the world.

Żaneta sat in the corner of the room with Anna. Nadya had noticed the two girls spending more time together, and perhaps it was nothing, but she was secretly delighted that the girl who had tried so hard to pull her away from Malachiasz was drawn to a Vulture.

Katya and Ostyia were playing some game with elaborate tiles that frequently ended in them yelling incredible insults at each other after every turn.

Malachiasz returned, using his crutches to almost elegantly lower himself down next to her where she had moved to a fur rug in front of the fire, a blanket tucked around her shoulders.

"You've adapted unnervingly fast," she said.

"He'll have to relearn to walk when we get him a false leg," Serefin said before Malachiasz could respond.

Malachiasz shot him a dirty look and Nadya could almost see him contemplate launching one of the crutches at Serefin's head. He glanced at her. "So, I was going to bring you tea, but . . ." He shrugged ruefully. "Haven't really figured out a gait that won't spill it everywhere."

"He's going to milk acting helpless for years if we let him," Rashid said as he entered the room, carrying the abandoned cups of tea. He handed them to Nadya and Malachiasz, dropped a bottle of wine in Serefin's hand, and gave a cup to Parijahan as she settled down at Nadya's other side.

"Did you get tea from Akola?" Nadya asked, sniffing the air.

Parijahan made a happy sound as she stuck her face in the steam wafting from the cup. Rashid flopped down alongside them.

"What are you going to do about Akola?" Malachiasz asked.

"Stop running," Parijahan replied. "We'll see what they say when they finally come for me."

They may not have achieved peace for their fragile countries yet, but they had achieved some kind of peace here, and for now, that was all Nadya needed.

epilogue

THE BOY WHO
WAS A MONSTER

It whispered, the book that had once been soaked in his blood. It always whispered.

He had taken it to the Salt Mines, left it in a vault. But the girl who walked without fear in the mines said that it was probably not the best place, that there was too much magic in the air it could feed upon. Reluctantly, he'd taken it into Grazyk. He'd had a vault built in the corner of his study, and even though the girl would wrinkle her nose at it each time she entered the room, there it remained.

But he could always hear it. The insidious whispers were constant. Even when he shut the door and went to bed, it bled into his dreams.

They needed to destroy it, he said.

To destroy it would be to release him, she would reply.

And they would argue for hours, eventually leaving it to its corner with its locks and chains.

He spent most of his time trying to hold together the fragile shreds of magic left in Tranavia. Long days locked

in his study, some alone with the whispers, but most with the girl. Her blond hair like snow and honey. A glove shielding her left hand even though she was told time and again that no one would look twice in Grazyk. Who read his notes and pointed out inconsistencies, finding all the places that he could not with her strange, incomprehensible magic. Sometimes his brother would perch on the back of a chair, his boots on the seat, and frown deeply at the notes Malachiasz had gathered, moths fluttering in his neatly trimmed hair, only to be pulled away by the quick smile of his general. Or he would tug the *prasīt* into his study to find a pattern in the numbers, the tension in him diminishing, just slightly. Or the healer would work with him to discover what was possible in this mortal life, leaving flowers in his wake.

The god he had agreed to let in never spoke.

Only the whispers, constantly.

But that was all they were. Whispers could do no harm. There were greater things to worry about. Tranavia and Kalyazin needed to be rebuilt. The time between war and peace was dangerous and tense.

But magic was everywhere, and what was locked away was simply waiting for the door to be opened.

The girl tapped him on the temple, stealing him from his thoughts. She smiled, taking his hand in hers—no glove, only stained skin and curled claws next to his tattooed fingers.

Today, everything was quiet.

ACKNOWLEDGMENTS

In 2015 I started a book about a girl with the weight of divinity on her shoulders, a prince traumatized by war, and a monster who makes all the wrong choices. It is completely unfathomable to me that I've managed to pull this off not once but three times. Reaching the end of a trilogy is truly incredible and I wouldn't have made it here without the help and support of so many wonderful people.

Absolute first and foremost, thank you so much to Vicki Lame, for taking all my weird ideas and making them weirder and so much better, for embracing my odd cast of monster kids and my desire to throw genre conventions into a blender and see what happens.

Thank you to Thao Le, for suggesting this book that I never thought I would get to write in the first place, at the start of it all.

Thank you to the rest of the SDLA team, Andrea Cavallaro, and Jennifer Kim.

Thank you to DJ DeSmyter—every day I feel so lucky to get to work with you! Thank you as well to Alexis Neuville and

Brant Janeway. Thank you to Meghan Harrington, publicist rock star (sorry about all the eye clusters).

Thank you so much to the Wednesday Books team: Sara Goodman, Eileen Rothschild, Melanie Sanders, Anna Gorovoy, Janna Dokos, and Olga Grlic. And thank you to Mark McCoy for all the deeply black metal cover art.

And to everyone behind the scenes who worked on these weird books: Creative Services (and Michael Criscitelli who so *totally* understands what it means for something to be Extremely Metal), School and Library Marketing, Sales, and Audio.

Thank you to everyone who listened to me and provided such needed help as I agonized over this book, specifically Jessica Cooper, R. J. Anderson, and Hannah Whitten.

Thank you to one specific frog-themed discord, Marina & Hannah, and the literal all-hours encouragement. Also Hannah, please, write your book. And A. Clarke, who suffered my unhinged descent during the last stages of this book.

And to another, knife-themed group chat, you all remain the best. Claire, please, your book.

This trilogy was embraced by so many incredible artists that I can't even name them all here, but I am so extremely grateful for the exchange of art that has happened with this series. I treasure every single piece of fan art that I see.

It would be remiss of me to not mention all the truly wonderful Reylos I met online in the wake of the last Star Wars movie who turned to my books as a balm. Sorry we had to meet under those circumstances, but I'm glad my weird villain romance brought some joy, and you all have been so wonderful!

Thank you to the team at Owlcrate for all the support; you guys rock!

Thank you to all the incredible booksellers who supported these books, but especially my local indie, The Learned Owl. And thank you to my coworkers at the library and all the rad librarians I've met through this avenue of the book world.

The past year was a rough one for me, and so inevitably I'll have forgotten someone in this list, so if it was you, I do apologize, but know that your support has been so extremely appreciated. To all the readers, everywhere, who embraced my eldritch horror fantasy kids, thank you so so much; I couldn't do this without you all. And thank you, as ever, to my family for their support. Again, as ever and even more important now, let's keep making weird art.